ALADDIN'S CURSE

Mark Pickvet

Nightmare Press
Shepherdsville, KY

Dedicated to my poker-playing pals through the years: Paulie, Billy, the Dougster, Ron, Ed, Dave, Pedro, Bob, Joe, Dan, and John

......and as always:

"Be careful what you wish for, lest it come true."

Ancient Chinese Proverb

ALADDIN'S CURSE

Mark Pickvet

PART I: ANCIENT TIMES

"Lasciate ogni speranza voi ch'entrate!" ("All hope abandon, ye who enter here!") - Dante Alighieri, *The Divine Comedy* "Inferno," Canto Ib. III, 9

CHAPTER I

The asteroid belt of misshapen vibrating rocks, some the size of miniature planets, is located between the orbits of Mars and Jupiter, the red planet and the big one with the bloody crimson dot. Like too many balls whisking about the table, pinball-like collisions between the asteroids within the belt breed meteors or shooting stars that occasionally penetrate Earth's atmosphere. If a meteor of some size fails to burn up due to its high velocity, it will slam into the Earth and from that point on, it becomes a meteorite. Every few years, someone discovers a meteorite on Earth immediately after its fall. It is primarily by chance or luck of the draw when someone is able to see where it lands. Since humans have colonized the planet nearly as successfully as ants, an exceedingly rare meteorite has punched through the roof of a human dwelling. The probability is quite small but not fully within the realms of the impossible. It is what happened to Dr. Billings on a cool October morning in the year 2025, the 7th, a lucky day if there ever was one.

Dr. John Billings was forty-four years of age, slightly built with dark hair that was graying more prominently day by day. He had a dark moustache with a little gray but a goatee nearly as silver as a pre-1965 U.S. coin. He worked as an associate professor at the University of Sacramento and thus, had a PhD rather than a medical degree. He happened to be working in his personal basement laboratory when he heard a strange noise like a crash, perhaps something falling over. He flipped off a Bunsen burner, strode upstairs, and performed a cursory search of the house. Finding nothing, he went through the exterior kitchen door that led into the attached garage. The two-car garage with nothing more for natural light than two small windows was usually a bit dark and dingy, but it happened to be radiating now for some unknown reason.

Meteors are usually extremely cold, colder than anything on Earth, and ordinarily remain that way despite the intense heat experienced after penetrating the Earth's atmosphere. Aside from transmitting an eerie glow, this one was also inordinately symmetrical in shape, nearly a perfect cylinder, a couple of inches in diameter and about six inches long. Dr. Billings eyed it with scientific fascination and his initial thought was from whence it had come from.

The small but precise hole he saw in the roof along the backside of the garage answered his question. Out of a burning curiosity, he approached the object gingerly, bent down to pick it up, but halted. He decided to touch it lightly at first, much like someone would do to find out if they needed a potholder to take a hot pan off the stove. The garage floor was 4-inch-thick poured concrete and the object had broken through to the literal ground beneath it. After a couple of quick finger pokes, it felt cool to the touch. He put his hand around it, squeezed, pulled it up, and brought it back to his lab. His first puzzling question was, "How could anything lit up like this be cool to the touch at the same time?"

He had picked up the little cylindrical object at 11:17 a.m. At 11:36 a.m., his wife Judy came through the front door during her lunch break. She worked as a librarian barely two miles away at a branch of the Sacramento Public Library. Judy ordinarily did not disturb her husband in his lab and John, preoccupied with his work, did not realize that she had come home. This was a normal occurrence for him while working. She parked in the driveway but did not notice the hole in the garage roof since it had gone through the rear side of the roof facing the backyard. The breakthrough had been fast and clean, neither time nor enough prolonged contact to set anything on fire like asphalt shingles or wood rafters. There was no smoke or smoldering either.

Analyzing the cylinder further, it was shiny black in color with smooth lines like obsidian, a glassy-like substance formed from intense heat, as from volcanoes. Worried about the glow, he discovered that it was mildly radioactive when it registered slightly, but distinctly on his Geiger counter. The last thing he needed was to suffer the fates of the famous Curies given their extensive work with radium. There did seem to be a faint outline of a circle near one end as if it were a capsule with a lid, but it was dirty. He tore off a paper towel, ran a small amount of water on it, and rubbed off some of the grime. To his amazement, the cylinder moved outward slightly more than a centimeter, maybe half of an inch.

"John, Oh Johhhhhhn, telephone," his wife called out from upstairs. It was the landline, and he felt his pocket for the cell but realized that he must've left it out in the car charger. Even in 2025, cell phones still had reliability issues and the Billings were one of a growing minority who still kept a landline.

"Hold on a minute," he shouted back. He hastily ran up the stairs to get the phone. It was the university wanting to know if he was coming in today. He looked at the digital clock on the counter; it read 12:01 p.m. "Oh my god," he thought to himself. "I'm uh, uh, I'm not feeling good today," he sounded a bit lame and unconvincing. "Could you get Dr. Rose to fill in for me?"

"Yes, okay," answered the secretary, normally used to absent-minded professors.

"Joey should be there too," he added referring to his lab assistant.

"Yes, he's here. It's all good."

"Bye," and he hung up the receiver. He had been so engrossed in his work, he had forgotten the noon lab for his introductory chemistry class.

"Who was that honey?"

"Oh just the office," he answered while heading for the basement stairs.

"What did they want?" She asked inquisitively.

"Nothing important," but he knew that he would not get off that easily since his wife was one of those who wanted or had to know everything. She was a librarian after all, used to grinding out details.

"They wouldn't have called the house phone if it wasn't important."

"Yeah, I left my cell in the car; I missed a lab is all."

"Well, not all of us can sit around all day and play with our little toys. I've got to get back to work, see you later."

"Joey can handle it on his own but Dr. Rose will be there too." He kissed her good bye and hurried back downstairs. Much to his fascination, the end cap had moved out a good five centimeters or two full inches. He picked up where he left off only this time, he used a clean rag to rub and polish it. To his growing surprise, a dense, grayish cloud of gas slowly escaped from its home within the cylinder, rising a little over seven feet in the air. It was rather funnel-shaped, tapering down to a point at the top of the cylinder, and expanding several feet in width at its widest point above what resembled a large, rounded torso. Then there was a bald head at top, two narrow slits for eyes, a wider one for a mouth, and it even seemed like a pencil thin moustache and thin goatee was forming into an off Middle Eastern, or perhaps, an Oriental-looking face. It was hard to determine. It folded what resembled beefy arms and then it began speaking!

Dr. John Billings was immediately alarmed and actually had a gas mask somewhere in a box, but he failed to smell anything, and the color was more of steam and it ended abruptly. Still, he couldn't locate the gas mask after some frantic searching but did grab an old antique bronze lamp sitting back in a desolate corner on an old shelf. He had paid a dollar for it at a rummage sale wondering if he might have a use for the metal since it was of sturdy construction, rather heavy at that. It was one of those obsolete items that looked more like a teapot with a handle and spout from whence the flame spewed out. The inside was hollow, and he popped the top off.

In the meantime, the cloud was hissing, but Dr. Billings did not recognize it as language and promptly stuffed the cylinder in the lamp. To his further astonishment, he heard what sounded like a "nay" or "no" coming from the mouth of the cloud, but as soon as the cylinder was enclosed in the old lamp, the smoke filtered in with it in a rush like a high-pressure vacuum. He dismissed the voice as no more than hissing steam. There were some brief banging sounds as if the cylinder was crashing against the lamp walls, some vibration as the lamp skittered about on the stainless steel countertop; a little steam poured out of the spout of the lamp, and a faint metallic smoky smell, as of burned or welded molten metal. Then there was silence.

Dr. Billings went to grasp the handle and "Ah!" He burned his hand as if he had placed it directly on the burner of a hot stove, and raced to the faucet to run some cold water over it. A nice stinging red welt that would probably blister appeared on the palm of his right hand. He filled a beaker with cold water and with the rag handy, he poured some water on the lamp; it sizzled as steam poured off like an old locomotive. A second beaker full made it steam a little less. This time he gingerly grasped the handle with the rag and the warmth quickly played through the cloth. He picked it up high enough to notice a nice discolored circle that had burned into the stainless steel and sat it back down as it heated up again.

He walked over a few paces to a sidewall where there were water lines and a sink. He filled up the sink with cold water, grabbed the lamp with the towel, rushed back to the sink, and plunged the entire object within it. A new batch of steam arose but it tapered off and seemed to do the trick. He touched it under water with his left hand, the water had warmed, but the metal object had cooled enough to touch. He left it there for a few more minutes, pulled the plug to drain the water, and then filled it again with cold water to be sure.

All was quiet on the western front, but his hand hurt where he had burned it. Like a bad or unlucky penny, he had briefly forgotten about it but now the pain resumed as burns usually do. He stared briefly at the lamp, wondering if he was dreaming, but his scientific mind kicked into gear. Where did it come from? Maybe it was the neighbor kids launching payloads in their model rockets, but it had some heft and glow to it. Where would kids get something mildly radioactive? There were low grades of uranium, some once used in glassware to give it that little extra greenish or Vaseline like glow.

The object had pierced through the garage roof and had broken through the cement floor; that meant that it had likely traveled at a high velocity. The most probable conclusion was that the military had launched it, or it had come from outside the planet. "Is it a UFO?" He voiced allowed. What bothered him was the uniform cylindrical shape, and how it appeared carefully crafted somehow. The military might play out in the desert some, but he lived in a subdivision of Sacramento. Maybe it was space debris. Various countries had so much junk up there that more and more of it seemed to be falling back to Earth with some regularity.

He drained the water again, pulled the lamp out safely as the exterior had cooled, and tugged at the lid. It would not budge. He pried and pried with his hands, found a screwdriver, then chisel, and a small pry bar, but it would not give. He thought that would explain the molten metal smell and heat. He sat down on a stool and stared at the lamp for a moment. The lamp completely shielded the faint light or glow that the cylinder had given off. The composition of the lamp was bronze, an alloy of copper and tin and a little iron, severely tarnished due to long years of neglect. He picked up the lamp and still felt a strange warm feeling and he tried one more time in vain to remove the lid.

It was getting late in the afternoon and Judy would be arriving home soon. He wasn't sure if he should tell her just yet until he had a chance to figure it out. In the meantime, he'd have to round up a shingle or two from the garage to patch the roof. He had kept a half a bundle from when the contractors had last replaced the roof a few years back. He had a full class schedule tomorrow and needed to do a little prep work for that too. The lamp and the cylinder inside of it could wait another day or two. It certainly wasn't going anywhere, so he thought.

"Don't have the spirit of contradiction. You will only burden yourself with foolishness and annoyance. Let prudence plot against it. Finding objections to everything can be ingenious, but the stubborn person is almost always a fool. Some turn a sweet conversation into a skirmish, and are more of an enemy to their friends and acquaintances than to those with whom they have no dealings. The bone of contention is the hardest when the morsel is the sweetest, and contradiction often ruins happy moments. They are pernicious fools who add nastiness to beastliness." - Baltasar Gracian, *The Art of Worldly Wisdom*, 135

CHAPTER II

A t 4:36 p.m., Judy came home. A few minutes after that, Joanie arrived as well. Their daughter Joanie, an only child, had been a bit of a disappointment to them over the past few years. She was 20 years of age, in her third year of college, and had only just become a sophomore. She had been to two other colleges besides the current one and had not made up her mind as to what she wanted to do. Her current interest, which probably would last for all of three months at most, was theater. John had little use for religion and was more of an agnostic; however, despite being a scientist, he still felt that there was some higher power out there responsible for the miracle of life on earth. His view was that the ability to create was the end of the evolutionary process, not likely completed by a single individual or god. Judy was raised Catholic and rarely missed a Sunday mass and had brought up Joanie in the same system complete with private schools and the sacraments of baptism, communion, and confirmation; but it looked like it was going to end there for Joanie.

As Joanie drifted through the liberal arts despite her father's personal view that such things as English, history, sociology, psychology, and so forth were not conducive to practical employment, she switched religions like she did jackets – there was the Buddhism phase followed by Hinduism, then a brief bout with Unitarianism, and lately she seemed to just have dropped them all in favor of atheism. At five-foot five-inches in height, Joanie was an inch above average, certainly within a single standard deviation of the norm, less so with her weight, at only 115 pounds. She had short black hair, dark brown eyes, somewhat flat chested to go with her slim figure, and overall, was not exactly a knockout, a bit more plain and ordinary, but she did dress up nicely like a French girl and always had a steady flow of boyfriends and dates. Her parents were not very happy with the numerous piercings and various holes in her ears, nose, and eyelids, enough to give a prairie dog community a run for its money. If that wasn't enough, she had a few tattoos as well, but fortunately, just some small ones on her shoulders, neck, hips, feet, and a couple in some private places that her parents were unaware of. The only battle that she had lost with her parents was getting her tongue pierced. A bit of tough love would have been the consequence, no more tuition money, and a possible eviction from the home, so Joanie caved in on that score.

As far as Joanie was concerned, her parents were just out of it, typical generation gap; they didn't understand her or the modern world. She would argue sex, politics, and religion readily and ticked off her mother of late by denouncing Catholic myths like the failure to recognize evolution over creation to explain the existence of higher life forms. Her dad seemed a little more open but to keep peace with her mom, his attitude was not to mix up science and religion for the greater goal of peace. Her mom on the other hand felt that sex was for making babies, and polite well-mannered classy girls did not discuss it or spread their legs for every boy that so much as winked at her. Joanie already had five times as many lovers as her mother; nevertheless, five times one is still five. Just thinking of her parents doing the nasty was an awful thought, but in a way, she felt a little sympathy for her dad, wondering if he got much out of mom who seemed a bit old school prudish and seriously uptight.

On the evening of October seventh she made a small note to self on a three-inch square yellow sticky note pad that said "Pick up Lamp" that she placed on her nightstand. She had a part in a play about Aladdin and the Arabian Nights and they happened to need a small article that Joanie promised to donate to the cause, an antique bronze lamp. She had been with her dad several years back when it had been fun to go rummaging. He was always looking for old tools, metals, and other junk that he could use in his lab while he would buy her old games, Lego blocks, CD's & DVD's when they were a dying thing, and whatever she would yell for if it was only a dollar or two. As far as she knew, the somewhat dirty and tarnished bronze lamp had been resting on a dusty shelf in the basement ever since without any purpose or use whatsoever.

**"Spheres of Light,
Atoms in the Universe."**
Mark Pickvet, "The Stars"

CHAPTER III

T hursday, October 8th, had all the makings of a wretched day. At the early break of dawn, it was dreary, cloudy, overcast, and the sun would play hide and seek, but mostly the former as the rain commenced. The droplets would go on and off all day, sometimes a light sprinkle, at other times a downpour, if only for a minute or two. Two minutes could make a huge difference whether it was a fire, a heart attack, or lack of breathable air, halfway to total suffocation and lights out for the brain.

After breakfast with his wife, Dr. Billings, not to mention the strange happenings with the lamp to his wife or daughter as planned, decided to attend his morning class sections, which he rarely missed. Unlike the labs where he could slack off some, the main course was his baby. He cross-referenced Chem 496 as both graduate and undergraduate work, one of his most important classes. Grad students generally had to do more than did the seniors, including a 75-page final paper and additional work as assistants in the lab.

Chem 496 was a 9:00 a.m. class for two hours straight followed by an 11:30 a.m. sophomore level course, Chem 221 that lasted an hour and a half. He was gone by 8:00 a.m. Any further play with the lamp would have to wait until later in the afternoon or early evening provided that he had his paperwork completed, the usual nightmare of grading lab assignments, homework, and quizzes. Judy would leave about 8:40 a.m. for the library with little or no reason to go to the basement if he was not there. Joanie would wake a little after 9:00 a.m., not having much to do until her theater class at 11:00 a.m.

It was fall and a bit cool, so she put on a short skirt and a long jacket, dressing in a leisurely, unhurried fashion. Her legs were thin as her hips, but she had no problem whatsoever finding boys who sought to land between them; nevertheless, the boys would not be enjoying them today. She recalled her note and scurried downstairs peeling a banana dangerously as she skipped along the steps. She approached the dust-ridden corner and peered at the relatively clean white circle where the lamp had rested for years. "That's bizarre," she said aloud and scanned the basement for some clue to the lamp's disappearance. There it was, sitting prominently on her dad's main worktable. "Shit, I wonder what he's been using it for," she mumbled. She thought about calling him but realized that he would not have his cell on or maybe not even with him in the classroom. "What ta hell," she said and grabbed it; after all, it couldn't be that important and she planned to return it in a few days.

It did have some black residue on it, and it was severely tarnished, no glow whatsoever. She took it upstairs and sat it on the kitchen table. Her mother had inherited a few pieces of sterling silver from her grandmother, namely a tea set and some candlesticks. Judy Billings kept a special can of tarnish remover under the kitchen sink. Joanie grabbed it and a soft polishing cloth and sat down. She poured a little of the thick liquid on the cloth and began rubbing the lamp vigorously. It wasn't long before the whooshing sound of a leaking bicycle inner tube filled the room as a grayish-white smoky-like steam poured forth from the spout of the lamp. Joanie scooted back and nearly fell out of her chair as she stepped away.

"What ta hell!" She said, and then it seemed to answer!

"Vell, vhat is your vhish?"

"Holy shit! You, it, what, you're talking!" Joanie couldn't quite speak coherently. She stared at the towering cloud with two thin slits for eyes and a small-lipped mouth that widened up the cheeks in a sly, troubling grin. The features slowly came into focus like binoculars with the proper adjustment. It appeared to be on the Oriental side, mostly bald headed with hair above the ears leading into a ponytail, and with a tipped goatee and thin moustache "Are you for real?"

Struggling with English since it had been untold centuries, the ghostly form crossed its thick arms and replied menacingly "I yam veady to obey vu as slave."

She sat thinking for a minute or so while what she could only fathom as a Djinn, or Djinni, or Genie as kids would call them. It sure looked like one. "What did you say?" she finally replied.

The Djinni absorbed her words carefully, filing them away like a computer to enhance his own language skills. It could speak a wide variety of languages and dialects as experienced from these pesky humans. "You," he repeated, "Have three vishes."

"Hmm," she answered. Her conclusion was that this was some outlandish experiment her father, the mad scientist, had been working on secretly in the basement. Genies, some talking cloud, must be a toy of his she considered. He was always a heartbeat away from a viable invention. "Okay Genius or Genie or whatever," she said for the fun of it, "Tell me how the world, you know, the Earth, how was it, um, created."

Interpreting this as a proper vish or wish it now noted, the plan was in motion. The Djinni withdrew to its home.

"Cute," said Joanie thinking that it had merely been a joke or just a weird invention of her father's. She stepped forward once the smoky cloud had retreated into the lamp, tentatively touched it, it was warm but not too hot, and then started polishing it again.

Time travel was not one of the restrictions in its makeup, though 13.75 billion years is no ordinary amount of time. A brief period of darkness enclosed Joanie's entire field of vision.

Everything about her gradually disappeared, first the table, then the kitchen, the walls, the house, the yard, the street, the entire neighborhood, the clouds, the sky, and the planet too. She sat as an independent observer wide eyed, rapidly closing and opening her eyes to clear her vision, but it didn't work. She found herself in a different place at a different time, clutching the bronze relic tightly that was responsible for her journey into this new amazing illusive dimension.

An intense absolute quietness filled her senses. The deafening silence was so complete that the little noises which are ordinarily screened out by the human mind were absent; the faint whisper of the wind, the familiar screeching of a cricket, the chirp of a bird, the buzzing of a fly, the clamor of a passing car, the hum of an air conditioner or furnace, the occasional crack in the drywall of a breathing house, the pitter patter of pets, the ticking of a clock, and so forth. Faint dots began to appear in the blackness, distant stars light years away. One blue colored star out of the millions appeared to glimmer with a much greater intensity and grew in volume as it approached center stage.

Stars with a great deal more mass than our own sun have relatively short lifetimes, perhaps only 10 million years. Our own familiar yellow orb, though small , has a lifespan of about ten billion years. All stars are primarily made of hydrogen, the most abundant element throughout the universe. Hydrogen is the core of a star and gradually fuses into helium. When all of the hydrogen is exhausted, the normal nuclear process halts and the central core can no longer withstand the pressure of gravity. As a result, it contracts and seems to lose heat once the nuclear reactions end; however, the gravitational pressure forces the smaller denser core to retain and increase heat as it condenses. The ball of energy in the pressurized core forces the outer layers of the star to expand and turn a crimson color. Surprisingly, red is a cool color for a star compared to yellow, green, and blue, which in turn are hotter in temperature respectively, like when one kicks up the oxygen flow when using an acetylene torch. The primary ingredient in acetylene is hydrogen.

The red star becomes an enormous red giant as it expands. Red supergiants are rare stars so massive that they burn through their hydrogen supply quickly and become incredibly and inconceivably colossal. Our own sun in time will become a red giant, but is far too small to become a supergiant. When it reaches this stage, it will expand to such an extent that it will swallow the current orbits of Mercury, Venus, and the Earth within its boundaries; thus, incinerating them like paper in a boiler. The name for the final explosion for a lesser star is nova, or called going nova.

Within a red super giant, the helium core goes through a complex process which transforms it into heavier elements like carbon and then on to iron. The core is continuously losing energy but responds by heating up to temperatures more than 100 million degrees due to extreme pressure. Unlike anything else in the core, iron absorbs energy rather than produces it. High-energy photons like light bullets or gamma rays of radiation can pelt and break up the iron forcing the core to absorb even more energy. The spiraling process eventually burns out of control. The core deteriorates but continues to heat up catastrophically as the gravitational pressure only intensifies into an orgasmic climax. The end is near as the pressure and heat reach a point where the core collapses, bounces outward with a cosmic force to the star's outer material, and explodes like nothing else conceivable apart from the original Big Bang itself.

The star that was approaching Joanie happened to be one of the rare stars that would become a red super giant. Like time-lapse photography, ten million years compressed into ten minutes for her viewing pleasure. The star was not necessarily approaching, but rather growing and expanding, a million times greater than its original girth as it changed from blue to purple to red. Joanie had to shield her eyes from the intensity laid out before her. Suddenly, the supergiant exploded in a glorious but silent burst. Sound travels in waves like light or heat, but unlike them, sound travels by making molecules vibrate. So, for sound to travel there has to be something with molecules for it to travel through. On Earth, sound travels to your ears by vibrating air molecules. In deep space, the large empty areas between stars and planets, there are no molecules to vibrate. There is no sound there.

The supergiant explosion was so immense in scope and mass, it cast away illuminated particles as large as planets and normal stars. This super nova where the star had literally torn itself apart, not only produced solid space debris, but huge clouds of dust and gas with several lesser objects in the general vicinity of the clouds. After a billion years or so which was condensed for Joanie's view to within a few minutes, one relatively small cloud of gas consisting almost entirely of hydrogen collapsed into a familiar yellow sphere with a few tiny objects revolving around it in elliptical orbits. The third object from the yellow ball became the focus of attention.

Since her wish had not mentioned anything about returning to her own place and time, the Djinni set her down on the recently developed planet. The ardent temperature was so hot that water only existed in the atmosphere as steam vapor. The lamp normally may have melted too, but the strange home of the Djinni resisted the high temperature. The Djinn originated from ancient, forged fire of the gods, and thus were immune from its affects. Unfortunately, for the Djinn, they are vulnerable to certain kinds of metal, especially copper and iron. This Djinni lay encapsulated and bound in a bronze object that was mostly copper mixed with a little tin and iron. In such a predicament, it became subservient to the master of the lamp.

Back on the smoldering planet, Joanie had witnessed something no human eyes had ever seen, but after a few minutes, the only relics left behind were the lamp and her skeleton; within an hour, the newly formed planet's atmosphere incinerated even her bones to fine ash and dust. It would take a long, long time to cool down, time that quickly diminished for Joanie.

"For my own part I would as soon be descended from that heroic little monkey, who braved his dreaded enemy in order to save the life of his keeper; or from that old baboon, who, descending from the mountains, carried away in triumph his young comrade from a crowd of astonished dogs – as from a savage who delights to torture his enemies, offers up bloody sacrifices, practices infanticide without remorse, treats his wives like slaves, knows no decency, and is haunted by the grossest superstitions." - Charles Darwin, *The Descent of Man*, Ib.

CHAPTER IV

THE LAMP NOW OCCUPIED a spot amidst stone and the makings of soil sheared from the rock. In the beginning, Planet Earth was nothing but a lifeless, desolate wasteland comparable to the current surface found on our Martian neighbor, only Earth was blistering with much higher temperatures. As it cooled nonetheless, the steam in the atmosphere inexorably cooled into a common liquid form known as water, the key component in the development of life. The earliest known life form was blue-green algae and fungi arising from the pooling waters. Algae and primitive bacterium known as prokaryotes made their appearance around 2.6 billion years Before Present (B.P.). Under untold and unobserved millennia, intrusions from volcanic eruptions and plate tectonics aided in the formation of landscapes, mountains, valleys, plains, and islands. By 600 million years B.P., bacteria, marine algae, and true microscopic plant life had formed in the warmer more pleasant waters. Even eukaryotes, primitive organisms from all kingdoms were scurrying about.

Evolution, the constant changing and adaptation of a living thing to its environment, attacked the planet like hungry locusts in a cornfield. Of course, living things do not develop specializations over night; rather, it takes thousands of years, sometimes a few million in an agonizingly slow process of gradual change. Hundreds of land plants along with the first air-breathing creatures appeared around 425 million years B.P., but it is within the vast oceans where the dominance of sea creatures progressed long before those on land walked about. Primitive fish had beaten air-breathing creatures on land by a few million years. To get from one source of water to another, albeit a lake, river, or stream, sea denizens gradually develop small paddles or flippers and these appendages eventually become feet and toes over thousands upon thousands of years. By 350 million years B.P. give or take a few million, the first amphibians were routinely hopping from water to land and back again.

Some of these amphibians adapted to conditions on land so well that they morphed into reptiles 300 million years B.P. Many were able to escape the sharks and other large carnivorous fish that patrolled the vast waters on the planet. To the bane of nearly all land-based creatures, annoying insects made their appearance as well. To aid them in their new land environment, reptiles with a few mammal-like rudimentary features appear around 250 million years B.P. With the higher concentration of oxygen in the atmosphere, reptiles develop massive lungs, and consequently giant bodies; by 200 million years B.P., dinosaurs come about along with colossal sea predators. They would rule the planet for well over 100 million years leaving their footprints and bones behind for the world to discover in the 19th century.

Around 70 million years B.P., about five million years before the killer asteroid would strike the Earth and accelerate the end of the giant reptiles, the first true primitive mammals along with modern birds appear. When the reptiles could not readily adapt to the cataclysmic events forced by the devastating impact of the comet, the mammals survived and even thrived, and have basically ruled the planet ever since; only insects could possibly make the same claim. The world cooled and the ice age mammals like the saber-tooth tiger were present 40 million years B.P. Between thirty million years and ten million years B.P., man's closest ancestors enter the fossil record—apes and monkeys—the first primates. Somewhere around 2 to 2.5 million years B.P., the vital link or transformation occurs whereby the first creature that resembled a man more than an ape walks upright on the Earth. Since then, this species has violated the planet in every way.In the meantime, the lamp, set down in what is now a mountainous region on the continent of Africa, remained in the exact condition as it had been in the hands of Joanie Billings. Ordinarily, it would have totally decayed after a few hundred years, but the mysterious substance encapsulating the Djinni resisted any rust, corrosion, or deterioration despite the temperature and atmospheric changes through four-and-a-half billion years. The Djinni's essence had everything to do with that. It was in a dormant stasis, waiting for the next victim or brave soul who dared to rub the outer surface of the lamp to awaken the demon within. The Djinni, like a universal translator, could easily adapt to most spoken languages, the more primitive the better since it had been around long before the earth had formed, not a fallen angel, but more like a balancing force; after all, one can argue that there cannot be good without the equilibrium of bad or evil.

This Djinni wreaked havoc on earth before, long in the past, and, like all of its kind, someone captured it, denied it freedom, bottled it up, and imprisoned it in the asteroid belt like so many others, such as Hades or Hell, only there was no fire, just eternal darkness. When freedom was within its grasp once again, some odd little man had accidentally stuffed it into a receptacle with a high concentration of copper, one of the banes of its existence, sort of like kryptonite to Superman. The black extremely hard cylinder-like projection within the bronze lamp also contained some copper along with burnt iron, iridium, and obsidian, a near perfect tomb for a creature of its kind. Still, there was only one possibility of freedom, three totally unselfish wishes from an individual which was about as likely odds as hitting seven consecutive blackjacks or the same number coming up four times in a row on a roulette wheel; still possible but highly improbable.

Communication was necessary for a human-like creature to converse with the Djinni, but man's vocal cords, tongue, and larynx didn't invert until one million years B.P., which was the basis for the development of primitive speech patterns. Partly responsible for the advancement of speech, bipedal movement freed man's hands to allow for the creation of simple tools as well as the ever-increasing size of the brain. Opposable thumbs too were a great evolutionary gift in terms of tool making and manipulation. New home bases representing living sites rather than temporary sleeping places distinguished man from apes along with larger brains, manufactured artifacts, and the beginnings of a cultural system.

The predecessors of modern human beings existed in Africa, Europe, and Asia some 150,000 to 200,000 years ago in small bands or tribes as hunter-gatherers. The men dominated the hunt while the women gathered what fruits, berries, nuts, and edible roots that they could find. Two of these rival tribes lived in the hilly and mountainous regions of Eastern Africa near the great mountain of Ras Dashan, over 15,000 feet in height.

Zondoro, leader of his tribe, looked expectantly at the sky hoping that the great rains would soon be upon them. The drought was always worst at the end of the dry season, after all water drained from the land The sun was quite intense at the equator as well. Even the great river to the west had become little more than a narrow furrow with its supply of water near exhaustion. In a few shallow spots, it was little more than moist mud.

At twenty-seven years of age, Zondoro was both the oldest member of his people, and the tallest, at 5'11". Most of the men barely made it to 5 feet while the women were several inches shorter. A common trait amongst his people, Zondoro's skin was as black as coal to cope with the blazing rays of the equatorial sun. Like most who reached his advanced age, he had lost two more than half his teeth, and another precariously jutting outward would not be around much longer.

"Khama, we must hunt soon and we will need more spears."

"Yes Zondoro, I have made two more this morning and will have this one finished soon," replied Khama. Khama stood a half a foot shorter than his chief but was still above average. He weighed perhaps 110 pounds and was very skilled at his craft. Khama was the toolmaker who fashioned crude spear points by chipping stone. The women would aid in fastening them to straight sticks utilizing little more than strong gnarly vines.

Zondoro's mate or wife Quini was twenty years of age and had born him two surviving sons, boys of five and three years respectively. He looked with pride upon his family for he was the only one in the tribe at present who could boast of two living children. Death was an ordinary part of living. A man rarely made it to his 30th birthday while children were far more vulnerable to plague, disease, and above all else, predators. While the men were away hunting, the females stayed with their children near the home cave. The cave's location was conveniently located near a deep-water hole, a perfect place for hunting, but also one where the predators gathered and patrolled. A human, especially a small one, was one of the easiest things in the world to catch out in the open.

"If only we had the sticks of fire that Nagante's tribe uses, you would not have to worry Quini."

"But we have done well enough without them Zondoro."

"Not so, we have lost two children and a good hunter during the last three moons while Nagante's people have lost none. It is because he has the fire and we do not."

"Yes, but we have tried to keep the fire, but it does not stay. It is always lost to the wind. We do not have the magic that Nagante has."

Walking away from his woman, Zondoro said, "We need the fire and we will have it."

Earlier in the year, Nagante found a burning stick after a severe lightning storm that had caused a great brush fire. He had many experiences with fires as did Zondoro, but both groups had trouble sustaining them. Nagante was able to bring his glowing stick back to his own cave and carried it deep within. He dropped it carefully near a small hole in the floor. After the wood fell through, the fire continued mysteriously projecting itself from the hole. Nagante dropped to his knees and gave thanks to the gods above, knowing they somehow had favored him. The small holes actually extended miles below into the Earth to a large reservoir of natural gas. A slow but steady seepage from this reservoir kept the fire going. People have long attributed the unexplainable to divine intervention, until science catches up.

Nagante and his people quickly found new uses for this recent incredible prize. By using piles of wood, he created light where there had only been darkness. It kept his entire tribe of sixteen warm during cold nights, but more importantly, all the animals both large and small were utterly terrified of the sizzling light. The protection factor was unheard of, except by Zondoro and his own people.

As the day progressed, the virtual unbearable early afternoon temperature decreased which signaled the time for the hunt to begin. Zondoro, Khama, and three others, including Chaaca, the best hunter, set off, each with an armful of spears.

"We will not travel far for there is abundant game near the waterhole," Zondoro stated confidently. The dry season had its advantages. All animals needed water, and when it became scarce, they had to frequent what remained. There were disadvantages too. Game generally moved away from dry regions. As it became scarcer, competition increased between the remaining predators.

"Today, I will try to get the wooly monster and his pointed-white horns will be a present to my wife," boasted Chaaca. Chaaca was speaking about a gigantic mastodon with huge ivory tusks. The size of a fully-grown mastodon easily dwarfed that of a modern elephant. Stout, as well as a formidable hunter, Chaaca was fearless. As a young man of fifteen, he had killed a wild pig, and while attempting to drag it home, a brown, panther-like cat stalked him. The three-hundred-pound cat had not eaten for a few days and was desperate for a meal. The bloody smell of the dead pig was too much to pass up. Chaaca may have been an inch shorter than Khama but weighed 155 pounds and was much broader in the shoulders. Most cats are silent ambush predators, and when the beast timed his leap, four razor sharp claws raked Chaaca's back before he knew what hit him, from the upper neck sliding down the entire length of his lower back.

Fortunately, for Chaaca, the cat was far more intent on acquiring the pig, but Chaaca was not willing to give it up. While Chaaca had been knocked to the ground and was bleeding heavily, the cat snatched the pig within its powerful jaws, and was about to make its getaway, when Chaaca recovered and made his move. He had no spear, but grabbed a nearby rock and lunged at the cat, screaming from both the searing pain and ferociousness of his own attack simultaneously. He hit the cat squarely on the head. Now it was the cat's turn to be dazed as it dropped the pig trying to shake it off. Chaaca hit it again, and again like a jackhammer. The fourth blow crushed the cat's skull and it flopped on the ground, dead with a big bloody tongue hanging out where it had bit its own self. Chaaca, though weakened, was so proud of his victory, that he used his adrenaline to drag both the cat and the pig foot by agonizing foot several miles all the way back to the cave. Ever since, he shows off his scars proudly to commemorate his bravery.

Mastodons ordinarily stuck together in grazing herds, and it would be virtually impossible for a band of hunters to bring one down, especially an angry bull. Chaaca would be the one foolish or brave enough to attempt such a fete. As the band approached the watering hole, they used extreme caution, always on the lookout for predators. Their luck was good today as a small herd of antelope were busy drinking. They were alarmed and on high alert, but water was frightfully scarce, and they had to drink before they could run.

The brothers, Gunte and Genga, under orders, crawled through the brush to get to the opposite side. Chaaca would flank the herd from the right while Zondoro remained in the front behind a tree. When they were in position, Zondoro signaled Khama to run out screaming hysterically to set the herd in motion. Khama got them moving and the majority of the heard turned toward Zondoro.

When a doe was about to pass close to his position, Zondoro leaped out and hurled his spear. The sharp stone point caught the upper portion of the rear leg of the doe, but it was more of a glancing blow, not a serious one. At the sight of this new intimidating creature, the herd of about fifty changed direction on a dime and headed to where the brothers were waiting. The wounded doe turned too, which caused the spear handle to drop off lodging the spearhead a little deeper internally. She began to run with a limp, significantly slower than her kin. The herd became quite confused at the raging appearance of the brothers. The water hole was now on their left, Chaaca was on the right, Zondoro and Khama were behind them, and the brothers were now in front. The hunters closed in. The antelope panicked and burst out in all directions. Gunte was closest and managed to hurl his spear into the flank of the doe that Zondoro had hit as well.

Though seriously wounded, the doe limped off faster than a man could run. Unfortunately, she couldn't keep up, and her kind left her. Gunte signaled for the others to follow, and all five men were quickly in hot pursuit. The bleeding intensified as the doe's movements accelerated. Finally, she collapsed, and the hunters were on it like flies on a bloody carcass. Chaaca pulled out a stone-chipped knife and severed the doe's throat to end its misery. With a razor-sharp spear, Chaaca then cut a neat line down the vertebral column followed by another one from the chin to the end of the stomach. The others joined in and started hacking off sections to take away immediately. Gunte and Zondoro reclaimed their spearheads as scavengers had already gathered impatiently waiting for the hunters to depart. Carrying what they could, the men made a quick getaway for the cave. There would be enough meat to feed the tribe for three days, but Zondoro was not satisfied.

"We could have brought the entire kill with us if we had the fire."

"We have lived our entire lives without fire and we don't need it now," Quini said. "If we don't get meat, we can always live awhile on roots and berries." Usually, the women provided as many meals for the tribe as men. Aside from roots, berries, and nuts, the women gathered figs and even eggs too. Humans could always be scavengers if the need arose, and eating worms and insects was not out of the realm of nutrition either. If one were hungry enough, that one would eat nearly anything that was remotely edible.

Zondoro was becoming more envious of Nagante day by day to the point of jealousy. Jealousy is the condition that arises when one wants something that is difficult to obtain, especially when another already has it. Zondoro's jealousy would continue to grow and fester with Nagante's continued success.

Jackie: "Who... what are you?"

Shendu: "I am the keeper of the Talismans, I am the Apocalypse of which legend speaks, and I am, for once and for all, your executioner." - *Jackie Chan Adventures: Day of the Dragon*, #1.13, 2001

CHAPTER V

A few weeks later, the torrential transcendent rains effectively ended the dry season. Lowlands, soft spots, and sink holes that filled with water reduced the hunting land that could easily be walked a short time ago. With the rains, an abundance of life sparkled and materialized throughout the region. Creatures lying dormant awoke and the eggs of many fish, insects, and amphibians hatched. An orchestra of noise followed many generated from little beings' intent on attracting a mate or food. Most importantly to the emerging tribes of men was the arrival of vast herds of grazing animals.

The cave that Zondoro's people had chosen was quite small, barely 50 feet to its end, but adequate for shelter, one of the three most basic needs of human survival to go along with water and food. The cave sloped downward facing the mighty Ras Dashan, which was only a few miles away but seemed so much shorter. Mountains in the distance were much a desert mirage. The cave kept them dry, and had only one entrance, making it easy to defend. A handy supply of sticks and stones that could readily break bones lay piled adjacent to the spears, even deadlier in the right skillful hands. Brandishing any of these primitive weapons combined with some whooping and screaming was enough to drive off the most vicious of intruders.

Staring across at the mountain across the plain, Zondoro decided to take a relatively short trip to the other side to visit Nagante. He had not seen his rival leader for several weeks and he wished to view the precious fire again. He dreamed of it while sleeping and more often as he was awake. It had become an obsession. Taking Chaaca and Khama with him, Zondoro set forth. The brothers Gunte and Genga would have to provide for the tribe for a few days. It was only a one-day journey to Nagante's home, and they would not stay long.

With little more than their spears, the three men set off. They did have to detour to higher ground since it was still raining and many of the low-lying areas had transformed into lakes and streams. As they were walking in and around the hills, they came upon a raised canyon area. They hugged the rim as Zondoro cautioned those behind him to mind their footing. Some of the severe drops fell to a depth of 300 feet, far enough to break a man and the majority of his bones into little pieces given the rocky slopes.

As the sun advanced toward the horizon, they reached Nagante's home, a cave on the side of Ras Dashan that was much larger than Zondoro's, four times the length, and it had two entrances or exits depending on how one viewed them. It also had a few passages in between and one of these routes led to Nagante's precious fire. As they approached the cave, Zondoro noticed instantly that something was different. There were a lot more people as Nagante came out with another man at his side.

"Greetings Zondoro my son," said Nagante. Zondoro was temporarily speechless. His rival was of the same age and stature, but Nagante held his head high with an unexpected arrogance as he spoke down to him. Nagante also wore a magnificent robe that had once been on the back of some large spotted animal, likely a leopard of sorts.

Zondoro recovered and said, "Greetings Nagante."

"Please come in my children and warm yourselves, we have food and water."

Zondoro was immediately interested at the prospect of warming himself since it would likely involve fire. Sure enough, Nagante had a small fire going inside the cave near the mouth so the smoke could flow outside. "Nagante, who are all of these strange people?"

"They are a band of hunters from the North who have joined my humble band. I lead them now as I do the others," he boasted with puffed chest.

It was not hard for Zondoro to surmise that Nagante no longer considered them as equals, and though jealous, Zondoro was impressed with Nagante's extension of his leadership. As the evening progressed, Zondoro learned that Nagante no longer led the hunts or even hunted at all! This was unheard of, for it was a man's duty to hunt, but Nagante had others hunt for him. He had become a shaman, a powerful religious leader for his growing tribe. It all had to do with controlling the fire. Zondoro's emotions turned to anger for many reasons. Nagante for one acted as his superior. Nagante was also getting soft, fat, and lazy by not taking part in the hunts. What really got Zondoro's dander up, was when Nagante asked him to join his tribe. Nagante would naturally be the leader of all. Zondoro vowed that he would not add to his rival's growing power.

"I am sorry Nagante, I cannot join your tribe, we are content with our present home and do not choose to leave it," Zondoro stated firmly.

"Very well, if you do change your mind, you know where to find me," Nagante consoled.

After spending the night, Zondoro was up early the next morning, "We must get back and hunt for our people," he said to Nagante.

"You just got here my son, why don't you stay another day or two?"

"We really must get back, but I would like to know...," Zondoro hesitated.

"Yes?"

"Where or how you get your fire?" It was the question he wanted to ask last night as well as the main reason for the visit.

Nagante stiffened and seem to stretch on his tiptoes, but he was still shorter than Zondoro by several inches, "No one but I, Nagante, is allowed to see the fire. Certainly one as you could not hope to have such a thing," he said oh-so-smugly.

Zondoro got the gist of Nagante's rising hostility and several of Nagante's old and new warriors had their hands on their spears. Zondoro was not exactly feeling unhostile, but raised his voice, "Farewell Nagante."

"Safe travels," said Nagante in a dismissive tone.

When the trio traveled far enough away from Nagante's home, Zondoro said to the other two, "Just because he has the fire, he thinks himself a god."

"Yes," said Chaaca grimly, "Nagante is no longer himself."

As mid-day approached, the men stopped for another rest after a steep climb. They followed trails previously made by animals like wild goats. It finally stopped raining for the first time in a week, and the sun appeared from behind the clouds. They continued onward when Khama spotted a small sparkling glimmer of golden light about 18 feet to the right of the trail. Unless there was a little gold dust in the bottom of a shallow stream, shiny metals in raw form were virtually unheard of.

"Hold on!" Shouted Khama who had been bringing up the rear. The other two had gotten a bit ahead of him but returned to the sound of his voice.

"What is it?" Questioned Zondoro.

"Look, over there," Khama pointed in the direction of the light. It was easy to see the glittering sparkle of light as the sun played upon it and the three strode off to investigate it with Zondoro in the lead. Shifting sands and rains managed to expose it at exactly the time of their passage. A golden or more bronze-colored tip protruded from something buried within the depths of the wet sandy soil. Zondoro bent downward, tentatively touched in, and then tried to pull it up, but he could only grip it with his thumb and forefinger. It was thoroughly stuck and all three jumped in with able fingers to loosen the muddy soil about it. Eventually, what seemed like ages but was only a few long minutes, a good 80% of the lamp was exposed. The three stared at it in fascination and awe, afraid to touch it as the two shorter and younger men looked to Zondoro for guidance.

"What is it?" asked Khama.

"I don't know," replied Zondoro. The three Old Stone Age inhabitants had no idea what metal was since it had rarely been seen other than as dust or veins in rock. This was the first any of them saw it separated or melted. They examined it closely but could not figure it out. Zondoro was brave enough to pick it up. It seemed heavy for its size but a lot of that was due to the build-up of mud and dirt that covered most of its surface. There was just enough shine to confuse them as to its origin and general make-up. Something so refined would have been a surprise in the Bronze Age, but more of a miracle in the Stone. Great magic was at hand that could only be the work of the gods.

"Let's take it home and examine it there," said Zondoro. He handed the other two his spears, grasped the handle of the lamp with one hand, and placed the other on the bottom. Zondoro then continued onward with two hands on his new possession and resumed the expedition home. When they arrived at the familiar site of their cave, the rains had started again. The other members of the tribe came out to meet them.

"Look what we have found!" Khama said pointing to the grimy possession in Zondoro's hands. The other members stared in confused fascination except for the four small children who seemed to take no interest whatsoever.

"What is it?" was the common question of all.

"We don't know," said Zondoro. A few touched it, but after the initial interest of the lamp wore off, Zondoro took it deeper into the cave to his sleeping area. He stared at it admiringly and began to brush some of the dirt off it with a blanket hide. A peculiar thing happened. A slow swishing sound filled the air as a funnel-shaped cloud morphed before his very eyes. It was broad-shouldered above as a slant-eyed face materialized before him and spoke, "What is it that you wish?"

Zondoro immediately fell on his knees. If this was not a god, then what was? The god was speaking to him in some odd language and Zondoro slowly lifted his head to sneak a peek at the god. Zondoro spoke, "I do not understand my lord."

The Djinni cocked its head at the voice inflection, it was odd and clicky, but somehow familiar from long ago, a Stone Age African dialect combined with body motion and gesturing. "I am ready to obey you as your slave, what is your wish?" The Djinni was able to adapt and spoke in words that Zondoro could understand.

Zondoro was speechless trying to sort out his thoughts. He slowly sat up and pondered as to how a god could act this way as my slave when it should be the other way around? He sat mute, daring another look at the portly figure hovering menacingly above him. After a few minutes, the Djinni gave up and returned to the inner sanctuary of the lamp. Zondoro finally realized what the thing was trying to do for him, but it was too late. Maybe it is how Nagante got the fire, the gods were here to help, one need only ask. Zondoro hastily rubbed the lamp more vigorously this time and the Djinni appeared as before.

"I can only appear three times to the same person. Do you have a second wish master?"

Money or great wealth or vast material goods were not part of man's greedy culture just yet, but Zondoro knew what he wanted, and that was fire. He swiftly had to think of how he wanted it as time was running out. The Djinni could only appear for a precious few minutes.

"I would like a stick glowing with fire at one end about this long," Zondoro raised his hand level with his own significant height. To Zondoro's astonishment, the stick appeared immediately from a tiny flame the size of an ordinary match. Zondoro held the stick staring at it as the Djinni hissed back into its home. A stiff breeze that wound through the cave struck Zondoro in the face, but the miniscule flame at the end of the stick did not survive it. One thing the Djinni required was specific details. Without them, the Djinni simply filled them in itself and the result was usually not to the benefit of the wisher.

What Zondoro had really desired was a long-lasting torch he could use repeatedly, like Nagante was able to do. The last remnant of the smoke coming from the end of the stick was enough indication that he had not quite gotten what he had wanted. Now he was down to his final wish. This one would require careful thought. Putting the lamp aside, Zondoro walked out of the cave to get a little fresh air and think things over.

Later that night while the rest of the tribe was asleep, Zondoro lay awake pondering what he would ask for. "Nagante has it and I do not," he thought. At last, after deep thought in his little brain, he knew what he would do, "I'll ask for a fire so great and show it in front of Nagante's eyes that he, and all those that follow him will now have to follow me." With that, Zondoro fell asleep.

The next day, Zondoro sent the brothers Gunte and Genga to bring Nagante and his tribe to them for a great occasion. The brothers were in the dark, as was everyone else, as to what Zondoro was planning, but he told the brothers enough to convince Nagante to come see this newfound magical object of Zondoro's.

Zondoro hid the lamp in a corner of the cave, half burying it in the dirt while covering the top portion with a small pile of stones.

"When you look into an abyss, the abyss also looks into you." - Friedrich Wilhelm Nietzsche

CHAPTER VI

Nagante, both wondering and curious as to what the great occasion was all about, left his home with a little over half of his entourage, which still added up to more than Zondoro's entire tribe. He left some men behind to guard the way to his precious fire. Traveling faster than usual, Nagante's tribe made it to Zondoro's cave with barely an hour of sunlight left.

"Greetings Zondoro my son, what is so important that you wish me to be here?" Zondoro led his people and his visitors to a clearing outside of the cave. A grove of about 20 fig trees interlaced with some scrub brush lay in front of the group. Zondoro had been walking in the middle of the band with a carefully wrapped package, concealing the lamp from Nagante's view. Zondoro had also ordered his people to say nothing of the artifact. At the designated place, Zondoro strode forth in front of the gathering cloud and lifted the lamp from a soft hide. He stretched out with both arms and displayed it prominently above his head.

"This is a present from the gods!" Zondoro shouted for all to hear.

Nagante's fascination level rose as did the others, but he was not impressed just yet, "Just what can you do with that thing?"

"Watch," Zondoro said as he rubbed it with the furry hide. All of the people stared wide-eyed with mouths agape. Some even dropped to their knees when a towering cloud materialized into the intimidating figure of the portly Djinn.

"What is your final wish master?"

Zondoro indeed had his wish thoroughly planned this time as he instructed the Djinni: "I would like this entire bunch of trees to burn with a fire that reaches the sky!" With his final request, the Djinni retreated to its home while conjuring the plan into action. A deadening silence filled the air. It had rained most of the day and everything was still dripping wet, but it was not raining now.

"Nothing is happening," Nagante said smugly, "Zondoro has played a trick...," but he stopped in midsentence. Lightning flashed once without thunder and a burst of flame appeared in the middle of the trees. It grew larger and larger as the seconds ticked by. Suddenly, in one gigantic leap, the flame surged into the low-lying clouds as lesser bursts leaped out from the base. These bursts shot out in all directions, many whizzing by the heads of the onlookers. The people slowly moved backwards, their eyes glued to the blazing spectacle, as if they were in some sort of hypnotic trance. This was powerful magic. Unexpectedly, Zondoro's three-year-old son, too young to display fear of the elements, was so engrossed in the magnificence of the fire, that he began running toward it.

"NO!" Shouted Quini, but the boy did not hear. Coordination is not a strength mastered by a 3-year-old, but the boy almost reached the edge of the trees when he stumbled. The fire now spread to the outer trees, defeating the wetness as it combined to produce a dense dark gray smoke, darker than the Djinni itself. Quini was in hot pursuit of her son as the boy struggled to right himself. The smoke curled and then spiraled around him blinding his eyes and polluting his tiny lungs.

When Quini reached him, the boy had slipped into unconsciousness. She grabbed him but failed to hold her breath. As she tried to stumble out blinded by the smoke and coughing loudly, a fiery branch from a perimeter tree hit her on the head and knocked her senseless. It was only the beginning of the growing conflagration. Smaller flames leapt out that seemed to turn into arrows of fire aimed directly at the crowd. Screams filled the air as members from both tribes caught on fire and danced about unnaturally in cursed delirium.

"Quini! Quini!" Zondoro shouted as he reached her seconds after she hit the ground. He tried to pull the branch down but burned his hands; it was too heavy and too hot. If there was any luck at all, it was Quini's, who lost consciousness as her body burned away. The boy was not as lucky as his screams rose above the tempest while his tender skin blackened and peeled away. On a spur of the moment, Zondoro felt that he had one last chance. Coughing from the smoke, he rushed back to where he had dropped the lamp and frantically rubbed it. He rubbed and rubbed but nothing happened.

"Come out, come out!" Cried Zondoro, but nothing happened. In a fit of rage, he picked up the lamp, brought it to the edge of the fire, and threw it in as far as he could. The lamp was now in the middle of the fire, but the flames did not consume it. Zondoro fell to his knees and began weeping, "What have I done? What have I done?"

As the fires died down, blackened smoldering bodies filled the plain. Zondoro lost over half his tribe including Khama, three women, and three additional children including his other 5-year-old son. What was left of Zondoro's tribe joined with Nagante, who had survived but lost six of his own people. Within the thin wisps of smoke, Zondoro lie down and fell asleep in the grass. He woke up alone for all the others had left with Nagante. He staggered over to the charred remains of his wife and youngest son, but they were beyond recognition, scorched to the bone in some areas.

He then wandered into the ashes where the trees and brush had burned away and found the lamp easily enough. If anything, it shined brighter than ever as if it was newly forged. He picked it up with his sore burn-blistered hands and blankly stared at it. He was in a state of severe depression, more like shock, a condition way beyond anger, sorrow, or grief. The pain in his hands intensified as he squeezed the lamp.

Finally, he left for the higher elevation of the mountains. He returned to the same cliffs he had crossed with Chaaca and Khama during his trip to Nagante's home. With the lamp in hand, he stopped at the rim overlooking the canyon below. He sat staring at the tiny stream some 250 feet below which had only existed recently due to the rains. Going over in his mind the events that had transpired, he felt so old and tired, and that life was simply not worth living any longer.

"Why?" He asked himself, "Why?" He had lost everything that mattered, his wife, his children, his leadership, and all his people. He could go and join Nagante, but there was pride at stake, not to mention that Nagante might not have him because of his evil fortune. Even if Nagante would take him in, he could not live with himself or face the others. With that, he stood up, flung the lamp over the cliff, and followed. The lamp could easily sustain the fall; Zondoro could not.

"Believing as I do that man in the distant future will be a far more perfect creature than he is now, it is an intolerable thought that he and all other sentient beings are doomed to complete annihilation after such long-continued slow progress. To those who fully admit the immortality of the human soul, the destruction of our world will not appear so dreadful." - Charles Darwin, from *Life and Letters*

CHAPTER VII

THE STREAM THAT HAD formed at the bottom of the elevated canyon swelled as the rains and runoff from above intensified. The enlarged stream swallowed the lamp and caught it in the swift current before any thoughts of sinking happened. Since it was in a mountain stream, where else could it go but down? There were bends and twists combined with rapids and tiny waterfalls. A crocodile even attempted to make the lamp a meal mistaking it for a bobbing fish; nevertheless, instead of gaining anything, the big croc lost a few teeth for the lamp's alloy was harder than a rock. The lamp's course found it weaving and bobbing until the stream ended in a small but deep lake. Over time as the continents shift and raised some more, the lake became a little shallower and more pond-like during the dry season, even drying up on occasion during a severe drought. The cycle would continue for thousands of years, a good 140,000 for the lamp to be exact give or take a few hundred years.

During the last ice age, there were four major periods of glaciations. At one time, ice covered thirty percent of the land on Earth above sea level. By the start of the twenty-first century, it was down to ten percent, and has been on the decline ever since due to global warming. Antarctica accounts for the majority of it in modern times. The third period was a very warm one. During the receding portion of the age, bridges between Asia and North America opened for a while allowing man himself along with some ice age mammals to travel to the New World. Those bridges were only temporary and quickly closed.

Glaciers do move slowly, just an inch or two forward or backward every year. The fourth and final period closed the bridges, but as it receded, it left water in its wake, the Bering Strait for one. As they inched backward, the northern parts of Europe, Asia, and America were uncovered. Consequently, the land became dryer leading to the reappearance of vast deserts and the extinction of old growth forests and many species of life forms that had previously not only adapted to but also depended on the cold.

From 150,000 years B.P. to about 10,000 years B.P., man made significant advances. He passed from the Old Stone Age to the Middle and then to the New. His upright walk advanced, he grew in height, and his brain swelled to new proportions. The increase in intelligence led to an incredible number of specialized tools, hundreds where there had only been a handful previously. Man developed heavy stone cleavers for more efficient dismembering of carcasses, followed by scrapers, needles, knives, engravers, harpoons, a wide variety of spear and arrowheads, and especially the hand ax and bow. Aside from stone, bone, antlers, and wood became tool-making material. Improved hunting led directly to significant advances in lifestyle.

Around ten thousand years ago, women started agriculture. They tilled and cultivated with hoe-like instruments, planted seeds, and discovered grains such as wheat, rice, and barley followed by an incredible array of fruits and vegetables: apples, cabbage, spinach, pears, lettuce, onion, garlic, plums, beets, parsnips, carrots, cherries, radishes, and grapes. The Native Americans in the new world had started vast corn farms combined with certain vegetables like potatoes, pumpkins and squash before the Old World caught on; nonetheless, the gap was a narrow one at best.

At this time, man was still much a hunter-gatherer, but the advances in hunting, agriculture, and fishing too allowed him to produce a surplus. Surpluses were stored in granaries or underground bunkers, and as a direct consequence of them, not only did the population increase, but man found himself with a strange new dilemma, and that was leisure time. In his spare time, painters used cave walls as their canvas, comprehensive language developed, social organization came about, and vast improvements included the mastery of fire, better clothing, and the beginnings of organized religion. The burying of the dead and though there was no tangible proof for it, the concept of a mysterious inner substance that would eventually be referred to as the soul came about as well.

"Since the days of Nimrod, the first hunter, every household has been stirred to its foundation every now and then by a male member stalking in with some wild thing 'plucked from the forest' and demanding that 'you cook it.' Then it is that the faithful wife[1] trembles with emotion. All eyes are upon her. Her ability in the estimation of her husband will rise or fall with that goose." - *A Book for a Cook*, The Pillsbury Co., 1905

---

1.   http://www.foodreference.com/html/q-wives.html

CHAPTER VIII

Naosha stared in fascination as the sun inexorably receded behind the great mountain of Ras Dashan. Her rich, but sun inspired raisin-like skin caught and held for a moment the last fading glimmer of sunlight. She walked back slowly to the brush shelters and caves passing by the tiny fields where most of the vegetables grew. At 47 years of age, she was the second oldest member of the tribe and well respected because of it. Her hair was mostly gray, thin, and wispy, and she was down to her last two functional teeth. She was overflowing with knowledge and her main occupation was dispensing advice and telling stories. She would tell one tonight to the 30 odd members of the tribe gathered about the fire.

"My grandmother's grandmother Nurobisi told the story to my grandmother who told it to my mother who told it to me and now I tell it to you. When Nurobisi was a young girl, it was her job to gather food from places far away and bring it back to the tribe to eat. She walked with the older women of the little village who always gave her too much to carry. So, on her way back, Nurobisi would stop off the trail and throw some food away to lighten her load. She did this for many days always throwing the food in the same place. The next year, many foods grew at the very same spot. The year after that she did the same thing, only this time, she threw the food over where our fields grow now. The next year, the food grew there and Nurobisi told everyone what she had done, and now, because of her, we have lots of food."

The people of the village now knew that it was the seeds that made the plants grow as they cultivated, planted, and hoed the undesirable weeds with their crude hand tools. Agriculture and food gathering remained a woman's job though young boys and old men sometimes helped. Just like people needed to drink water to quench their thirst, they learned too that plants required the most precious of resources to grow and thrive. Before widespread use of irrigation, they watered them by hand if dry.

The hunt for the men was still as important as ever, particularly in proving one's manhood. At twenty-three years of age, Leos, the son of Naosha, was highly skilled with the bow and arrow. At five foot, five inches tall, he was an inch above average height for men with dark black skin and dark brown eyes. He was slender barely tipping nonexistent scales at 110 pounds. Along with his weapons of choice, he carried a substance of great value and danger. Within the guts of his little pouch, which had once been part of the abdominal cavity of an infant deer, were a few tiny plant stems that grew wild in the forest. Within each seedpod was enough poison to kill a full-grown elephant. The hunter had to treat it with caution for if it entered his own bloodstream, he was a dead man.

Leos, with his best friend Gusho, decided that it was time to go out on a hunt. Gusho, an inch taller and significantly heavier said, "Why don't we go over to the lake and see what we can find there?"

"Yes," replied Leos. The lake was getting a little smaller everyday now that the rainy season had passed. When they reached the lake, they were careful to scout the perimeter searching for hungry leopards, panthers, crocodiles, and other predators that had no fear of attacking a man, especially if they were hungry. A group of noisy elephants was frolicking on one side of the lake, washing themselves and blowing water with their trunks wherever they pleased. There was little if anything in the world that would dare attack an adult African elephant. Babies might be vulnerable to lions, but the mother elephants gathered in bunches to protect their children. A few zebras at a time approached the water meticulously while the rest of the herd situated in various lookout positions ready at any moment to sound the alarm. A few crocodiles basked in the sun as they were mostly inactive during the daytime; but, due to their cold-bloodedness, the temperature of their blood rose and fell with the changing weather. Like a battery, the sun recharged them ever so slowly.

Gusho and Leos were not interested in elephants or zebras; the former were too large and formidable, and they could get rather nasty if attacked. If they dropped a zebra, it was a bit too much for the two of them to carry back; at best, they could hack off a hindquarter before the big cats would converge upon them.

"There is what we want right there," pointed Gusho.

"I see it," answered Leos.

"He's still a little one, but will do just fine," said Gusho. They were talking about an immature wild boar, very tasty eating. His tusks were only a few inches long, ones that could still prove treacherous at the precise angle of attack. The two hunters opened their pouches and carefully dipped their arrows into the sappy poisonous liquid within. A stiff urine soaked and dried vine was what they slipped the rear end of their arrows into as they pulled them back. Gusho was the first to shoot, and at barely thirty yards, he did not miss. His arrow struck the rear foot of the beast. The boar screamed and snorted in agony and ran directly at the men as best it could somewhat dragging its bloody rear foot along. It could still move on its three good feet.

"Shoot! Shoot!" wailed Gusho.

"Ah...," Leos murmured as he dropped his arrow in panic. The boar was 20 yards away and closing. Gusho started running. Leos picked up the arrow a split second later and thrust it into the bow. The boar was 10 yards away and screaming madly as if it were insane.

"Run! Run!" shouted Gusho.

For Leos, aiming was not necessary at this range; he pulled back and fired. Just a few yards ahead, the arrow landed smack in the left eye of the boar. Blood poured forth and another scream wailed from the boar, but it kept coming! Frozen with terror, Leos could not move. The boar, bellowing like a beaten bull and limping like a one-legged man who had lost his crutches, took one last plunge aiming its tusk for the guts of the man who had shot it. It landed short of its mark at the feet of Leos. The boar was still alive but luckily for Leos, the poison in its foot had finally taken effect while it was airborne. The last moment before death, Leos, breathing easier now, felt a little sympathy for the boar.

"That was a close one," said Gusho who had returned and patted Leos on the shoulder, "Why didn't you run?"

"I couldn't," was all Leos said.

The wild hog was a delicacy for the tribe as well as being the ancestor of all domesticated swine throughout the world. They all shared in its roasting and there was ample praise for the successful hunters. Gusho and Leos would later recreate the story, exaggerating the details a bit to make themselves look strong and brave. It was still an impressive story with the remarkable eye shot, especially to Zebo. Zebo was the last man in the tribe to kill a boar; however, he suffered a severe goring in the upper leg before completing the difficult task of killing it. Now he could hardly walk, only by hobbling around on a stick that acted like a makeshift crutch. His hunting days appeared to be over, which left him much like a burden to the clan, a situation that he felt overwhelmingly guilty about; thus, the taste of the new boar was somewhat bittersweet for him.

"The fear of some divine and supreme power keeps men in obedience." - Robert Burton, *Anatomy of Melancholy*

CHAPTER IX

As the circle of life would have it, it became hotter and consequently dryer as the rains had ceased. The lamp lay at the bottom of the lake, the very one that was a favorite hunting spot of Gusho and Leos. Even though it had not moved, it was closer to the surface as the lake transformed into a much smaller pond. As far as the hunters knew, the lake had never gone completely dry in their lifetimes, even in the worst of droughts.

At the very bottom, a lazy hippopotamus lay asleep. As her air supply dwindled, she would have to surface for another gulp. With a vicious kick, she propelled herself to the surface; nevertheless, the kicking motion did something that so many others had not. It dislodged the lamp, which had been rooted to the lake's foundation for thousands of years. Hippos carpeted the lake bottom. The movement of others created underwater currents that brought the lamp closer and closer to the shore before its weight sent it back to the bottom.

As the lamp was swirling about, Leos and Gusho departed the village for another hunt. Ninte and Maola, the respective wives of the two, were busy grinding wheat on stones used solely for processing grains. As it was ground, the granules fell into primitive baskets created by the weaving of certain flexible sticks and vines. It would either be stored in the cave or in a couple of the spare huts that were set aside specifically for that purpose.

"That's the last of it," said Ninte as they finished up for the day. Grinding by hand with stones was a slow arduous process.

"That ought to be enough for a long time," replied Maola.

"Let's put the baskets in the hut and go out to the lake."

"Yes, there should be some good fishing today."

It was that time of year when fish were easy to catch. Many spawned in small streams and tiny waterways that diverted from the larger river that flowed into the lake. As the mother fish left hundreds of eggs, she was often too exhausted to fight her way back to the lake, especially since the water levels had dropped off. Many of the fish were stuck, becoming a ready meal for some hungry beast or bird.

Ninte, at a hair below five feet in height, was still taller and rounder than Maola. Consequently, Leos and Ninte presented a rather odd couple with her being short and chubby while he was relatively tall and thin. Maola with dark, deep-set eyes walked slightly stoop-shouldered with sagging breasts from feeding her children. She had a boy of seven years and a girl of five. She was thinner than and not nearly as strong as Ninte. Children were a burden in so many ways and required carrying before they could walk, and it was routine for mothers to tie them on to their backs while working in the fields. They would stay behind under the watchful eyes of Naosha the elder, among others in the village as Maola and Ninte went off to catch fish.

"Don't forget a basket Ninte," Maola said.

"I've got one right here."

The two women set off in hopes of returning with something worthwhile in their basket; but today, they would catch something else that they would not have conjured in a thousand dreams. They did have to be on alert for dangerous beasts that lurked about the watering hole. The big gray elephant herd was there, monopolizing one part of the lake; then again, who was going to deprive them of that privilege? It was always wise to keep one's distance from the descendants of mammoths. Walking part way around the lake, the two women approached the stream up a few hundred yards until they came to a narrow rivulet that sprung from the main stream.

"Here we are," Ninte stated the obvious.

"Look at all the fish there!" Maola cried out as she pointed downward. Many were dead and the smell was powerful. There was a logjam at a sandy uprising in the stream where the water was only an inch or so in depth. Normally, the fish could scoot or even jump to pass it by, but enough dead had accumulated to cause a blockage. The harsh drought lowered water levels virtually everywhere.

"Let's pick up a few of the good ones here," said Ninte.

"I can taste them already," answered Maola.

They picked up a few that still had an ounce of life left in them, filled the basket three-fourths of the way up and proceeded back toward the lake taking turns carrying the heavy basket. Out in the lake, just a few yards away, a faint golden-like glitter caught the eye of Maola as Ninte hefted the basket.

Maola grabbed Ninte by the arm. "Look over there, do you see it?"

"No, what are you pointing at?"

"That light, right there."

"Oh! Now I do, what is it?"

"I don't know," Maola said as the two stepped closer to the edge to get a better look. Ninte dropped the basket for a moment as well. "I'm going to get it," said Maola. "Keep an eye out, will you?"

"Be careful," said Ninte nervously as her eyes scouted about for predators, but nothing of consequence caught her eye.

Maola waded into the lake. As the water encircled her waist, she reached down to where the light had glimmered and scooped up the gleaming artifact.

"What is it?" called out Ninte.

The lamp looked as good as it had been in the basement of the Billings' home, even better since the dust and most of the tarnish was now gone. Maola stared at it in fascination as metal was virtually unknown at the time, particularly in any finished or manufactured form.

"I am not sure what it is," said Maola as she handed it to Ninte. Ninte turned it over carefully inspecting the handle, spout, and the little bell-shaped finial on top of the cover mysteriously welded to the base. She turned it over again, but this time her fondling created enough friction to trigger the interior substance. A lofty, shimmering cloud of smoke seeped from the spout revealing a portly figure of Middle Eastern origin.

"What do you wish for woman?"

"Whaaaa....ttt? Whoooo.....are you?" Ninte stammered.

The Djinni glared down at her pretentiously awaiting a proper response.

"He wants you to make a wish," said Maola who was strangely calm and seemingly unafraid. "Hurry up because I don't think you have a lot of time," she added intuitively as if she sensed the urgency.

Magic was nothing new to them because they had heard of it in stories and experienced things they could not explain like thunder, lightning, heavy rains, rainbows, and basically anything odd that happened.

"But what should we wish for?" Ninte inquired.

"Let's ask for good crops!" Maola ventured.

The request was a likely one since it was comparable to what the men did on a major hunt. They often made the paintings on the cave walls just before the hunt took place as a good magical omen. Some came afterward as a commemoration of success.

"Good idea Maola," said Ninte as she directed her attention and voice to the menacing figure above her, "We would like to have good crops this year for our village."

With that, the Djinni quickly withdrew to its prison and the project was set into motion. It was an unselfish wish since it would truly benefit all and not just one. Little did the women know, two more like it could dispose of the Djinni from the planet for good.

"Do you think it will come true?" Ninte asked. She did appear shaken.

"I don't know what to think," reasoned Maola. She had shown no fear to the amazement of Ninte who tried to emulate her in turn.

"Let's talk to Naosha, she'll probably know what to do," said Ninte.

"I wonder if it will come true," Maola answered, "I think we have some more wishes left too, that thing or whatever it is did ask for your first wish."

"What else do you think we should wish for?"

"Let's think about it on the way back," replied Ninte. Ninte grasped the lamp as Maola bent down to pick up the basket of fish. "Wait, feel it," said Ninte. Maola touched it and it was warm, "Maybe I could get a bow made for Leos out of this same material," added Ninte who was fascinated by the smooth hard surface of the lamp.

Maola picked up the basket of fish, "If our crops are going to be good, we may need more huts."

"Then why don't we just ask for our huts to be filled with food? It would be less work," added Ninte.

"Now that's a better idea," Maola agreed. They continued to ponder the possibilities of their wish. As they approached the village, they stopped near the fields.

"Do you think we should tell anyone besides Naosha about this thing?" Maola questioned.

"I don't think so," said Ninte, "Let's hide it in the bottom of the basket." When they finally approached the village huts, they sought out Naosha immediately. The huts were large enough to hold about three adults, perhaps four if two were children. Naosha was in one of them with Ninte's baby while Maola's children were playing with others outside.

"Ah, there you are Naosha, we wish to speak with you about something important," said Maola.

"Well come in and sit for a spell," ordered the heavily wrinkled elder.

Ninte dropped the basket outside while retrieving the lamp from beneath the fish, "This is what we wish to talk to you about." Ninte produced the bronze artifact.

Naosha gazed at the lamp both thoughtfully and superstitiously. One did not reach her advanced age of 47 without acting with reason mixed in with a good dose of caution. Her own intuition told her that something wasn't quite right. "Do you know what it is?"

"No," answered Ninte.

"We were hoping that you could tell us," declared Maola. Maola and Ninte added what had happened to them when the spirit had appeared and explained about the wish.

"Let me get a closer look," Naosha gestured. Ninte handed it over while the elderly woman turned it over. "From what you say about this spirit within, I cannot tell if it is a good one or an evil one. You say that you wished for good crops?"

Maola and Ninte both nodded in the affirmative.

"Then perhaps we should take a closer look at the fields," stated Naosha. They strode out to the fields slowly since Naosha walked hunched over at a snail's pace. Ninte's daughter followed along behind them. An amazing site struck them at once as they stared at the fields in awe. Everything had grown so tightly together that they could not see any dirt between the rows.

"Look at the cabbages and the lettuce!" Ninte cried out. The heads were twice as big as they had been the previous day.

Maola pulled out a few carrots, "Look at these!" She held them out and they were over a foot long, nearly three times as big as they usually harvested. Everything was significantly larger than before.

Naosha scratched her head, thinking that it could only be a good spirit to do this for them. An evil one would not; yet, she had some doubts. She then commanded Ninte to do what she had done earlier to call the spirit forth.

"But we need to have a wish ready," Ninte protested.

"We thought that we might wish for some more huts to be filled with food," suggested Maola.

"I think we have too much food now and it will rot before we can eat it all," reasoned Naosha. "The men can build another hut or two to store some of this excess."

"Well then, what shall we wish for?" Ninte asked.

In the distance, Maola observed Zebo barely getting by as he limped along. She felt pity for him as did the others. "I know, we'll make a wish for Zebo so that he can walk again and hunt like the others."

"That sounds like a good wish," responded Ninte.

Both younger women turned to Naosha for confirmation. Naosha nodded affirmatively; after all, Zebo was her son. The old woman sat down waiting patiently for the spirit to appear. Ninte began turning the lamp repeatedly, but nothing happened.

"Where is the spirit?" Naosha inquired.

"I don't know," said Ninte, "It came out earlier when I did this." She began shaking it vigorously, turning it over and over, and then finally rubbed it.

The Djinni hissed out of its home menacing above them as it directed its attention to Ninte, "What is your second wish woman?"

Naosha shifted backward unconsciously as she craned her neck upward. The hairs rose on the back of her neck and goose bumps formed on her leathery skin. It certainly didn't look like a kind spirit with mean, vengeful, slanted eyes and a hissing voice. With an inner or sixth sense, Naosha sensed trouble, but Ninte's voice interrupted her thoughts.

"We would like for Zebo to walk again like the rest of us do." The cloudy spirit evaporated back into the lamp at the end of the request.

"Look at Zebo!" Maola exclaimed. Zebo dropped his stick and was walking, then hopping, and then running, shouting as he went along.

"I can walk! No! I can run!" The woman readily heard the cheerful screams of Zebo as Zebo danced about.

Naosha still had her doubts. As an old saying not yet invented but generally accurate went: "You can't get something for nothing," as something similar had crossed Naosha's mind. It was too easy, and anything worth anything was usually hard, at least in her experience. She had a sinking feeling that the spirit would want something in return. Would there be a price to pay? She couldn't get over how awful and even hateful the way the spirit looked. It had a sly nasty grin. Perhaps the curse it placed on her blinded her. One thing Naosha did not know was the fact that Ninte's second wish was another unselfish one, a third like it would rid the world of this mean looking thing.

"The difficulty in life is the choice."
George Moore, *The Bending of the Bough*, Act III

CHAPTER X

G usho, Leos, the newly mended Zebo, and nearly all men of the village except for the very eldest, gathered for a hunt. They could live on grains and vegetables and had been forced to in the past when game was scarce, but hunting was so ingrained in their culture that they would do it unless the surplus of meat was as great as that as other food sources. That was virtually impossible since meat never kept for long in the hot heat of Africa; however, the taste of it was preferred. Young boys too had to prove their bravery and coming of age with the hunt, traits that would not leave them when they became men. Naosha spoke to the village of the newly found artifact in one of her stories. The site of Zebo, Naosha's son, and the abundance in the fields was proof enough that they were favored by a magical being.

Kao was the master painter of the tribe and his works on the cave walls illustrated man with bow and arrow adjacent to the beasts that he killed. His tools included sticks with hair and fur attached to the end that served as brushes and paints made up from plants, flowers, and even blood. Prior to the hunt, he had been busy painting a magnificent buffalo with two hunters armed with bows and arrows. The hunters resembled crude stickmen, but the buffalo, brown, formidable, and life-like, had been a more patient work of art. The hunters believed that painted illustrations appealed to the spirits around them to aid them in their quest.

Ninte was alone with the lamp and was suddenly feeling very important, so far, she thought to herself, "I have been the only one to summon the spirit." A sense of recognition of her power crossed her mind. After the pre-hunting ceremony with the painting on the wall, she was thinking, would if her mate, Leos, was the one to shoot one today all by himself? No one ever before had killed the exact creature on the wall particularly for a single hunt. Leos could become chief if he could perform a few deeds like this. "I could arrange them too and become the wife of the chief. Then I could have more children, maybe a son and he might become chief after his father. I would be the most important woman in the village," she smiled to herself, "Yes; this spirit could prove to be quite useful!" Ninte did not know that she had only one wish left. No one had asked the Djinni about rules, obligations, or even simple questions. There were some limitations and the Djinni would willingly spew information but only if specifically asked. She rubbed the lamp and the spirit came forth.

"What is your final wish woman?"

Ninte, in her haste, did not really hear that 'final' part and broke out hurriedly, "I want my husband to kill a buffalo during the hunt all by himself, for us!" She was counting her days until she would be the wife of a chief as the Djinni, with an ever so slight sly grin on its face, retreated. Unlike the first two, this was a slightly selfish wish.

The hunters, armed with bows, arrows, poison pouches, knives, cleavers, and a variety of other tools, set off for the hunt. They traveled south to what is now the lands of Kenya. The upper north-central portion of this land contains a sizeable lake, much bigger than the one close to their village; once again, a popular gathering place for all sorts of thirsty animals. When they reached the lake, they split into small groupings, two groups of three and two more with two each.

Leos, Gusho, and Zebo consisted of one such group. A few wildebeests came into view and Zebo, anxious since he was newly back on the hunt, recognized them as prime targets. With horns and horse-like manes and tails, wildebeests were like large African antelope with ox-like heads. Zebo set his arrow, strained the bow, and fired. The arrow pierced the hindquarters of one of the beasts. Gusho and Zebo reacted immediately and engaged in hot pursuit. Leos had an arrow ready but retracted it when the wounded animal ran, and consequently, fell several steps behind the other two as he eased it back.

Suddenly, an enormous white buffalo, shaggy maned and hump-shouldered with huge horns crossed directly in the path of Leos, but behind Gusho and Zebo. Too occupied with the injured wildebeest, the two hunters in front of Leos did not notice the great buffalo, but Leos didn't miss it. Strangely enough, the buffalo stopped and glared blankly at Leos. Leos also stopped. He carefully dipped his arrowhead within his pouch, placed his arrow in the bow, and launched it toward the buffalo at point-blank range. As the arrow penetrated the shoulder of the white monster, a violent scream erupted from the beast as it charged in Leos' direction. Leos quickly strung a second arrow not bothering with the poison for there was no time. This one struck the charging beast in the chest just below the heart, but it kept coming. The buffalo bellowed out an ear-splitting wail, but its speed and momentum never wavered despite the two deep poison-tainted wounds.

Leos, realizing that it would take additional time for the poison to work on such a large specimen, turned and sped in the opposite direction from whence he had come. The shaggy beast followed at full speed dead ahead. The fastest man can run a mile in just under four minutes; however, a charging buffalo needed only a few seconds over two such minutes to cover the same distance. This one could run much faster than could the puny man in front of him.

Leos was running for his life, but it was only a matter of seconds before the buffalo closed the gap between them. Leos could hear the pounding of the hooves, feel the rumbling behind him, and then the moist hot bloody spray on his back from the angry snorts and steaming breath. Leos could only pray the poison would work rapidly, but timing was the key factor, especially for Leos who was running out of it. Leos reeled in time to see the deadly eyes of his pursuer as the full force of its horns buried themselves so deeply into his chest that the tips protruded out his back. The two were locked together in their last breaths with neither having the strength to unlock itself from the other. It was not necessary that either had to die, but they did, together, each at the hands of the other.

Ninte knew that Leos would kill the buffalo and bring great glory to their family, but the death of Leos was something that she had not counted on. His was not the only tragedy of the day. During the duel between Leos and the buffalo, while pursuing the wounded wildebeest, Zebo ran straight into the path of a massive boa constrictor.

The thick, lengthy snake was on its way to the precious water when the hunter rudely stepped upon it. It happened to be hungry too since its last meal had been over two months ago, a small baboon that it had fully digested. The crafty serpent couldn't pass up a gift horse, or in this case, a gift man in the mouth as it grasped the former injured leg of Zebo and pulled him downward. It coiled around the human several times and then did what it did best, constricted until it squeezed the life from Zebo. Zebo's cries never registered for he had no sound nor breath to exhale.

Gusho had moved forward with his full attention upon the wildebeest; when he realized that Zebo was not by his side, he turned back to see the end of a deathly struggle, the end for his companion. Gusho, letting the wildebeest go, was too late to help Zebo as he rushed backward, pulled a knife, and lashed and slashed at the snake some twenty times, but Zebo's last breath had been long gone like a homerun to center field. The snake did not fare well either from Gusho's berserker-like onslaught.

Frustrated, Gusho gave out a loud emergency signal cry for the other hunters to come, and they did. The men assembled from one killing site to the other, taking turns cutting up the remains of both the snake and buffalo as quickly as they could. Time was always of the essence particularly around such a big kill scene. They tried to pull Leos off the buffalo, but the buffalo's horns welded him in place. With their cleavers, they chopped the horns off with Leos still attached to them. The snake was softer and had uncoiled thanks to Gusho slashing it so many times. Gusho was sad for Zebo but wept even more over the loss of Leos, his best friend.

"They were good hunters," remarked one.

"Yes," said some while others nodded a tribute to the dead. Normally at the village, Zebo and Leos would have been given a proper burial, but out on the hunt, the two, along with the carcasses of the buffalo and snake, and the wounded wildebeest, though it had escaped the human hunters, would all become presents for the hungry lions, hyenas, jackals, vultures, and even insects; all on their way. Rarely did anything in the wild ever go to waste. The men would carry what they could from the buffalo and snake.

Sorrow cast upon the villagers when the news arrived. Those affected most were Ninte and Naosha for one had lost a husband, the other a son.

"It is all my fault," cried Ninte.

"How so? He was hunting and the buffalo killed him, how could it be your fault?" Naosha questioned. Ninte broke down and told her how she had summoned the spirit and wished for Leos to kill a buffalo. Naosha was horrified and that sick feeling she had about the spirit came to light, no, it was not a spirit, but an evil demon. "It is the fault of the demon spirit Ninte, not you, and the demon must be taken away from here, far away. It is your duty to rid us of this thing."

"What shall I do?"

"Take the spirit over the mountains far away and throw it back into some water," said Naosha.

Ninte left with the lamp, never seen again. She had crossed Ras Dashan, descended to a valley on the other side, and tossed the lamp into a slow-moving river, one that would become a flowing rapid during the heart of the next rainy season. Weakened, she became a meal for a leopard family and gave no resistance when the mother leopard pounced on her back and bit deeply into her invitingly soft neck.

Naosha told the complete story, a story that she would not like to repeat, for it was tragic, but she did. Kao painted Leos and the buffalo in their deadly grip as well as a fallen Zebo wrapped about a snake on the cave wall. A picture of the lamp was included with the dead signifying that it belonged to evilness. A lone figure of Ninte far off to one side of the wall was walking away with a strange blobby shape within her grasp.

"Living fearlessly is not the same thing as never being afraid. It's good to be afraid occasionally. Fear is a great teacher." - Michael Ignatieff, *O Magazine*, April, 2007

———◉———

CHAPTER XI

———◉———

SOME YEARS AFTER NINTE had perished, Nambo, a lean and wiry hunter with more scars than someone who flogged frequently with a whip, was the next to find the lamp. Naturally, it was in the dry season and the lamp had come to rest between some rocks along a sandbar in a shallow part of the river as the depth of the water had fallen drastically. When he pulled it out, wiped it off, and the Djinni appeared, Nambo was so frightened that he flung the lamp back into the river before the Djinni could finish more than three words. The smoky like substance flowed back into the lamp as Nambo ran several miles to distance himself from the demon. Unbeknownst to him, it was a good move for Nambo.

"Homes in empty logs
Or a hollow tree
Little perfect hexagons
Patterned intricately.
Infertile tireless workers
Always on the wing
Working hard and guarding
With a deadly sting.
A mission to the flowers
To return with pollen-filled legs
To serve the royal giant queen
Who'll lay a thousand eggs.
When the work is finally done
And the months have passed
It's time to sleep forever
For the combs are filled at last."
Mark Pickvet, *Honeybees*, 1989

CHAPTER XII

The lamp had found its way north along the Nile beyond Lake Nasser and the future place of the Aswan Dam. Considering the vast geography of the world, the population of man thousands of years ago was quite limited. It would take another series of advancements and nearly four thousand years before someone discovered the lamp again.. Once man began using tools, the progress toward bigger and better endeavors was simply stunning. The San hunters gradually became nomadic rulers of Africa for some millennia, and existed until farmers, followed by European invaders, claimed most the land by the nineteenth century. The San were highly adaptable establishing small reusable campsites during different seasons for untold generations. Shelters stood in the open, built with sticks, brush, bone, and grass. Fat layers of grass made comfortable beds inside the homes. About the only problem was that indoor grass did not stop millions of bugs from nesting cozily indoors with their generous human hosts.

The San lived and collected food everywhere across the continent. They gathered nuts, fruits, roots, and other foods in the rainforests. The same nourishment grew in the woodlands, with the addition of vegetables. The San herded cattle in the open plains and in the savannah, and even stole some from neighboring San tribes. They gathered seeds seasonally, then planted and cultivated them. Fish were caught in shallow pools or rivulets, and then with the use of boats in deeper waters. They fashioned animal snares from plant fibers. Newly honed grinding stones processed foods more efficiently. Hunting was still a major source of food and the persistence of toolmakers brought on the development of more advanced weapons. Hunters discovered new poisons in which to dip their arrow tips. Microliths, or tiny stone-chipped arrow barbs fitted to wooden shafts, were used with superb accuracy and devastating killing power. Kinship ties were very important with the San. They traveled in bands of 10 to 30 as they set up their camps. Inner marriage within bands kept most all of them closely related; furthermore, parents named children after their parents. The lack of abundant new names did cause confusion, especially if several grandchildren had the same names. Gokoa, the name of a young man as well as three of his cousins from nearby tribes, belonged to a San tribe where some serious unrest was brewing. Gokoa was tall and lean with a heavy Cro-Magnon face. Cro-Magnon peoples differed much from Neanderthals in that they were more modern with thinner faces, high-domed foreheads, and much taller where Neanderthals were short, stocky, had flatter heads, and were quite strong. The Cro-Magnon had one key advantage above all others, and that was a considerably larger brain.

Gokoa relayed some of that restlessness to his good friend Mhanto, "Khoro is getting very old and must give up his leadership soon."

"I agree, but how can he turn it over to Nimpopo? We all know that Nimpopo is weak and does not think like a leader should," said Mhanto. Mhanto was also lean but not as tall or as strong as Gokoa.

Khoro must break tradition, he cannot allow his halfwit son to rule," stated Gokoa.

"That has never been done before. All leadership of all people is passed from father to son. You had better not mention that to anyone," said Mhanto uneasily.

"If Nimpopo becomes chief, then I shall leave and join another tribe," declared Gokoa. "I believe that I would make a better chief or anyone else for that matter than Nimpopo."

"I agree," said Mhanto uneasily again. It was easy to say that Nimpopo would not make a good leader, but it was more dangerous to suggest another aside from the chief's son. It was nothing more than treason.

Nimpopo, the son of Khoro and the grandson of another Nimpopo, since deceased, was not the sharpest arrowhead in the pouch. His mother Ibisi had complications during birth and nearly died. Nimpopo's oxygen was cut off a little too long which in turn destroyed many brain cells; thus, hampering his proper development. To put it in modern nomenclature, he suffered from mild intellectual disability. That fact, combined with his poor eyesight, or more accurately, nearsightedness, made him a terrible hunter. If he could not lead a hunt, how could he lead an entire band?

"It is not right," protested Gokoa, "No way must we allow Nimpopo to lead us."

"I don't know," said Mhanto, "His grandfather was a good leader and Khoro is a good leader. It will be difficult to get others to agree to break tradition."

"It must be done," stated Gokoa emphatically. Gokoa was by far the tallest, strongest, and best hunter, and possessed most every other quality a leader would need. His problem was that he belonged in the New World where leadership with the native population was not based on hereditary, but on skill, not so in the Old.

"I will help you Gokoa," Mhanto said at last, giving in.

"First I will speak to Lenga for she is wise; after that, we will go in search of honey."

"Would you like me to go with you to see Lenga?"

"No, I do not want to get you involved yet. I will meet you at your hut when I am finished." Gokoa strode off to seek out the elderly woman.

When Gokoa arrived at her hut, he said, "Greetings Lenga, I would like to talk with you if it is convenient for you."

"Ah Gokoa, sit, sit my son," asserted Lenga. The elder referred to everyone as son or daughter for she was old enough to be the mother of all, at least in her own particular band. "What is troubling you my son?"

"It's about...," he hesitated.

"Go on."

"It's about Nimpopo, I am afraid that Khoro is getting old and can no longer perform his duties as chief. No matter how old and weak he gets, he will always be able to lead far better than Nimpopo. I do not think that Nimpopo will be able to lead at all."

Lenga, old and withered, continued cracking nuts slowly but steadily with a hand-sized flat-edged stone. She thought a moment before speaking as all wise people do. "I remember two great chiefs named Nimpopo. It is our law that the new leader be the first born of the chief. It cannot be changed. It will be our duty to work harder and help Nimpopo, no matter how badly he performs."

"I do not know," said Gokoa.

"It is law. You are young Gokoa. If you cannot live under Nimpopo with your own people, then you must move on to another tribe. Nimpopo will become leader whether you like it or not, it is our way. No good can come otherwise."

"Thank you for your time, I must meet Mhanto to search for honey. I will bring you some when we return."

Lenga smiled revealing her three remaining teeth, "Good luck my son and always beware of danger, it can come when you least expect it."

"Goodbye old one."

Gokoa went along to Mhanto's hut, "Are you ready?"

Mhanto stepped forth immediately, "Let's go."

They carried a few tools along with bow and arrows. The essentials included flint for making fire, a hand ax, and some hollowed out gourds. The ax sported a wooden handle with a sharp cut stone for the blade. It was capable of downing a modest tree or for cutting up smaller branches and logs. Though not all that edible, they saved the seeds of gourds ever year and replanted them. Hollowed-out bottle gourds made excellent water holders. Artisans used other gourds as bowls and containers, decorated and painted them, and as masks, hats, net floats for fishing, and on this day, possibly to transport honey.

Their first stop was to find a bee, and what better place than where the gourds grew? Many gourds were in the beginnings of their development stage and hundreds of large attractive bright blossoms called to the bees. It was a symbiotic relationship as the plants readily advertised their pollen, and the bees hungrily sought it to build their honeycomb hives. As the bees moved from blossom to blossom, they inadvertently pollinated the gourd plants. Within the vines, the two men were roaming freely with at least a hundred bees moving about. They focused on certain bees, but the ones they sought seemed to be in no hurry to leave. They wandered from white blossoms to yellow to orange and then to red when finally, one in front of Mhanto rose up high in the air with legs overloaded with pollen.

"I've got one!" Mhanto shouted, "Follow me!"

"Stay with him," said Gokoa as he jumped up and started following Mhanto following a bee headed straight for the nest. It was making a straight direct course, a beeline so to speak, never changing or varying its altitude by more than an inch. They followed it diligently for nearly half a mile when the bee suddenly shot upward fully fifty feet high into a large hollow branch of a fig tree.

"That's it," Gokoa said pointing upward. He passed Mhanto during the run and was not short of breath.

"You....are....right," Mhanto spoke between breaths.

"Look at all of them," Gokoa said as there must have been hundreds flying about. The average wild bee's nest could easily contain fifty thousand bees. "One of us is going to have to climb up there and chop that branch off," Gokoa was thinking.

"How will we keep from being stung?"

"We'll have to use fire and smoke them out," answered Gokoa.

"I suppose both of us could go up, one chop the branch and one wave a lighted stick," suggested Mhanto.

"Well I guess that I do not have a better idea," confessed Gokoa, "If you can smoke them some, I think I can chop faster."

"Good with me," said Mhanto. They gathered some dry twigs, spongy brown rotted moss, brown dead leaves, and a four-foot-long dead branch that would serve as Mhanto's torch. With several strikes of the flint, they quickly ignited their materials. Many thousands of years in the past, Zondoro would have believed that they possessed magic for their ability to make fire on demand.

"Let me go up a little first before you follow," said Gokoa.

"Be careful," warned Mhanto.

Gokoa stepped from branch to branch and made it safely halfway up. "Bring it."

Mhanto climbed carefully with burning stick in hand and gingerly passed Gokoa. As he moved upward, slower going now, Mhanto waved the stick back and forth, even more vigorously as he approached greater numbers of the swarming insects. The bees sensed intruders but were afraid of the brightness and the smoke of the burning stick. Those caught in the smoke experienced disorientation, and by natural instinct, flew away from it; however, many from the hive were now on high alert and made a beeline for the intruders. Gokoa chopped quickly and frantically but not quite fast enough. The flame at the end of the stick was expiring. The smoking end that was petering out gave them a few extra seconds, but still not enough. Some of the angry bees attacked through the smoke; others joined in more aggressively once the smoke thinned. The two men scampered down the tree fighting off bees as they ran away like the wind. Several bees managed to administer their suicidal stings.

When they made what they felt was a safe distance, Gokoa spoke as he was pulling out black stingers from his arm, "You all right?"

"Yes, just a few pains here and there," answered Mhanto who was rubbing the stings all over his bare legs.

"Are you ready to do it again?" Gokoa grinned. He was not one to give up easily.

"Uh, yes, maybe," answered Mhanto who was not quite as enthusiastic this time.

"It will be easier, I almost made it through this far," Gokoa spread his thumb and forefinger to reveal about three inches of the four necessary to get through. "Let's go light another torch!"

"Well, all right," said Mhanto. "Maybe we should get a bigger fire going on the ground."

"Great idea, let's do it!"

The branch fell with a crashing thud as Gokoa broke through before Mhanto's torch expired on the second attempt. Angry confused bees dashed about this way and that, everywhere it seemed while the two men rushed down to the relative safety of the fire they had built. The precious, thick liquid that they were seeking was seeping out of the shattered branch. They worked quickly adding to the fire, each grabbing a newly lit piece of wood so that they could approach the fallen honey-laden branch. Mhanto swung his branch about while Gokoa boldly grabbed the prize branch and dragged it closer to their fire.

The extreme heat and excessive smoke were enough motivation to scatter what remained of the bees in the broken nest. The precious honey was now theirs for the taking. They thrust the hollowed-out bottle-shaped gourds where the oozing honey was flowing forth. Gokoa lifted it to pour it out more efficiently and aim it into the respective containers. Their undertaking had been a success, and those back at the encampment would praise their efforts.

The bees had taken his mind temporarily away from the Nimpopo situation, but Gokoa returned to it and thought of some new questions for Lenga to consider. He brought the old woman some honey in a somewhat tiny, underdeveloped gourd and said, "Greetings Lenga, I have brought you some honey as promised."

"I have heard of your adventure, many thanks my son. Please sit and visit with an old woman."

"I would like that." Gokoa related the brief story of how they had acquired the honey somewhat accurately, exaggerating a detail or two here and there. He would embellish it even more later for the rest of the tribe. Now, he was more interested in Nimpopo and maneuvered the conversation in that direction. "I am still concerned about our band and Nimpopo. I have been on hunts with him and others. Many of us have had to save him for he does not see well. What would happen to our people if he died?"

"This has happened before," she said. "I learned of these things from the great meetings that many different peoples attend. The first son of a chief in one of my cousins' tribes died, but he had a younger brother who took his place. Another small tribe of only 12 people lost their leader and they broke up, joining other tribes."

"Nimpopo has no brothers and I think that our tribe of 28 is too large to break up," stated Gokoa.

"Then as I told you before, you and the others must help Nimpopo as best as you can."

"You are wise," said Gokoa, "I will do my best to see that he does not get hurt."

"You are good to say so Gokoa, go now so I may rest."

"Goodbye," Gokoa said as he left.

The next day Gokoa and Mhanto, as part of their duties, went to check on the fishing nets set up in narrow tributaries that branched from the Nile. They worked separately each removing fish captured within the crudely woven fibers held up by the hollow gourd floats. The gourds functioned as floats and location devices. They only had to spot the gourds to find the nets.

Gokoa was in the process of hauling a net out of the water when his eye focused on something sparkling beneath the water's surface. He reached in and plucked out a somewhat dark golden object. It was the lamp, well preserved since it had last been touched eons ago. Gokoa gazed at it curiously, not having a clue what it was.. No toolmaker of our people or anyone like our people would have made this he thought to himself. The metal itself was not too surprising since arrowheads and other sharp implements were sometimes made from bits of natural pure metal pieces like iron, copper, and even gold when it was chipped and separated out of rocks every now and then by the toolmakers. He smoothed over the water droplets on the surface, which had bubbled as it dripped off. The rubbing motion was enough to compel the Djinni from its imprisonment. Pssssshhh! The sound the smoke produced as it exited the spout.

"Ah primitive man, what is it that you wish?"

Gokoa dropped the lamp in fright, and he was not one to ordinarily exhibit fear. The smoky somewhat transparent portly figure shimmered before him and remained upright despite the lamp resting on its side. Although advanced much over those before him, Gokoa was still a primitive man as the Djinni suggested, and his first thought was that this was some sort of god.

They already had their share of superstitions that included many gods like the sun, moon, animal spirits, and angry ones that caused storms, but this one was like none other. Although scared, Gokoa understood the words spoken in his own dialect and realized the god was here to serve him as it hovered impatiently above with thick arms crossed and what looked like an odd covering upon its bald head. Gokoa decided to ask for something and succeeded in his request before his time expired.

"I would like to have someone besides Nimpopo lead our people in the future." With that, the Djinni vanished into its resting place. Gokoa stood, stunned, not knowing what to do with the lamp. He had asked it to do something that went against their way, even after the wise counsel of the elder Lenga. He decided to leave it hidden. He selected the largest gourd, a giant that was big enough to house the lamp. He had to break a wider opening to accommodate the lamp. He secured it firmly within by fastening vines about the opening. He continued to gather fish as before.

Back at the camp, Nimpopo had become very ill. Ibisi, the healer, tried all her remedies and collective knowledge passed on to her by San healers that came before her, but she could not restore Nimpopo's health. Nimpopo expired before the sun the very same day that Gokoa and Mhanto had gone on their fishing expedition. Gokoa felt a great sense of guilt. He knew inside that it had been his fault. This is not how he wanted it to happen, and he shifted much of the blame on the god he had found. The very next day he journeyed by himself without telling anyone. He picked up his hidden object hoping that the god would not speak to him anymore. It did not because he failed to rub it in any way. Gokoa traveled north an entire day's journey on foot, which exceeded thirty miles. He dumped the lamp back into the great river where it would rest under water for another lengthy period. He returned to the camp the next day, the day when the official burial of Nimpopo would take place.

There was both sorrow and a small amount of jubilation mixed with Nimpopo's death. The future of the tribe was at stake for one. Khoro was naturally very sad at the death of his son, but he was also experiencing relief for he would not have to pass the leadership to what had been his inept and embarrassing son; however, this led to a new question. Who would lead? He, like all others at one time or another, consulted the elder woman Lenga. She relayed what she had told Gokoa, but this did not help Khoro. In the end, Khoro decided to choose a new leader from within the band, and Gokoa was the obvious choice. Under Gokoa, the band grew and survived well under the new director. There would also be further productive chiefs named Gokoa in the future. The Djinni apparently had been satisfied with the pound of flesh that had been Nimpopo.

———◉———

"BENEATH THE RULE OF men entirely great,
    The pen is mightier than the sword."
    Edward Bulwer-Lytton, "*Richelieu; or the Conspiracy,*" 1839

CHAPTER XIII

Like the perfect predator, time, relentless and unstoppable, continued to pass, wiping out virtually everything in its wake. Farmers began seizing prime land for cultivating and as grazing grass for their ever-growing herds. Grindstones became all the rage increasing in both quantity and size as man honed them into near perfect circles for milling domesticated grains, carefully selected and developed strains that produced several times greater than did those in the wild. Farming tools like hoes, sickles, ground-edged axes, shovels, and hand plows for cultivation increased in abundance as well.

Unlike the San, who time pushed aside, the new breed of farmer altered the environment to suit him. They cut down trees and burned away greater tracts of land. People, especially farmers, cut back on their mobility with more permanent settlements. They built superior huts of pole and mud that remained standing for two solid decades. The creation of raised bins in which to store cereal crops also thwarted animals from plundering. In a food-producing culture, it was critical that it be stored in quantity. Man settling down was the birth of land ownership, inheritance, and the beginning of a class culture, and of course, all the problems that followed.

For one, relying too much on agriculture has its side effects. Primitive farming techniques combined with an occasional drought produced famine, which in turn, could lead to many, many deaths by starvation. In good years, Old World crops of wheat, barley, and various cereal grains were stored in granaries in sufficient quantities to make it through the non-growing season. Many, many favorable years led to spikes in the population which came crashing down in those not so good; yet, once man got his foothold into permanent settlements, the overall population has steadily increased ever since to the billions and billions today.

Animal domestication was another advancement to ensure survival. Young creatures and at times, even entire wild herds were captured alive and penned up. Eventually, certain species of goats, sheep, hogs, cows, dogs, chickens, and so forth were obviously tamed, but no one really knows for sure when it began precisely. It is a very complex process requiring much more than just capturing and nurturing wild animals; many, like zebras for instance, were untamable. Selective breeding had to take place since wild sheep for example had no wool. Wild goats and cows only produced milk for their young, and untamed chickens did not lay surplus eggs. The first step was usually to isolate them from their wild relatives to achieve these alterations.

As farmers settled down in one place, they expanded outward from these settlements little by little. Settlements grew into villages and villages became cities, and civilization with orderly rules and laws arose amidst the chaos. Some of man's very first cities sprung up in Mesopotamia and near the Nile River Valley. The general fertility of these regions aided in this development for the mighty Nile flooded its banks on a regular cycle. Flooding brought new silt and sand producing ideal growing conditions. Hand-dug irrigation trenches controlled these floodwaters to drench the crops, but not drown them out completely. Crop surplus supplemented by cattle and fish led directly to population explosion and leisure time as well, at least for some. Free time aided in the evolution of social, political, religious, and even artistic endeavors. Leisure time meant that people had time to think, and thoughts, like the pen, could be far more dangerous than the sword.

Another factor in the rise of civilization was commerce, or more precisely, trade. In the beginning, farmers bartered with items like food, clay pots, simple gifts, and tools. Later it became metals, jewelry, cattle, salt, and even slaves in ever-increasing quantities. New markets and new inventions sprang up to meet the demands of commerce. The invention of the wheel enabled men to haul trade goods from one place to another. Painted pottery, in near perfect symmetry, in all shapes and sizes, became ready for export. As farmers increased their yields, it freed up others to work as stonemasons, copper workers, weavers, potters, and a host of other more specialized tasks.

As society progressed, class distinctions, in all their pain and glory, did too. A hierarchy of bureaucrats such as merchants and landowners stood above tradesmen and craftsmen, followed by the masses of fishers, farmers, peasants, and sailors who were next in line, and then, ultimately at the bottom, were the slaves, those often captured in war from neighboring peoples. Little has changed today, only semantics as workers are little more than slaves to corporate and political management.

By 3,000 B.C., copper specialists produced both ornaments and weapons from the distinctive shiny metal. The smelting and casting of copper with other metals like tin led the world into the Bronze Age. Kiln fired pottery appeared too at this time while large powerful but domesticated animals like oxen, horses, and mules were hitched to wheeled carts. Three thousand B.C. was also an important time in history for ancient Egypt because a powerful pharaoh unified much of its people. Writing held an important role in this unification as the Egyptian developed hieroglyphics. The written law was far more powerful than just word of mouth.

Complex tools removed this new Egyptian society far beyond the limitations imposed by the stone ages. Metalworkers fashioned pins, flat axes, daggers, swords, knives, helmets, armor, boxes, and jewelry frames to hold precious polished stones. Out of the upper classes came the all-powerful despotic rulers, and so arrogant was their attitude, that they declared themselves gods. Kings or pharaohs became the ultimate power and their profound belief in resurrection led them to build the great pyramids, tombs in the present that would serve as homes in the afterlife, so they believed. Construction of these pyramids took a tremendous waste of human effort, but they also presented the permanence of Egyptian society, which would endure for over two thousand years.

"But love is blind, and lovers cannot see the pretty follies that themselves commit." William Shakespeare, *The Merchant of Venice*

CHAPTER XIV

The day was not going well for Chenes. Her newborn baby boy desired too much nursing during work time. Her other child, a girl of three years, was too large to carry but too curious to remain within her mother's field of vision. Chenes, like her husband, was a peasant farmer, but today, her children were hindering her ability to hoe the weeds as well as to loosen up the dirt about the precious plants. Twice she had to stop to retrieve the girl and several more times over to cater to her fidgety son wrapped around her neck. To add insult to injury, it was hot as sweat pooled wherever her skin met that of the baby. Temperatures in the 90's during the day in the growing season were not usual, but they did help balance out the cold nights that could readily fall to 40 degrees. Although the humidity was a bit low, vigorous work in the fields had a way of draining one's energy, even without the weight of a 20-pound baby.

As she moved about aiming the blade of her hoe with precision at the weeds and not the grain, she heard a splash followed instantly by loud wailing, namely that of her daughter. She rushed to the sound as she deftly leapt over irrigation ditches. Her dexterity was amazing considering that she carried the dead weight of a baby during her leaps and bounds. There, in the bottom of one of the trenches, stood her daughter with water up to her neckline. Chenes reached in with one strong arm and pulled her out.

"There, there," Chenes comforted, "Maybe you will learn to be more careful," she lightly scolded. After that minor infraction, her daughter stayed near her the rest of the day. With the girl temporarily behaving, Chenes' problems were not over with yet. One of the ditches had plugged up during the night as part of its bank had collapsed. Water was flowing out of it, threatening to flood and drown out the plants in one particular region within the field. For both plants and humans, too much water could be as bad as too little. This section of land was in a corner, one of the last pieces she had to hoe. In short, it was well into the afternoon before she had discovered the breech.

Getting to the overflowing makeshift dam was no easy task in and of itself. She ordered her daughter to remain on dryer ground as she set forth into the overflow. Water soaked the ground thoroughly and every bare-footed step sunk ankle deep if not deeper in what had turned into muck. Slurping and slopping noises filled the air with each hard-fought step forward. When she finally arrived at the breech, several river plants, mud, roots, and tiny stones converged around something on the bottom. Chenes stepped directly into the water with her baby still clung to the backside of her shoulder. Halfway through the mess, her hands encountered something larger; it was metal by the feel of it. She at first thought it was a good-sized rock, but it was very smooth and a tad lighter. Its form revealed itself more clearly as she lifted it out of the water. It was the lamp.

She was feeling exhausted with her day's work and decided not to wash or rinse it off immediately. She was pleased with it, but it was nothing too much out of the ordinary since bronze objects were now in abundance. The Celts had been working with an alloy of about 10% tin and 90% copper for hundreds of years in much of Europe to the north, and this new bronze conglomerate was at least twice as strong as any pure metal. The techniques for making it gradually drifted south and to Chenes, this bronze object in her hands definitely had value. She would bring it home to her husband and perhaps he could take it into town to the marketplace and exchange it for something more useful, and that was what he did. She and her husband would be one of the lucky few who actually profited from the lamp without paying some sort of price. Her husband returned with a young cow plus the weight of the lamp in salt.

Ahmose the trader had been shrewd, but the farmer had put up a good fight. Ahmose recognized the fine workmanship, and he was sure that he would receive much greater compensation from the pharaoh's advisers. They were always looking to acquire fine pieces for the living ruler, especially for his grace when he passed on. First, he would have to clean off the dirt and mud as it was apparent that neither the farmer nor his wife had bothered. He found a piece of woven fabric and dipped it into some water. Before he could begin wiping it, another barterer interrupted him.

Ahmose was a gaunt spindly man whose dark skin had wrinkled and tightened around his boney face due to constant exposure of sunlight on the market street. There were no trees and thus, very little shade. Getting beyond the age of 30 further sunk his eyes deep within his face. His hair was thinning and turning gray with age. After acquiring some knives for some more salt, he turned his attention back to the lamp. He picked it up with nervous hands and fingers that were seldom still. He applied the damp cloth to the artifact's surface and began rubbing. To his astonishment, a slithering form shaped itself intimidatingly in the air above him as it sputtered out words!

"What do you wish peasant?"

Superstition had long been deeply entrenched in man's past; unfortunately, it would continue into his future as well. Ahmose, although shaking in his sandals, could not tell either way; on the one hand, it was very evil looking with menacing dark eyes that pierced his soul, while on the other, it was offering him a wish. As a shrewd trader, he did realize when it was time to strike out with a bargain and when to hold back, now was the time to act. He decided to wish for something he lost three years ago, but during his wish, Nemenes—one of the pharaoh's men—happened to observe him.

"I would like a new wife." Ahmose had been lonely since the death of his mate and as soon as his statement was finished, the Djinni returned within the bronze relic.

"What is it that you have there, Ahmose?" Nemenes pressed forward.

"Uh, uh, I'm not sure," answered Ahmose who was rarely at a loss for words. Nemenes had unknowingly placed him in a dilemma. He originally wanted to trade the lamp at a great profit to this very person, but on the other side of it, the object had the potential of providing him with all that he could ever want, and maybe even more. Like a swarm of gnats, the possibilities were running rampant through his head.

"Let me have a look at it," Nemenes demanded.

Ahmose reluctantly agreed as he handed it over. One did not ignore someone of Nemenes' stature, and much less disobey.

"I like it Ahmose and the Pharaoh will be most pleased with it, what is your price?"

"I, I do not think that I would like to part with it just yet," Ahmose answered hesitantly.

"Come now Ahmose, I will give you enough grain or cattle to last you four months." The Egyptian calendar was well in use by this time.

"No," Ahmose said more firmly, "I do not wish to trade it at this time."

"Listen Ahmose, my final offer is enough grain for five months, but no longer."

"I told you that I do not wish to trade it." Ahmose became very agitated for he felt that he may have gone too far in trying to keep the lamp, and he was right. Nemenes may have been an inch or two shorter, but he was much heavier, 50, maybe even 60 pounds more as the pharaoh's men ate well.

"I will have it one way or another," Nemenes raised his voice as a vein stuck out in his broad forehead, "Remember that the Pharaoh is always seeking slaves for his new buildings. I offer you one last time, do you accept the grain or not?"

"I accept, I accept," Ahmose answered hurriedly but reluctantly. The threat was a vivid one, and one that could easily become reality.

"Good Ahmose!" Nemenes slapped him heartily on the back, which nearly bruised Ahmose's kidneys. "I will take it now. I will also have your grain delivered later today." Nemenes took the lamp and left.

It was what Ahmose wanted to avoid. He at least wanted to keep it until he got the grain, but that was not to be. Nemenes had been most insistent. It all happened too fast. If Ahmose would have had more time to think about it, he might have taken a chance to keep it no matter how angry Nemenes became. He could easily have asked the god inside to take care of Nemenes and whatever men he might return with, but now it was too late. Then again, Nemenes could have taken the lamp at will in the first place.

The god granted Ahmose's wish nevertheless. Somehow, a spell cast upon him and he fell in love with a fat, gross woman of twenty-four years of age, past her prime and previously unmated with anyone. In a way, it was a bonus for him as she was a virgin. No one had ever shown a serious interest in her, and her disposition was anything but pleasant. Her parents had failed to arrange a marriage for her as well. His new wife would rule him sternly for his last remaining years and made sure that he traded for food more often than not. She became even more obese over time, but Ahmose loved her until his dying day.

In the meantime, Nemenes had seen what Ahmose had been up to with the lamp. He believed that Ahmose had somehow conjured up a powerful spirit and he would attempt to do the same. Nemenes had been far enough away that he had not heard the words spoken between them, but he had viewed the apparition. He took his new-bullied possession back to the imperial palace and on to his own personal quarters. The building was huge and made of stone from slave labor. It housed several advisors and many times more than that number of servants. On a crudely fashioned stone bench, Nemenes sat down with the lamp and began cleaning it with a cured hide like how he had observed Ahmose doing. It worked. The Djinni came forth.

"What is your wish?"

The spirit hovering above shocked Nemenes, but he quickly recovered. If someone weak like Ahmose could deal with such an entity, then so could he. Ah, so this is what Ahmose was playing with Nemenes thought. He wondered if it indeed worked and laughed inwardly as he regained his confidence and general level of arrogance, "All right spirit, if you are so powerful, then turn me into a cat." One might be thinking that this was not a particularly good idea. The Djinni retracted while Nemenes turned into a sizeable black cat. Things were not as bad for Nemenes as it seemed. If one was ever going to be a cat, this was the time. All cats were highly regarded, much like royalty, in ancient Egyptian. The price for killing a cat was one's own life in return. They led a life similar to that of the pharaoh himself, tremendously pampered.

Coincidentally, pharaoh began to miss Nemenes about the same time the big cat appeared. The dark cat became one of the pharaoh's favorites, so favored that the pharaoh requested or more like ordered his most trusted priests to bury the cat with him when he died. The basic idea was for the pharaoh to have him as a companion in the afterlife. Nine months later, when the pharaoh died, one of pharaohs' men slit the cat's throat, and laid it to rest in a massive tomb adjacent to the pharaoh; both had their organs removed and bodies mummified. They discovered the lamp and added it to the pharaoh's burial chamber as well amongst various items including two mummified servants, two additional chests of treasure, an altar, numerous clay pots, fabrics, beads, and so forth.

The son of the old king had made sure that his father would be quite well off during the next life. To ensure his father's grave would remain unmolested, he had it dug deeply, and the only entrance was booby-trapped to cave in on whoever might enter it. The burial site was in a sacred place around twelve hundred B.C., which would be later known as the Valley of Kings. The lamp may have been lost forever and may not have needed three unselfish wishes to dispose of the force within; yet, this was not to be. It would not be long before grave robbers figured out how to either circumvent or spring the traps, and then still get the goods.

"Idleness among children, as among men, is the root of all evil, and leads to no other evil more certain than ill temper." - Hannah More

CHAPTER XV

Menkhamen vowed that he would not live as his father had. Menkhamen was 15 and now would be responsible for the duties as man of the house. His father had died when a huge stone collapsed upon him crushing him as effectively as a man would step on an ant. Ordinarily a farmer serf, Menkhamen's father had been called to aid in the moving of massive stones for pyramid building. Along with moving rock, they would have to dig irrigation canals to maintain Egyptian agriculture. It was a bit like jury duty only there was no chance of getting out of it. When the state called, one answered or risked its wrath. Punishment was the same for those captured in battle; namely, the end of one's family, friends, and way of life as one fell deeply into the bottomless pit of hopelessness and despair – the hell of permanent serfdom.

When the neighbors were humbled, conquered, and even permanently destroyed, the prisoners worked as slaves on public works projects; the lucky ones became domestic servants or sex slaves, the unlucky labored like Sisyphus and died in the heat when their muscles fizzled, and backs broke. When there was a shortage of prisoners, the state recruited peasants, especially the strong ones, for duty. Many made up the pharaoh's army, but some, like Menkhamen's father, were there to push heavy stones along logs or upon a barge for transport to the building site. Once the slaves achieved a bit of momentum moving something weighing many tons, those within its direct path should get the hell out of its way. Menkhamen's father happened to stumble, and was then pancaked like roadkill from a semi.

Menkhamen was able to remain as a farmer, but he did not particularly enjoy the life. Like his father, he was about average in height, but strong, broad in the shoulders. Unfortunately, he became a bit of a bully amongst his peers. If another boy did not agree with him, he knocked that boy to the ground. He picked on those smaller and weaker than himself too. These qualities attracted the army's attention. At the height of Egyptian prosperity, they boasted an army of 20,000 men made up primarily of mercenaries and peasant recruits. Soldiers were paid in grain to support their families and their sons were put on the fast track to join the army too. Menkhamen did at least support his mother.

When not assigned to fight foreign invaders or establishments, the army, like unsupervised children, could not remain idle without getting into some sort of trouble or mischief. Menkhamen temporarily had the unpleasant task of collecting taxes or tribute. The Egyptian government was wise and routinely sent three or four big strong army lads to do the dirty work. What many scribes or clerics higher up in the government did not realize was the extent of the corruption in the lower ranks. The servicemen overtaxed the peasants, taking their cut from the surplus, and Menkhamen was no exception. Being the son of a farmer, he knew many of the tricks that the peasants used to hide their grain, and when he discovered their hidden and undeclared caches, he punished them both physically and financially.

At the age of twenty, Menkhamen married a peasant girl of sixteen named Cherops. She was short and a little on the plump side, but her parents were overjoyed since her station in life would rise with marrying a soldier. Her parents gladly gave her away despite the little fact that she did not love him. Menkhamen was somewhat shy, awkward, and inexperienced around girls. They had avoided him in the past because of his bully-like nature, but Cherops was feisty and had a strong will of her own. She was not one bullied person could bully, and was in fact much of an overbearing person herself, especially in the way she treated Menkhamen's mother after she moved into the family hut. She ordered the thin, somewhat gaunt woman around as if the elder was a child, particularly when her husband was away.

Menkhamen loved her dearly and in a battle of wills, Cherops may have won, but Menkhamen was gone far more often than not. When not fighting battles, he continued in his tax collecting duties. Cherops never questioned him when he came home with unnaturally large amounts of grain. She was greedy in her own right, secretly welcoming them and admiring her husband for it. She understood the workings of a tax collector and if he exploited others, that was all right with her.

The two produced a son that Cherops named Peti, and Peti inherited the undesirable traits of his parents. Unlike his parents however, life was easier for him as he was not raised a peasant. Nor did he have to learn the value of hard work. Peti would also not gain an understanding of what extreme exploitation was like. The intent of his parents was to see him trained in special schools with tutors for a career as a military officer, or perhaps something even greater beyond that. Unfortunately, the goals of parents for their children are like autumn leaves in the wind; some sail to fruition while others die in the dirt.

It was at these schools that Peti began stealing. At first, he pinched little things like paper from the papyrus pith and paintbrushes with ink for writing. Next, he implicated his friends without their knowledge by pilfering their completed homework, copying it if it was acceptable and then discarding or destroying the original, usually by fire. Gradually, he moved on to bigger endeavors. Since the schools were part of the training provided by the state, they were located near the imperial palace within government owned buildings. Peti's military training provided him with the ability to scale walls and open locked doors, crafts that he perfected with a good deal of practice. His adeptness at these functions outpaced his peers and brought on an entire new set of possibilities for his thieving ways.

It took Peti some years to find a co-conspirator with similar motives. Mosie impressed Peti by stealing the scroll one of the teachers was going to lecture about the next day. From then on, they became fast friends and eventually partners in crime for life, literally. They were already scheming and planning heists while they were still in their early teen years. From the jewels and personal possessions of government officials, to some of the royal treasures of the pharaoh himself, allowed the two to turn their backs on their parent-chosen military careers. By their late teens, they had become full time professional thieves, a rather dangerous calling.

Though not always written, Egyptian laws were quite like Hammurabi's Code, a system that was used widely east in Mesopotamia for centuries. An eye for an eye, death to builders if their construction failed and killed others, loss of a surgeon's hand if his patient died, and for thieves at the very least, the loss of one or both hands when caught. How could one survive in the ancient world without hands? Loss of both hands ordinarily meant death.

The most ambitious undertaking of the two thieves was grave robbing. Aside from the rulers, the tombs of high-ranking ministers, high priests, record keepers, and noted scholars contained valuable artifacts buried with them. The work did require some brute physical force in terms of digging and chiseling, much more so than the skill of sneaking into locked and guarded rooms. Over time, the rewards were significant in terms of copper, bronze, and even a little gold treasure.

Grave robbing eventually brought them to the Valley of the Kings where some time had passed, and the valley was not as highly

regarded as it once was. Although still deemed sacred, there were
no more guards. Peti and Mosie, as they were digging in a favorable
spot, discovered the very tomb with the lamp. On their way in, they
had found three crushed skeletons.

"We are lucky today," said Peti, "These three have already
sprung the trap. Look how the roof is caved in, we must remember
how this happened in case we find another like it."

"Be careful," warned Mosie, "There could be more traps."

"I don't think so, notice that part of the door supported the
roof. When these idiots broke the door down, the ceiling fell in."
Peti was right, when they cleared the rubbish aside and dug deeper,
the inner burial chamber revealed itself with no more traps.
Together, they heaved the two chests out of the tomb and placed
them in the cart trailing their two hitched horses. It proved to be
an excellent find, one that could support them the rest of their
lives, but as fate would have it, neither would rise the morrow
morn. From the distance an unsavory pair, two more dangerous
and violent than themselves, had followed them. As Peti strode
back in the chamber for one last look, Mosie brushed the dust from
several artifacts including the lamp, and the Djinni slithered out.

"What do you wish for?"

"What?"

"A wish, you have three of them thief."

Mosie was confused, scared, surprised, and then as was his
nature, greed formed at the front of his mind as the portly
somewhat Mid-Eastern-Asian-like form hovered over him. "I wish
for all of this treasure here to be my own," Mosie stated. As the
Djinni whooshed away, two arrows slammed into Peti from their
followers as he exited the chamber, fulfilling the wish almost
instantly. The treasure was Mosie's, all his own.

Mosie acted fast, as thieves, despite lacking honor, are generally
on guard for quick getaways. He flung the lamp into the cart,

jumped in, and jerked the horse reigns as he sat low in his seat. Just as he bent downward, two additional arrows whooshed past his head. He didn't give a second thought to Peti who lay dying with two vital organs pierced and oozing out his life's essence. The treasure was still his own, but not for long; after all, there was no time allotment connected with the wish.

Just like in America's future Old West, a rider with cart, stagecoach, wagon, or buckboard was never a match for lone riders without such encumbrances. It took all of 6 minutes for them to catch up to Mosie and fill him full of arrowhead holes. Amazingly, he did not die, but fell out of the cart as it came to a stop, bleeding profusely from no less than four wounds; nevertheless, unlike Peti, they did not connect with any internal organs. Still, the followers bludgeoned him to death with crude wooden clubs before seizing the treasure.

The new batch of robber bandits had not seen the Djinni, nor did they further clean any of the objects prior to dumping them on the nearest merchant back in town. The inner workings of the lamp did not activate when the merchant traded it away. It ended up in the hands of the last pharaoh, or more precisely, a speck in a vast treasure store; yet this ruler's burial would not be as elaborate as his predecessors.

As Egyptian culture had developed about the Red Sea and the southern Mediterranean, Mesopotamia was rooted in the Tigris and Euphrates River valleys. Mesopotamian culture would be a major influence on the nest word power, Assyria. Assyrians migrated from the Arabian Desert settling on the north end of the Tigris; against great odds, they expanded rapidly from there.

The Assyrians were simply Bad Ass, not a nice neighborly group of people; nevertheless, the location of Assyria made it a prime target for foreign invaders. The likes of Kassites, Hittites, the Mitanni, and the Semites all attacked. Assyrian farmers rarely worked their lands alone, as they routinely doubled as soldiers. With new iron weapons, these farmer soldiers gradually evolved into the best military force in the region by 1,000 B.C. Sometimes the best defense is a good offense and the Assyrians launched offensives against their neighbors. Arabian Desert nomads, mountaineers, Hebrews, Phoenicians, Armaens, and Mesopotamians all fell victims to the power of the Assyrian sword. Assyrians developed cavalry forces to near perfection to both supplement the infantry to decimate their enemies.

Assyrians deliberately introduced a system of terrorism and torture to spread the word of their formidableness. They strung up conquered chiefs to have them publicly whipped to death by Assyrian kings. Prisoners had their toes, fingers, hands, feet, arms, legs, and even private parts severed. The skins of those conquered hung prominently on city walls, while the corpses of many enemies lay across a river to create a bridge the conquerors. As Assyrian exploits pooled outward like so many ripples in the water, some minor bands, tribes, and settlements surrendered without a fight rather than risk the wrath of such a brutal enemy.

A good deal of Assyrian dominance occurred in 900 B.C. Those conquered had to pay tribute to the central government in the Assyrian homeland. The empire lasted for nearly 3 centuries as the entire civilized Near East was under the control of Assyrian kings during this time. The glory days of Egypt were long in the past and it was easily conquered, and her treasures taken since to the victor go the spoils. The lamp, a now somewhat dusty relic lost in a vast hoard, found itself in their possession, but the Assyrians would die out before its secrets emerged.

A negative side effect of the Assyrian terrorist policy was that all they had conquered hated and feared them. With an ever-expanding territory and declining army constantly depleted in battle after battle, it slowly became impossible to repel the foreign invaders combined with the internal revolts. The Semitic tribes combined with the Medes, a fearsome group of northern barbarians who had adopted and imitated Assyrian fighting techniques; together, they brought down an empire that would plunge the West and Near East into a century of darkness and unrest until a new power would arise. A similar fate would strike Rome that had not yet risen.

Like Egypt and Mesopotamia, and then Greece and Rome, Assyrians made some positive contributions to what was once a tiny, civilized world. They encouraged trade and brought down regional barriers. They adopted and expanded the beauty of Mesopotamian architecture in the form of temples, palaces, sculptures, and stone works. Libraries and the ancient cities of Nineveh, Calah, and Ashur became near mythological wonders. Assyrians were also some of the finest early historical writers since they compiled journals and diaries of military conquests and campaigns attempted.

A new batch of Homo sapiens migrated from north of the Black Sea to the Near East, and they would outdo the Assyrians in terms of empire building and culture. The Persians were far more even tempered and more like tame cats compared to the brutality inflicted by the Assyrians. As they fought and conquered, the Persians accepted surrender on favorable terms. They did not slaughter captured kings and they accepted the gods of their subjects even going as far to support their continued worship with financial resources. Like nearly all great powers in history, the Persians relied heavily on their military might. After laying waste to the Medes, they expanded by conquering the minor nations around them. After relying on professional soldiers from their own ranks, they gradually recruited new warriors from those they conquered. The Persians were the first in history to assemble a powerful navy, made up mostly of Egyptian, Greek, and Phoenician crews.

One of the great early Persian kings was Darius. Darius proclaimed himself absolute ruler, the one and only who could make laws, judge, and rule his subjects. He divided the great Persian Empire that extended from India to Greece including Egypt into 20 separate districts, and then appointed a trusted friend or relative as governor in each one to personally report back to him. He would then send government inspectors to check up on the management of these regions and would readily remove said governors who did not please him. He made sure to have tax records from each region carefully maintained.

The empire lasted a bit longer than that of the Assyrians, but problems from within eventually led to the decapitation of the Persian beast. The Persians were not overly progressive and often lapsed into ancient, or more accurately, obsolete ways. Due to heightened corruption within the government, late-ruling kings spent much of their time and effort surviving mortal plots from family members, officials, and even servants. Little energy for ruling the empire remained. Rebellions broke out as one after another local governor strove to become king of it all. The constant onslaught from outsiders combined with internal rebellion signaled the end. The final blow came with the rise of an extraordinary conqueror from the West in the name of Alexander the Great. In 330 B.C., Alexander closed the book on the Persians by running roughshod through much of their territory and killing Darius III, the last Persian king.

Without the old there could be no new. The Egyptians, Mesopotamians, Assyrians, and Persians, along with hundreds of tiny developing civilizations all unknowingly prepared the world for a new West. Absolute monarchies, tax systems, militaries, bureaucracies, recordkeeping, laws, complex agriculture, technology, trade, transportation, social systems, iron & bronze weapons, art, writing, libraries, and on and on, were all created by them. The major problem was that once a system was established, the various extinct cultures were hesitant to change and rarely improve significantly upon them; thus, spelling their doom. All along the lamp's secrets remained hidden, but not for long.

"It is not light that we need, but fire; it is not the gentle shower, but thunder. We need the storm, the whirlwind, and the earthquake." - Frederick Douglass

CHAPTER XVI

With Alexander's impressive victories, the Greeks came into power and soon made significant advances in every school of thought. Scholarly pursuits in mathematics, medicine, science, literature, astronomy, philosophy, and many other fields would be unequaled until the end of the Dark Ages. Political and cultural life, economic enterprise, the arts, and an interesting multi-deity religion all flourished with the Greeks. The Romans would take up where the Greeks left off and Western Civilization would prosper for hundreds of years until the fall of the Roman Empire.

Damo, along with his father, and his father's father, and a few fathers before that, were eupatrids in Lydia, a Greek-controlled territory in Asia Minor. The first usage of money for commerce occurred in Lydia in the 7th century B.C. From the very beginning, money was trouble. It created chaos as those with money routinely cheated peasants, who did not know the value of their goods in terms of money. In the old days, if they traded a nice breeding pair of sheep for ten bushels of grain, they knew what they were getting straight up. If they traded those same two sheep for five silver pieces only to find out that 10 bushels of grain cost 10 silver pieces, then they discovered the concept of usury the hard way from the moneylenders.

A eupatrid was little more than a wealthy moneylender who loaned money to the peasants. In return, the peasants took an oath to repay the loan with interest with rates that would have made modern loan sharks and credit card companies envious. Forty-percent annual interest was tough to repay and, in the age-old tradition that started here, the eupatrids not only acquired peasant land, but their labor too for repayment. Their practices forced peasants to rent the land back at a payment of perhaps one-sixth or one-fifth of all produce subject to a minimum. Those who could not make the minimum became slaves sold for additional profit; win-win for the eupatrids, lose-lose for the peasants.

Monetary wealth led directly to political power; sadly, a fact that has rarely changed today. Because of the great unrest in the region, eupatrids were constantly siding and supporting one military power or another. Damo fortunately fell in with Alexander. As with most generals, Damo had already been a man of some influence and was an obvious choice for military leadership. Generals received rewards with each conquest, and that is how the lamp fell into Damo's hands. When not fighting for a larger empire, Damo had all that he could handle keeping his own little one together which left him little time for rare glimpses of his collected treasures. Luckily or unluckily, depending on one's view of the matter, Damo never discovered the lamp's mystery, but his son would.

Dameus, son of Damo and Ariad, was primarily raised by his mother. At the age of thirteen, he had been tutored somewhat in most subjects of the day, but his father expected much more from him. Damo sent his son to the city of Athens to learn under the instructor of Alexander, and that was Aristotle. Aristotle would become renowned as the last of the three great Greek philosophers, and he was the pupil of the second, who in turn had been a pupil of the first. The first was Socrates, a sculptor who became a self-taught philosopher of significant influence. Socrates believed in doing all good and no evil to convince people good was the right path from a moral and spiritual sense. His highest virtue and eventual downfall consisted of pursuing knowledge no matter what the consequences.

The method of Socrates was to pummel one with relentless questions until the error of those who claimed to know something was exposed. He would then further question them until they arrived at the truth by way of precise definition and logic. He believed the objective truth existed, and that's ignorance prevented him from discovering it, and so Socrates made it his business to enlighten.

Socrates attracted many followers in public forums, particularly the youth of the day, many from the higher-ups or noble families. Since his teachings were quite radical, the elders were not exactly ecstatic about him. His constant questioning and ideas got him into trouble with the state, which accused him of corrupting youth and sentenced him to die in 399 B.C. He was given a chance to escape, but rather chose to abide by the state's decision of death by poison. He drank the hemlock and died a poor man at the age of seventy.

Socrates was a single man who changed the current of human thought. Like Jesus, he wrote little of anything, but unlike Jesus, he did not preach a doctrine. Socrates left his mark by simply talking in the streets of a city that he rarely left.

After the fourth century B.C., Plato, the prize pupil of his master, Socrates, founded the Academy, a school for the privileged youth of the time. Plato would spend his life as a teacher and writer, putting many of the ideas of his master down on parchment. Plato became a philosophical idealist and expanded upon the work of the Pythagoreans, a group that had centered on nonmaterialistic endeavors in science and mathematics for the greater good of learning.

Unlike Socrates, Plato did not get into trouble with the state; rather he embraced it and wrote *The Republic*, a discourse on the duties of the state. A good philosopher-king who will put the specific talents of his subjects to work must run the state. Plato supported the dictatorial form of government, and his work soon became much like a guide as to how Greek society should operate.

Aristotle came to Athens from northern Greece specifically to study at Plato's Academy. Platonic idealism greatly influenced Aristotle, but his approach was different, and he founded his own school, the Lyceum. Aristotle dabbled in philosophy and politics, but he was also a scientist and the inventor of logic. Dameus was enrolled in the Lyceum with the hope of his father that he would become as educated as anyone and as accomplished as Alexander himself, but such was not to be. Dameus spent too much time and energy pursuing religion rather than practical scholarly engagements. As was common, he worshipped and prayed to many different gods. He did not comprehend philosophy and substituted superstition, astrology, and the supernatural rather than the more valid ways of reasoning to explain worldly matters. To Dameus, the answers belonged to the gods, not with his human teachers.

After 4 years at the Lyceum, Dameus returned to Lydia after receiving correspondence about the unexpected death of his father. As custom dictated, he inherited his father's wealth and responsibilities of the state including the care of his two younger sisters, his aging mother, and control of some 200 peasants or so. At age seventeen, Dameus was not quite ready for the authority and responsibility thrust upon him. At the start, it may have been best if he had just left well enough alone.

Artimus, his father's chief steward and overseer, managed the peasants well, exacting their labor or rent as needed, pressuring or beating those who did not measure up, or even deciding to sell the slackers off. Dameus' father was often gone for great lengths of time before his passing, and no revolts or major problems arose mostly due to the iron fist of Artimus. Like the Russian serf system and much of Europe's feudal years that would last until the 19th

century, the estate functioned in an orderly fashion with the master's frequent absence.

"Greetings mother, how are you?"

"I am so glad to see you Dameus," replied Ariad as she hugged her son, "Look at you Dameus, you're a man now! You've grown so much and now everything is yours." She cried.

"Now mother, you didn't answer me, how are you?"

"I'm still mourning for your father. He was a brave and courageous man just like I know you will be my son. I am much better now that you are back. Come, your sisters will want to see you." She led Dameus inside the dwelling that was now his.

It was not a particularly large home for people of their stature. It was made of stone, as were many of the furnishings, except those cast in marble or metal his father had delivered from as far away as Athens. The nine rooms were tall and spacious, with ceilings rising twenty feet. It looked bigger from the inside given the cubic space derived from the ceiling height.

"Greetings Ariel," said Dameus. "It looks like it is about time to find you a husband."

She blushed before saying, "Greetings Dameus, father was already looking before he became ill." Ariel was fourteen and of marriageable age.

"It is one of the first things that we will have to consider very carefully," chimed in their mother.

"And you will not be far behind your sister," added Dameus to his other sibling who was now eleven years of age.

She blushed more furiously but Ariel came to her aid, "All this talk of husbands Dameus, when will you be taking a wife?"

Dameus smiled crookedly, "In good time Ariel, in good time." He was not particularly attractive with a round soft face and large nose. Like many of the privileged class, he did not have to toil in the fields, and he had not tasted battle; as a result, he was soft all over. "I am hungry now but first we must pay tribute."

Dameus led them into a prayer session to various immortals including one they had never heard of. It was quite lengthy, and they were both surprised at some of the choices and relieved when it was finally over. Initially, these lengthy dissertations were few and far between, but as time went on, they gradually became worse to the point of obsession. A fresh goat was killed for the celebration of Dameus' return, the skin cured into a container for wine. Breads along with various fruits completed the meal. The servants appreciated these rare celebrations, since they were the few times during the year they ate well and could drink.

Dameus spent the first few weeks visiting relatives, family friends, and other nobles from the surrounding area. Good contacts were essential especially when sisters needed husbands. Dameus needed a wife too to bear him children so that his legal heirs could inherit wealth. By this time, he was now personally leading prayer sessions in the morning at sunrise, at night, and after all meals with his mother and sisters. Gradually, he incorporated the house servants into these services. It would not be long before he forced the outdoor workers into larger gatherings.

Artimus, the head overseer, along with his band of slave drivers and lesser overseers were quite adept with the whip. Many peasants who were little more than slaves sported scars on their backs, backsides, and arms where they had tried to block the blows rained down upon them. The estates of the nobles often lived or died based on the amount of food they produced. For sixteen years, the aging Artimus had kept them afloat in good years and in bad, but that would soon change under the directorship of Dameus.

"Thank you young master," Artimus bowed in respect, but looked with disdain upon Dameus. In a physical sense, the boy would never be the bear that his father was. To Artimus, Dameus was soft, weak, and did not present a commanding or authoritative presence for one in his position. The boy slouched and had a habit of staring at the ground rather than looking one in the eye.

"There are some small changes Artimus that I would like to discuss with you concerning the workers."

Artimus was instantly alert for this was something his master rarely discussed with him. "Dameus, my young master, do not concern yourself with them. You have matters of concern that are far more important. They are not worth your attention."

"I am afraid that I will decide whether or not they are worth my attention," he said snidely.

"As you wish," Artimus answered as he bowed, not particularly liking this boy who was trying to be a man. To the annoyance of Artimus, his squeaky voice sounded more like the higher pitched vocals of a girl; neverthless, he did give him a slight amount of credit for not being told what to do.

Dameus id give some ground when he said, "All that I want them to do is to give praise to the gods along with the rest of us in the morning. I would like you to gather them near the house at sunrise in the field in the west side; it won't take very long at all."

"It will be done as you say," answered Artimus.

The next morning a little crowd of over two hundred gathered to hear Dameus give his morning speech. Various gods and goddesses from Z to A, including Zeus, Poseidon, Hades, Athena, and so forthwere asked to favor them, the crops, the house, and most anyone and their brother and sister that Dameus could think of. He ran out of things to say after a 20-minute discourse.

"Glad that's over," Artimus mumbled to one of his assistant slave drivers.

"They loved it though," responded his companion who gestured to the serfs, "Anything to get out of their work makes them so happy. They'll just have to work that much harder to make up for lost time."

"Now that's a good idea," said Artimus, "I hope that this is the only one for a while." It wasn't.

Dameus approached him in the evening with the news that he was going to do this every day, even on the 7th day, the traditional day of rest.

"Why do you bother master? The gods do not favor them at all or else they would not be slaves."

"Maybe not Artimus, but we have been blessed with good crops and good land for years. We should be thankful and do nothing to bring disfavor to us."

"Yes Dameus I agree to a point, but is it necessary to do it every day?"

"I believe so Artimus. I even think that once a day is not enough, we should have them pray in the evening too."

"But Dameus, they will not work as hard and the crops will not do as well if they are constantly praying and not working."

"The gods Artimus will favor us if we pay tribute to them as often as we can." With that, Dameus left before Artimus could protest further.

Dameus was now devoting nearly all his time to composing speeches and lectures for his twice-daily audience. Little by little, the time involved continued to increase. There was a third session added before the slaves' only meal of the day and the time away from hard labor began to measure in hours rather than minutes. Artimus did his best to inform Dameus of the consequences, but he may as well have been speaking to an insect. Twenty minutes a day had been manageable but making up hours times nearly two hundred workers was impossible. It was not long before it took its toll on the estate.

To help improve upon his lectures, Dameus raided the little treasure room to build a temple. The room itself was like a modern-day closet accessed only by removing a shelf to expose a keyhole. It was in his new room, the one that once belonged to his father. To the best of his knowledge, Dameus, along with his mother, were the only two that knew of its exact secret location, and he was right. Through his escapades, Damo had stocked it well with jewels, ornate weapons, and several thousand of the new coins: coppers, silvers, and even a little gold. The lamp was among the assorted cache buried beneath the surface of one of the wooden chests.

Dameus had been in the storeroom a couple of times since his return, but now he set out to separate some of the pieces there and collect enough to erect his temple. He gathered up mostly coins and jewels to hire an architect as well as a sculptor. His efforts at sorting and sifting brought the lamp far up enough that the spout, lid, and part of the handle rose above the sea of coins, but no further. He felt that he had enough without digging deeper to put his plan into motion.

He had a small temple erected on a small hill in a small field. He would have bigger plans later. The structure was in honor of the goddess Athena, daughter of Zeus, from whom the city of Athens took its name. It is where Dameus learned of her as a student. The temple itself sported a roof, alter, a sculpture of Athena on the altar, and a small, raised platform from which Dameus could look down upon his audience, all of 10 feet. Dameus was disappointed with it after a few lectures. He found this facility far inadequate for his needs.

There was a somewhat larger medium-sized hill on the property and Dameus envisioned a much larger work for Zeus himself, the king of gods. Naturally, this would require a much greater outlay of capital. The further raiding of the treasure store hoarded by his father is what finally brought the lamp to the surface in full view. As Dameus held it free in his hands it felt warm, almost hot compared to the coldness of everything else in the room. To Dameus, it didn't look like anything special, and he would have cast it aside if not for the feeling. Subconsciously, he felt the need to rub or clean it for some unknown reason. He pulled up the folds of his robe and brushed off some of the accumulated dirt and grime. A sound of a hissing serpent commenced as a large, rounded form consumed much of the space in the storeroom as the Djinni sprung forth:

"Ah, a young master? What is it that you wish?"

Dameus exhibited some signs of surprise, but not nearly as most who had shared the experience. "You must be a messenger from Zeus since I was going to build his Greatness a temple." Dameus was getting quite excited, "I would like you to do it for me!" On record, it was probably one of the fastest first wishes, but Dameus of late was losing more of himself into the realms of the supernatural world. It occurred to him in an arrogant way that it would not be long before he would be speaking to those above. It was simply a logical extension of his efforts. The Djinni condensed itself into the lamp after Dameus uttered the request. Word came to Dameus almost immediately after he exited the secret room with the lamp tucked safely inside.

"Master! Master! Come see! Come see! A new temple by the forest, come see master!" The servant was quite excited.

"Yes I know, calm down," Dameus said smugly, "Take me to it."

A few hundred yards from the house on a hill near the tree line of the forest sat a beautiful structure. Tall columns, golden rectangles, a fountain, and a marble statue of a bearded menacing Zeus threatening those below with a lightning bolt in hand graced the temple. Awe overcame Dameus for this would have taken at least two maybe even three years to complete by an experienced crew of master craftsmen. Dameus' first thought of making an addition to the regular schedule of practicing reverence. Everyone would visit and recite a short note of thanks after the usual morning lecture.

Upon studying it further, Dameus suffered some disappointment in a practical sense after the initial elation. Once again, it was not very practical for him to deliver his oratories. The reason was that too many trees contributed to a lack of open viewing area. It was virtually impossible for more than twenty souls to gain a clear view of the speaker at the front of this new testament to the king of gods. The more he thought about it, he would have to pick out a better and more specific site before giving instruction to his personal messenger.

Contrary to what Dameus believed despite the true word of Artimus, production by his peasant workers decreased a full twenty-five percent. The gods were just not picking up the slack. Artimus was at a loss as to what to do. From a priority standpoint, his first duty was to obey his master; nevertheless, peasant worshipping, and down time did not set right with Artimus. The plebes seemed to enjoy their worshipping more than working. They were beaten and flogged worse if they showed a hint of unruliness or disrespect at any of Dameus' special meetings. They learned quickly to sit still and quietly as it sure beat toiling by hand in the fields, especially on hot days. Artimus felt uneasy about the situation and something about Dameus did not sit right with him.

It took Dameus numerous hikes and a full two weeks before he discovered the perfect site a full half of a mile south of the house. It happened to be one of the tallest hills from miles around with a slight inclination and a nice level area at the top. It was a little rocky and scraggily with few trees, but it did present enough open area to accommodate hundreds of viewers. With the site picked out, all he had left to do was to order the messenger to produce what he wanted.

He started to run back home but had to slow to a walking pace halfway back since he was not in very good physical condition. It did give him some time to think and there were issues to consider. He already had temples dedicated to both Zeus and Athena. He worried about offending Zeus by building a larger temple for someone else. An idea did cross his mind and that was to build an architectural wonder for himself, but with the intent of preaching and making offerings to the various gods. With a few more details to work out, he headed for the treasury to gather up the messenger.

He brought the lamp all the way back to the top of the hill, held it at arm's length and commanded after resting several minutes to catch his breath, "Come forth messenger." Nothing happened. He had forgotten what he had done to summon it the first time. He began shaking it violently, "Come out, now!" Still, nothing happened. He shook it again, "Come forth!" Finally, he sat down and carefully went over what he had done previously, and a small light went off; he remembered. With the cloth of his robe, he rubbed it and the messenger appeared.

"What is your second wish?" It glared down at him menacingly.

"I would like a much larger temple than the last, placed here to fill up this entire spot but facing north. I would like the altar placed at the very edge with a raised area behind it for me to stand and look down upon all of those who will be gathered below. Finally, I would like a statue of myself inside," Dameus finished as he gestured behind at the to-be-determined invisible altar.

To the Djinni, it sounded like more than one wish, but since Dameus had had two remaining and given that it was all going to be part of the same, the Djinni granted the wish. A beautiful white marble altar appeared beneath a roof supported by tall marble columns. The frieze sections that made up the front roof facings sported carvings that resembled angels blowing trumpets, but up close where no one would really see until the temple would fall, was that the eyes of the cherubs were dark and sinister, like that of a Djinn.

With the lamp in hand, Dameus walked behind the altar when suddenly he had trouble breathing. The fluids within his body began to harden and his circulatory system shut down. It was as if he had stared into the face of Medusa or some other gorgon as the process of stone petrification seized him and did not let go. The last thing he was able to do was raise his hand about to the height of his head before it froze. The left hand remained down, and the lamp fell to the ground behind the altar as Dameus became the statue for which he had wished.

When Dameus missed the evening meal and the one next morning, his mother ordered a search, and it was only a matter of hours before the discoveries of both new temple and the statue of Dameus. To add insult to injury, it started raining and both thunder and lightning followed, but that was not all. The ground began to vibrate, ominous cracks formed in the rocky soil, and someone yelled "Earthquake!"

One large crack resembling that of an artery, raced up the hill straight toward the temple of Dameus as veins and capillaries sprung from it. Two peasant men had been examining the new statue while the other was just about to put his hands on the lamp when the pillars came tumbling down and the roof caved in upon them. They died instantly. The statue of Dameus toppled upon the lamp, breaking the statue into hundreds of pieces without even denting the lamp.

The movement of the earth was only just beginning as it trembled northward, leveling the home, and taking Dameus' mother and younger sister with it. Ariel managed to escape outside and become the lone survivor of the family. The other temples collapsed as well. A crack swallowed Artimus and both overseers and peasants alike ran from the chaos. Those who survived, including Ariel, would view the place as cursed. Dameus had obviously angered the gods and had suffered their wrath. The lamp fell beneath a pile of rubble and bones, and it would be some time before someone uncovered it again.

"Veni, Vidi, Vici." ("I came, I saw, I conquered.") - Julius Caesar, after his victory against Pharnaces II, King of the Pontuso, City of Zela in the year 47 B.C.

CHAPTER XVII

The next empire to rise in the Western world was that of the Romans, a simple but great extension of the culture created by the Greeks. A little village called Rome founded by Romulus and Remus in the 4th century B.C. was little more than seven hills in the beginning, all just east of the River Tiber: Aventine, Caelian, Capitoline, Esquiline, Palatine, Quirinal, and Viminal. In the history of man, the Greco-Roman world brought about the concept of man's well-being, rationality, an ordered universe, man's capacity for good, and man's growing political nature. To expand by conquering, great battles had to be fought, and the Punic Wars were just that.

The first Punic War began in 264 B.C. and would last two decades. It would lead directly to Roman domination of the entire Mediterranean after the first defeat of the powerful Carthaginians. The second Punic War led to the defeat of Hannibal, the greatest of the Carthaginian generals. Hannibal had crossed the Alps in 218 B.C., one of the major achievements of the war, and caught the Romans by surprise. Hannibal won several battles, but over the next sixteen years, he was beaten back despite making it to the outer walls of Rome. When the Romans defeated the Seleucid King, Antiochus III at Thermopylae in 191 B.C., their domination of the Western world was nearly complete. The final blow came with the total destruction of Carthage during the third and final Punic War from 149 to 146 B.C. The Romans slaughtered 450,000 Carthaginians and enslaved some 50,000 others. There would be many more minor skirmishes, but the Western world now belonged to Rome.

With great empires come great leaders but Rome had its share of poor ones too. Julius Caesar invaded Britain in 55 B.C. and conquered Gaul (later France) a short 5 years later. He returned to Rome and claimed himself emperor, a title that the Roman Senate did not appreciate. When the senate tried to remove Caesar from power, civil war broke out. Caesar ultimately won the war by destroying Pompey; but died by assassination in 44 B.C. Octavian, the adopted son of Caesar, assumed control after defeating Marc Antony and Cleopatra at the battle of Actium in 31 B.C. Octavian established the official Roman Empire as Emperor Augustus, a new title meaning "The Illustrious One" given to him by the senate.

With the help of his wife Livia, Augustus would reign over Rome for forty years and many consider him the greatest Roman Emperor in history. Under Augustus, there was the establishment of new reforms and a significant peace throughout the empire. He supplied cheap grain, police supervision, economic security, and entertainment for the masses. He beautified the country with roads, supply depots, military posts, public services, temples, and architectural wonders from aqueducts to great buildings. The 300,000-man army mainly defended the boundaries of the empire so as not to overextend them, a common problem with would-be conquerors. He inspired the people to be patriotic, loyal, and devoted to public service, all for the glory of the empire. Unfortunately, he was not able to pass down the whole of his efforts to his successors.

Tiberius, the adopted son of Augustus, was rather suspicious, distrustful, and rid himself of those he remotely suspected of threatening his power. Though more accepted at the time, his penchant for playing with little boys did not make him a popular figure from an historical perspective. Caligula, whose sanity was virtually nonexistent, ruled for four short years before his assassination. There was hope with Claudius, a capable intelligent ruler, but his timidity, physical ugliness, and several poor wives combined with even poorer advisors outweighed his accomplishments. Nero was arguably the worst. In the end, he killed himself, his mother, two wives, several senators, and hundreds of Christians. Nero was quite wasteful and emptied the once bountiful treasury on his own personal whims leaving the state broke at the time of his suicide.

From 14 A.D. to 68 A.D., Rome was plunged into political turmoil after renowned general, Vespasian, seized power only to pass it on to his sons Titus and Domitian. All were tyrants who did not excel at the more moderate and successful Augustan system. Vespasian did initiate the building of a massive coliseum in 70 A.D. originally named the Flavian Amphitheater, later known simply as "The Coliseum," to which no others for countless millennia could compare.

Vespasian happened to be the founder of the Flavian Dynasty, but he would not live long enough to see its completion. Titus would open it to the public in 80 A.D. with an inaugural ceremony that would last for more than 100 days. With the death of Domitian in 96 A.D., the empire would return for a time to the good old days and even reach its peak in prosperity under a series of leaders known as "Good Emperors."

It was in this transition from the tyrants to the good that Pero, a fairly old girl or young woman as one would have it, found the lamp. The curse of Dameus had been lost to history, and good fertile lands, especially those cleared or partially cleared, became rewards for army officers. Pero's father was a cavalry officer, moving up the ranks over time until he led as many as a hundred men into battle as a faction of his general's soldiers. Her father was much a trusted and dependable captain, rewarded with lands that encompassed the fallen temples of Dameus. Unfortunately for Pero, she was not only heavy set, but she sported an unsightly raised mole on the side of her face that was larger than a typical Roman Silver Denarius, a common trading coin. She was born that way and many a suitor was discouraged despite the best efforts of her parents to find her a husband.

Pero would never suffer the plight of the pretty girl with too much bothersome attention thrust upon her. In a time when the view of the weight of a woman was far more generous than in modern times, there was still a threshold for obesity, and Pero was getting on that way as the time and hope for a husband was diminishing. As the daughter of a successful veteran cavalry officer, Pero's life was too easy, and a lazy one at that. With a ferocious appetite and little in the way of required physical activity, she put on the pounds like a hog at an endless feed trough. Being isolated on a farm, combined with the fact that girl's rarely received schooling, she had a good deal of leisure time, or in short, much in the way of alone time. When not eating, she spent many a sunny day exploring the old ruins about the property. When she noticed a bronze tip sticking out of the ground under a broken altar upon a hill, she dug it out with her fingers and wiped the dust upon it.

"Do you have a wish?" A voice that formed from a portly cloud instantaneously hissed out at her.

"Sure," she said, hardly thinking beyond a tiny amount of surprise at the talking spirit like form before her, "I just want someone to love, to be loyal, and handsome, and, and, obedient too! Yes, that would be nice." The cloudy figure retreated, and she stared more in confusion when it was gone. "Ya, I'd like to see you do that one," she said somewhat sadly thinking that it was just another cruel joke in her life. Suddenly, a gorgeous dark gray wolf, almost black, appeared before her and began lapping her leg with its tongue.

"Aya!" She screamed, but the wolf just knelt down at her feet and put one paw on his head in submission. She reached out tentatively for his head, and he nuzzled her. He was a big one, probably 90 pounds, and when she discovered that he was not a danger to her, she came to realize that in a way, her wish had been granted; after all, what is more loyal and obedient than a canine?

"No, no, no!" She said aloud, "That's not it!" She grabbed the lamp and wiped it again not really knowing that that was what triggered the form from within. When it hissed out as before, she interrupted when it was about to speak, "I meant a man! I want a man who is handsome, loyal, and obedient to my every wish!"

As before, the spirit form disappeared, and a naked man materialized before her eyes. He seemed a little thin and not overly endowed, but he had a handsome bronzed angular face, long hair, dreamy eyes, and just as she was taking it all in with a smile forming at the corner of her eyes, and as he reached out his hand to her with a friendly smile, the wolf attacked. The animal feared for his new master and took the outstretched hand as a terrible threat. The wolf leapt at the man, knocked him to the ground, and tore his throat out.

"No! Bad wolf! Go away!" But it was too late, the wolf whimpered off a few feet after the scolding, but the man bled out. "That's it, just another cruel joke," she said and buried the lamp where she had found it. She even pulled a piece of the broken altar over it and vowed never to visit the fallen temple again. She turned her attention back to the wolf with the bloody muzzle and then down at the corpse, "You may as well come along," and he jumped after her with the command. They left the body to the scavengers. Although Pero would never marry, she would never have a more loyal, trusted, and loving companion for the next 11 years or so for that is how long the wolf lived.

When Domitian passed away, Nerva ruled for only two short years, but he was a wise old man elected by the senate. Most importantly, near the time of his death, he chose Trajan as his heir apparent. Trajan ran an open honest administration while winning several important military victories. Under his rule, the great empire extended to Mesopotamia, Arabia, and the Balkans.

Hadrian, Trajan's immediate successor in the year 117, traveled throughout the countryside on a mission expounding peace and material well-being for all favored citizens. Hadrian created a postal system and codified Roman law for the entire Roman population, which was approaching seventy million at the time. Antonius followed in the year 138 and earned the name "Pius" from the senators due to his good character and intelligence.

The Golden Age of the Roman Empire reached its pinnacle with Marcus Aurelius in the year 161. He was reasonable, philosophical, serious, politically aware, and above all, sensitive to others' needs. Marcus Aurelius brought a deep sense of duty combined with a willingness to work on the empire's constant improvement. The beginning of the decline of Rome would not begin until his death in 180.

Rome borrowed a good deal of religion, literature, art, science, philosophy, and other facets of its cultural identity from the Greeks. Many of the gods remained the same but with the names converted to Latin. The four basic elements that shaped the lives of Rome's people were homes, farms, wars, and religion. Greek poems, tragedies, histories, and important writings were translated into Latin as well.

In the early years, Greek slaves tutored Romans. The writing and historical style of such great Roman writers like Virgil, Cicero, Horace, and Ovid could readily be traced to the Greeks. In architecture, the Romans took much of what was only theory by the Greeks and transformed it into roads paved with rock, aqueducts to bring precious water to the cities, and stone bridges some of which still stand today. Where the Greeks built simple forms with straight lines and rectangles, the Romans mastered the arch and even domes.

One final Roman accomplishment that cannot be understated was the ability to spread their superior culture and achievements to the backward peoples that they conquered. Once the empire expanded, government officials, soldiers, and trade merchants spread Roman ways across the countryside. By funding new schools and public works in old settlements and previously unoccupied areas, new towns arose with a distinctive Roman flavor. With a robust population, new settlers overran the old grounds of Dameus. The lamp would be unearthed again.

In the meantime, the incomparable and unequaled Roman Coliseum had stood for two centuries and served as the pinnacle for mass entertainment; nevertheless, throughout the lands and especially in the larger cities, many smaller arenas sprung up. In one such lesser venue located in the town of Ephesus, a former slave named Cacius selected his favorite weapon: a net and a three-pronged spear known as a trident. The goal of course was to entangle one's opponent in the netting and then jab him with the trident, a formidable combination when it worked and not easily defended. The thief, a smaller man with skinny arms, made a poor selection by choosing an overbearing sword with a blade that was a full two feet in length from hilt to tip. The thief was not physically large enough to handle such a massive weapon. The two men entered the arena for a fight to the death.

"Cacius will make easy work of him," said Marius to his father from his spectator seat. Even though the outcome would be obvious, there was always a little hope for the underdog and the thrill of combat. One could slip or be ill or be bleeding internally from a past wound or any number of downers. Marius was always excited with the games no matter how uneven the matches.

"I believe you are right Marius," answered his father, "But watch Cacius play with him some."

Cacius was fully two yards and a little over a hand span tall which equaled six-and-a-half-feet in height, a giant of a man at the time. Marius had that much in common with the slave. Cacius circled his opponent while feinting jabs with the trident in one massive hand while twirling the net in the other. The little thief began making desperate wild plunges with the big blade; nevertheless, they ended in a clumsy stagger with the lack of balance from the momentum of the thrust.

Cacius felt at ease and knew that it was necessary to put on a good show. The rewards for showmanship could mean more food and maybe even time with a whore. Cacius felt that if he gained enough popularity, freedom would be his, and he could retire. Being a slave was not much worse than the games since he had been beaten, whipped, and then put back to work breaking up rock for one project or another. The whippings were particularly bad after his thwarted escape attempt. He had the haphazard scar lines across his back and shoulders to prove it. Given his size and unruliness, he was a perfect fit for the games.

Enough fooling around Cacius thought to himself. He was beginning to sense the impatience of the crowd as the thief tired. On one of the thieves' wild off-balance juts that turned him halfway around, Cacius sunk the sharpened tips of the trident deep into the buttocks of the thief. The crowd roared with approval, cheering, and laughing simultaneously. The thief did not disappoint either as he ran screaming around the arena with a 3-pronged spear dragging from his ass. Cacius smiled too as the effect was better than expected.

The thief, wounded, made one last mighty effort with the sword that turned out to be a rather feeble effort indeed. He backed up to gain a running start and made straight for the heart of Cacius. The run turned into a pained galumph and Cacius easily sidestepped the effort as the little man lost his sword. As the thief passed on by, Cacius looped the net over the little man who went tumbling into the 12-foot wall that separated the combatants from the spectators.

Cacius picked up the sword easily in one paw and held it over the tumbled and pinned pitiful excuse for an opponent. Before he finished his role in this mortal combat, he waved the sword and free arm about for the crowd to decide. The crowd roared with delight and approved of the kill as there would be no handkerchiefs waving frantically or thumbs up to spare the life of the petty thief. Cacius sighed and plunged the sword through the back of the thief to finish the job. Blood pooled like rainwater drifting lazily over an overflowing bucket.

"Cacius! Cacius!" The crowd chanted repeatedly.

Marius gave a half-hearted clap, as he was somewhat disappointed, "He was hardly worth it."

"Yes, he was quite overmatched but remember the man was a thief and got what he deserved," said his father, "Cacius is not a man that I would like to meet myself, at least not down there."

Marius was thinking about how he would battle the brute Cacius but kept his thoughts to himself. The contest with Cacius had been the grand finale as it had been now for five weeks in a row. Cacius boasted an undefeated record with twelve wins and gained a reputation as the greatest gladiator Ephesus ever witnessed. Ephesus lay two hundred miles east of Athens across the sea and about forty miles west of Marius' home. The town leaders had the Greek amphitheater in which Cacius fought converted into an arena used exclusively for entertaining fights. The seating capacity increased to seat an audience of 10,000 souls.

The theater shared many of the same characteristics as its giant cousin in Rome. They were both elliptical in shape, both had an upper gallery for more important spectators, both sported sand-covered wooden floors, both contained mechanical machines beneath the floor complete with chains and pulleys that slaves worked to hoist animal and/or human cages up to the level of the arena, and both unsurprisingly were utilized for the same purpose. The most significant difference was that the Roman Coliseum held 50,000 people, 5 times that of Ephesus. Rome's floor area was fully 285 feet by 180 feet, but the one in Ephesus was only 130 feet by 75 feet, less than half in linear dimensions, but fully 80% smaller in area than the big one in Rome.

The majority of the gladiators were slaves, criminals, or prisoners of war. Some freemen enlisted to fight for money and fame as well. At times, even knights, senators, women, and Commodus, one of Rome's emperors, fought within the arena battle zones. Those of importance received superior weapons or advantages over whom they were fighting, whether it was armed chariots up against unarmed foot soldiers, or other cavalry verses infantry, or uneven manpower that was largely in favor of the privileged. At times, those running the shows took bribes to offer those advantages.

Many a contest took place during celebrations, such as war victories, aristocratic marriages, holidays, solstices, and even funerals too. Larger venues like the Coliseum often featured wild beasts in the morning and gladiators in the afternoon. Cruel battles were justified by the government in that they hardened and desensitized Roman citizens to the sight of bloodshed, and thus, allowed them to endure war. The games lasted hundreds of years, until the year 404 when Emperor Honorius banned them long after the empire had begun to crumble.

After Marius, his father, and the thousands made for the exits, Cacius enjoyed a large meal and a full 15 minutes of whore time. She was a bit heavy set, used up some, sweaty, and cursed with syphilis; however, none of it mattered to Cacius who had no trouble doing his business. A long-confined man has very little standards or choices. The winning warriors were not only well fed, but received medical care too if needed, but Cacius had not gotten as much as a scratch today.

Marius was a large lad for seventeen and likely avoided recruitment for the army because of his father's trade. His father made concrete by mixing lime and volcanic earth with water. Concrete, an earlier Roman invention was an unusually strong, hard material, and workable before it cured or hardened. Marius apprenticed under his father as trades, for it was common to pass trades within one's family. He learned to mix the proper amounts of sand, gravel, and crushed rock to form concrete blocks. The less water used the stronger the concrete would be, though too little would lead to premature crumbling. Too much water was just as bad. The Roman arch reinforced the concrete.

Marius had been helping his father for as long as his memories allowed. The years of shaping and lifting these blocks were directly responsible for his large muscles upon his naturally formed broad shoulders. He was a big lad, bigger than most including his father who was also no small man. His father was getting on in age and the backbreaking labor had taken its toll. Marius's father now walked stoop-shouldered, seemed to be constantly weary, and had trouble getting out of bed in the morning due to the stiffness. It would soon be Marius's time to become the headmaster of the trade.

Where Pero's family, like that of Dameus, had living quarters south of the hill where the lamp lay within the temple ruins, Marius and his father lived and worked a little north of the site. As the centuries passed, the population increased in all directions. His father built a concrete house in a large open area that had once been part of the farmlands owned by Dameus and his father alike. As a curious boy in the countryside, Marius had wandered about the ruins, but had not dug sufficiently or with any purpose to unearth the lamp. Earthquakes were not altogether uncommon and minor tremors in the past had shifted some of the rubble on top of the lamp, burying it further; however, a last-minute aftershock during the most recent movement reversed the trend by uncovering the lamp's handle.

The days went by quickly for Marius, hard 12-to-14-hour days left little time for leisure except for the 7th day of rest. Given the distance, his father only allowed them to travel to the games about once a month, despite them happening weekly in Ephesus. It frustrated Marius for he deeply enjoyed the games. His father would not allow him a horse or the money to go on his own more frequently. With nothing much to do on that 7th day, Marius set out in a walk to explore the old ruins. He was walking aimlessly through the weeds and brush when he came to the base of the hill where a piece of a rear pillar remained standing behind a broken altar. Various grasses had grown around the fallen stone pieces and combined with the recent past tremor, it seemed that some of the debris had shifted about.

Marius strode up to the hill wandering with no particular goal in mind when he saw it. A tiny golden twinkle stood in direct contrast to the graying decayed cement and green grass as the sun blinded him for a split second with its reflection. Marius blinked a longer interval than usual as a brief blackened vision clouded over as though some minute cells had died somewhere deep within his eyes. He was young and such things tended to regenerate faster. An instant later, he was beside the object tugging and clawing at the dirt around it. Marius's fat-but-firm fingers could not grip the fragment for it was barely exposed.

Marius sat back and thought a moment, looked around and about, and then moved a few feet to retrieve a nice hand-sized stone, which he proceeded to use to smash the old cement around the thing. It took him fifteen minutes of brute force to bore a few inches down just to expose enough to achieve a solid grip. Much of the handle of the lamp glowed dimly in the bright light of the sun. He grasped it and then pulled with all of his might. The blue veins in his taught arms popped out but the lamp would not budge. He stopped pulling and sat down again staring blankly at the little divot he had dug around the thing. He was a little disappointed since at first, he thought that the sparkle was gold, but upon closer examination, it turned out to be just bronze.

He rested a bit longer before picking up the rock again. He had nothing better to do today anyhow since his father did not wish to go into town. It was a long walk back to get a shovel, but he had made some progress and figured he could free it without wasting all of that time.

He took a different approach by working on the ground around the opposite side of the lamp. This side contained thick grasses and roots to boot. When he pulled directly on the weeds, they only broke off at the top. Bit by bit he bore into the earth with his heavily calloused fingers removing fragments of roots, still wondering if maybe retrieving a shovel wasn't such a bad idea in the first place. After another fifteen minutes most of the spout was now exposed, at least enough to get a second handhold. With both hands, he braced himself and with a strained mighty tug, it came free. He fell on his back from the force of the pull with the lamp lying on his chest, but both hands remained firmly upon it, one firmly on the handle and the other just as firmly on the spout.

Se slowly sat up and placed the lamp on the ground as he brushed the dust from his tunica. He picked up the lamp and began brushing some of the heavily incrusted dirt, roots, and cement debris from it as he turned it over and about, examining it closely. Then it happened. The metal thing that he had pried from the earth had a warm pulsating feeling as a strange murky substance streamed out of it. Marius dropped it but the substance continued out as a round somewhat cruelly grinning face stared down at him and began barking out words:

"You may have three wishes boy, what is your first?"

"Who, whaaaa...who are you?" Marius stammered as he backed up a step.

"I am a Djinni and I am ready to obey you as your slave, what is your command?"

Marius composed himself and it dawned on him that somehow this thing came from the heavens, or Mt. Olympus, specifically for his use. There was only one obvious wish for Marius, the only thing he admired and ever wanted to be.

"I wish to fight in the arena and win!" Marius said triumphantly, replacing his fear with excitement and enthusiasm. The substance slowly withdrew and was gone as quickly as it appeared. Marius picked it up and went home. With no one watching, he smuggled the lamp into his room.

Another agonizingly slow week dragged on for Marius. His only thoughts centered on enlisting and fighting in the games and he would soon get his opportunity. Nearing his eighteenth birthday, Marius split with the family on his next visit to Ephesus. He was of an age that he could wander some on his own and then meet back with the family before the games began. This day he had an overwhelming unstoppable desire to enlist. One look at his size and eagerness made him an easy choice for the local official. It was not often that healthy robust freemen enlisted.

When Marius failed to show at their accustomed seats, his father was somewhat concerned but he too thought that Marius was old enough and big enough to take care of himself. Maybe, just maybe his father thought that a young girl had distracted Marius for he was certainly old enough for that too. His father smiled at the thought of young perky upright breasts, the fresh taste of kisses that mattered, and the flowery smell of a girl's washed and perfumed hair.. With that thought, he led what remained of his family into the arena entrance without Marius. His concern multiplied tenfold into absolute fear and shock when Marius entered the arena clad in battle gear for the first kickoff fight of the day.

"Marius! What are you doing? Are you mad?" His father shouted but the cheering of the boisterous crowd drowned it out.

The local governor, who sat above all others at the highest point of the covered gallery, stood up and raised his arms for attention and silence. The crowd quickly hushed, as they were not to speak when the governor made the opening announcement. There were always numerous guards patrolling to silence them physically, if necessary, arrest them, and even make them part of the games if they were particularly obstinate or unruly.

"Greetings Citizens!" The governor announced. "We have a new warrior with us today who has committed no crimes!" There were several hushed chuckles. "He is a free man! I give you Marius the Magnificent!" As he said this, he gestured down at Marius as the crowd roared its approval. The official let them carry on a few moments before he raised his arms again. "Today, Marius will fight his first battle against a soldier from Germania, an enemy of the Roman people." The soldier arose in a monstrous cage ordinarily reserved for animals waiting beneath the stadium. The boos from the crowd made Marius smile, for the spectators would at least be on his side.

They had dressed Marius much like a Roman legion. He wore leg protectors called greaves, a leather breastplate, and a crested helmet, which he now placed upon his head. He received a shield made of wood and leather along with a one-handed battle sword, also known as a gladius. Even without Djinni's help, his opponent probably would not have posed much of a threat to Marius. The

German barbarian was an older man who was lame from a battle wound that had severely damaged his right leg. He was only of average height, which left him nearly a foot shorter than Marius. He hobbled out of the cage lacking armor as his temporary prison lowered. He had not eaten in several days and drank only a little survival water.

The official at the lower arena side signaled the games to begin by lowering his outstretched arm sharply. The barbarian backed a little away from Marius cautiously and there was obvious fear in his eyes for he thought wrongly that he was fighting an experienced soldier, like the one who had maimed him. The prisoner took a dull shorter sword barely larger than a dagger. Marius's adrenaline rush combined with his over eager youthfulness caused him to rush the German head on. The prisoner barely sidestepped in time and managed to stick out his good leg at the right moment to send Marius tumbling to the ground. Wrestling and bullying his peers did not exactly prepare Marius for mortal combat. There would be more than bruises, a fat lip, or a black eye within the arena.

Had he not been crippled and malnourished, it may have been the end of Marius. As his opponent limped over with dagger raised, Marius was able to rise in time to ward off the blows with his shield. Though Marius was not injured, the barbarian prisoner gained a little confidence especially when he viewed the youthful appearance of his adversary up close and personal. He was thinking that there still might be a chance as Marius approached him again.

Irritated and embarrassed at his fall, Marius came at him like a mad man and yelled as he charged. The sword of Marius rained down on him with all the youthful vigor that Marius could muster. The poor German was able to avoid most of the blows and even block a few with his pitiful blade, but the lack of a shield and a longer stronger blade was too much to overcome. The energy of the boy seemed to be endless and when he tried to sidestep off his bum leg, he fell to the ground near exhaustion. Another sword blow of the boy caught the German's hand as he attempted a feeble block from his inferior position. The blow severed two fingers completely from his right hand and left a third hanging by a thread of skin.

"Ahhhhhhh....!" The German grunted out in pain, but he was not quite finished yet. Marius swung again for the kill without any finesse or technique, but the German managed to roll out of the way at the last second while grasping his own short sword in his good left hand. Marius swung again simultaneously while the German lashed out from the ground connecting with the ankle of Marius. A wide bloody gash leaked from the ankle as it was Marius's turn to cry out in pain; nevertheless, his own sword had cut deeply into the left shoulder of the German. Marius's momentum carried him over the hunched barbarian, but the German had dropped his sword from the force of the blow. Marius had unwittingly nicked an artery of his opponent as blood sprayed and soaked the breastplate of Marius; luckily, it was not his own. The German barbarian was fighting a losing battle, not only with Marius, but with his own consciousness. Blood flowed freely from the missing fingers and the shoulder was spraying like a hole in a water pipe under severe pressure.

Marius was able to get up, but he was now limping as his adversary had been at the beginning; however, all the fight had gone out of the German as he was quickly bleeding to death. The crowd had been yelling and cheering but grew silent as Marius stood above his vanquished opponent. It was the time to ask them for their blessing though the German's time was already quite short. He looked around the crowd noticing a few handkerchiefs waving for the German, but not all that exuberantly. Marius was a bit confused but finally looked up at the governor. The quick downward point of the governor's thumb was all Marius needed. He tossed the shield aside. With both hands he thrust the sword through the back and then through the heart of the barbarian prisoner. Death had already been a mere few seconds away and it was almost a relief as darkness covered the German's eyes forever.

The sight of all the blood along with his throbbing ankle did not seem to bother Marius as much as it probably should have. The adrenaline was still flowing as soldiers led him out; the crowd waved, cheered, and shouted his name. Marius was never happier as he departed in a dream-like state. He was a star, and everybody loved him, but the cheers would be much louder later in the day for Cacius. Cacius would go on to win his thirteenth consecutive battle. Marius did get the benefit of skilled surgeons who stitched and dressed the ankle expertly. The cut had not gone to the bone and would only take a couple of weeks to heal properly; nevertheless, in that time, Marius would leave home for good.

"As the lion, king of the beasts, is reckoned chief among animals, for its strength, speed and bravery, so is the faculty of wisdom reckoned chief among mental states helpful to enlightenment." - Samyutta Nikaya, V. 227

CHAPTER XVIII

"Why Marius? Why"

"You do not understand father," answered Marius.

"Why don't you tell me then?"

"It's a job. I can get more pay than I do now and have my own place to stay."

"But Marius, you have an honorable job, and this house will be yours one day. Those games are dangerous and in the long run, everyone who plays in them gets killed."

"No father, look at Cacius, he has not lost a battle yet," countered Marius. It was obvious as to who Marius looked up to.

"Yes, but his time will come and what do you think would happen to you if you had to fight him?"

"I do not know but did you see how I killed that German prisoner today? It was not hard at all," he boasted. Like an expanding fish tale, he would embellish it further and further as time went on.

"Come to your senses Marius, that man was old, lame, without armor, and plus they gave him an inferior weapon to use. With all that against him, he still nearly came close to getting the better of you. You were lucky Marius and that is all."

"My mind is made up father, the arena official has already provided a place for me to stay, and I have agreed to it. You cannot do anything to go against it," he added defiantly.

"Marius, Marius, you are my son and I have taught you everything I know. Mark my words boy, these games will only lead to your death. Sons are supposed to bury their fathers, not the other way around. One day soon, you will come up against an opponent that you will not be able to dispatch. I am begging you one last time, please change your mind Marius, I'm sure that we can still get you out of this." His father was thinking that a hefty bribe to the official might do the trick.

"No father! It is my life; I will do as I please!" Marius wanted to tell him about his secret weapon, the lamp, but he thought more about it and decided otherwise. "You will see father, you will see."

"Then pack your things and leave Marius, we want nothing more to do with you. Say goodbye to your mother and sister and get out." With that, his father left angrily and vowed not to attend any games in which Marius fought; nevertheless, he would break that vow. Marius packed his belongings and stowed the lamp away in a trunk beneath his clothing. He said his final farewells and headed for the city.

Being a free man, Marius became a public employee on the territory's payroll supported by the average citizen's taxes; furthermore, the governor liked him and admired his bravery to the extent that he allowed Marius to stay in his own house, which was more of an elaborate stone palace. The structure was not nearly the size of any of the numerous palaces set aside for high central government officials in Rome like senators, but it was the largest single housing unit in the city of Ephesus. The local mansion had a servant's wing with enough room for 26 occupants, two spacious inner courtyards, numerous guest rooms, rooms for other officials on the government payroll, a bath wing, dining quarters, and much more. It was also a mere three blocks from the stadium.

There was a personal physician on hand, and he certified Marius' ankle had healed enough for combat. Though it had mended just fine, there was an ugly scar left. With the surgeon's approval, Marius would fight again. Pending a shipment of slaves, it appeared that Marius' next opponent would not be human. Battles between man and beast, or even animal against animal, were not rare.

The Romans captured and imported animals from all over their part of the world including lions and leopards from Africa, tigers from India, bears and wolves from the north lands, and everything from wild boars to hyenas, the wilder and fiercer the better. When the governor of Ephesus paid handsomely for animals, he wanted to get them in the ring as soon as possible, as the death rate for caged animals hauled a long distance was quite high. Marius would have to wait some time before getting his call up, and while he was waiting, he was not even sure of what he would be fighting. It would likely be a survivor from the early contests.

The first match of the day lasted all of two minutes. An African male lion dispatched an Indian tiger that outweighed him by a little more than 80 pounds. The lion was able to grasp the tiger's head, pull it down, and then rip open the back of the tiger's head. The crowd was stunned because the majority had bet on the bigger tiger despite 3 to 1 odds against the lion.

When it came to determining the true King of the Jungle, it wasn't necessarily a tiger, and it was even debatable whether it was indeed a lion as so often assumed. Orange and black-striped Bengal tigers, though generally bigger than lions on average by about one hundred pounds, are more solitary, lone hunters. Tigers typically defend a larger territory and only mingle during mating season. Lions on the other hand are unique in the cat world as they are far more social, especially the females. A male lion must survive by constantly fighting with other males generally for the first six years of his life, until he either dies trying or is big, strong, cunning, and experienced enough to take over or even form his own pride of devoted female followers.

Once a lion can take over a pride, then the lionesses coordinate the majority of the hunting. His job was then twofold. One was to protect the pride from other male interlopers, and the other was to mate with all the females, an exhausting task in its own right. The Roman Empire was vast, stretching into three continents; as a result, they were able to bring animals together from different habitats and regions that ordinarily would not cross paths in the wild.

Though larger, a wild male tiger was simply no match for the undersized but more ferocious and experienced male lion. One area where the lion is truly larger and stronger than that of a tiger is in the forelimbs. A conventional lion, or more often a lioness, overpowers her quarry by grasping and pulling her victim down with these strong forelimbs, followed up by a fatal bite to the neck, or perhaps by the clamping of her jaws over the victim's mouth and nostrils. Lionesses suffocated many a prey animal in this manner.

A tiger on the other hand relies much more on dense forest and grass cover with the striped coat providing superb camouflage. The Siberian tiger, a subspecies, is longer than a Bengal. The white coat with the black stripes enabled them to blend with the snow-cover and exposed rock in the higher elevations of the northern mountains. Unlike lions, tigers thrive in lakes and rivers and are powerful swimmers. In their old habitat, they did not have as much to fear from watering holes as lions.

Is the lion truly king of all beasts? For one, the largest carnivore in old Africa was the Nile crocodile, and it wasn't even the largest of crocodiles on the planet at the time as those in Australia were even bigger yet. On the other hand, the Nile version dealt with far more formidable prey, not the least of which included hippopotamuses, water buffalo, and perhaps an unsuspecting lion attempting to cross a river or maybe just stopping by in the dry season for a much-needed drink. The Romans had difficulty catching big crocodiles as well as transporting them. Most died due to a lack of water for their outer bodies while little ones grew so slowly that they too succumbed to conditions outside of their environment before reaching prime fighting size.

Once, more than a million wildebeests made an annual migration across the plains of old Sub-Saharan Africa. A downright spooky sight was that of a large concentration of Nile crocodiles lying in wait for the feast. The wildebeests, like insects, played the game of numbers. As long as more were born than were lost each year, the species remained viable. When a baby wildebeest was born, it had to get his or her legs going in a matter of minutes. Those that didn't kept the lion prides happy and fed.

As wildebeests crossed rivers bloated with crocodiles, there were losses. An adult male Nile crocodile could reach twenty feet in length and weigh up to an old English ton, or two thousand pounds. One disadvantage was that crocodiles couldn't chew, but they could grasp and lock on, then pull their prey deep below in the water to drown them. To feed, they grabbed mouthfuls of flesh, and then rolled and thrashed their bodies to twist and break off portions small enough to swallow, which were still quite large.

Since something big like a water buffalo was too big to eat in one sitting, they often hid the remaining carcass beneath a sunken tree limb or rock in the water. It was a smart move as the Nile crocodile was once arguably the most intelligent of all reptiles living at the time. The added benefit was that when the body decomposed further, it softened up some; thus, making it easier to consume. On the flip side, during the congregation formed exclusively for the wildebeest migration, it was virtually impossible to hide a carcass with so many competitors on hand.

In the water, a lion had no chance against a croc. Crocodiles have a keeled, vertically flattened tail that propelled it quickly and efficiently through the water. On the other hand, like most reptiles, they tire quickly and only have the energy for a quick burst forward, two at most. If they could clamp their jaws on something, they could then drag their intended victim under water and quickly suffocate and/or drown them within a few minutes. Able to crush the bones of the largest of animals, few others could match the sheer chomping power emanating from the jaws of a formidable crocodile, certainly not a lion.

One disadvantage of a crocodile is that it can't focus its eyes very well, especially underwater; furthermore, a protective eyelid further blurred its vision outward. On land, they could still make a quick burst forward; nevertheless, the agility and superior vision of a lion would make short work of it. Those who live near alligators and crocodiles know that if they run in circles, it will confuse and blur the reptile's ability to adequately track them and thus, give them a better chance of escaping. Does that mean that the crocodile is essentially King of the Jungle? Not necessarily. When it came down to it, habitat and environment play a crucial role; in the water, the croc wins, on land, it's the lion.

The same held true for the American alligator, another crocodilian-style predator with a slightly different tooth configuration, along with a wider, less pointy snout. With a jaw snapping force that could reach three thousand pounds, there was little to challenge it head on; yet jaguars and black bears once roamed in alligator country. Though smaller than a lion, pound for pound, a jaguar is stronger, but a bear is even stronger yet. The alligator is superior in the water, but not on land.

In the old South American rainforests, the jaguar is king. Stealthy, mysterious, dangerous, and reclusive like an African leopard, yet, a six-hundred-pound, forty-foot anaconda could squeeze it to death in a matter of a few minutes. In the old Asian jungles, the small but nimble mongoose was perhaps the best snake-killer of all time. Few could walk around anywhere without some type of danger, even the largest and strongest of the predator class.

In the unending debate of animal superiority, alligators are not necessarily at the top when it comes to water-based predators. Great white sharks can tear up saltwater crocodiles in head-to-head battles. Sharks of all species on the other hand, usually avoid killer whales who can hunt them in packs. Larger denizens yet included sperm and blue whales, not to mention giant squid that still roam and hunt the very deepest parts of the ocean.

A large adult hippopotamus can use its teeth like antlers, flipping its huge gaping mouth open while clashing its teeth and jaws to assert dominance. An angry hippo will split an old African bull shark or an occasional crocodile in two. Like crocodiles, hippos prefer to congregate in and around water. A large social grouping of hippos is nothing any sane creature with an ounce of intelligence would dare bother. Large animals like rhinos, hippos, and elephants were a bit problematic to catch and exhibit, especially in the smaller arenas. Transport could be difficult and clean up after the kill could take some time as well.

On land, hippos lose a little of their buoyant mobility and advantage. Say on land, a pitch battle between that of a rhinoceros and hippo, like that of a big cat and a crocodilian, favors the flabby hippo in water, but the more muscular rhino on land. As part of its fighting technique, a rhino can hook its horn around a hippo's back leg and use its bulk and charging momentum to flip it. If the rhino could pull that off, then it could gore the hippo to death with its unique frontal weapon. It wasn't that different from a gladiatorial battle between men, a martial arts match, or an ultimate fighter contest with more liberal wide-open rules. Once one participant knocked the other off his feet, he was then usually at a distinct disadvantage. Usually, one had to rise again to have any hope of victory, or at the very least, knock the opponent down to grapple at ground level.

A rhino's extremely sharp pointed front horn is one of the deadliest natural weapons in the animal kingdom. With three to four tons of body mass packed with taut muscles, combined with a thirty mile-per-hour charge, one had best get out of the way of an enraged rhinoceros. Yet, that wasn't difficult to do as a rhino's poor eyesight and short chubby legs make it difficult to maneuver, especially when it comes to turning quickly. Nature has a way of balancing strengths and weaknesses. About the only rhino verses hippo battles occurred in the Coliseum at Rome, and the rhinos usually won.

The largest land-based mammal in old Africa was the elephant, who exceeded hippos and rhinos by as much as three tons. A massive white rhino, the largest of its kind, might hit eight thousand pounds; an African bull elephant could top fourteen thousand. There was nothing to challenge an adult elephant in the wild except for man.

Only the babies of these large grazing animals were vulnerable to predators, and few protected their own like a group or family of elephants; furthermore, since elephants are a matriarchal social society, they emphasized protection of the young even more. Elephants also had eleven-pound brains making them some of the smartest of all land-based grazing animals. For the most part, foraging and plant-eating animals avoided conflict with one another as many could graze and feed in the same regions peacefully, unless man thrust them together in a cramped arena.

In round two, a four-hundred-pound male silverback gorilla rose into the arena in a cage from which he almost escaped. He was so strong that he was in the process of bending the bars before they released him into the arena. His opponent was a leopard that was barely half of his weight. Primates held an advantage in intelligence and male gorillas were usually about twice the size of females. Though a herbivore, the male gorilla sports much larger canines than does his female counterpart. An experienced silverback leader of a social grouping threatens first with a tremendous roar while beating his own chest repeatedly in a clear display of dominance.

If an intruder persists after this show of exhibition, the male will rear back its head and charge at full speed, a sight every bit as heart stopping as that of an angry rhino. At this intense moment, it's a toss-up whether he will turn away at the last moment or, engage in fighting. With extremely powerful forearms and strong hands, a beating by a gorilla often proves fatal to whatever it is attacking, whether it is another gorilla or an unwary leopard. It's generally unwise to provoke something that has the strength to topple a 3,500-pound automobile.

In the arena, he and the leopard were both out of their element. The leopard raced around the oval sides of the arena, leaping wildly as it tried to find a way out, but the walls were too high even for it. The gorilla sat mostly agitated and confused by the crowd and the running leopard. This went on for several minutes and the crowd became somewhat bored as they shouted encouragement for the two to engage. The leopard finally stopped and lay down in the shade at one end of the arena. The gorilla had backed up some and the two rested a good 100 feet apart as the arena was 130 feet in length on the long side. At a signal from the governor, the arena official sent in two archers on horseback to encourage the animals to fight. As a last resort, their job would be to wound one or the other or both.

Things got quite interesting then, at least to the crowd. The moving horse looked much like a typical grazing animal to the leopard, and its predator instincts kicked in. The archer made a feeble attempt at shooting it, but the leopard was on the move about the time the arrow flew from the bow. In the small arena, the leopard caught the half trotting horse along its rear flanks and raked it unmercifully with deep slashing claws. When the horse reared up screeching in pain, the rider fell, and the leopard promptly ripped his throat out.

Meanwhile the other archer shot the gorilla at point blank range in the shoulder, which caused the gorilla to bellow out in pain and charge. The gorilla was not entirely ignorant and had realized with definitive certainty as to who had wounded him. When the horse rode by, the gorilla leaped at the man upon its back and took him to the ground, and then pounded and pummeled the man to a bloody pulp, sort of like a blanket party with aluminum baseball bats.

The crowd was really getting into it now, but despite the wild activity, the gorilla and leopard avoided each other. The horses were trotting around the perimeter, one with blood streaming down its flanks, the other unscathed. The men at the side gates were able to rescue the horses and exit the arena too. The leopard was busy chewing on one man while the gorilla, breathing heavily, hovered over the pulpy mass of the other.

The governor conferred with someone and had a message sent to the arena official at ringside to send the lion back in. The first thing the lion saw was the leopard, and this lion was closer to 500 pounds than 400. Predators in the same class have a way of knocking each other out to reduce the competition, and the lion made short work of the much smaller leopard. Like what a tiger would do, the lion grasped the head of the leopard and bit clean through it. With a freshly bloodied and stained maw that had barely dried from the tiger, the lion now focused on the gorilla and began stalking it. Despite their relative size and strength, gorillas and other primates were generally mortally afraid of big feline predators.

The lion had proven itself a ferocious fighter and the gorilla was another obstacle in its way of mastering the territory of the arena. In the wild, this lion had held a pride for several years and was well experienced in combat. He trotted around in a circle, closing in little by little. The gorilla still had an arrow lodged in its shoulder and it hurt. The silver on its back meant maturity but advanced age too.

The lion finally came head on and leapt into the chest of the gorilla, pawing for the head with the goal of sinking its teeth into it, but the sheer strength of the gorilla was able to resist, but not without consequences. The lion slashed and thrashed with its sharp claws opening long deep gashes down the gorilla's chest that drew warm fresh streams of blood. The gorilla released his grip to pummel the lion on the sides, but it gave the lion the opening that it needed. The lion got a hold of the gorilla's throat but suffered some bruising shots to its ribs and rear haunches before it could rip out the gorilla's carotid artery. One of the gorilla's blows broke the lion's left hip before the gorilla bled to death.

The lion limped about in victory, not knowing what to eat. The crowd cheered it madly for today the beast had truly proven that it was king. There were the collective carcasses of two men, a leopard, a gorilla, and even a bloody spot from the dead tiger removed from the earlier fight as the lion sniffed about confused. To add to that confusion, the men pulled up in a cage from below and coaxed the lion in with a nice raw rack of lamb to get the lion out of the battleground. The lion's fighting days would be over nonetheless. The hipbone had pierced the outer skin and it would be dead in three days from infection. With some cleaning and butchering, workers cleared the arena for round three.

In round three, a big European brown bear faced a strong and agile prized black bull imported from Spain. The breeders took special pains to sharpen the bulls' horns to extreme points. The governor was an older man of 55 years and wise. He was one of the few that had ever seen this type of battle in Rome and he kept the secret to himself. He had been trying for years to find a bear in the same weight class as the bulls and had lined up a dozen for the bear to fight, but he would present them one at a time. He would bet on the bear for several of the earlier rounds encouraging his friends and colleagues, at least the ones he favored, to bet on the bear, and he was not wrong.

Like gorillas, foraging bears were so unbelievably strong that they could knock vehicles over, break out windows, pull off doors, pop tires, and do whatever else was necessary to gain entry, particularly if an opportunity for acquiring food was involved. The biggest European brown bears were not much smaller than grizzlies and Kodiak bears in the New World, a rare one might reach 12 feet in height and weigh 1,500 pounds or even more, three to four times that of a gorilla.

A bear's fur was so thick that bullets could barely penetrate their hides and give them an annoying pinprick at most. Experienced mountain men from the Pacific Northwest learned that shooting a bear in the head or between the eyes was about the only proven way to significantly injure, kill, or drive it off. Many repeated shots to the hide did little more than anger the bear, a precarious situation no one would to face. Bow and arrows in Roman times rarely penetrated as well as the modern bullet.

Despite its bulk, a bear may not have had the quickness of a tiger; nevertheless, a big bear could move at thirty miles-per-hour, far more agile than man. The only hope against an angry bear was to run away, or perhaps up a tree, but that tree had better be a big one. Even the lowly black bear at a few hundred pounds, can rip away average size logs with the sheer strength of its forearms and long claws. Given enough time and motivation, a grizzly could take down a tree if it was larger than one it could readily tip over. The governor had featured black bears in the past, but never a monstrous brown bear from the northlands like they had today.

The betting was ferocious, but the matches were not. The first bull, as expected, made a direct maddening charge at the gargantuan brown bear. The bear nonchalantly, in a matter of a few precious seconds, crushed the bovine like a fly with a fly swatter. One extremely powerful massive blow to the bull's skull forced what little brains the bull had out its nose, mouth, ear, and between the numerous cracks and breaks within the shattered bone itself. The bear was a solid 1,500 pounds, roughly the same weight as the bulls.

Eight more bulls suffered the same fate, brought out one at a time. Numbers four and seven suffered only a glancing blow; nevertheless, the bear had the strength and ability to grab the proverbial bull by the horns, and then twist with such an incredible force, that the thick neck of their adversary would snap like a toothpick. The bear often applied this technique against caribou, elk, deer, moose, and anything else that sported antlers.

Frustrated with the accumulating piles of dead bovines, the bettors against the bear switched allegiances just when the bear was suffering telltale signs of exhaustion. The governor finally started taking the bet action against the bulls and won with bull #9. The tired bear stumbled against #9 and suffered a deep goring wound. The fresh bull charged repeatedly, adding several piercing shots until the bear stopped moving. The bear would end the day at 8-1 but despite the impressive record, the one loss meant death. As for Marius, since there were a few healthy bulls left, he was getting closer to becoming a bullfighter long before the sport would become popular.

In round four at the Ephesus venue, a group of four prisoners went against four tusk-heavy wild male boars. The slaves received crude wooden clubs and on average, the boars outweighed them by about sixty pounds each. The boars were not nearly as smart as primates, and did not proceed in a coordinated attack. A couple sparred with each other while one did not like the look of the men and charged. The four men ganged up on him and clubbed him to death, but not before the boar was able to sink a tusk deeply into the rear thigh of one of the men. As bad luck would have it, the tusk penetrated the femoral army and blood sprayed out as if it was under pressure from a punctured spray can. Now it was down to three on three.

The three men spoke different languages and could only communicate by gesture; nevertheless, one was of African descent and approached one of the lightly sparring swine duo from behind. He motioned the other two men to do likewise, and they followed, gladly allowing the dark-skinned man to take the lead point. The dark-skinned man wished that he had a nice long spear rather than a small wooden club half the size of a modern baseball bat.

Unbeknownst to his followers, the dark-skinned man designed his own survival plan. He strode lightly in the sand and got close enough to wallop the occupied boar a stinging blow on its rear haunches. The boar screamed in agony and turned furiously to engage the intruder. The dark-skinned man deftly ran behind the other two men who were not as ready to bolt. The wild and angry boar drilled one of the men hard in the chest and for an unlucky moment could not extract its tusks from the chest cavity of the man. The tusks penetrated the man's ribs, sticking within them. The man's organs were bursting in alphabetical order while the other man and the dark-skinned man used the opportunity to wail on the boar's head with their clubs. At the end of the skirmish, it was now down to two on two.

In less than a minute, the wild hog that had been sparring a bit with the other that was now dead, charged the men as well. The dark-skinned man hunted with his tribe in Africa and was far more cognizant of the danger at hand. The other man froze as the dark-skinned man actually tried to push him out of the way, but the boar came on fast just as they were finished clubbing his companion.

These new tusks hit the prisoner in the side, busting up the large hipbone. The boar kept boring in, a second, then a third time, as his tusks were not stuck like those of its dead companion. While the wounded prisoner was screaming in agony, the dark-skinned man was able to land two solid blows to the boar's head. The first dazed it, the second knocked it out, and then a follow-up third finished the wild hog off for good. The wounded man was still alive, but his hip was severely broken, and blood was gushing from several holes where the tusks had penetrated the flesh. There was no way for him to walk, but he remained conscious.

The last boar stayed out of the fighting and was over sixty feet away. The dark-skinned man had been both lucky and skillful in not having to take one of the boars head-on like the others. He felt bad for his barely surviving companion but thought his best chance was to lure the boar toward the wounded man. He could use his fellow prisoner as maybe a decoy or shield, and furthermore, the boar might get a little bloodlust going given the strong scent that the bleeding man was giving off.

The wounded prisoner rested on his knees clutching his hip with one hand while using his club as a prop for the other. The dark-skinned man backed off some, picked up a 2nd club from one of the dead men, and then walked gingerly toward the boar trying to get its attention without having to get too close. The last boar seemed somewhat bored and uninterested in the man. The dark-skinned man fell back toward the wounded prisoner, dropped one of the clubs near him, and retrieved a third club from the other dead man. When he approached the boar again at a distance of about thirty feet, he hurled one of the clubs and scored a direct hit!

The dark-skinned man was no amateur hunter, and he was already running while the club was still in the air. He grabbed the second club adjacent to the wounded man when it finally dawned on the wounded man what his fellow prisoner had done. The boar sped on a beeline straight for them both and the dark-skinned man moved about easily while there was no hope for the wounded man. Boom! Three hundred pounds at approximately twenty-eight miles per hour crashed into the wounded man and propelled him a full two yards backward as the boar would have eaten him for breakfast had not his brains been bashed in by the dark-skinned man lying in wait. The outcome of round four was prisoner men four kills, wild boars three. The spectators cheered the dark-skinned man, who would live to fight another day.

Finally, it was time for Marius. He had already invoked his second wish with a simple: "I wish to win my battle today." The problem that he shared with some before and several afterward was that he did not listen closely when the Djinni warned that there were only three wishes. Marius thought that they would go on indefinitely.

For hundreds of years, large fierce toros bravos, or brave bulls roamed wild over the plains of Spain. They were caught, bred, and quite common in Rome, maybe a little more difficult to acquire in outlying towns like Ephesus, but the governor had made a deal to get them. At this point, it was about all the fighting animals he had left, and the only decision to make was whether to use number ten, eleven, or twelve, or the one that had bested the bear. The governor called for number eleven, a fresh one, a nasty tempered black bull with a massive head of razor-sharp horns. Since the Romans did not care for the art of bullfighting, there would be no banderillos or picadors to weaken the big bull. Picadors were horsemen who lanced bulls to weaken their neck muscles while banderillos carried darts mounted on shafts two-and-a-half feet long, which thrust into the muscles just behind the bull's neck. Romans simply did not bother with them.

Marius was clad once again in his Roman soldier uniform, carefully cleaned following his first match. The new pair of sandals was about the only thing different, as the first contest ruined the originals. With his sword at the ready, the bull rose in a cage from below the arena. Marius's father decided to show up after all. He could not bear the agony of waiting several hours as news traveled slowly across the forty miles between his home and the arena. He held grave misgivings against his son's choice, but secretly he wished him well and may even have admired a little of the courage of the boy. He did not cheer with the crowd as Marius brandished his sword back and forth. The crowd quieted momentarily as the governor signaled the official, who in turn made his announcements and introductions. Without further ado, the door raised and the beast emerged. As the chains rattled, the cage slowly disappeared from view leaving man alone with bull.

Marius had never observed an animal quite like the intimidating bull that was huffing, puffing, and attempting to get its bearings. Sure, he had seen docile cattle at times but they were generally unaggressive and dwarfed in comparison to the massive black Spanish beast stomping before him. The bull staggered around shaking its big head back and forth while its eyes attempted to adjust to the daylight. Like all bulls and cows, the eyesight was not good.

The crowd of people appeared as a blurred noisy bunch to the beast as he strode more confidently around the perimeter of the arena. He was searching for an escape route through the wall; finding none, he quickened his gate. Sensing no way out, his anger arose, and he slammed directly into the wall at various places, but the wall held. One vicious hit dazed him some and he stopped, looked more toward the center of the ring as his state of disorientation wore off. That is when he noticed Marius.

Marius had been on full alert observing the bull as it blundered about, not knowing what exactly to do or maybe how to best approach the beast. He just moved as the bull did to keep it within his full range of vision. Mario's perplexity became a moot point as the bull started angling toward him. Marius crouched and deftly maneuvered the gladius into an attack position. The movement of the highly polished shiny sword captured the bull's full attention as sunlight sparkled from it like a shard of untarnished crystal on pavement.

Stamping his foot and puffing with a clear target in full view, the big black bull broke into a gallop. There was something to direct its rage on and the breastplate of Marius flashed as the sword had; thus, giving the bull a clear and present target. Near the final moment of impact, Marius leapt to the side as be brought the sword down into the face of the bull, but Marius had misjudged its speed. The sword landed behind the head and on top of the broad neck. The sword cut some into the thick muscle, but the wound was not a deep one.

The bull ran on a little further before halting and then turned to face his adversary again. It was a little confused for all its previous battles had been face to face with its own kind. The wound if anything angered it, and since it was a being of low intelligence, it charged again on instinct alone without much in the way of thought. Marius repeated his move away but timed his thrust more precisely. As he neatly sidestepped the bull rush, Marius severed the bull's ear and it flopped into the dirt.

The crowd was cheering wildly as they were completely engrossed in the battle. Enraged more than ever before, the black beast did not stop or hesitate this time and swung around with amazing speed and agility. This caught Marius unprepared as he paused to bow and play to the crowd. With lowered head, intense machine-gun-like snorting, and two long pointed massive horns that would have done Lucifer proud, the black monster roared and zeroed back in on its target. Marius was a tad late in adjusting and as he tried to leap aside, the bull caught one of its horns in his left thigh ripping deeply within the muscle and tendon of Marius's leg.

Marius screamed out in agony as the horn hooked, bucked, and lodged itself deeper, twisting his body completely around so that his head lay on the underside of the bull. The roar of the crowd drowned out his screams of pain. The crowd was on his side shouting encouragement and many voices yelled out for him to use his sword.

"By the gods, Marius! Use your sword!" It was his father, caught up in the action, but he was too far away for Marius to hear, but other voices came through loud and clear. The bull staggered about with the young man caught on his horn and stopped, then shook back and forth while Marius struggled to adjust both hands on his weapon in preparation for an upward thrust.

The horn was stuck so solidly that it would not allow much in the way of flowing blood, much like a cork in a bottle. Marius still had the strength in his arms to wield the gladius. Marius aimed for the middle of its chest, but at the precise moment of contact, the bull jerked and shook its head violently once again as it tried to shake off the attached burden. The blade veered off to the side from his intended mark, but still buried itself deeply within, piercing skin, muscle, and most fortunately, a lung of the creature. Filled with a new source of horrific pain, the black monstrosity bellowed out loudly as Marius desperately tried to extract the blade for another shot. His efforts were in vain as the bull began running wildly all the while dragging Marius somewhat underneath and behind him like a rag doll.

The energy and movement of the bull caused its own blood to flow freely as its heart pumped and pumped. Some of that blood soaked the breastplate of Marius, who, despite being dragged and dirtied, was suffering an occasional kick as well. Not by choice, Marius tasted the bull's blood as it streamed down upon his face and caressed his lips. Finally, the horn broke loose from his leg. It had not gone completely through but rather through the top above the knee just grazing the large femur bone beneath the thigh muscles. Marius, left bruised, battered, and bloodied, soon felt the flow of his crimson liquid upon extraction of the horn. With his upper body covered in the bull's blood and his own leg gushing, the crowd for a moment thought he was dead as he lay unmoving for a moment. The spectators grew quiet as a deathly hush filled the air.

The bull was still staggering around on its feet but breathing laboriously with the punctured lung. The gladius was hanging from the left side of its chest, but it still turned and decided to make another pass at its grounded opponent. To the delight of the crowd, Marius rose gingerly on one leg. In his heart, Marius trusted Djinni and felt that he was destined to win this match. The audience thought otherwise, for Marius had no weapon and did not appear to be in any condition to fend off another charge.

Although the simple mind of the black beast from Spain wanted to attack, its body did not seem to agree. With a somewhat feeble effort, the bull's halfhearted charge ended in a collapsed heap. Marius hobbled over on his good leg and was able to extract the sword with one good yank. Marius could see fire mixed with anger and pain in the eyes of the bull, and he could not help but admire that look. Marius felt faint and did not have the time or energy to play the crowd nor ask for their approval, he just thrust the sword deeply within the center of the beast's chest touching its heart by accident with the tip of the blade.

The light of life left the bull's eyes and the crowd cheered, "Marius! Marius the Great!" With a slight smile on his face, Marius collapsed into a state of unconsciousness directly on top of the dead bull.

At ringside, the stadium official quickly signaled for the grounds crew including the emergency call for stretcher-bearers for Marius. The surgeon would be waiting immediately below. The crowd was still cheering as the crew did their best to rope, cable, and hoist the bull back into the cage for removal from the arena. As part of the festivities following the show, the dead animals would be roasted, and their meat sold.

Expectedly, the arena finale featured Cacius who would claim his 14th consecutive victory over another prisoner of war. Unfortunately, for Marius, his injury would not allow him the choice of the many prostitutes made available to him by the governor to celebrate his victory that evening. Roman parties could be wild affairs with much in the way of eating, drinking, and carnal activity. Marius's deeper wound would take longer to heal than the inconsequential slash in comparison given to his ankle in his first battle, but he would gain another proud scar and another story to embellish too.

Later that evening, with all the influential and most important leaders of Ephesus gathered at the governor's main dining table, an announcement came that directly affected Marius and Cacius. The governor was quite pleased with the arena that both had helped to fill, and he decided to pit the two against one another. Many believed that Cacius was a hero and deserved his freedom while they respected the newcomer Marius for both his bravery and guts for enlisting freely on his own.

Marius's reputation had already been growing and the forthcoming announcement would cause quite a stir. Even though he would charge four times the usual entrance fee, the governor announced that it would be the grandest match in the history of Ephesus. For Marius, his salary would double if he won. For Cacius, victory would win him his freedom. Both would be allowed to fight one more battle since the governor wished "To give Marius a little more practice after his injury," as he put it.

Cacius was no more than a confined prisoner and knew little of Marius. He saw many men and animals come and go in the arena, mostly go. Rumors both false and true reached his ears from both the guards and fellow inmates. True ones about Marius' bravery, size, and courage along with others not so true such as Marius being a great soldier, weapons-master, a giant of a man, and a superior fighter all found their way to Cacius. Cacius did not really know what to think one way or another but listened to them all, nonetheless.

Marius exhausted his third and final wish in the previous fight. Had he known better, he would have saved it for the latter fight. He won his third round of combat easily against a scrawny cowardly criminal who had lost one hand previously as punishment for stealing. The one-handed man's knowledge of fighting was even more limited than that of Marius and he could not even support a shield if he'd had. The criminal had no way of blocking the rough amateur-like downward swipes of Marius's sword. One of those blows sliced the criminal's head open as its grayish brain-like material oozed outward along with a stream of blood.

The match ended quickly, and Marius was beginning to like what he was doing so much that he felt invincible. It seemed to be getting easier and the cheers of the crowd left him in a constant state of euphoria. His conquests combined with the favorable chants of the crowd filled his dreams at night like a kid on Christmas Eve. Little did he know the governor purposefully provided him with a weak opponent to build up the match against Cacius.

"So live your life so the fear of death can never enter your heart. Trouble no one about their religion; respect others in their views, and demand that they respect yours. Love your life,

perfect your life, beautify all things in your life. Seek to make your life long and of service to your people. Prepare a noble death song for the day when you go over the great divide. Always give a word or sign of salute when meeting or passing a stranger if in a lonely place. Show respect to all people, but grovel to none. When you arise in the morning, give thanks for the light, for your life and strength. Give thanks for your food and for the joy of living. If you see no reason for giving thanks, the fault lies in yourself. Touch not the poisonous firewater that makes wise ones turn to fools and robs them of their visions. When your time comes to die, be not like those whose hearts are filled with fear of death, so that when their time comes they weep and pray for a little more time to live their lives over again in a different way. Sing your death song, and die like a hero going home." - Tecumseh, Shawnee Indian Chief, Early 19th Century

CHAPTER XIX

On the morning of the big match, the crowd gathered early for admission into the stadium. The quadrupled admission charge discouraged very few as the arena would fill with spectators sooner than usual. As had becoming his custom, Marius pulled out his secret weapon in his room while he was alone. He began cleaning rubbing, polishing, and even massaging the smooth metal but nothing happened. If his listening skills and comprehension had been sharper, he might not have gotten into this desperate situation. The last time the Djinni was out of the proverbial bottle, it had asked Marius for his third and **FINAL** wish. Marius rubbed and rubbed until a blister formed, all the while demanding the spirit come forth, but nothing appeared.

"I don't need you anyways!" Marius shouted. With a tremendous heave, he threw it out the window and it landed in some shrubbery within the governor's gardens. He then left for the stadium when summoned, trying to hold back the inevitable fear. The Djinni had made him confident, even when it looked as though that big bull was going to eat him for dinner in his most desperate match of the three so far. The other two matches against the criminals had seemed easier, but now he was completely on his own, no hidden ace up his sleeve or rabbit's foot in his pocket. Unlike Cacius, Marius had knowledge of his opponent and that slight advantage belonged to Marius, but that was all. Cacius was an experienced older fighter, the lion so to speak against the youthful tiger; only the weight difference was negligible.

It was turning out to be a poor day for a fight. Light rain came off and on like a faucet, with some unknown hand turning and twisting it back and forth, sometimes partly on, sometimes off, and sometimes all the way on. It halted temporarily with a beam of sunlight at the beginning, but the dark slow-moving clouds battled it and destroyed it as light rain showers prevailed. It would be a day without any lightning or thunder, at least up in the sky, just mostly sprinkles coming and going with the whim of the wind. The crowd held mixed feelings as the rain served to reduce the heat, but also left them irritatingly wet.

Another five rounds of fighting were scheduled and the fight between Marius and Cacius would be the last or marquee event. The local odds makers set them at five to two against Marius giving Cacius the edge in experience. Marius stood at three wins and no losses, while Cacius was up to fifteen wins and no losses by the time Marius had healed enough to return. Naturally, very few surviving gladiators had any losses since one loss was not only the end of one's career, but life too.

The first fight featured a wild boar, the type of animal that seemed easy to acquire in and around Ephesus, and a house slave. The house slave was a scrawny man barely an inch over five feet, and he had tried to smother his master in his sleep. The master had fought him off, called for help, and then had him whipped. After that, the slave could not be trusted and his master sold him to the governor's men for the arena. The slave wielded a long heavy spear that he had trouble balancing.

With the rain, the sand upon the wooden arena floor had quickly turned into the consistency of dark brown sugar with some muddy sinkable spots here and there. It did not faze the big boar who had been used to wallowing about wetlands. When the cage door withdrew, the animal seemed possessed by a demon as it flew madly about in a rage. Boars had nasty tempers and could approach thirty miles per hour at full speed. This one was no exception on both accounts and made for the man without hesitation.

The slave was woefully unprepared and trembled at the sight of the angry charging beast. His mind told him to move out of the way, but his body did not react in time as the left eight-inch tusk of the boar plunged into his right side. He died without lifting the spear into an attack position. The boar would be retired for the day and as a reward, they stripped the dead slave and threw him in with the boar in its more permanent cage, at least permanent for a few short weeks. The boar would win another fight in two weeks, but the third time was not a charm. In the following month, a large African slave, who was a seasoned hunter and knew how to use the spear, would face the boar. Case closed for the wild hog, but for now, it would live and eat well for a few more weeks until it wound up on the governor's dinner table.

Round two of combat was a very interesting one. As rare as animal-on-animal battles in Ephesus, three women, two who were prisoners of war and the other a criminal, stepped into the ring together. The arena official at ringside announced their crimes against the state and added jovially that they were not fit to be whores. One was quite fat, another was ugly, and the third was both fat and ugly. They were fitted with unusual weapons, gloves with rusty spikes attached to the ends along with elbow pads with similar spikes protruding out the back. That was all. It turned into a long grueling but entertaining match with the smallest, who was not really that small, dying first. The fat ugly woman ended up winning the match after tearing the throat at the jugular of the other fat woman, but she suffered some deep slashes too. The winner would die in two weeks after contacting blood poisoning and tetanus from her lacerations.

The next two fights were nothing out of the ordinary, just individual matches between men. War prisoners, unruly slaves, criminals, undesirables, and on and on: the why or wherefore mattered little once they were in the arena. One man dead, another alive in round three, the same in round four. The rain spouted off and on, but the soaked crowd did not dare leave as they held out impatiently for the big one. The governor took his turn to announce the two big men, making sure the people knew he set up this match.

Marius was once again in his soldier's uniform complete with the same polished gladius that he had used to defeat his last three opponents. He had his shield too. The uniform was in fact another slight advantage since Cacius only wore standard clothing. Physically, there was very little difference between the two. They were both big strong men. Marius had built his muscles laying concrete blocks and stone while Cacius had spent some time digging waterways by hand. Cacius may have been ten years older, but his strength was far from deteriorating.

There were so many bets placed on the fight that the cheers were nearly equal at the announcement of each man; however, Marius felt that they had been a bit louder for Cacius. Cacius felt some concern in return for he was convinced that he was about to fight a bona fide experienced Roman legion. He had also not fought a man as large as himself, at least in the arena. The youthful appearance of Marius hid beneath the fancy crested helmet and since he had not shaved in some time, he had the makings of a beard that gave him an older gruffer look as well. Cacius got to pick his weapons and he chose his favorites: the trident and net, which had not failed him yet. Marius received the same option, but he stayed with sword and shield. Then the fight began.

They slowly circled each other, cautiously at first as one took the measure of the other before lunging or striking out. Cacius took the offensive thrusting his longer 3-pronged spear closer and closer as he circled inward. Feinting left, attacking right, the trident thrusts were vicious and snappy. Marius fell back as he did all he could do to ward off the blows with his shield. Then Cacius slipped in a muddy footprint when he nearly had Marius driven to the back of one of the walls. Marius had a momentary opening and brought his sword down in the general direction of Cacius' head, but he hesitated ever so briefly where an experienced soldier would not have. Cacius rolled out of the way and was up on his feet in an instant. Cacius exhibited surprising quickness for a big man and blocked the second downward follow-up blow of Marius's sword with his lengthy spear.

After those two brief defensive moves, Cacius again regained the offensive; nevertheless, the wet conditions hampered his attack. The mud caked up on his sandals and he was unable to move about as quickly as usual. As the fight wore on, the mud hampered both men, but eventually, Cacius was able to back Marius up against one of the 12-foot walls along the short side of the arena. His net was not working well because it too had grown heavy with wet rain combined with a little dirt. He flung it every so often but with little authority, and Marius, up to this point, had been able to avoid it. On the umpteenth throw, Marius slipped in some mucky footprints and the net caught his ankle. Immediately, Cacius yanked it with all his might and Marius lost his balance and tumbled upon his back.

Cacius had been waiting for that moment. As the net came back in one hand, the trident came forth with the other. There was no hesitation like that earlier by Marius. With deadly aim, the 3-pronged spear was on a direct line for the face of Marius. Marius turned to avert it but was too late as one of the prongs ripped a deep gash across his cheek. A second prong embedded itself between Marius's helmet and face. "Ooohs" and "Ahhhs" sprang from the crowd, not to mention a painful yell by Marius as the helmet ripped completely off when Cacius retracted the trident. The helmet stuck to the spear but no matter, Cacius tore it off losing the prong in the process. It left him with a "bident" or "dident" if there was such a thing, and it gave Marius a brief second or two to rise to a crouching position. Marius smeared the blood from the deep cut across his cheekbone when a nasty kick from the older man landed square upon his exposed chin.

As Marius lay sprawled out on his back, the plant foot of Cacius slid in the mud and he stumbled face forward into the muck. Cacius was not dazed like Marius and was the first to get up. The older man advanced with his weapons as Marius was attempting to rise from the ground. Cacius lashed out with a spear thrust and somehow Marius blocked it with the shield, but he was weak and the blow off his shield nearly put him on his back again. Cacius was tiring too as each step in the cake-like soupy mud took a good deal of effort, and he had been doing more of it than Marius.

Marius was young and still had some reserves as he caught his breath. Doing about the only thing possible, he summoned what energy he had left, rose, and just started swinging wild blows with no particular aim except in the general direction of his oncoming attacker. The newfound exuberance took the older man by surprise when the sword of Marius knocked the net out of his hands leaving him only with the 2-pronged spear. Wild blows continued and now Cacius was doing his best in the thick mud to avoid them. Marius dropped his shield and gripped the gladius with both hands. He was like a man possessed swinging and swinging and swinging.

The skill and experience of Cacius appeared to win out as he landed both prongs deep into the side of Marius when the younger man overbalanced from one of his wild thrusts. As the spear lodged within, the momentum of one of Marius's downward lurches caught the forward thrust of Cacius' spear arm. Both howled loudly in pain. Marius dropped his sword, fell to his knees, and tried to pull out the two-pronged spear. Cacius lost hold of the spear as the sword sliced deeply into his right arm, deep enough to connect and chip the bone. Cacius still had one good arm;

Marius was as good as dead. The prongs in his side were too deep; one punctured his lung. Marius struggled to breathe as the lung completely collapsed, rasping something awful like an asthma attack.

It was a fight to the death, and both had understood this from the very beginning. No approval was necessary one way or the other from the governor or the crowd. Cacius picked up the fallen sword in his good arm and plunged it into the chest of Marius. It was then that Cacius got a good look into the youthful eyes as the light abandoned them.

"You just a boy," he muttered, realizing at that moment just how young his challenger had been. A sense of pity and regret filled the mixed emotions that ran through his head. What had this boy done? He thought. Thieves, murderers, war prisoners, and the usual suspects had all deserved to die in his opinion, but this battle had been with a mere boy, one who should have had a better life. Marius was no soldier, Cacius realized that now; then again, when it came down to it, it was kill or be killed, and he had no option but to kill for his own survival.

Huge cheers of "Cacius! Cacius! Cacius!" filled the air. Cacius shook off any regrets, he was one win closer to freedom, and only the healing of his arm would delay him. Tears were flowing however from several spectators in the crowd, namely the family including the parents of Marius. They had witnessed it all and still his father could not accept what his son had done, "Why Marius, Why?"

"He who is not contented with what he has, would not be contented with what he would like to have." - Socrates

CHAPTER XX

Near the end of the fight, the governor's gardener was outside digging small trenches to alleviate some of the flooding in certain low spots. He was an older, gaunt man who worked at a rather slow but steady pace. His work took him under the window where Marius stayed and noticed the lattice-worked shutters above were still open. He immediately notified one of the house servants concerning the window and they would likely take care of it without the governor knowing. To allow rainwater into any of the rooms above could be a beating offense. The gardener wandered back and stumbled on an object caked with mud, it was the lamp. Just as the crowd was beginning to exit the amphitheater, he picked it up and wiped some of the mud with his tunic. To his surprise, it was as if steam poured forth into an overweight form like that of a murky Mideastern foreigner:

"What is your wish dirt man?"

The stunned gardener worked in the rain and was a bit of a muddy mess. He stared upward into the cold lifeless eyes that were nothing but tiny black slits in a nearly formless gray face, but it was coming more into focus the more he stared. It was not the god of his daily prayers, but he could alter allegiance on a whim.

"You mean that I can have any wish I want?" The gardener replied hesitantly.

"I am ready to obey you as your slave, so what is your first wish?"

As the somewhat bald head with hair forming at its sides and chin stared down upon him impatiently, the gardener's surprised and frightened look gave way to one of greed and even power.

"Well let's just see then if you can do as you boast. I would like a pile of money this high." The man held his hand level with his forehead.

As the evil being vanished, the gardener heard the sounds of approaching voices from the governor's mansion, as Marius had known, was only a few blocks from the coliseum. When the Djinni was completely gone, an outline of a new form appeared in front of the man's eyes. A miniature perfectly symmetrical mountain with its peak just a few inches less than the height of the gardener himself slowly shimmered and faded in and out progressively becoming more real as the seconds passed. Then it happened. At the gardener's feet lay a miniature pyramid-like pile constructed of Roman coins. It was mostly silver with a little copper and gold mixed in, and every emperor's face in Roman history up to that point was upon them. The sun decided to peak out for an instance, and the reflection of its rays off the coins temporarily blinded the stunned man.

The gardener's jaw dropped first and then he covered his eyes to shield them from the blinding vision. When he was able to look again, he stood awe-struck and frozen as if total paralysis swept through his bones. He tentatively reached out with one hand to verify this new reality. Metal tingled in his fingers and fell down the side. He then forced both hands into the heaping mass drawing forth handfuls upon handfuls of precious coins.

"Oh by the great gods, I'm rich! I'm rich!" He tossed handfuls lightly in the air and they tingled and clanged as only metallic objects can against one another. Meanwhile, a block away, people were pouring out of the arena in drives like a cattle run. The gardener's shouts garnered the attention of the approaching crowd, and their gazes could not help but fall on to the true source of the disturbance.

That is when the gardener's troubles began. When he had wished for such a vast amount of money, he did not consider how difficult it might be to move it or hide it away, especially since it lay enticingly in the open. It may have taken a few hours to move the coins with a small cart; at the moment, he had no cart, no box, or no bucket, just a shovel, the lamp, and a lot of money. Then all chaos broke loose. The first few passersby looked at the money and a wild dirty looking man throwing it around, but they ignored the man and went right for the pile. They swarmed upon it like hungry bees in a fresh field of blooming flowers at first dawn.

"No! No! You are not allowed here! Get out! Leave immediately! Get out I said!" The gardener's words were not enough to stop them as the horde intensified. He then tried to stop them by throwing wild punches and kicks, but the numbers increased so rapidly that people trampled the poor gardener. Normally the guards of the small palace would have prevented the first few from entering the palace grounds and perhaps could have averted the entire mob by stopping the initial batch of intruders; however, there were only two left as the vast majority had accompanied the governor to the games. The two had chosen to remain inside out of the rain and did not realize that anything was wrong until there were well over 100 people outside stuffing their pockets, purses, hats, and whatever they could use to haul away as many coins as possible.

Word spread faster than wildfire and in fifteen minutes or so it seemed that half the stadium crowd of spectators filled the grounds about the governor's home. The coins lasted less as several greedy hands sought the stray ones that rolled away. The crowd stepped on and kicked poor gardener repeatedly, but he survived with a concussion and numerous cuts and bruises. He even found a lone silver coin in his palm despite leaving the realm of consciousness for many minutes. Overall, it led into one big disaster as numerous fights broke out. Once the crowd scooped up coins, there seemed to be nothing much left to attract interest; still, the riot had started, and it was impossible to stop without some bloodshed.

The palace guards returned to immediate orders to disperse the crowd. They beat and killed some, but they were too few. Upon getting word, the governor dispatched a message to Captain Conas, leader of an entire legion of soldiers stationed in Ephesus. A force of 200 men in full battle gear, some on horseback, finally ran through the crowd with their blades slashing and ripping until the crowd finally ran for their lives. A few wounded men who resisted would find their way into future arena games.

Except for a few scattered coins in the mud, the neat shimmering pile disappeared like so many scattered dead leaves in a brisk wind. The gardener would recover and find a buried low value copper coin a week later, but the lamp was gone. Out of curiosity, Captain Conas had picked it up himself, as all others appeared to have ignored it in favor of the coins. The gardener would be the only one who knew the mystery behind the money pile, and he would tell no one for fear of his own life. If the governor found out he were responsible, he would have faced execution or been thrown into the arena.

Though a little wet, the lamp was clean, as the gardener had managed to rid it of mud. Conas strapped it on to his mount and returned to manage the mop-up duty. He ordered his soldiers to rid the grounds of the wounded; they executed those whose wounds were untreatable. The governor's own staff of slaves would be busy the rest of the day cleaning up the bloodstains and stray body parts that the legion would leave behind.

Career soldiers like Conas served for twenty-five-year terms, recruited from the general populous of Rome. For such a lengthy period, it was for all practical purposes, a lifetime. It was a rare man indeed who survived, intact, twenty-five years of service. The officers who steadily moved up in rank rarely retired even if they did reach the vaunted twenty-five-year threshold. The military system instituted by Augustus was going strong in the 2nd century. About the only significant change was that of widespread recruiting. It spread outside of Italy into the ever-growing provinces. The life of a soldier was not necessarily a bad one as they received good payment, training, clothing, and food. Those who survived their service received pensions, the higher the rank the better the payoff in terms of land and money.

Soldiers were inherently vital to the security and defense of the empire, but almost as important, the legions brought the advanced Roman culture and way of life to backward peoples living on the outer frontiers. The assimilation of these peoples into Roman ways expanded the empire. By the time Conas reached the rank of captain, it was a particularly fortunate time to be part of the army; then again, it was not necessarily favorable to the empire as a whole. After the banner time of Marcus Aurelius and his incapable son Commodus, a new struggle broke out for control of the imperial office. A general who had been born in Africa named Septimius Severus seized control in the year 193. Although he ruled in prosperity for 18 years, he would set in motion the beginning of its decline.

Under several Severi-related emperors up to the year 235, the army became the focal point of the empire in favor of the general populous. These emperors constantly raised taxes on the people, as huge material rewards went to the army in terms of increased pay, pensions, promotions, and even civilian appointments. Bureaucrats, governors, and other officials were recruited from the army, as Rome gradually became a police state with little in the way of inspiration or advances. Rebellious army units that tried to elevate their own generals into higher and higher positions of authority created little more than chaos. In the next fifty years, nearly twenty emperors ruled, as more and more generals rebelled with the hopes of seizing ultimate power. Massive civil wars broke out as emperor after emperor did little more than burden the state to reward or buy the loyalty of their troops.

Additional taxes and further intrusions into the outer independent city-states were necessary to pay the rewards promised to the soldiers. It was a herculean task to keep 50 million people happy and the new militarized society could only do so by the threat of force. An autocratic severely regimented economy might bring some measure of peace, but only on a temporary basis until the people rose and rebelled against it.

Aside from dissension from within, there were always increasing threats from the outlands. A new dynasty of Persians strengthened and threatened Rome from the East. The numerous German tribes from the northern European theater were not only rising again but banding together. Families abandoned farmland along the frontier as the barbarians upped their raiding. Erosion, mineral depletion, and the lack of technological advances led to a severe crimp in food production. Suddenly, the empire began to experience a decrease in population and the loss of laborers added to the crisis at hand. The double hit of wage control and heavy taxation upon the lower classes reduced their standard of living to little more than servitude, and they were certainly not happy nor content.

When times are tough, the lowest and poorest members of society often find consolation in religion. Support for the ancient Greco-Roman gods intensified, but they didn't seem to listen. The Romans conceded some privileges to the Jews but were still suspicious and repressive of any threat of independence. Fanatics became wanted criminals and Jesus was no exception. During the glory days of Augustus, Jesus was born, and he would disrupt the entire Jewish community. A new form of Christianity would throw the empire into turmoil from a philosophical religious standpoint.

Great prophets and missionary preachers arose and spread their messages throughout the empire and beyond. The suppressed peoples listened very carefully and took solace in the belief that the meek just might inherit the earth after all.

Religious holidays supplanted the existing Roman ones. Easter now marked the beginning of spring along with the belief Jesus was reborn and rose from the dead. Christmas supplanted the winter solstice. The teachings of Christianity reached into the deepest recesses and needs of the common people. A caring and loving god from the New Testament compared much more favorably to the punishing god of the Old Testament. The ultimate sacrifice of his son to redeem man, eternal salvation based on the individual's worth, banishment to hell for sinners, and universal brotherhood were promises from the new church. The church itself became so politically powerful, that it shared the same abuses as the Roman government – increased wealth, influence, promotions from elder to priest to bishop, and disputes over beliefs led to an entire new host of problems from an empire that was reeling.

A second Roman empire developed. Since Rome was still the center of power in the Western World, the bishop of Rome evolved into a rank of great power. By the year 285, the bishop of Rome had a new promotional title, that of pope, which meant, "Father." The decisions of the pope in terms of religious doctrine were accepted as law.

Great spectacles arose to further the appeal of the religion such as splendid balls or pageants, fancy robes for priests, bishops, and the pope himself depending upon rank (not unlike the military), emotional worship, mass praying rituals, and elaborate churches decorated with fantastic paintings, art, and sculpture, all brought the church into a new sense of wonderment and splendor.

Where the government ignored and failed with the lower classes, the church did not. Donations and aid to the sick, diseased, lepers, orphans, criminals, slaves, poor, widows, elderly, and so forth, all added to the growing popularity of the church. In turn, the church gained much of its strength from this vast demographic.

Religion placed a massive internal strain on the failing Roman system and it was too much when combined with the barbarian pressure along the outer borders. The rise of Christianity caused such problems that the Roman government began persecuting them around the year 220, and these persecutions increased. The government outlawed Christianity, rounded up the followers, and crucified them or executed them by other means, such as throwing them into the arena to fight lions or other beasts, or gladiators.

Before the year 300, the Franks and Goths were making serious inroads with one successful invasion after another. Constantine and Diocletian nearly saved the empire as both tried to institute desperately needed reforms. Constantine reunited the eastern and western split and made Constantinople the new capital over Rome. To pacify the unconquerable Christians, Constantine issued the Edict of Milan in 313 that legalized Christianity, and he actually became a Christian on his deathbed in 337. Constantine may have briefly halted the decline, but like a slow-moving avalanche, there was no halting the slide down the proverbial slippery slope.

During the next century, the empire faced invasion from every direction. The German tribes from the north did the most damage from a military standpoint. Around 370 to 380, attacks came from the east from a wild bunch of nomads called the Huns. The Huns were particularly destructive in that they destroyed everything in their path. The Huns would find the lamp stored away in the home of Captain Conas' grandson. None of the Conas family had ever discovered the secrets of the lamp and neither would the Huns, but they took it anyway. Anything with the smallest hint of value or appeared to be some sort of treasure was naturally taken in their raids.

Theodosius, the last emperor of the united Roman Empire ruled it all from 392 to 395, until it split permanently into western (Rome) and eastern (Constantinople) parts. A series of weak rulers ended it all. Alaric, the King of the Visigoths, sacked the once unconquerable City of Rome in 410. Attila, Chief of the Huns, decimated several of the eastern Roman provinces, wiping many settlements off the map by burning them to the ground. The Vandals picked up where the Visigoths left off, and destroyed the once unequaled City of Rome in 455. The official end came somewhere between the years 476 and 493. Four-seventy-six was the year that Odoacer, a formidable German chieftain, overthrew Romulus Augustulus, the last Roman emperor of the western half. Odoacer then became king of Italy.

The lamp went east with the Huns. Somewhere within their armies, it was lost in Asia. A soldier who had been carrying it upon his horse among other loot died in combat. Despite its mortal wounds, the horse managed to run without a rider for two miles before expiring. When the horse fell, the lamp fell into the sands beneath it. Wandering wolves, foxes, vultures, and lastly, insect scavengers all discovered an easy equestrian meal. The bones did not even last long between the mini marauders and the scorching sands. Occasional heavy rains softened the ground beneath the lamp, worms and other boring critters constantly worked the soil below, and the lamp fell much into a tiny sinkhole. There it would lie buried for a long time, but not indefinitely.

PART II: CHINA

"By three methods we may learn wisdom: First, by reflection, which is noblest; second, by imitation, which is easiest; and third, by experience, which is the bitterest." - Confucius

CHAPTER XXI

Next to the Egyptians, the Chinese civilization was the oldest one founded by humans. They were vastly different from the Western world, especially in the way they approached and solved problems. The first of the great dynasties, the Shang, was founded 3,800 years ago during the Bronze Age, and would last 650 years. The Shang set up little foundries for casting, invented the horse-drawn chariot, built walls about their important cities, and most importantly of all, developed writing. A king who had numerous advisors led the government; nevertheless, the vast majority of the population consisted of peasant farmers and artisans. Non-Shang peoples captured became slaves or sacrifices to the Shang's ancestors.

Given the immense size of China geographically, it was difficult for a single ruler to maintain control. This resulted in its many divisions into states. The Chou assumed control from the Shang a little over 3,000 years ago. Chou kings appointed subordinate rulers over certain territories or states, but the continuous loosening of the bonds between king and powerful territorial warlords led to the decline of the Chou; however, the Chou Dynasty lasted 800 years, longer than that of the Shang.

Philosophers of the Chou brought writing to new heights with men like Tao, Mencius, and the greatest of all, Confucius. Confucius was a failed politician who became a great teacher and statesman. He did not promise salvation but rather drew up a code of ethics on how to live in this world to bring peace and harmony in the next one. He stressed that one man best ruled centralized government and that the advisors be intellectuals. The various emperors then and beyond had little trouble with this philosophy especially when Confucius advocated that knowledge could only be obtained by hard work.

The Han Dynasty came next just a century or so before the birth of Jesus. The Han leaders were the first to claim the Mandate of Heaven, the divine right to rule by a single person, namely the emperor. To justify his holding of the mandate, the emperor had to maintain order, establish harmony, repair roads, fend off enemies, and see that justice prevailed. Should he fail, a challenger could overthrow him.

The Mandate system would last until 1911. To maintain order, the outer provinces or states within China had three administrators. One was a civil governor who collected taxes, supervised construction of public works, maintained roads, and performed other civic duties. Second was a military commander who did the policing of the region. Finally was a censor. The state censors reported to the Grand Censor in Beijing on the other two.

Under the Hans, Beijing was the capitol and there were two major centers of power in and around the emperor. An inner court was made up of his wives, close friends, family, trusted advisors, and personnel attendants. An outer court consisted of intellectuals, military bureaucrats, engineers, and other professionals. Potential members underwent a vigorous testing procedure so that only the best and brightest could become part of the bureaucracy.

The Han Dynasty would last up until the early third century, but before the end, they would have to deal more with foreigners than past dynasties. Nomadic invading tribes were a constant problem, which led to the beginning of the construction of the Great Wall. The goal of the wall was to keep foreigners out of China. When the Han were overthrown, a new lasting dynasty would not come until the early seventh century. It was no easy task trying to maintain 36 or so different provinces in a country as large as China.

When the Han were no more, a new religious force swept through the entire country. A man from Indian named Siddhartha Gautama had a unique but elegant solution to combat suffering and pain. His ultimate goal was for one to give up the idea of one's self to obtain perfect peace, a state, which he called Nirvana. Once he obtained it for himself, he sought to spread the method to all who would listen. His influence may well have eclipsed that of Jesus, as Gautama soon became Buddha.

Although the influence of Buddhism had its roots in China as early as the first century, it did not become overly popular until the rise of the Tang Dynasty. The Tang ruled from 617 to 907 and Buddhism not only became the most popular religion in China, it also strongly influenced art. One could find great monuments, sculptures, and paintings depicting a plump Buddha throughout the country. The Djinni, trapped within its lamp, resembled the Buddha somewhat if one could put a mean nasty sly frown in place of the peaceful or humble profile of the Buddha. Like Christianity, Buddhism appealed widely to the peasants for its simplicity.

The basic system of Chinese government did not change all that much with the Tang, or with the Dynasty that followed, the Sung. Confucian ideals remained, but the Tang did manage to build a much bigger palace in the center of Beijing. Walls surrounded the palace and the roads within the city bisected at right angles. The Sung reigned from 960 to 1279. Confucianism became even stronger with them while Buddhism still held its charm to the masses. To become a member of the government, even more stringent standards and testing were required under the Sung.

Invaders from the North had always been the most troublesome to the Chinese, but none was more so than the Mongols. The Mongols were little more than desert nomads, but to the dismay of the Chinese, they were also some of the most skillful and fiercest cavalry fighters ever to invade the homeland. The Mongols could strike quickly and unexpectantly, withdraw just as easily, and then strike once again.

Under one of the most feared leaders in history, Genghis Kahn of the Mongols conquered the northern and western areas of China first, and then finally drove to the southeast. The great Kahn would conquer more territory and rule the largest empire in history, and it was his goal to wipe out all the Chinese; nonetheless, there were just too many. The Mongols would be the only foreign force ever to conquer China and under their rule, they treated the Chinese as inferior. They leveled entire Chinese towns and villages, and it was state law that any Mongol could kill any Chinese at any time without rhyme or reason.

When Genghis died in 1227, he had not quite conquered all of China. His less-than-capable sons took control of his empire, and China would eventually come under the rule of Kublai Kahn, a grandson of Genghis. Under Kubali, 1279 was the year that the Mongols conquered the whole of China. Much of the Chinese way of governing remained intact, but they paid heavier taxes. The most significant change that would alter the history of the world was that Kublai began trade with the West. Silk routes were established, and the Western world prized the superior pottery created by the Chinese. Two important developments under the Mongol or Yuan Dynasty were cotton and paper.

The Mongols strengthened the rulership and even allowed Europeans to hold government positions. Marco Polo was the first. When Kublai passed on in 1294, a series of weak emperors, rebellion, and general chaos within and outside the borders brought the Mongols to ruin. A Buddhist monk named Chang led rebel armies from the south and overthrew the Mongols in 1368.

Ten years before that, a Mongol horse soldier of little consequence was in the process of building a small fire in the very spot where the collapsed horse of the Hun soldier had died upon the lamp. The soldier was in the process of digging a pit in which to start his fire when he partially uncovered the bronze relic. Fascinated, he dug around and about it, and with one good yank, pulled up and out of the sand. He examined it very briefly and flung it aside. In all of five seconds, he determined it was not half as nice as the gold and polished gemstones he had acquired from past raids; furthermore, a soldier had to travel as light as possible, and he had no room for bulky items of low value.

This particular soldier had been a veteran for a number of years and had participated in countless raids. He had enough items including a carved jade statue of Buddha to be choosey in what he kept and what he tossed aside. There were younger inexperienced members of his band and the junk of one man could be worth something to another. One of the younger members was a boy of sixteen years. The actions of the older man had not gone unnoticed by him. The boy strolled over to where the lamp had been thrown, picked it up, and stuffed it into some loose rags around his horse which doubled as containers for his meager worldly belongings. The band left early the following morning heading east.

The lamp and the boy ended up twelve miles north of Beijing but still south of the ever-growing Great Wall. The wall itself lay twenty-five miles north and stretched about 1,500 miles from east to west. It was twenty to thirty feet tall with forty-foot guard towers every few hundred feet. Its thickness varied from fifteen to twenty-five feet. Only about ten percent of China's land is suitable for agriculture and half the land consisted of desert and mountains. The wall served a dual purpose in that it repelled invaders while separating the fertile soil from the desert sands.

When the band raided a Chinese village some two months later, the boy tossed the lamp aside without discovering the secret within. Like the old man, he had treasures that were more valuable. The son of a poor farmer found it and his father traded it for a couple of fish at the market. The merchant trader named Lu Ching held on to it for several years without selling or cleaning it. Eventually he gave it to his daughter as a present since it apparently had little value. Meanwhile, a new dynasty reigned over the Chinese empire after the Mongols' departure.

With much of the country's resources allocated to war appropriations under the Mongols, the roads, canals, buildings, and the Great Wall itself suffered serious neglect over the last few years of Mongol power. The Ming restored them all and even added hundreds of miles to the wall. The very first Ming ruler lowered taxes and gave land to the peasants, who in turn improved it. Not only did agriculture and industry thrive, including the production of porcelain, but also cash crops arose in cotton, silk, hemp, mulberry, and so forth.

The Ming era happened to be the greatest time when Europe sought these high-quality items. The discovery of America happened when the Europeans were trying to find quicker trade routes to China. Columbus failed in his primary objective during all four of his voyages west. The Ming government shared much of the attributes of its Chinese predecessors. They built the Forbidden City within Beijing, and Beijing became the greatest and largest city in the world. The Ming would rule for nearly three hundred years before corruption, cheating, neglect of public works, and infighting from regional warlords collapsed the government.

The merchant's daughter named Lu Lin accepted the lamp humbly and graciously from her father, careful to show just the right amount of emotion. It was vital for Lu Lin not to anger or upset her father in any way and to remain on best possible terms with him. When it came to family matters, Chinese fathers had much power as they were little more than dictators. Fathers made all the important decisions including the choice or final say on future husbands for their daughters. Worse than that, the father could have any member of his family put to death legally if he so desired. Lu Lin's father had never gone that far but he had sold two of his lesser children into slavery. Her father had nearly killed one of them, but he was a shrewd greedy man; if there were a way for him to profit, he would take that route.

Lu Lin felt safe from this because she was the daughter of her father's first wife, the dominant female of the household. Her mother controlled all domestic affairs and would do what was in her power to keep her own children unless they somehow brought great dishonor to the family in some way. Lu Ching's oldest wife had urged the selling of one of those children from a lesser wife into slavery, and she had gotten her way. Though not nearly as powerful as her father, the first and eldest wife held the most influence with the man of the house.

Lu Lin's father belonged to the merchant class of buyers and sellers of goods, and it was not really an honorable class. Had there not been slaves and servants, the merchants may very well have been at the very bottom. Merchants received little respect because they did not produce anything. At the very top of the scale were the wealthy aristocrats like landowners, censors, and advisors to the emperor. Next in line was the scholarly class and obtaining an education was about the only possibility for a commoner to enter government service. Farmers followed by artisans were still higher up the ladder than the merchant class.

Lu Lin's father inherited his own father's business, who in turn had inherited it from his father. No one really knew the origin of the family business only that one of the ancestors had been a fisherman along the Yellow River many generations back. He was so successful that he and his family began trading the excess fish for other necessities like rice, clothing, utensils, tools, and whatever held value. The sons and grandsons that followed eventually gave up the fishing portion of the business altogether, at least the actual work of catching the fish.

They became middlemen for other fishermen, buying their surplus and the trading it at the marketplace in Beijing for higher prices. The Mongols nearly ruined the business by sweeping through many of the markets, taking whatever they desired and striking down or even killing anyone who resisted. Since the Mongols retreated to the deserts in the north, business flourished as the population of Beijing soared.

Lu Lin was more than just being in her father's good graces; she was his favorite. Her father had four wives and fourteen current children, not counting the two sold into slavery. Though many parents try to raise their children fairly and equally, undoubtedly one or two children in a large family are favored over others. Since girls were not educated as much as boys, Lu Lin, with her father's consent, was able to obtain some degree of literacy. She learned from her brother who attended classes with another group of boys under a common tutor. Since there was no Chinese alphabet, she learned hundreds of Mandarin symbols. To be literate meant that one had to be an artist too and this is where Lu Lin excelled. She mastered calligraphy skills with grace and fine lines and this talent pleased her father. It was no small feat considering that she learned most everything second hand from her not-so-gifted brothers. Even moderate literacy required one to be familiar with some 3,500 characters.

Lu Lin's father took full advantage of her skills in his business. Not only did she help with the paperwork, but she also drew up a new sign that hung on the spacious lot owned by the Lu Family in the marketplace. She also sketched tiny characters on little slips of paper that contained fortunes slipped into oddly baked cookies sold at the market. Her father owned two ovens that were more like miniature pottery kilns; nevertheless, he baked various breads and cookies in his. Although not as important as rice, other grains like wheat and barley were common in China. The Lu family founded their business on the fish trade, but as time passed, they expanded into whatever they could find. During the trade, they might end up with goats, chickens, rice, or other animals. Since gold and silver were not as common as in the West, rice was often the basis for the Chinese trade economy.

After her father dismissed her with a nod, Lu Lin carried the lamp into her private quarters. She stared at it partly in contempt for it seemed to her to be a big awkward ugly looking thing. It didn't even open; therefore, it had no use as a container. On top of that, it was very dirty, and it looked as though it had been centuries since its last cleaning. She was right. Since it was a brand-new gift from her father, she would have to keep it at least until enough time passed when she figured that there was little hope of him remembering it. If she had her way, it would not be long at all. Her sights were set on a son of another merchant and much of her energy and thoughts went into maneuvering her father into looking with favor upon her suitor. It was a crucial time in her life to remain on the very best of terms with her father, and now was not the time to do anything rash. Accepting the lamp as one of the greatest things that he had ever given her was just one small way in which to please him.

Her miniature room barely contained enough room for her 5-foot bed, a small storage cabinet, and a tiny crude wooden table. She set the lamp upon the table. She noticed with mild disgust the dirty brown smudges on her fingers from touching it. First, she cleaned her fingers and next the lamp. The sound of compressed air being released burst from within and a grayish form nearly filled half of Lu Lin's sleeping quarters: "Do you have a wish Chinese girl?"

The Djinni spoke with an odd accent, but she understood perfectly. The same wide-eyed shock expression possessed her face as many before her when the god-like presence scowled down upon her. The ceiling was less than 6 feet in height and the cloud-like figure appeared shorter and wider since it was unable to stretch out to its entire 7 feet in height. It seemed to cover the entire wall opposite her bed. She thought and wondered to herself, "What kind of magic in this present had her father given her?" She grew bold and decided to try it out. She bowed her head in acquiescence as she had done to her father and said, "Please allow Lao Shung to be my husband."

The mass that had covered the wall streamed back within the metal present as quickly as it had appeared. The Chinese, not unlike the Greeks, Romans, and other ancient cultures, were a superstitious lot, and none had much of a centralized religion. Many practiced Buddhism, but to different degrees; some took it seriously, others did not. There were many gods, demons, religions, white magic, dark arts, and a host of other beings from the occult.

"I wonder if it worked," Lu Lin said aloud after pondering what had happened for several minutes. She ran a thin hand through her black hair nervously and stretched out on her bed. She was short enough that neither her head nor feet touched the ends. Strangely, the thing reminded her of fortune cookies. The thing inside was probably asking her to choose a fortune that it promised to make true she surmised. She smiled, as it all seemed a bit silly. She finished cleaning the dirt off it while humming slightly as she did so. She rubbed long and hard and when she was nearly finished, the thing came out a second time nearly shouting within the confined space of her tiny room: "Do you have a second wish Chinese girl?"

Lu Lin laughed this time. She was having fun and since she was thinking about the cookies and the new fortunes that she would create. She decided to share the gift of her father with others; that is, if it worked. She had little confidence that it would, but she would try anyhow: "I want all of my fortunes that I write in my next batch of cookies to come true." She giggled like the thirteen-year-old that she was, and the thing closed itself up again.

It was a game to her and the Djinni was just a funny plaything. Her doubts about the lack of seriousness of the thing would arise when her father took a sudden interest in this young man Lao Shung. He invited the lad for tea the next day and her father would uncharacteristically gush over him. Before the little tea party, she was fast at work writing 20 or so fortunes for the next batch of cookies.

One of the biggest problems with the Chinese language was that one Mandarin symbol could stand for more than one word, and not just two or three, but many. The demon inside the lampwould shuffle the possibilities and interpret some of the fortunes quite differently from what Lu Lin intended. Besides this fact, Lu Lin did not necessarily write all good or positive fortunes. The majority of what she wrote was okay, but in this particular batch, she would even them up a bit; after all, it was only in fun....

Then they came true. Unknowingly, Lu Lin had found a way to transform a single wish into twenty. She had no idea the toy her father had given her was capable of what was about to happen. One of Lu Lin's half-sisters prepared the dough for the hollow cookies. Before baking, she folded the little slips of neatly written characters and placed them inside. She then used a little thin strip of dough to seal the opening, and then shoved it back into the oven for a few minutes longer.

Sometimes they gave away the cookies as a bonus to certain traders or suppliers. Three days after she had last rubbed the lamp, the cookies were ready for sale. The lamp remained unused on Lu Lin's table. Thoughts of Lao Shung dominated her mind; he would be dining yet again with her family for a third consecutive night. It would not be long she believed that the two respective families would be hashing out a dowry for the marriage; prior to that however, the fortunes within the cookies were set into motion.

The beginning of the day was a little off, a few clouds in the sky, but nothing wicked or ominous. It was windy however, but that would die down as the sun heightened in the sky. The weather in Beijing was similar to that of modern-day Chicago, only windier. The beginnings of summer and spring were busy times at the market, peak season so to speak. Lots of people ordinarily meant lots of business. The novelty cookies with tiny paper fortunes were not a new idea, but the surprises within Lu Lin's special batch would sell quickly.

One of their key suppliers, a fisherman named Wen, was the first to receive one. Wen was a man who owned three boats. The junks were on the small side and not very seaworthy, but they were flat and made of wood, and most importantly, they floated. Wen was an older man in his forties, but the heavy wrinkles from working in the direct sun along the Yellow River made him seem older yet. Within a few short years, his hair would be white. He nipped the cookie taking extra care in not chewing up the little parchment within. He thought to himself that the cookie did not taste great, but the novelty of the fortune t interested him.

His fortune read: "Today will be pleasant, your life will prosper." The sun shone brightly, the wind hung around just enough to maintain a comfortable breeze, and Wen's fishing lines were unusually vigorous that day, and then fairly consistent for the remaining six years of his life. A bite from a large catfish took a pebble size chunk out of his arm and he would die from infection a month short of his fiftieth birthday. Whether the Djinni had anything to do with that, one can only wonder; nevertheless, his fortune had been a good one, the next one was not.

A woman named Chang Ling purchased the second cookie. She purchased one the previous week and now bought one as a gift for her husband. Ling had shared her last fortune with him, and he had showed some interest, at least in the fortune as he often neglected her. She was a round, short, stubby thing with stout thighs and a burn scar on her face. It did not make her attractive in the least, but her husband seemed to enjoy her more when the lights were out.

After a bowl of rice with some wild onions, she presented him with the cookie. He busted it open with his hands before eating the cookie and the paper read: "Your next dream will come true." Lu Lin had liked this one so much that she had written it twice, and it would show up again. That very night he dreamt of falling off a cliff, but woke up right before his body hit the ground. Barely a week later after climbing a rather small mountain, hardly more than a hill, he slipped and fell, but did not wake up. Against all odds, his head had collided with the only rock protruding outward from the incline for several hundred yards around.

A somewhat lesser merchant known to the Lu family was wandering around the market when he happened upon the Lu booth. He stopped briefly to speak with Lu Lin's mother and commented upon the cookies, "Ah, I see that Lu Lin has been at it again," he said agreeably.

Ever the dealmaker, Lu Lin's mother said, "Would you like to gain your fortune today?"

"Well why not? I could use some good luck." He traded an old hat that he had been wearing but was not particularly fond of for one of the cookies. The stitching within the fabric of the hat was loose, frayed, and even ripped in places, and on top of that, he owned two other hats that were in slightly better condition.

The trade was acceptable to Lu Lin's mother as the cookies were nothing of great value; nevertheless, this batch was unlike any other. The Lu family did not know it at first, but certain members would suspect it later after many strange events.

The cookie and the man who had bargained for it returned to the man's space in the marketplace. Within the comfort of his own lot, he bit into his treat. He retrieved the miniscule parchment that read: "Poor investments will bring financial ruin." He grew a little red in the face and displayed his irritation by crumbling up the paper and tossing it into the dirt. Then he stepped on it for good measure like someone extinguishing a cigarette.

"The damnable stuff is just a bunch of lies," he muttered under his breath, "That despicable Lu family probably gave that one to me on purpose," he added.

"Did you say something?" His wife had said as she slipped out of the tent behind him.

"Nothing important, nothing at all," he muttered.

"Oh," she said and went about her duties. Her husband looked as though his mood was not a favorable one, so she did her best not to bother him further.

A few days later with the crumpled paper mostly forgotten, the lesser merchant purchased a large load of fish at an exceptionally good price from a fisherman who had seemed just a little overeager to rid himself of them. The lesser merchant had spent nearly all that he had and borrowed some too to pay for the shipment. The problem with the fish was that they were a few too many days out of the water and nearly spoiled. The fisherman had put only the freshest and best-looking ones at the top of each sample basket and it took two additional days to transport them all to the market. By that time, the fisherman received his payment, but most of the fish were beyond their usefulness. The lesser merchant had not inspected them carefully before paying and only sold a few until the stench of rotting fish drove his customers away from his stall. He could not survive the loss nor pay his creditors.

Since he had no other skills, combined with the lack of respect merchants received, he could not find another means of living. Luckily for his future offspring, he had only had the one wife and she had not given him any children. His parents were dead, and his family had long since broken up and moved elsewhere. His wife left him over the incident with the fish, and he resorted to begging.

He had kept the little paper fortune and stormed with it back to the Lu family, blaming them for his misfortune. Lu Lin's father eventually reported him to a government operative, who had the lesser merchant picked up and forced into servitude. He would die partly from physical exhaustion from moving rocks for the Great Wall. As he rested, a portion of the wall that he and others had been repairing collapsed upon him. His wife returned to her family, young enough to be the fourth wife of a more prosperous man. Her life was not much better. Aside from being a sex slave to the man and bearing him two children, being the youngest wife meant that she had to serve the other wives as well.

A man named Po pedaled his wares on a hand-drawn cart. He was highly superstitious when it came to fortunes, fortune-tellers, astrology, religion, and the like. Out of everyone, he would likely take the words most seriously. His main occupation was that of a farmer who raised goats on a plot of land a few miles outside of the city. He had two goats tied to the back of his cart and they went where he went ambling along on tethers. They had little choice in the matter. He would trade them at the market for rice and chickens to bring home to his wife. Within the cart, he carried products made from goats, mostly cheese and milk. He would trade a small wedge of his cheese for two of Lu Lin's cookies. With the goats gone and his cart stocked, he would save the cookies to open with his one and only wife once he journeyed home.

Po loved his wife dearly, but she did not care much for him. Like most marriages of the time, theirs came with one small twist. They would not meet until the day of their marriage. Her father had honed into her that being a goat farmer was an honorable profession that could provide well for her. She had been receptive at first, but what she could not stand was the smell. She had grown up working in the waters of the rice paddies away from animals. The odor of goats was nearly intolerable, especially when confined in small pens or shed-like enclosures. What was worse was that Po smelled exactly like them no matter how much he cleaned or washed himself. To sleep with the man was like bedding down with a goat.

Po did have his good points. He was a kind generous man and treated her like a princess during their three years of marriage. He was eleven years her senior and earned enough to support two or three additional wives, but one seemed to be enough for him. They did not have children mainly because she allowed him very few opportunities to try. He accepted her excuses and did not force himself, as was his right under Chinese law. He was too nice a man to treat her badly in any way and was rather thoughtful and considerate of her needs, like bringing her the gift of a cookie with a fortune stuffed within.

Po's wife could be a little domineering, but she was not mean to him constantly. She liked him some but did not love him. He was not a man that she would personally devote her life too, but the decision had been beyond her control. Leaving was not an option since it would bring great shame to her family, and they would likely disown her. She did most of her wifely duties with a moderate but steady flow of gripes that Po would attend to if it was within his power. The one he could not fix or cure was the smell of the goats. She would have absolutely nothing to do with the goats and

Po accepted that; after all, women maintained the household, not the animals. That was his duty.

When he arrived home, she complimented him on his good trades. Despite being a kind and polite man, Po had no trouble bargaining. If the price was not to his liking, he never raised his voice in argument, but bowed politely and went on to someone else until he made the best deal. The amount of competition was the one great advantage of the vast trading grounds in Beijing. Po's wife uncharacteristically exhibited some excitement with the cookie and a simple smile upon her face was all that was necessary to sustain Po's own happiness for days on end.

She opened hers first as he patiently waited, "You will make a change for the better." Po read his next, which stated, "Your dearest wish will come true." Po's fondest wish was that his wife would learn to love him. There was only one way to accomplish this. Within minutes of his unspoken subconscious wish, Po's wife lost her sense of smell. With the horrendous smell of the goats removed from her, she did indeed learn to love her husband more over time. They would still not have children despite the increased frequency of their lovemaking; it was a small price to pay given the dark magic emanating from the entity within the lamp.

A little man named Chu barely a hair above five feet in height was also a goat farmer like Po, but that is where the similarities ended. Chu spent his spare time and money in and around the seedy gambling establishments around Beijing. Chu wagered on most any game of chance, such as Nim, Mah Jongg, Go, and many others. He had much difficulty in trying to find a wife. Most daughters convinced their fathers that Chu was not right for them and that their unhappiness would be interminable. When the fathers learned of Chu's gambling addiction and growing reputation, they would not dare part with their daughters for such a suitor. The Chinese accepted gambling in moderation; addicts received no respect. Chu did have a chance once with a plump girl who was nearly double his own 114 pounds, but he declined.

If one gambled enough, there was bound to be a good day. It was not often that he came out ahead at the tables, but today was one of them. He was in a good mood with a long string of coins as he strode about the marketplace like a rooster proud of his harem. He bought things on a whim that he ordinarily would not have given a second glance. One of his fancy purchases included the sixth cookie. He chose the smallest cookie on the tray of 15 as if something had compelled him to do so. He joked with Lu Lin's mother saying something about a small cookie befitting a small man. Lu Lin's mother laughed along with him and bowed slightly as Chu left with his cookie. Though staged and empty, her laugh was often necessary as a sales tactic.

On his way home, Chu stopped a little way out of the trading grounds to eat his cookie. He had not known that there was a paper inside until he felt that he was chewing something that had the texture of a dried leaf. He pulled most of what was left of the paper out of his mouth. The front one-third was missing or too gooey to decipher, but there were still a few legible characters on the remaining portion. The lady had not told him about the surprise but no matter now. If he went back and complained, they would likely laugh at his ignorance, and he would lose face. Chu could not read very well but he knew one or two of the symbols. One was something about gambling, because that particular character had adorned many a hall where the games took place. Another symbol was something that meant a curse or hex but he wasn't exactly sure. He couldn't make out anymore. In frustration, he just tossed it away and swallowed the rest of the edible part of the cookie.

"No matter," he mumbled and finished his trek home. The fortune that he could not read stated, "Do not allow the evil of gambling to overtake you." But it did. Chu would gamble away his goats, his plot of land, his little fingers, and then his own servitude. When he could not repay his debts, his creditors sold him to the government. He became an army porter on a supply train and would die during a surprise raid by archers two years later.

A good friend of Lu Lin's mother named Li received the seventh cookie as a token of friendship. Like Lu Lin's mother, Li was also the first wife of a merchant trader. Li was thirty-four years of age, married nearly twenty years, and had eight children of her own. There were seventeen other children by her husband's other four wives so that Li had her hands full managing such a large household. Much of her duties centered on children for when she was not pregnant with one, she cared for many.

Li, like that of Lu Lin's mother, had the look of a no-nonsense manager. Both delegated responsibility to the younger wives and older children so that all remained busy with various tasks and obligations. Failure to perform their duties as head wives meant facing the wrath of their respective husbands. Both were strong experienced leaders and to cross them meant trouble. It was common for a wife further down the food chain to replace a weak first wife. Since the booth that Li occupied was only about 120 feet down from that of the Lu family, it was easy to visit back and forth during slow times.

"It is a good day we are having," said Li to Lu Lin's mother.

"Yes, many people have been here already, and it looks like more are coming."

"We have been very busy, how are things here?"

"Very good so far, would you like one of our cookies Li? You know that Lin works very hard at them." Lu Lin's mother offered the dish with 13 remaining.

"Why thank you very much," answered Li. She bowed lightly as was custom and selected the one nearest to her. She thanked Lu Lin's mother again and then left. It would be nearly an hour before she would get an opportunity to consume her gift. The trading grounds were very busy with much of the time spent haggling over prices or deals. As was custom, one started way low and the other too high and a significant amount of time passed before they ended up in the middle somewhere. The customers had no choice, it was bargain or pay too much, and the merchants looked with disdain on those who were poor bargainers. The most people were poor and could ill afford not to barter.

Li bit into the miniature pastry on one end. She then removed the paper from inside and promptly handed it to one of her teenage sons to read it to her. He gladly did so.

"You are gentle and graceful like a butterfly."

"Now that is very sweet. I will have to compliment Lin on her fine choice of words the next time I see her." Soon after, Li started to feel restless and light-headed, very light-headed. She left her son in charge as she had done before when she had gone to speak with Lu Lin's mother. She walked far and wandered completely off the trade grounds. Her light-headedness seemed to infect her entire body, growing like a cancer from within. Soon it felt to her as if she were no longer walking, but rather floating along. Her body became lighter, and lighter, and lighter. She waved her arms, but they felt as light as feathers. She was drifting as if on a current of air and then miraculously she was! Memories faded out, legs disappeared, clothes fell to the ground, and tiny brightly colored yellow wings with dark spots sprouted where her arms had previously connected to her body. She was fluttering and flapping and then swept away by a current of air.

Her thoughts became little more than instinct centering on plants, flowers, and to gain control of her destination. It was so difficult and nearly impossible to fight the strong winds, but easier to go with the wind flow. Their power swept her away for what seemed an eternity. A huge giant bird barely missed making a meal of her as a gust of wind not only controlled her but saved her life too. When the wind eventually calmed some, she was able to gain control of her motions. What thoughts remained centered wholly on eating and breeding. She would need a suitable mate if she were to lay her eggs and die before the coming of winter. Li was now a butterfly and would survive only a few more weeks, but just long enough to set into motion a new batch of offspring.

An old man with his head bowed walked very slowly with the aid of a bamboo walking stick. Bamboo worked well since it was both strong and light in weight, tough enough to support a man but light enough for easy transport. Ping was his name, but it was Master Ping to his students. Ping was a monk who had dedicated his life to a certain oriental philosophy. He was not necessarily a religious priest, but the sect that he belonged to did sport a small Buddhist shrine within their complex. They were simple and humble farmers, but intelligent scholars as well. Only after they had mastered skills and disciplines could students leave. They could leave on their own at any time, but it was dishonorable to do so. Some did, while dismissal came for those who did not meet the teachers' expectations by age twenty.

The skills required included reading, writing, poetry, survival, etiquette, philosophy, self-defense training, gardening, or farming, and a little Buddhism mostly to develop respect of nature and natural things. The primary goal was to lead a fulfilling life fraught with peace, harmony, and respect. Many of the monks or masters specialized in one field or another. Apprentices who successfully completed the training became monks. Monks could either stay on as a teacher or leave at any time much like an honorable discharge.

Ping was bald with a white moustache and a long thin white beard that tapered to a point nearly a foot below from the bottom of his chin. Monks and the students regularly shaved their heads, but Ping no longer had to do so. When one became an official monk, beards and moustaches became optional. Although Ping walked with his bamboo cane, he did not stoop. He walked straight with his head characteristically bowed down as was expected of all monks no matter their age. One of his favorite proverbs that he drilled into his students was that "A wise man walks with his head bowed." A little pride was all right if one did not show or flaunt it. Better to be humble and polite and those traits should reveal themselves in one's walk according to Master Ping.

Ping was walking slowly but confidently around the marketplace in his white sandals and white robe. He approached the Lu family's sizeable lot that was marked off by stones from the adjacent ones. He noticed Lu Lin's mother conducting trade negotiations with another, but out of the corner of his eye, he observed a rather shifty character in the corner. It was a man, but a very young one who had only recently achieved that stature in Ping's reckoning. He was likely only seventeen or eighteen years of age in Ping's estimation, but the boy had his eyes riveted on Lu Lin's mother. He seemed to pretend to look at things in the booth and occasionally looked all around with a nervousness that Ping could not help but notice. Ping kept his head planted to the ground and was not oblivious to the fact that the young man's eyes fell upon him, but Ping did his best to play ignorant. Ping shuffled along slowly, and the young man dismissed him as no threat.

Suddenly, when the young man was sure no one was watching, he hurriedly snatched a clay pot filled with rice and concealed it beneath his ragged garments. He tried to look natural and nonchalant as he walked away, but there was haste and nervousness in his movements. Lu Lin's mother had been temporarily manning the booth alone while one of her sons and a daughter were away. She was in a heated negotiation and did not see the man swipe the pot. As the man walked a little further away, he was just beginning to feel a small sense of relief that he had pulled it off when out of nowhere, the old man in white appeared before him. The younger man nearly ran into him, muttered a quick excuse, and then tried to walk around the elder. Ping anticipated the move and walked directly in front of him.

"A man who takes what is not his is apt to lose a hand or maybe both," Ping stated.

"Get out of my way old man," answered the younger quite rudely. The thief turned to run but Ping threw the bamboo cane, quick as a flash, in front of his legs. The young man was unprepared for such a maneuver and fell headfirst as the clay pot spilled its contents upon the ground. Two pounds out of nearly five contained within the pot now lay exposed.

"Why you dirty old bastard," shouted the thief, "I'll show you some respect." Leaving the rice for the moment, the younger man leapt to his feet and produced a hidden rusty blade from under his rags. He made a rush at Ping. Ping was patiently waiting for such an action. Demonstrating amazing agility for his age, he sidestepped the charge, and as he did so, the hard endpoint of his bamboo cane thrust into the midsection of the robber. The double force of the blow from Ping's strike combined with the forward motion of the younger man broke two of the thief's ribs and knocked the wind out of him too. He doubled over in pain but before he fell, another hard blow from the cane smashed down upon his back, effectively silencing him for the moment. Ping pulled the blade out of his hand as the younger man lay sprawled out upon the ground.

A small crowd of 18 or so people had gathered to witness the proceedings. Ping knelt again to where the rice had spilled. He picked it up carefully with his fingers to minimize any dirt as he placed it back into the clay pot. He returned it to Lu Lin's mother who was still oblivious to what was going on. Ping briefly explained what happened as he presented her with the pot. One of the military policemen on horseback galloped to the scene to check on the commotion. Those around the groaning thief explained to the officer what had happened. The officer thanked them and Ping too, and then took the thief into custody. The thief would lose a hand later that day.

"Thank you," Lu Lin's mother said to Ping as he was about to leave. She bowed lowly.

"It is my pleasure and duty mam," he bowed in return.

"Wait, I would like to give you a small token of appreciation," Lu Lin's mother said as she presented him with the plate of fortune cookies. "Please take one, my daughter writes the fortunes inside," she said proudly.

"Many thanks," answered Ping and bowed again. It would have been rude not to take the offering, so he selected the smallest one that he could observe. Lu Lin's mother bowed again in return as Ping smiled, nodded his head, and then walked away.

Ping did not open his cookie until he was over two miles away from the marketplace. He followed a similar route home, which led partly along a stream. The same stream flowed through the land, which belonged to all monks and teachers at the monastery. Ping stopped to rest at a small rock outcropping in view of the softly flowing water. He noticed a tiny water bug scooting along the surface unaware of the carp stalking it silently from below. The jaws of the carp opened ever so stealthily and in one quick dash, the water bug vanished. Ping smiled at the wonders of nature. The carp did not wander off and Ping remained silent and motionless so that he would not be the cause of it if it did.

When the carp finally sauntered off, Ping removed the dark tanned snack from his pocket and took a tentative bite out of it. The taste was not altogether pleasing but he did manage to pull the strip of paper out from within without damaging it. On a whim, he tossed the remaining uneaten portion of the cookie into the stream. From out of nowhere, the carp reappeared and snatched it as quickly as it had downed the water bug. Ping laughed as it moved off again. He read the paper: "You take a reverent attitude towards life and are most capable in guidance to others." He smiled again, pocketed the paper as a keepsake, and resumed his journey. Out of the many fortunes along with those the Djinni touched, Ping's life would not change nor be affected in the least.

The ninth cookie held the same message as the second one. "Your dreams will come true." Unfortunately, like Chang's husband who had fallen from a small mountain, its interpretation was literal. An elder woman named Tzu had purchased the cookie. She broke it in half first to retrieve the message before eating the cookie itself. Her taut face further wrinkled into a pleasant grin, but it changed somewhat after she tasted the cookie. It was a bit on the salty side, and she noted that she had tasted better, but she ate it just the same. Food was valuable and not to be wasted. Tzu's husband had long since been dead and she lived with one of her sons and his family. Elders were always cared for and given a high degree of respect in Chinese society. Tzu helped as much as she could and expected her grandchildren to help her out in return, as needed, a solemn family duty. In turn, Tzu told them stories and she was a good source of knowledge and wisdom to their inquiring minds based on her vast experiences.

The very night that Tzu had purchased the cookie, she had a hazy dream. She was in the woods searching for something, but it seemed as though something was searching for her as well. That was about all she could remember when she awoke in the morning. Three days later, she'd completely forgotten the dream. Another four days passed with dreamless nights.

She took two of her granddaughters into one of the forests to hunt for mushrooms. Each carried gallon-sized hand-woven containers in which to gather the mushrooms in. It was a good 4-mile trek to the edge of the forest. Tzu knew it well for her own mother had taken her here decades in the past for the same purpose. The granddaughters of Tzu did not, so Tzu would not let them wander off far on their own. They walked nearly two additional miles once they had entered the trees. The pickings were scarce.

"You girls stay in my eyesight while I lie down and rest a moment," Tzu declared. She sat on a fallen log while the energy of the young girls seemed unending. Extremely tired, Tzu was not looking forward to the long walk back. Her eyes were not as good as they once were, and she squinted through the trees to catch blurs of the girls here and there. She called out once or twice to them and they answered immediately. Tzu was pleased and was confident that they would not wander far.

Tzu began thinking back to a time when she was a little girl just like them, only now it had been over 50 years in the past since that time. Life was so uncomplicated, no cares, no worries, no man to please, few responsibilities, strolling through the trees, skipping, hopping, singing along with her sisters and stepsisters, talking to the animals who rarely answered......she dozed away with pleasant visions meandering through her tired mind. The dream she had a week earlier resurfaced only it materialized more clearly now.

She was here in the woods. She had been walking and something was definitely following her now. It was only in her dream that she sensed the presence of another, or so she thought. She woke up into the cold hard stare of emerald green eyes, only they were not the eyes of a person. An old tiger as old as Tzu in tiger years peered at her cautiously. The beast was momentarily confused as it expected her to run or at least attempt a get-away. She did not move. Tzu was frightened and her first reaction was to scream or call out to the children that she could not see, but she bit down hard on her bottom lip instead, enough to draw blood. The tiger smelled it and licked his own lips in anticipation. Tzu gathered up her courage and strangely was no longer afraid to die; her only remaining fear was for the kids. Part of her life flashed before her with older memories more vivid than new; that life had been complete and maybe it was just time.

She stood up and faced her attacker, "Come, let's get it over with." She thrust her face out aggressively and the tiger sprung. She put up no resistance as killer canine teeth punctured completely through her wrinkled neck. She died soundlessly with just the briefest amount of pain. It was like the end of her dream that she would not remember. The tiger had always been a little afraid and hesitant of these tall 2-legged creatures, but it had just learned with Tzu that they were amazingly easy to catch and kill. The tiger would get several more before its long life would end as well. Since Tzu filled the tiger's belly enough for several days, the granddaughters were able to return home safely. Tzu's son would search for her later in the forest without avail.

The day at the market continued to brighten. People crowded around the numerous booths occupied by dealers. The stock and holdings of the Lu family increased as the merchants in general obtained more than what they traded away; it was how they made their basic living. With their excess, they traded for food. The way the day was progressing, the cookies would not last long.

The wife of another supplier arrived, and received a free cookie. Lu Lin's mother did not particularly like this woman named Yu. Yu was one of those somewhat mouthy, highly critical women with a lot of attitude. She was unfriendly and treated most everyone with contempt. Yu was so rude and insensitive that the other merchants much preferred dealing with her husband than her. Yu did not even thank Lu Lin's mother for the cookie, and she only bowed her head ever so slightly as if she was someone in power acknowledging one of her subordinates or subjects. Lu Lin's family sighed with relief when Yu conducted her business quickly and left. Yu ate the cookie as she was walking away but she did extract the fortune: "Your life is but a moment in time." After reading the message, Yu felt faint. She immediately blamed the bad taste of the salty cookie, and since she hadn't gotten far, she decided to return and complain.

"This is the worst tasting piece of pig dung that I've ever eaten, whatever did you put in them?" Yu demanded to know.

"They are made mostly of wheat with some other spices." Answered Lu Lin's mother, "Would you like to try another one?"

Yu started laughing bitterly, "The last one made me sick, and you want me to eat another one? Are you trying to kill me?" She laughed so hard and loudly that tiny spittle bubbles formed in the corners of her mouth. She wiped them with the back of her hand. "If I were you, I'd throw the rest of them out." Before Lu Lin's mother could respond, Yu stormed off partly in anger, but also satisfied that she had voiced her dissatisfaction.

Yu's faint feeling returned , stronger, and more frequent each time like pregnancy contractions. A short few hundred steps away from the marketplace, her chest started to burn. Sharp, stabbing pains followed as if a knife was working its way in and out of her chest. Her left side grew weaker and weaker as a paralyzing numbness set in. She collapsed dead from heart failure. Her moment was up.

The noonday sun had reached its zenith about the time Lu Lin and another stepbrother showed up to help their mother. The sun would then follow its path to further heat up the day and then rise in the new world.

"Lu Lin! I am glad that you are here. We have been busy today and much has happened." She related the story to the two about the robber and the old monk. She turned to her stepson and said, "Watch things here for a while, I have something to speak to Lu Lin about in private." She motioned Lu Lin into the covered tent-structure at the rear of the lot.

"Yes mother, what is it?" Lu Lin was a little agitated when she asked this and wondered if she had done something wrong.

"No need to worry," said her mother who was sensing her daughter's uneasiness. "I think that your father is going to arrange your marriage soon, maybe today, to that young man, Lau Shung."

"Oh thank you mother!" Lu Lin threw up her hands in excitement and hugged her mother. She left the tent humming to herself with sweet thoughts running through her mind, "Maybe wishes do come true," she mumbled aloud. At that moment, she developed a picture of the lamp in her mind and considered, "What if that thing really did have the ability to make wishes come true?" Her sunshiny smile gradually morphed into one of sorrow, "What about the cookies? Are all those fortunes going to work? No, probably not." She shrugged it off, not knowing the exact circumstances behind the elderly Tzu, the disappearance of her mother's friend, the collapse of Yu, and the others. By that time, the rest of the cookies would be gone.

An important man named Yang toured the market on horseback accompanied by four guards. Yang served as a captain of the guard and reported directly to the local military commander. The vendors feared him nearly as much as the censors and tax collectors. One of Yang's guards had removed the thief earlier and he led Yang to the Lu family plot within the market. The four guards dismounted first before Yang stepped down among them. Lu Lin was just finishing up with a customer when the five horsemen arrived. The customer quickly left in the direction opposite the soldiers. Lu Ling muttered a nervous frantic greeting and bowed as low as she could without toppling over. She held her bow while Yang waited impatiently for her to rise.

Yang turned to one of the guards and said, "Is this the woman?"

"No sir, the other was older, probably her mother." By this time, Lu Lin had risen some but kept her eyes and head fixed at Yang's feet.

"Is your mother here?" Yang commanded.

Lu Lin rose further, nodded in the affirmative, and hurriedly ran back to the tent to fetch her mother. Her mother came out as fast as Lu Lin had come in. Lu Lin stayed behind as her mother greeted Yang in much the same fashion that Lu Lin had.

Yang, though impatient, sensed her agitation and said, "Relax, I am only here for two reasons. One is to apologize for the thief. He is in our custody and has been punished accordingly. I am not sure if he will survive since he lost a lot of blood with the loss of his hand." A couple of the guards snickered. As a deterrent, the prosecutors often shared the sentencing and consequences of a crime with the people.

"Thank you, my lord," Lu Lin's mother said with her head deeply bowed.

"The second is that I have heard of your famous fortune cookies, I would like to purchase 5 of them." He motioned to one of the guards who produced a small, carved wooden box with some exquisite detailing. "I have this to offer in exchange." He handed the box to Lu Lin's mother.

Her eyes lit up for carved in the top of the box were two pheasants, a pagoda, and mountains hidden in the clouds in the background. It was beautiful and valuable. "I will find the cookies," she said as she hurriedly stepped over to one of her tables. She uncovered the dish with the cookies and presented them to Yang.

"Is the box acceptable payment for the five?"

"More than enough," Lu Lin's mother said honestly, "Please take them all."

"Five is all that is necessary." Yang selected half of what remained and placed them in a similar box that he had just given away, only this one was larger. He thanked her, mounted up—as did his fellow guards—and left. Lu Lin's mother sighed with relief as they rode away.

Lu Lin rushed out of the tent and said, "Is everything okay mother?"

"Yes Lin, everything is fine, look what the man traded for your cookies." She placed the elaborate carved wooden box into Lu Lin's outstretched hands.

"It is very pretty; he gave us this just for the cookies?"

"Yes, for only five of them."

Lu Lin was a little confused and slightly suspicious as her thoughts wandered back to the last present that her father had given her. "That is wonderful mother," she said with a little enthusiasm; nevertheless, there was a vacant far off look in her eyes.

Later when the sun buried itself in the eastern sky, Yang gave each of his five wives a cookie. Yang received the wives over time, as he was an important man and only twenty-four years of age at that. At 5'8" in height, Yang was quite tall and broad-shouldered too. He carried 180 pounds well. He was a distant cousin to the royal house, and was to resume the duties of regional military commander as soon as the current elder died or retired. Unless one obtained a high degree of education, about the only other way to importance was through relation. To go with his commanding physical presence, Yang was a somewhat polite and reasonable man. He often listened to both sides of an argument before acting, and then acted quickly, efficiently, and brutally if necessary. He still had a little impatience with youth, but he would work that out in the end.

All of Yang's wives had come from the upper classes as well. A common practice with this class of females was the art of foot binding. Foot binding was a painful procedure to restrict the growth of one's feet to enhance a girl's attractiveness. At a very young age, a girl's feet were wrapped extremely tight with bandages about two inches in width. After a few years, the four smaller toes in each foot would bend into the sole. With the sole and heal nearly joined, about the only thing left unbound was the big toe. It was terribly painful to say the least. Besides increasing her attractiveness, it was in theory supposed to prevent her from straying or getting into trouble. Since one could barely walk, and hence, do little else, it was indeed a grave deterrent to mischievous behavior. About all a foot bound woman was good for was sex, and as a healthy twenty-four-year-old virulent male, Yang took full advantage of the situation.

Although there were many servants, the wives of Yang had the special duty of serving him exclusively. They washed him when he bathed, hand fed him if desired, served him tea upon request, massaged his aching muscles, and catered to his manhood upon demand. In turn, personal attendants served the wives as they only spent a miniscule part of their lives in servitude to Yang. After all, there were five of them to wait on a single man.

Yang was sweet to them, and, unlike Lu Lin who had to fake it with her cheap father, the wives showed genuine pleasure when he purchased things for them. They were excited with the cookies and acted much like sisters fighting and bickering with one another, but all in good fun. All were teenagers and did have a bit of maturing to do; nonetheless, it would not be long as two were already pregnant. They all giggled and cracked open their cookies at the same time. They each read their own fortune privately before sharing it with the others.

One of them said to another, "What does yours say?"

"It says that I will be blessed with many children," she smiled again for the first of twelve was already on its way. She would spend the next fifteen years pregnant several times, and many of those pregnancies would be difficult.

"Mine says that life to you is dashing and a bold adventure," volunteered the second wife. Her bold adventures with many different men, including two of the young house servants would get many of them killed. It was not wise to mess with the wives of an important man, even if she initiated such affairs. The second wife placed her potential lovers in precarious positions, and not just physically. On the one hand, she would threaten them with punishment if they did not obey her wishes; on the other, if she became bored or displeased with them, she would let news of their indiscretions slip out. The actions of this wife prompted Yang to seek the services of a Eunuch for the sole purpose of keeping a better eye upon them.

The third wife read hers aloud: "Someone is speaking well of you." It was Yang himself for she was his favorite of the five. She had a quiet demeanor, but was a tigress in bed. Out of all the wives, she would remain forever faithful and loyal to him; consequently, he would speak well of her for years and years.

The three who had shared their fortunes now stared at the remaining two. Both started reading theirs at the same time, stopped, and giggled, each insisting that the other go first. Finally, one of them took charge, held up her hand to the other, and read, "You will be fortunate in everything you put your hands to." Yang could already attest to that, but his fourth wife was skilled in other areas as well. She would become a master at weaving, stitching, embroidery, and practiced calligraphy with a finer hand than ever before. With so much use of her hands, she would develop arthritis early on. By forty, she could do little with her hands.

The fifth wife read hers aloud which simply said: "You are broadminded." By far, she was the most intelligent of the wives, but the snippiest of all. She read much and added the composition of poetry as a hobby soon afterward. She was much smarter than Yang himself and had difficulty at times trying not to make her husband look bad or feel stupid. She became his least favorite as her intelligence threatened him. She liked to argue, far too much. Yang would have to slap her around more than the others, and she learned not to argue directly with him, but to plot behind his back. She would poison him after two decades of regular beatings. Overall, vicissitudes exacerbated by the various fortunes filled Yang's life.

Ching was a hunter. As a boy his father taught him how to set snares, create bows and arrows, set fishing lines, tie flies as bait, dig pits and traps, and everything else to that point to be a successful hunter. Ching mastered them all and was doing the same things with his boys as his father had for him. Skinning, disemboweling, and curing were also part of the trade and Ching was doing just that with a deer slayed by his accurate arrow.

The last two or three winters were relatively mild which allowed the current deer population to explode. One harsh winter could probably cut the various herds in half, but for now, they were abundant and not too difficult to shoot with a bow by a skilled hunter like Ching. Ching routinely snared rabbits, pheasants, and partridges; fished frequently if the hunting was unsuccessful; and disguised his various pit traps with branches, leaves, and even a little food for the larger animals. Food for them was often the entrails from what he skinned. The skins and furs of some animals such as a panda or even a rare tiger were far more valuable than the meat. Certain organs like that of the tiger's gall bladder or even penis could keep them in rice for a month.

On occasion, Ching hauled a load of furs, game meat, fish, and birds on a flat makeshift wooden cart to the markets in Beijing. He did the majority of his hunting in the forests southwest of the great city. The cart he pulled with ropes had wooden wheels permanently attached to wooden axels. The wheels turned forward only but did not adjust for curves. Whenever a right or left turn was necessary,

Ching and/or one of his sons would have to literally pick up the relevant end and lift the entire cart into the direction that they desired. It was difficult hauling any sort of quantity this way and was the principal reason why he did not make the trip very often. Another reason was that he did not like to deal with many different people, but he had struck up a business relationship with the Lu family and he sought them out first.

Ching and his eldest son, who made the journey with him, traded their entire load with Lin Lu's mother. In return, they received a generous supply of rice, a long piece of rope, some herbs for cooking, a folk medicine or two for Ching's wife, and 2 of the remaining 5 fortune cookies. Ching was a good customer and always brought them quality fresh goods, and Lu Lin's mother used the cookies as throw-ins that were not necessarily part of the original bargain. If the customer felt they were getting a bonus, it made them happy; furthermore, Chinese society wasted nothing, and gifts of food were readily accepted and consumed. Ching was satisfied and glad that the deal had been a quick one-time affair. Before he met the Lu family, he could remember spending two full days once trying to get the best possible price.

Ching and his son made five good miles on relatively flat ground in about two hours before resting. They would push, pull, and lift the cart as needed for another two hours and four miles on some hillier rockier terrain before stopping for the night. For now, they rested. A drink of water and the cookies was a major part of their break. Ching had a cookie in the past and knew of the paper inside, but he forgot to tell his son.

"Father, what is this for?"

"It is supposed to be some sort of fortune."

"A fortune?"

"Words of advice," answered Ching.

"Do you know what it says?"

"No, I do not know these characters," Ching said as he tossed his own paper out. His son of 14 years stared at his own briefly and tossed it out as well. Both only knew a few rudimentary symbols in the Mandarin form. The fortune of the 14-year-old boy stated: "You will succeed in your chosen career," and that he did. The eldest son of Ching would have to take in more responsibility after his father's fatal accident. The boy would become a fine hunter, as was the tradition of the Ching family for generations before and after.

Ching's fortune was more of a warning: "Beware of the alligator." Lu Lin liked to use this fortune repeatedly with the only change being that of the animal's name. She could easily substitute bear, tiger, snake, or any number of dangerous beasts. Alligators were more numerous in China in the 15th century, and they would be virtually extinct some 600 years later. Like the crocs in Africa and Australia, the alligators frequented rivers, ponds, and swamps primarily south of Beijing where the weather was warmer and more conducive to reptiles.

It was nine days later, usually a lucky number in China, but not for Ching, when he encountered a gator. It was getting late in the day and the day's hunt had not been going well. When Ching was about to give up for the day, he spied a large takin drinking out of a small stream. A takin was sort of a mountain relative of the musk ox with curved horns that pointed straight up. A certain species of takin inhabited the same bamboo forests of the giant pandas.

Ching circled and approached it soundlessly from downwind, notched an arrow, aimed carefully, and at 52 yards placed an arrow into the chest cavity of the beast. It was a superb shot that nearly dropped the beast where it stood, but the tip of the arrow briefly plugged the heart of the beast and prevented it from bleeding to death, at least temporarily. The takin roared in pain and then staggered for nearly 200 yards before its activity loosened the arrow. With the plug pulled, blood filled its lungs and spouted outward too, and the takin collapsed along the streambed with its rear legs and tail dangling in the edge of the water.

Ching was ecstatic since it was only the second one that he had ever shot in his lifetime. The problem that arose was that the sun was nearly down, and he would be skinning it as the day darkened. The numerous predators and nocturnal scavengers caught the smell of blood. Watching hungry eyes from within the trees were all waiting impatiently and anxiously for an opportunity to spring forth. Ching was working fast to cut it up taking little notice of the growing activity around him.

From within the stream, an unnatural current arose. At an inch or two less than five feet in length, a young alligator caught the scent of the kill. Almost lazily and silently, it glided along as it crept up on the unsuspecting man with the takin. The alligator eased its rounded nose and eye out of the water. It created a few miniscule ripples but less than an average cruising fish. Ching heard something but then it was too late. In one mad dash, the reptile wrapped its jaws on the rear legs of the fallen takin and attempted to haul the entire carcass away. Ching grabbed hold of the front legs of the takin while the alligator pulled from the rear. The alligator was stronger and inched backwards. Ching realized that he was losing the tug-of-war and released the front legs.

Ching ran to the alligator before it could completely submerse itself and the prize takin within the stream. Bravely, Ching kicked the gator in the head, and then a second time. The alligator would not release its prey. On the third kick attempt, the gator anticipated it. In one swoop of its powerful jaws, the reptile released its hold on the takin and grabbed a hold of Ching's foot. In a matter of seconds, it pulled Ching underwater and drowned the man outright before it was able to adjust and completely snap the leg off the takin of the man. Ironically, the gator spit the clothed leg out as if it sensed something was not right or perhaps not edible or at least not part of its normal diet. The gator returned to the takin and pulled it away instead, leaving the man's corpse floating upside down.

Wang was not a happy man. He stood an inch below five feet in height and was unable to capture a bride until he reached the middle age of twenty-seven. He had once been sweet with a girl on a neighboring farm, but her father had given Mi to another. Mi was even an inch shorter than him. Both Wang and Mi were disappointed as they had grown up together and expected to be that way in the future. Mi's father, believing that he was looking out for Mi's best interest, chose a taller man whose family owned considerably more land. The tall man already had two wives but could easily support more. Due partly to his lack of height and relatively poor holdings, Wang had difficulty wooing another; nevertheless, he found one.

Far beyond the usual marriageable age for women, an unattractive woman of twenty-two years entered Wang's life. Her problem was the opposite of Wang's. She was five and a half feet tall, far taller than her typical suitors. She was a little on the portly side and outweighed Wang by sixty pounds. Men avoided women that big, feeling threatened by their size, and Wang was no exception. As was common, it was more of a marriage of convenience to save a little face between the two families. Older, unmarried somewhat odd children were typically an embarrassment and any marriage at all was preferable to none. Wang's wife proved to be overbearing and she used her considerable bulk to her advantage. Wang was afraid to confront her physically as was his right, not knowing if he could win such a battle. To deal with her, his strategy was to spend as little time around her as possible. He passed his time toiling in the fields often wondering if his life would have been better with Mi. There was little doubt in his mind.

Mi's life was little better. Being a third wife was not very pleasant, especially when the two above her station treated her like a common slave. Like a foot-bound member of the ruling class, about the only use her husband had for Mi was for sex, and he complained that she wasn't much good at that. She was tiny and her heart wasn't much into it. She would just lay there, do nothing, and silence her pain until her husband was finished. After a year or so of weekly visits, he ignored her. This gave the first two wives even more power over her, and her never-ending tasks of servitude continued. While she scrubbed pots and clothing, she could not help but think of her own childhood sweetheart, Wang.

As chance would have it, Wang and Mi showed up at the market on the same day; however, their paths did not cross. Both traded with the Lu family less than an hour apart. Wang was there first and with a little extra produce, sprung for the eighteenth and nineteenth cookies as part of his trade deal. Mi was better off and took the twentieth cookie as part of her more extensive dealings. Wang, like the goat farmer Po, was still thoughtful to his wife; unlike Po, he was not devoted to his much at all. On the other side, he still brought her the cookie which she promptly set aside telling Wang that she would eat it later. Wang was not too upset for he had long grown disappointed in most things that she did; instead, he drifted outside to enjoy his treat on his own.

His fortune read, "Your life will make a significant change." About the time Wang read his, his wife decided to eat her cookie as well. Hers said, "Now is the time to try something new." Her something new turned out to be a new husband. The next week while Wang was away, she packed up all her possessions along with a few of Wang's and moved out. The community she called home her entire life never saw her again. Rumor had it that she hooked up with a fat man at the marketplace and they moved south to the Shanghai area.

Mi stared at her fortune barely a few minutes after Wang and his wife had read theirs. She handed it to Lu Lin and asked her to read it for her. Lu Lin was a little afraid since she still had serious doubts about just how potent the messages truly were. She quickly scanned the symbols she had written and sighed with relief. The words were positive and she spoke them aloud: "Good fortune awaits you." Her good fortune turned out to be the death of her husband.

The tall man that was Mi's husband was in the process of fastening a plow to the harness of a horse. While doing this, he happened to be standing between the horse and the iron blades of the plow. A storm was brewing, and a sudden loud burst of thunder erupted across the plains followed by a bolt of lightning. The spooked horse bolted at that very moment. The man's body lodged under the blades, twisting in many directions as the horse ran. His screams as he was being sliced and dragged only propelled the horse onward faster and faster. Another rumble of thunder and the horse ran itself out of breath. No one would find him for several hours until the horse calmed down and returned home with pieces of the broken body lodged within the plow blades. With their respective spouses out of the way, Wang and Mi found each other, remarried, and a slew of tiny children.

When Lu Lin heard of the death of Mi's husband, it was far too many misfortunes associated with the cookies to be chance alone. It was enough reason for her to consider the disposal of the lamp. From within her room, she summoned the being within after some frantic rubbing. It poured forth and once again, despite hindrance within the limited height of her room, managed to hover over her in a look that was both foreboding and intimidating: "What is your third wish Chinese wench?"

Unlike the two previous requests, Lu Lin was afraid now but managed to say, "I wish that you would go far, far away like,

like......Nippon!" About the time the smoky substance rescinded, the lamp vanished. Lu Lin stared where it had been, not believing until that moment, "So you were real after all," she whispered. Lu Lin married Lao Shung several weeks later. She would go on to teach her daughters how to make fortune cookies, but none would ever be quite as potent as that batch of twenty.

PART III: JAPAN

"Given enough time, any man may master the physical. With enough knowledge, any man may become wise. It is the true warrior who can master both....and surpass the result." - Tien T'ai

CHAPTER XXII

The Japanese civilization was derivative of China and had its beginnings in the sixth century. Buddhism followed about fifty years later and became immediately popular. Japan borrowed much from China such as writing & calligraphy, painting, sculpture, religion, and architecture; despite this, the island nation did manage to remain a distinct and separate culture from the giant on the mainland. Japan entered many phases throughout their history with China. At times, they readily adopted Chinese inventions and traded extensively with them; during other periods, they wanted nothing to do with them and deliberately isolated themselves.

The first major period in Japanese history was the Yamato. In the year 552, a powerful chief named Yamato declared himself chief of all chiefs; nevertheless, it was a religious title, more like chief priest than that of a warrior. Much of this new Yamato period would last into the early eighth century, spent mostly in direct isolation from China. The man Yamato did not collect taxes but did live on his own estate in southern Japan where the climate was warmer. He had advisors from the rich aristocrats and became a figurehead emperor, one acknowledged as the chief authoritarian figure, but one with little in the way of real power.

Initially, Japan did not have a centralized government, but this changed by the year 645. For a time, the Japanese opened their doors to China in terms of trade, receiving Buddhist missionaries, new writings, new paintings, more sculpture, and even diplomatic ministers. The Chinese visitors lobbied the Japanese to adopt their system of government and empire management; nonetheless, their efforts failed. The Japanese emperor sent a letter to the Chinese emperor stating that Japan was the land of the rising sun, separate and distinct from the land where the sun went down. Soon after, Japan expelled the Chinese diplomats closed its doors to its neighbor. Since the Japanese emperor had nowhere near the power of the Chinese emperor, it was safer in Japan since there was little fear of being overthrown or assassinated. The Japanese emperor today is a direct descendant of the first emperor Yamato.

A military commander with the title of Shogun would eventually hold the real power in Japan. Japan did not create a major bureaucracy or central army like China. Since they were an island country, they had few invaders. Korea was the nearest country at about a hundred miles away. China posed little threat at the time as they were fully five hundred miles west and deep sea or ocean voyage was not the strong point of travels in the Orient. The Mongols at the height of their power tried twice; once in 1274 with 30,000 men and again in 1281 with 140,000. With the aid of devastating storms, the Japanese defeated both invasion attempts.

As is expected with a military culture, intense fighting was commonplace. The countryside divided into as many as two hundred territories at one time and a local aristocrat called a Daimyo ruled each. A Daimyo had his own army and appointed local officials in every village within their respective territories. Much like the feudal system in Europe, the aristocrats owned all the land. This was contrary to the Chinese way where peasant farmers did own small land plots. Japanese farmers were tenants only and had to work like slaves to survive.

Beginning in 710, Japan built a new central capitol called Nara, based on the Chinese model. It was a wealthy city where the emperor's palace stood in the center. A century later, Japan constructed the new capital city of Kyoto, which was far more glamorous than Nara. Kyoto was rich in money, art, writing, pottery, and virtually everything else. The wealthy lived in Kyoto, as did anyone who was someone outside of the local Daimyos.

About the year 800, the Fujiwara family integrated with the emperors in Kyoto, and the head of the Fujiwara became the military leader of the entire country around 850. The Fujiwara did not use the title of Shogun, but would after their downfall. The Fujiwaras would last through the year 1185. Local officials in all the outer territories collected taxes and sent shares back to Kyoto. Those who supported the local officials received tax breaks and incentives. As the feudal system became widely established, the local tycoons developed their own armies of highly trained men with some of the world's best swords and swordsmanship. The local Daimyos constantly fought battles against one another and two of these tycoon families eventually became powerful enough to bring down the Fujiwara.

A new and distinct military culture arose in 1185 with the fall of the Fujiwara. A warrior Daimyo by the name of Yoritomo became the first true Shogun and a new system of government named the Bakufu System was established and centralized. Under this new system, skilled combat, honor in fighting, even finer sword development, intense loyalty, and ritual suicide for dishonorable behavior were all benchmarks.

A code of ethics known as the Joei Code became mandatory for the warrior class. Much of it was rooted in religion, an offset of Buddhism known as Zen. Zen was an anti-intellectual religion based on self-reliance and intense discipline. Solutions to problems were supposed to appear out of thin air after intense meditating. Mental and physical fitness were part of the teachings and both aristocrats and members of the military made retreats to Zen monasteries. Landscaping and gardening were also part of the Zen way.

The Shogunate divided into three major periods in Japanese history. The first by Yoritomo—the Kamikura—lasted from 1185 to 1330. Japan re-established limited trade with China, but not for long. The military instituted four levels of hierarchy. The Shogun naturally was the head of it all, the supreme military commander, and the single most powerful person in Japan. Next in line were the Daimyo, military governors in control of local regions. Third in line were the Bushi, captains of small groups of warriors or troops known as Samurai. Bushi were experienced warriors usually appointed by the Daimyo. The Samurai were fourth in line and recruited from the best, largest, and strongest young men from the underlying peasant class.

The following period known as the Ashikaga lasted from 1336 to 1600. It was an intense one militarily as constant fighting took place. On most any given day, a petty or tiny little war raged somewhere in the islands, a nation barely the size of modern-day California only sliced into 200 distinct regions. Overlap and conflict were constant.

Though at the bottom of the military scale, Samurai were not without power; in fact, they held tremendous authority over the peasants that relied on them for protection. By law, a Samurai could kill any peasant on sight for any or no reason. During the Ashikaga Period, several larger cities arose, and some intense trading took place with China. As a result, the economy flourished. It was near the end of this period when the lamp resurfaced. It had been Lu Lin's desire for it to be shipped to China's little island neighbor, the Nippon as the locals referred to themselves.

It was just there. Tonara, a log cutter with beefy arms, had paused to rest a moment upon the massive log that he was chopping. He had dozed for barely a few minutes when he awoke to find an interesting object resting against his leg. He said something along the lines of "WTF" and then looked all around cautiously expecting to see some Samurai lurking about spying on him just waiting for him to do something wrong. They could be a touchy bunch. His eyes tracked slowly about in a semicircle through the trees, up and down, side to side. He swung his body around so that his vision could complete the full 360-degree circle. Satisfied that no one was watching, he picked it up and examined the lamp.

It was clean and shining from the rays of the sun that fought through the trees in little bullet-like trails to find it. He turned it about admiring it when he heard voices approaching in the distance. Quickly, he stuffed the lamp under some branches heavily laden with leaves and resumed his hacking. The forms of three men working their way through the forest to where he was chopping appeared as shadowy figures in the distance.

When Tonara recognized that they were indeed Samurai, he carefully laid down his ax, knelt to the ground, and stuck his forehead down upon the forest floor. Failure to do this as a peasant ordinarily meant the loss of one's head. The Samurai commanded the utmost respect no matter how humiliating. The party of three finely dressed with their swords—a short one and a long one—worn properly no less, stopped and conversed less than 15 feet from where Tonara lay. They acted as though he did not exist, like the dirt on the ground or the nearest tree. Finally, as they were about to leave, one of them spoke to him.

"You may resume your work boy. I will need extra wood to heat my bath tonight."

Obediently, Tonara rose and resumed cutting at a pace much faster than normal. The three watched him for a few minutes. Tonara was extremely careful to keep his headway down upon the log. To raise it ever so slightly, let alone meet their eyes, could lead to a beating or even a beheading. If the warriors for even a moment suspected he was acting like an equal, they would cut him without hesitation and remove his head if desired; furthermore, peasants did not speak to Samurai unless they required an answer.

The three wandered off and Tonara continued his vigorous pace for nearly 20 minutes until he was sure that they were not only long gone, but hopefully out of earshot. He wiped the sweat from his face and forehead and sat to catch his breath. His sole duty for chopping logs was to heat the fires of the daily baths of the Samurai as the one had remarked.

Sitting again for a moment, he made the same sweep of the region with his eyes before retrieving the lamp from its hiding place, grateful that his visitors had not discovered it. He brushed away the branches that had adequately concealed it and picked up his gift that had appeared from nowhere. He brushed the dirt away from it with his hand. Some of the dirt stuck to his sweaty hand and smeared all over the lamp; nonetheless, it was enough to release the inhabitant.

The tall cloud-like figure morphed into a fat human-like form far above the unsuspecting boy. Tonara's jaw fell to his chin as far as possible without breaking it, and he immediately dropped to the ground in reverence as if it was the Daimyo himself who appeared. He had his forehead stuffed in the dirt deep enough to make an impression when the god-like substance began speaking to him.

"What is it you wish peasant boy?"

Although his head was firmly rooted in the ground, Tonara's ears remained open. He listened carefully through long practice with the Samurai. Although he was too ignorant to know it, the words were distinguishable despite somewhat of a Chinese influence. Failure to miss a given order was as bad as disobedience to one and a swift decapitation could well be the result.

He had heard every word and paused, a wish? He was confused but grew bold and lifted his head ever so slightly. He then grew bolder yet and pulled himself up on his hands and knees, but not looking up in the face of the creature. Discipline and obedience were not only honed into him since birth, but occasionally beaten into him by the passing Samurai; therefore, he did not hesitate long to do what the thing had asked. Wishing was quite easy for a peasant lad. Tonara, sometimes painfully, knew the advantages of being a warrior well. He was in the one that served the other.

He finally grew bolder yet, partially looked the man-like spirit hovering over him in the eye from below, and uttered, "I wish to be Samurai." He had observed the face of the thing for a couple of seconds until it dissipated into a grayish smoke as the bronze object quickly consumed what was leftThe monolids, thin moustache, and goatee gave it an East Asian appearance. For a boy of fourteen, Tonara was of average height but far more muscular and broader in the shoulders for his size and age than most. Already he had years of experience chopping and gathering wood with nothing more than hand tools and hard work. Recruitment for him was a certainty.He set the lamp aside and would wait and see how the first wish turned out before attempting to summon the creature again from within. For now, he resumed his chopping and spent much of his time thinking as to how he could bring the lamp back to the village unnoticed. He concluded that it would have to be during the night when all were sleeping. Aided by the darkness, he managed to do so by concealing it within an old raggedy robe.

Like nearly all peasants, the dwelling he resided in was a group home. Most of it was made of thin paper with wood pillars as the main supports. There was no furniture. They rested, ate, and slept on the floor. Peasants could easily create one giant room by tearing down the paper walls, but there was little need for the peasants to do so. Each plebe ordinarily had his or her own private room except for the younger children who bunked together.

The Samurai lived in houses with architectural similarities only far more decorative. The same wood support pillars and removable paper walls existed for them; however, their individual rooms and the houses themselves were much bigger. Furthermore, there were extra rooms for tea, dining, and bathing. Where the roofs were flat and leaky in a peasant home, the Samurai would not tolerate such conditions if there were peasants to fix them. The roof of a Samurai's home was one of delicate curves carved out of wood. Tonara's dream that night blossomed into the luxuries he would experience as a member of the warrior class. They would partly come true the next week when he began his preliminary training as Samurai.

A powerful and rich Daimyo might build a large castle made of stone, and towns ordinarily sprung up around them. Castles were outlawed in the seventeenth century because of the difficulty the Shogun had overtaking them. In both the fifteenth and sixteenth centuries, castles were allowed if a Daimyo could afford to build one. Castles stood on the highest point within a Daimyo's territory. Since Japan is an island, there are numerous bluffs and many such high points. The Daimyo who established unquestioned loyalty and respect among his troops, and built a castle, was a direct threat to the Shogun himself.

Tonara's dreams did not take him to the level of Daimyo. He was content in his sleep to be Samurai. It may have been different if the peasants had as much respect as a Chinese peasant, but not so in Japan. Even the Japanese farmer garnered no respect from the warrior class. The soil was thin and poor and only twenty percent of the land on the entire main island was suitable for agriculture. The tillable land rested in the internal river valleys and three-fourths of it grew rice. The rest grew tea, mulberry, and a few other basic staples. Where the land was poor, the waters surrounding the islands were not. Some of the richest fishing areas in the world were found around the islands and ninety-five percent of all protein consumed by the people was seafood.

Tonara spent another week cutting down trees and shaping them into smaller convenient pieces until the Bushi himself paid a visit to Tonara's village on a recruiting mission. The Bushi or Captain named Mitsami accompanied by a contingent of warriors strode about the village as the peasants hastily scattered about the ground around him with their foreheads firmly entrenched into the dirt, grass, or even rocks. Mitsami had only to point to a man or a boy and two guards immediately lifted him off the ground. Mitsami would then approach the peasant, walk around him while sizing him up, feel the muscles in the candidate's arms, and even hit him to judge how he reacted to the blow. If they shuddered, cried out, showed any hint of cowardliness, or for whatever reason Mitsami was not satisfied, Mitsami rejected them. The guards would then throw the failed prospect back to the ground and move on to another.

Mitsami chose only one out of t fifty young men he had surveyed, and this boy appeared somewhat stronger and stoic than all the others. Tonara was not present in the village while the recruiting was taking place. He was off in the woods, but the peasants and Samurai alike faintly heard the sound of his ax. With the peasants face down upon the ground, the village was unusually quiet. One of the three Samurai who visited him the day the lamp mysteriously appeared consulted with his captain and the group, with the addition of their lone recruit, left in search of those faint chopping sounds.

Tonara had been swinging away for fully an hour in the heat. Mitsami ordered a silent stealthy approach by his warriors as if they were practicing an ambush. He also left the new untrained recruit further back for the moment. Mitsami did this to observe the boy working without interruption. Mitsami crept the furthest ahead motioning the others with hand gestures to remain where they were.

The training of true Samurai warriors was endless or more accurately, a lifelong occupation. He watched Tonara for ten minutes observing the sweat glistening off the boy's strong arms. He could see the numerous veins and sinews of the boy's muscles strongly defined in those arms. Here was a boy that looked stronger than nearly all he had recruited over the past several months. Still, the boy required further testing.

With another hand motion, the warriors came forward with less stealth and more noise as they entered the small clearing from all directions. Tonara was startled and literally fell down to the ground in honor of so many important men that gathered around him. Mitsami nodded and two soldiers lifted Tonara. Mitsami approached him and Tonara did his best to keep his head bowed in order not to meet the scrutinizing eyes of the Bushi. Mitsami stopped directly in front of him, snarled, and then pulled back his hand with knuckles out. He struck Tonara in the stomach hard enough to knock the wind out of an average boy but not hard enough to injure him. Tonara grunted but did not cry out, and just for a moment, he met the cruel eyes of the Bushi with a slight look of defiance before he dropped his head again. Mitsami noticed the look, and nodded slightly in satisfaction. He motioned his head to one of the soldiers in acceptance, and his second recruit of the day would well fill his quota.

The training began. Tonara had only thought of the good points of being a Samurai, but had no idea what it took to become one. Hours with the bow and arrow, sword play, constant combat, walking around with a heavy pole across his back with large rocks tied in both ends, running for miles, going without food and water for days to test his endurance, staying up three consecutive days without sleeping, and all the while suffering the abuses and insults hurled his way in an unending fury by his teachers.

The teachers beat him when he did not meet expectations. His first set of swords would be his last. He was to not only constantly wear a short straight model accompanied by a fine long gracefully curved one, but also guard it with his life. Failure to step out of one's home or living quarters without the swords meant death by seppuku, better known in the western world as self-inflicted ritual suicide with the short sword.

He was to give reverence every morning and night to the great Buddha statue lodged within a small temple. The statue was only three feet in height but cast solidly in bronze, surrounded by numerous candles replaced daily. Here they were to sing Buddha's praises, worship the spirits of their ancestors, vow to fight honorably and bravely in battle, and under the Daimyo's specific orders, consider the newcomer's religion as well. Christianity tried to gain a foothold in Japan with the coming of Jesuit missionaries only 6 years after the first Gaijin or European barbarians had arrived. A shipwrecked Portuguese vessel had landed accidentally in Japan in 1543.

The Christian God to the Japanese was strange, but not that different from Buddha. Christianity caught on in some limited capacity for a while and there was a mission erected near the Daimyo's castle and central city a few miles from Tonara's village. Unlike western ways, there was little fear in religion for the Japanese except for a select few that the Jesuits recruited. The goal of the Jesuits was to convert the top classes and work their way down; that is, begin with the Daimyo, the Bushi, and the Samurai.

The natives did not need or even care much for the new religion, and as a result, did not take it seriously. Many of the Daimyos converted only with the hope or even as a bribe in acquiring select trading opportunities with the European barbarians. If the merchant ship did not come in, then the religion was either neglected or discarded entirely. The Society of Jesus consisted of highly trained, disciplined, and well-educated intellectuals who learned Japanese culture and adopted many of their ways as long as it did not interfere with their religion. The Jesuits learned the language, the art of tea, to squat, and the necessity of a tearoom. They even bathed on occasion, which was foreign to European society.

Part of Tonara's training included time with the missionaries. Three such Jesuits lived in the Daimyo's town and the one assigned to Tonara's unit was Father Joseph. They referred to him as Joey or Master Joey because that was easier to pronounce. Overall, they liked the Jesuit priest. He was short for a European but as tall as most Japanese. He was round, overweight, jolly, and had lost most of his hair at a young age except for the sides of his head. He ordinarily wore long dark brown or black robes and always had a crucifix, the clear symbol of his religion, wrapped about his neck. He was intelligent, polite, and greeted all the Samurai with utmost respect, even the pupils in training.

Of course, he did this for potential recruits, but the pupils especially appreciated it. He was an interesting man from another land and was never at a loss for words. Master Joey, to the Japanese, could talk, and talk, and talk endlessly. He was a good man to talk to for the trainees for he thoroughly answered every question. They listened attentively for that is what the Bushi instructed them to do.

The training continued relentlessly, with a visit to Father Joseph nearly every other day for prayers and instruction; nevertheless, for every hour spent at the missionary, recruits dedicated twenty times that amount to combat. Tonara along with nine other recruits made up his class. Two failed after three weeks, then banished to villages foreign to them. It would have been too dishonorable to their families to return as failures. This worried Tonara. He was doing all right as one of the remaining eight, but it was difficult. He had managed to bring the lamp with him in his meager belongings and called it forth one evening when he found himself alone and tired at dusk. To ensure his goal of successfully becoming a good and true Samurai, he used his second wish.

Tonara bowed fully to the ground in reverence to the great god-like being before him and tentatively looked into its face while voicing his request: "I wish to do well in my teachings and to be the best warrior in my class." The smoke cleared as Tonara's second wish was set into motion. From here on out, he excelled a cut above the others; however, this was not necessarily good for one's health. To perish in combat was certainly the most honorable way to die for a Samurai if one demonstrated bravery and did not back down or away from one's enemy.

A battle between Samurai rarely involved armies or large bands, unless an ambitious Daimyo was attempting to overthrow the Shogun. As typical in most encounters, two smaller groups met in conflict, and each side ordinarily chose a champion to do the actual fighting. The champion naturally was the best fighter of the band unless it was a grudge match. The winner of the individual fight claimed victory for the entire band. It was a fight to the death and since Tonara had been demonstrating above average skill with his weapons, he would soon have his opportunity in mortal combat, one on one.

The original group of ten lost another trainee so that it now dwindled down to seven young men. His death came swordplay while practicing with one of his teachers. It happened now and then. The trainee lost his temper and wanted to show the instructor that he was the better of the two. He wasn't. He had tired of the wooden practice sword and challenged his instructor with the real long blade of the Samurai.

The training continued and the remaining seven held out for the required year to become official Samurai. Tonara kept the lamp carefully hidden and yet, did not have a good reason to make another wish. The seven were now ready to accompany the Bushi on his various duties, which covered three separate villages. Tonara was assigned to a village separate from the one he had grown up in, as were the other members respectively.

One of the primary functions of a Samurai was much like that of an overseer over slaves. They made sure that the peasants worked hard, collected taxes from them out of the goods they produced, and generally watched over them closely. It was their job to protect them too though the peasants did not always realize it. Rival Daimyos were constantly battling over territory and villages.

To own a village meant more taxing power. The more goods received, and the more villages controlled, the more powerful the Daimyo. The community Tonara was to protect was not an easy one for it was on the border of another Daimyo's territory, a place of frequent fighting. The ambitious neighboring Daimyo had been sending raiding parties across the border and this was one reason for assigning four of the new seven recruits here.

Before Tonara would fight his very first battle, he would meet the Daimyo first and swear his undying loyalty. The Daimyo Samoto, the son of the former Daimyo, inherited his title but not without proving himself first. Like his father, he constantly traveled throughout his lands to check on his Bushi, evaluate the troops, and hear their vows of loyalty personally. Mitsami gathered his soldiers into neat rows. They were all dressed identically to perfection with their swords hanging at the ideal height, neither too low nor too high. The Daimyo arrived and nodded his head from above his horse ever so slightly as Mitsami bowed low to him. Samoto dropped off his horse in a curt ramrod straight movement and his concierge followed.

Samoto, a seasoned veteran in his forties, had not led what one would call a pampered life. He, like Tonara, had begun as a

Samurai in training. After several successful battles, Samoto's father promoted him to Bushi. After Samoto had further proven himself as a leader, his father made him captain of his personal guard and successor to his title. It certainly did not hurt his career to have a father in such a position of power and the promotions came easily enough. With the death of his father, two Bushi and their men tried to overtake the throne but were defeated when they tried to storm Samoto's castle. Those taken alive committed seppuku as was expected of them.

Mitsami uttered a brief greeting, which Samoto barely acknowledged. The elder Samoto strode up and down the ranks of the Samurai who did not flinch, nor did they look directly into the Daimyo's eyes as the general stared at them with the harshest and cruelest looks he could muster. Samoto stopped in front of Tonara and seemed to spend forever eyeing him up and down like that of Mitsami upon his recruitment. Tonara did not stir, and the only visible movement was a trickle of sweat slowly streaming down his forehead. To his relief, Samoto moved on.

When he was satisfied, he returned and complimented Mitsami on what appeared to be a fine group of soldiers. He then gave them a brief speech on loyalty and discipline and then led several hearty cheers, which the warriors responded enthusiastically. The entire unit pledged their loyalty until life escaped them. When Samoto finished with the group, he took tea with Mitsami inside the Bushi's home, gave him orders, and was on his way off to the next group.

Mitsami was more relieved than his soldiers when the Daimyo finally departed. Mitsami's orders were to raid the neighboring Daimyo's region to acquire more territory. An aggressive Daimyo was the norm and not the exception. It was one reason why Mitsami had been doing more recruiting than usual. Mitsami gathered up seven soldiers including two of the new recruits. One of those was Tonara.

As the sun was about to rise, the band of eight began their journey east on foot to the outermost territory of the rival Daimyo, just across the border from that of Samoto's. They did not sneak or hide their cover for they would have done that at night if so intended; instead, they walked boldly in an open challenge.

The Bushi Yotara for the defending side received advance notification and assembled his own force to meet the challenge. The two captains said little to each other. They bowed in respect at an equal distance, but hard aggressive looks adorned their faces like junkyard dogs, neither revealing anything short of true grit and determination. Yotara chose one of his fighters, a man of only twenty-three but with many years of experience.

To Tonara's surprise, Mitsami chose him, but he managed to keep his face from showing any subtle changes. A slow gradual queasiness worked its way up from his stomach like an inchworm inching up a steep branch. It burned into his lower heart muscle before long. It was part of his teachings to hold firm and he did so on the outside while his innards were gasping like that of a drowning man who was sucking up too much water in lieu of air.

The two opposing forces backed up leaving somewhat of a makeshift arena where the two would fight. Tonara and his opponent bowed to one another and then drew their long swords simultaneously. Then they went to it. The twenty-three-year-old came racing directly at Tonara as if to split his head open from above, but he faked the blow; instead, he brought his sword around his back in an uppercut thrust aimed at Tonara's lower stomach. The only trouble was that the maneuver was a bit slow in developing, but more importantly, Tonara was familiar with the move.

The art of fighting was not much different between neighboring bands or all of Japan for that matter. Tonara, as taught, ducked to the opposite side, and slashed a deep cut into the foot of the bewildered attacker. Blood flowed freely on his attacker's sandal. Tonara's opponent grimaced in pain but did not cry out. He had lost his advantage, but the fight was far from over if he could still wield his sword.

It was now Tonara's turn to go on the offensive with his wounded adversary. He did nothing fancy, just rained hard muscular blows upon the injured man as if he were chopping wood. Tonara circled as he struck, and the injured man could not spin as quickly as Tonara on his bloody injured foot. The man had all he could do to block the strong blows of Tonara's long sword as it wore him down. As the rival Samurai attempted to turn, he let out a yelp as his injured foot failed to obey, and Tonara's sword laid open his arm, then a hip, and finally a lung as the rival Samurai bent and then collapsed on one knee. Without hesitating, Tonara removed his head with a final brutal slash.

Tonara's side cheered in unison as Tonara stepped over to his unit's side with blood dripping drop by drop from his murderous blade. Even the Djinni would be proud or at least temporarily satisfied. The two Bushi met briefly with the loser Yotara issuing a return challenge to avenge their defeat. Mitsami accepted, and they scheduled the match for two days later in Samoto's territory. The second would be more important for if Mitsami's side won again, they would be free to attack and raid the villages of Yotara. If Yotara won, then the two sides would be even once again and business would proceed as usual; or in short, Mitsami would have to lay off for a while any renewed attacks.

Mitsami was impressed enough with Tonara to use him again; after all, Tonara was the strongest of his recruits and it was up to the Bushi to use any of them as he saw fit. In the first place, it was the most honorable way to die in Japanese civilization. The second fight for Tonara would be like that of his first, only the scenery and opponent would change. The next man would be a better fighter than the first as Mitsami had constantly warned him. Yotara's band had much more to lose this time around so they would send for one of their best, at least one who could make the trip in two days' time.

Tonara's opponent was a little bigger and more muscular than the last man, but no bigger than Tonara. He seemed older, perhaps in his early thirties, and would be more experienced. This did not faze Tonara much. Tonara could not help but be a little nervous, but he calmed himself and was not afraid to do battle. He had used his second wish to become an excellent fighter and the being within the lamp did not disappoint him. A wish that involved killing or some other form of evil was one the Djinni most appreciated.

In his second battle, Tonara appeared to be possessed as if the magical being itself were a part of him or within his body somehow. He fought with speed and agility, easily blocking and avoiding the blows of the more experienced warrior. As he avoided them, he looked for openings or places where his attacker was vulnerable, and then carefully noted and then aimed for them when given a chance. Finally, the elder slightly overextended a thrust and Tonara was able to slice his sword hand across the knuckles. He followed up with a nice deep gash down his opponent's thigh, nearly ending the match. Swords clashed repeatedly as the older man displayed courage and fortitude, but as he weakened, he lost his maneuverability.

Tonara sprung on the offensive like a predator sensing weakness in his prey and closed in for the kill. In an act of desperation, his challenger threw away his long blade and yanked out his short one when he was near enough to wrap his arms around Tonara as if they were in a wrestling bout. Tonara saw it coming, back up, spun around, and leveled a vicious kick into his opponent's left rib cage. The long-curved blade of Tonara slashed the back of his challenger that brought him to his knees. A sharp but muffled cry of pain escaped from the older man's mouth as Tonara's sword whistled like a willow branch and sent his head tumbling. The painful grimace locked upon the dead man's face as it rolled in the dust, looking back at those watching.

Two years passed by, and Tonara, at the ripe age of eighteen, had become one of the top fighters in all Samoto's territory. They won village they had constantly raided in one final duel between Tonara and the Bushi Yotara himself. It was a great day for Tonara, and he received another wife as a reward. Samurai, like the Chinese, could have many wives, mistresses, and concubines. The new bride was Tonara's third. Tonara already had a six-month-old son with his first wife, and children of Samurai were automatically Samurai too.

The Jesuits had great difficulty from a moral and religious perspective with the polygamous ways of the Japanese, particularly the Samurai class and above. Father Joey, who had become a good friend of Tonara's, preached long and hard against it, but it did little good. A couple of Samurai held on to one wife and only one, but they were by far rare exceptions. They all listened politely and attentively to the Jesuits but did little to alter their basic lifestyle; still, Tonara did enjoy conversing with Father Joey, and they often drank tea together.

As part of his eighteenth year, Tonara would use his third wish from the lamp he carefully concealed in a hidden wall panel within his personal chamber. While still a teenager, Tonara developed a reputation for being a superb fighter, and as a result, others constantly chose him to fight. This troubled him to the extent of a dilemma. On the one hand, he enjoyed his hero status and popularity with his unbeaten and mostly unmatched record; on the other, he saw little long-term future in his occupation. He realized that on any given day, a lesser fighter might get lucky and beat the better one.

A good fighter could simply have a bad day; furthermore, there were many, many men in the world, not only in Japan if one could believe the tales of Father Joey. Somewhere out there, there was a Samurai who was bigger, stronger, and just better than Tonara. One day, the way things were going, he just might meet up with that man. He also realized there was another undefeated soldier in Japan; nearly all were. Except in rare instances, to suffer a single loss meant not only the end of one's career, but the life that accompanied it.

Instead of picking a fighter impulsively, Mitsami informed Tonara he expected him to fight. Mitsami stopped by that very day when Tonara was contemplating his future to inform him that there would be a match for him tomorrow. Tonara appreciated it, but it did not solve his dilemma.

When Mitsami left, he removed the wall panel that held his treasure. Before he had done so, he had ordered everyone to stay out of his room for he had wished to meditate alone. Tonara grasped the item given to him in the woods. He removed the old, ragged portion of robe that had encased it. The lamp looked the same as the day of its delivery to him. Using the worn robe, he rubbed it gently and as expected, the towering form rose from the spout and began speaking to Tonara for the last time.

"What is your third and final wish boy?"

Tonara bowed in respect and stated plainly, "I wish to lead and order other Samurai as Mitsami does; in other words, I wish to be Bushi."

The Djinni returned and Tonara sat looking at the lamp. He rubbed it again just to make sure he had heard right, nothing happened. Subconsciously, he knew there would be no more wishes. When the being failed to come out, it only supported what he now knew. It still might hold great value for another, perhaps there were three wishes for someone else. Tonara thought that there just might be a way to benefit from it again, and he was right.

The neighboring Daimyo named Muroji was very concerned about his decreasing territory. Tonara's own Daimyo, Samoto, had already claimed two of Muroji's villages, and was working on another. Word of the invincible fighter named Tonara had reached the ears of Muroji as twelve of his men over time, including two Bushi, had lost to this lone man. Muroji's solution to the problem was to find the best fighter in all his lands in an attempt to defeat Tonara. If he had not passed his fortieth birthday by several years, Muroji himself may have challenged the youth. The warrior that Muroji chose was another Bushi, one who had proven himself numerous times in both one on one and group combat. His name was Mokura.

The Bushi Mokura's record was even better than Tonara's. He had won sixteen individual fights over the years and had killed at least equal that number in large-scale battles. At five feet eleven inches, Muroji was quite tall for a Japanese man, a full two inches taller than Tonara. Tonara had filled out some in the last two years and though he was shorter, he weighed about the same. The two were about equal in strength as well. Aside from a height and consequent reach advantage, Mokura also had more experience. At twenty-eight years of age, Mokura had seen much and sported numerous scars to prove it. Tonara was younger and quicker, and had the Djinni on his side as well, a powerful though dark ally.

The Daimyo Samoto was on the offensive and pressing his rival Muroji at every opportunity. Mitsami, Tonara's Bushi, and Yotara, the Bushi for Muroji met formally in the village that had once been under Muroji's protection, it now belonged to Samoto. The big match would take place a few hundred yards from where Tonara had fought his first battle over two years prior. After Mitsami and Yotara dispensed with the formalities, the fight was on.

Tonara and Mokura faced off with a respective bow, and then both backed off drawing their long swords. The finely crafted models immediately clashed numerous times as Mokura chose to go directly on the offensive. That suited Tonara for it was his basic strategy to fight defensively at the start, gage his opponent, and then look for openings to exploit; nevertheless, Mokura did not leave any at first, and on top of that, his reach was quite long, longer than any Tonara had experienced in past bouts. Tonara did all he could do to repel the constant onslaught of sword blows that seemed to fly at him from all directions: overhead power blows that took advantage of gravity, upward thrusts, and roundhouses from the sides. Tonara was sure that Mokura could not keep up this level of intensity for long as sweat poured from the older man's face. The rivulets of sweat poured downward from Tonara's face in steady streams too no less than Mokura's.

For over 15 minutes, the level of intensity and concentration between the two did not waver. As Mokura slowed a little, Tonara, realizing that his defensive style was not getting him anywhere, switched to the offensive. He attacked with ferociousness but left parts of his body vulnerable; however, since Mokura was slowing, he was not quick enough to exploit them. A few near misses drew blood on the arms, legs, and midsections of both fighters, but nothing serious. The sword's that clanged, cut, and slashed were as sharp as piranha teeth and another ten minutes elapsed as both men were wearing down without either gaining a distinct advantage.

The long grueling battle continued and the youth of Tonara seemed to be taking its toll on his opponent as exhaustion was looming more and more for Mokura. Blood, dust, and sweat enveloped their bodies when finally, a glancing blow from Tonara's sword slid off Mokura's, but still cut deeply into Mokura's sword arm. Mokura dropped to one knee and could no longer grip his sword tightly. Tonara drove in for the kill and brought his long sword down upon the exposed throat of Mokura; simultaneously, Mokura was able to jerk out his short sword with his left hand and ram it into the upper thigh of Tonara.

Darkness covered Mokura's eyes as his head was nearly severed at the neck. Blood spurted like a fountain and closed off any sounds that Mokura may have uttered. Tonara let out a howl as Mokura died with his hand still on the dagger that had penetrated so deeply that it punched completely through Tonara's leg. The tip of Mokura's blade emerged on the other side.

Tonara removed the hand and yanked on the short sword. He managed to extract it while he gritted his teeth as blood gushed forth from opposite ends of the wound, lighter where the tip had been, but heavy at the entry point. He staggered for a moment, then collapsed. As his fellow shoulders rushed to his side, Tonara managed to pull himself up on his good leg, and then raise his sword in a victory salute before falling again. As the neighboring warriors picked up the body of the dead Mokura, Tonara slipped into the realms of unconsciousness as the loss of blood and cracked bone was too much to bear.

His fellow soldiers bound his leg as best they could and carried him to his home in the very village that he had fought for originally and had helped to win for Samoto. His comrades sent for a Samurai known for healing from another village. It would take time since an entire day's journey on foot and Mitsami sent his fastest messenger, a young slim man who had trained with Tonara.

A full day and a half passed before the healer arrived with a collection of herbs and other various folk remedies, but it was too late for his potions. Tonara was not dead, but blood poisoning had gained a solid foothold and long eerie looking greenish-red streaks were faintly visible up the side of his wounded leg. Another two days and they would show up in his good leg too. The healer had witnessed them before, but still applied a concoction of herbs and water and made a new dressing for the injury. He informed Mitsami that it didn't look good. In the Western world, they would amputate the leg, in Japan, the man would die.

Tonara's saddened wives waited on him hand and foot. They hand fed him rice and raised cups of water and medicinal tea to his lips while making him as comfortable as possible. Tonara weakened as the hours passed, and as a last resort, he called for Father Joey.

"Good morning Tonara," said the priest in a somber tone as he bowed politely. Tonara nodded his own head slightly in return. Father Joey held out his cross in both hands, a curious talisman that denoted suffering as Tonara understood it. It did seem appropriate. Father Joey closed his eyes and started chanting prayers that were leading up to last rites.

Then Tonara spoke faintly, "Joey, Joey," he whispered lightly, but the priest had closed his eyes and did not hear him. In a louder crackling voice, he repeated the priest's name once, "Joey...."

Father Joey looked down for he was kneeling against Tonara's pillows provided to him by his wives upon the floor, "What is it my son?"

With his arm, Tonara gestured toward the wall, "The third panel from the end," was all that he said in barely above a whisper.

Father Joey caught the meaning as his eyes followed the direction of Tonara's outstretched finger. He stood up and walked over to where Tonara was pointing.

"The third....panel......down."

Father Joey squatted and looked back at Tonara.

"Down," Tonara said as he motioned with his hand.

With a couple of look backs and gestures, Father Joey finally discovered what the young man was attempting to convey. The priest discovered both a small irregularity in the panel itself and a hidden handhold underneath. With a good tug, Father Joey pulled the panel from the wall. Inside the hidden cavity was an old robe wrapped about something else. Father Joey pulled it out and brought it to the bedside of Tonara. Tonara tugged at the robe feebly as the priest removed it for him. Father Joey was curious now; with the robe completely removed, he stared at it, but was not impressed. It was a decent work of bronze, but he had seen better in Europe. The intricately engraved silver chalice the head priest used daily was by far a superior piece of craftsmanship.

"Please, use....it.... for....me," Tonara uttered in a whisper.

"What do you mean?"

"Wish....to heal....my leg."

Father Joey stared at him with a confused look and then it struck him that somehow this bronze thing was some sort of religious object, maybe Tonara prayed with it or something.

"Please," said Tonara, "Rub.... wish." With a near-dying effort, Tonara grasped the robe, rubbed it on the lamp, and then thrust the silk cloth into the priest's hands.

Father Joey did as he was directed; after all, Tonara was on his deathbed and Father Joey was not about to argue theology or much of anything else with a dying man. He stroked the lamp softly with the silk cloth when a strange sensation penetrated his hands. The lamp seemed to heat up as if it had been toasting over or at least near a fire. As the heat subsided a little, something even more amazing appeared in front of Father Joey's eyes. The heat seemed to pour directly out of the vessel, unlike steam.

"My God in Heaven!" Father Joey burst forth for he was never one to be at a loss for words. The Djinni formed from the steamy cloud. It almost reminded him of Buddha, perhaps in size, but certainly not in demeanor: where Buddha was always looking restful, meditative, and peaceful, this being looked somewhat angry and impatient.

"What is it you wish priest?" The glaring somewhat angry looking face glared down at Father Joey.

Father Joey looked up with his mouth agape. Something tugging at his dark brown robe broke his look of amazement and confusion. It was Tonara.

"Please....Wish....Heal," Tonara was weakening now and his time would not be long.

Father Joey was a learned intelligent man for his time; all the Jesuits were, and he considered carefully before acting as a prudent man does. Maybe this was some sort of trick device or just a simple invention of the Japanese he surmised.

"Please," Tonara whispered.

Tonara was looking quite pale, and Father Joey had seen that look before. At that moment, he decided to do what Tonara asked. He stared up at the irritating-looking figure and said, "I wish for Tonara's leg to heal."

The cloud-like substance whooshed back from whence it came as the warm feeling from the outer surface of the lamp returned, but only for an instant. Tonara fell asleep but was not dead. Father Joey thought that he might have passed for good until he placed his head upon Tonara's chest and heard the telltale sign of a heartbeat. He then sat down on the floor cross-legged like the natives to try to sort things out. Above all he wanted to study and test the object again, did it really work? Was this an object from God? His Jesuit God? He did not think that Tonara would mind if he borrowed it for a while. In the meantime, Tonara was still dying. The injured leg miraculously healed; nevertheless, infection had spread to other parts of his body and the priest had not addressed anything further.

Tonara slept and slept while the Jesuit finished his last rites just in case. When Father Joey finished a long verse in Latin, he left with the lamp after he had covered it within the old, ragged robe. When he reached his own small quarters of the cramped missionary, he checked to see if any of the other priests were present. He was relieved to find it empty.

The mission consisted of five tiny structures built together; a chapel, a room for each priest, and the last addition consisted of a tearoom to meet with the important Japanese, namely the Samurai class and above. Father Joey took the lamp to his own private quarters and examined it like a research scientist. He was looking for a way to get inside of it, but the top would not budge in the slightest. To him, it looked like an ordinary piece of bronze. There were no jewels, gems, or hint of gold within it, not even silver, just copper and tin, maybe a little iron, common stuff or lesser metals.

He looked over the robe; there was something significant about it too. The priest unfolded it, turned it inside out, and went over every square inch of it, but found nothing unusual. As an experiment, he took one of his own robes and rubbed the rounded lower portion of the lamp. The first thing he felt was the lamp warming to his touch. He rubbed it harder and the entity from within sprung forward from the spout as it had earlier.

"Do you have a second wish priest?" the Djinni said snidely as it glowered.

This did not alarm Father Joey, for he had expected it. That at least eliminated Tonara's old robe as being anything special. "Who are you and why are you here?" Questioned the Jesuit, he wanted some answers.

The Djinni paused and said, "I am ready to obey you as your slave, so what is your second wish?"

"Not so fast, you did not answer my questions, who are you and why are you here?"

No response. The inhuman blank eyes stared down at him with no feeling or emotion. Had he made the request a wish, the Djinni may have answered he was much like a dark angel Allah created from smoke and fire, and how it was dangerous for mortals to interact with the Djinn. He may have told of the banishment of his race from earth for the troubles they caused; how they could bend reality and time, and how they were bound to certain metals, especially anything with copper, and, once they were indeed bound, how they must be a slave to the object's owner.

Frustrated with the lack of response, Father Joey tried the wish approach again. "I wish my friend Tonara will heal properly." The smoke vanished, the lamp cooled, leaving Father Joey in a state of confusion. A trick of some sort, he thought to himself, or maybe it was an elaborate toy crafted by a fancy metalworker. The Japanese did create the finest swords in the world with their metals, so they would have no difficulty creating this object.

Father Joey thought, "What about the smoke inside?" This was by far the most baffling to the priest. Coming out was easy, but how did it get the smoke to return? He had listened to the words more clearly too, wishes? No, he thought, that is not possible; then again, Jesus had performed miracles, but centuries had passed since. How could this thing obey one as a slave? There were still many slaves in the world and the peasants of Japan were little more than serfs, but was this thing a slave too?

Father Joey had no easy answers to his questions. He had inadvertently healed Tonara more thoroughly this time but did not take the time to check on his friend. The only thing he could think of was to wish for something more outrageous, then sit back, and see if this thing could deliver. Unknowingly, Father Joey was on the verge of dispelling the Djinni from the planet. It took three unselfish wishes to do so, and Father Joey's first two wishes qualified. Without another thought, Father Joey wiped the side of the lamp again.

About the time Father Joey had first witnessed the appearance of the Djinni, a Portuguese trading ship entered the port where Daimyo Samoto did business—a black ship that further enhanced the barbarian stature of the foreigners to both the Chinese and Japanese. The Portuguese had little in the way of desirable goods in bulk quantities to offer the Japanese; instead, they served as middlemen between the Chinese and Japanese.

In the 16th century, China loaded the ships with silk in return for Japanese silver. The Portuguese used the profits from this trade to buy spices. When they returned to Europe, they sold the spices for even more. The Jesuits were very important players in the trade. They spoke the difficult language of the Japanese, served as interpreters, and even took part in the negotiating process. This would require all three of the priests; however, before Father Joey's messenger arrived, he was able to test the Djinni with his third and final request. With a quick rub, the Djinni glared down at the priest in sort of a passive aggressive way after demanding the priest's last wish.

"I wish for a monastery twice as large as this one," Father Joey chuckled as the Djinni left his sight. "Let's see if you can do that one," he added a little sarcastically since he was convinced that the thing was merely a toy or perhaps even a trick. Father Joey's messenger arrived and before anything could be proven or disproven, the priest had to leave immediately to meet the Daimyo in the castle. When the Daimyo called, it was best not to delay. He left the lamp in the open on sitting mats directly upon the floor; after all, the Jesuits were under the protection of the Samurai, and anyone caught stealing would lose his head rather than just a hand or two. The penalty for theft and other serious offenses in Japan was instant execution.

The lamp was stolen, but not by the Japanese. Captain Garth of "The Seafarer" allowed all his men in small separate groups to set foot on land for a day while negotiating the sale of the silk they had loaded up from the eastern Chinese ports. He permitted them to visit only certain areas, and one of those was the missionary. From more of courtesy aspect than law, the tiny private quarters of the priests were generally off limits; nevertheless, the Jesuits did not have locks on their doors. Buck Heidel would be one with little in the way of morals to observe such limits. A group of visiting sailors first viewed the new monastery for which Father Joey had wished. Since this particular group had not seen the old missionary, there appeared to be nothing out of the ordinary to them. The size had doubled but the new half was virtually identical to the old.

There were only six sailors for that was all that Captain Garth allowed out on shore leave at any one time. The Samurai could be touchy and the last thing he needed was an altercation. The largest and meanest, or in short, the one the other sailors would not mess with was none other than Buck Heidel. Buck was a bit of a loner and kept to himself, but beyond his intense dark and furious eyes, rested an intelligence most underestimated.

A detachment of Samurai accompanied the sailors to guard and police them. Captain Garth ran a tight ship, and all landing parties had strict orders to not only respect, but to obey the wishes of the Japanese soldiers. The Samurai were only to discipline the barbarians in extreme circumstances. The Samurai regarded them nearly in the same light as peasants but could suffer the wrath of Samoto if they were to take off one of the filthy bearded heads. To compensate, they did indeed watch the sailors carefully, but let them roam around the mission freely.

Given that it was new, half of the mission was empty while there was nothing going on in the occupied half. Five of the sailors banded together while Buck walked around on his own. There were no locks on any of the doors and without a second thought, Buck rummaged through the private quarters of each priest. When he opened Father Joey's door, he could not help but see the lamp perched prominently on the floor as if it were beckoning him. It fascinated him as he drew closer. When he picked it up in his huge hands, it seemed to grow warm to his touch. There was something more to it and he decided to take it with him.

It wasn't going to be easy smuggling it back to the ship, but they had brought bedrolls to sleep on. First thing in the morning, they were to row back in the cutter so a new group could have their day's leave. The lamp was somewhat large and bulky wrapped within his blanket, but he was able to conceal most of it under his sizeable arm. The others did not seem to notice, and if they did, Buck was counting on them to mind their own business and say nothing about it. If one of them so much as glanced too long in his direction, he might break his neck. That was one reason why he had moved southward and signed up on one of the long voyage sailing ships.

Far north in the lands of Scandinavia, Buck had been minding his own business when a drunken man rudely staggered into him. Buck shoved him away none too gently. The man took great offense, picked himself up, and charged Buck with both fists flying. That was a mistake. Buck caught one fist and knocked the man down again with one solid punch to the jaw, nearly breaking it, and Buck had not even fully wound up. The man picked himself up a second time and rushed with head down like a bull directly into the midsection of Buck to drive the bigger man to the floor. Buck didn't go down; rather, he seized the man's head and twisted it so hard, that the man's head snapped like a rotted twig. Buck decided not to hang around for any judgments or trials; after all, he had a reputation of turning rather ugly, especially after several pints of grog.

At 6'3" in height, Buck wasn't the tallest man in the world, but he was big. Had he lived a few centuries earlier, he would have been an easy match for Cacius or Marius. He sported a broad barrel-shaped chest, huge shoulders, stout trunks for legs, and a neck that no man would ever be able to put his hands completely around, except for maybe his own sizable mitts. Had there been movies in his time, Buck could have played the Viking God Thor, the giant slayer. Reddish-brown hair emphasized his Scandinavian blood, and he had a beard to match. He could out drink any man he had ever met and about the only thing he lacked that Thor had was Mjollnir, the great hammer.

Buck stood in the doorway of Father Joey's room and looked cautiously about for the others. They were not there, but he heard their loud voices a few rooms down. He left quickly with the lamp and set it down near the entrance to the missionary, just long enough to retrieve his blanket, a makeshift bedroll left outside with the others. He hid the lamp within the blanket and strode out nonchalantly. The Samurai guards paid little attention and lost sight of him as he made for the dinghy. The priests themselves would spend an entire week housed at Samoto's castle and Father Joey would not miss the lamp for six days. By the time the priests made it back to the mission on foot, Buck would successfully smuggle it aboard and the ship sailed away.

In the meantime, Tonara slept for three days then awoke fully recovered. The Samurai healer would be dumbfounded at such a miraculous recovery. Tonara awoke weak with hunger and thirst, and so his wives fed him repeatedly. A scar was the only sign left of the wound. Tonara was grateful to Father Joey and except for Lu Lin who had turned one wish into twenty, Tonara received the full benefit of five wishes. Tonara still thought of the lamp as his but forgave Father Joey for losing it. Tonara ordered searches of all nearby villages, but the lamp remained missing. When he and

Father Joey put their minds to it, they were sure it had gone with a sailor on The Seafarer. Whatever the case, it was long gone and there was no chance of getting it back.

Tonara led a long successful career as a Bushi. Although he had the authority to order others to fight the individual combat, he on occasion chose himself. His wish of being a good fighter never expired and furthermore, the killing associated with it was right in line with the Djinni's evil nature.

Father Joey could only believe that a miracle or two of some sorts had taken place. The first was the recovery of Tonara; maybe he had healed on his own, maybe not. Father Joey would never know for sure. But what of the monastery? He confessed the events to the other two priests, and they were quite skeptical and had difficulty believing any of it; yet the physical proof of the enlarged mission was hard to refute. It inspired them in their work; nevertheless, new and more serious problems arose with the Jesuits.

The Japanese remained distrustful of the foreigners, along with the other missionaries that had arrived. Franciscans worked with the poor, Protestant Dutch followed along, and English Catholics set up shop as well. The differing religions clashed, but the Japanese would have none of it.

In 1578, they ordered all Europeans out. Strict enforcement didn't come until 1614, so Father Joey had a successful career and passed on before the Japanese his home to the ground. The foreigners left, their religions outlawed, and the few but true Japanese converts were either tortured severely or put to death. The Djinni would have approved.

PART IV: PIRATES!

" It's better to swim in the sea below than to swing in the air and feed the crow, says jolly Ned Teach of Bristol." - Benjamin Franklin

CHAPTER XXIII

The fifteenth and sixteenth centuries were a great time for explorers, sailing ships, and other historical achievements in the Western world. In the mid-1400's, Prince Henry the Navigator explored Africa's long coastlines. The Hundred Years War between France and England finally ended in 1453. John Gutenberg invented printing and moveable type as he ran off his first Bible in 1455. Christopher Columbus made his four disappointing voyages to the New World from 1492 to 1504. Leonardo da Vinci painted the Mona Lisa during the Renaissance in 1503. Michelangelo followed with the painting of the Sistine Chapel in 1509.

The changes continued and multiplied as Europe awoke from the Dark Ages, a time of unreason. The protestant movement began when Martin Luther posted his "95 Thesis" on a church door in Wittenberg, Germany. They summarized the current abuses of the church and sparked the Reformation. Knox, Zwingli, Calvin, and countless others spread much needed reforms throughout Europe.

In 1519, Ferdinand Magellan set out to circumnavigate the globe, but Filipino natives killed him in 1521; however, his ships did indeed make it around the globe. In 1524, Verrazano of France explored the northeastern coast of America and New York Bay. In 1532, Pizarro sailed to Panama and marched through Peru conquering the Inca Civilization. The Spanish would begin their domination of South America while France and England would battle it out a little later further to the north.

The sailing ships of the Western world proliferated like a successful group of breeding rabbits as the 16th century ended.

Monstrous Spanish and Italian fleets ruled the seas until the English bettered them and established their own unequaled navy. Francis Drake obtained the title of "Sir" in England by sailing around the world in 1580. With the defeat of the Spanish Armada in 1588, England claimed the title of King of the Sea. Europe emerged from medieval times as music, art, science, astronomy, literature, navigation, and about every serious realm of study flourished unlike any time since the days of Ancient Greece and Rome.

It took several months to return to Portugal. The Seafarer had to make two required stops to replenish food and freshwater supplies. Overall, there had been little trouble on the way back. They ran through a few minor storms, but the truly violent ones were somewhat rare. Buck Heidel was an able seaman and it seemed to him that no matter what ship he sailed upon, the task of hoisting or lowering the main topsail was his. Naturally, there was an additional long list of regular duties, but it took a strong man to pull the ropes to lift the heaviest of sails. None was heavier than those connected to the main mast with ropes and pulleys. Buck had little trouble even if the canvas was soaking wet against a strong wind. The officers rarely if ever had to scold him for his work. Most feared to do so.

Buck shared his berth on the vessel with five other sailors and the room itself was only about nine feet by eleven feet. Buck had one of the corners and each man had a small storage area under his respective bed. All the typical seaman owned for possessions was maybe an extra pair of clothes in addition to those on his back. Buck kept the lamp carefully wrapped within his spare outfit. He only removed it when he needed a change of clothes and he, like the others, could go two weeks or even more without changing. Other than that, the lamp remained under his bunk the entire journey home from Japan. No one would dare mess with his stuff.

The pay for the average able seaman was meager and most served on a ship because they had little else to do. It was adventurous, they were fed most of the time, and many stowed away on ships to escape trouble....out of sight, out of mind. Buck collected his pay and took a temporary room above a tavern. He would stay there a few weeks doing little but eating and drinking, or perhaps a lot when it came to drinking, at least until his money ran out. When he could afford no more, it was time to sign on with another boat. The room above the tavern was small yet big relatively compared to his bunk on the ship. It may have only been half the size, but he shared it with no one.

He felt alone and safe enough to unwrap the lamp without worry, and that he did. First, he wondered if it had any trade value for something else. If it did, he might be able to eat and drink a few extra days before sailing off again. He decided that he would have to clean it some to wash the dirt and grime from the saltwater spray that seemed to work its corrosive ways into everything, but that could wait for later. Now, all that was on his mind was food, drink, and maybe a woman, about the only things that mattered in life to him.

For three days, he did little else except for one brief fight. A man so drunk dared to challenge him and Buck simply punched him in the nose hard enough to break it. The man collapsed in a heap with blackened eyes and blood gushing forth. He then dragged the fallen man out of the tavern and threw him into the dirt, hardly anyone noticed. It was the beginning of his fourth day ashore when Buck would discover the secret of his stolen possession.

One of the tavern girls for hire spent the night with him. She was dirty, a little heavy and sweaty, and probably had more venereal diseases than a dog had fleas, but such was the norm at the time. Buck woke up in time to observe her rummaging through his things. She nearly found the thing when a huge hand gripped her shoulder followed by a hard shove that sent her sprawling across the room into the wall near the door. She was about to protest violently when she directly observed the look of what could only be described as a madman within Buck's fearsome eyes. She was out the door in a flash. He forgot about her the minute she left.

The lamp had originally lit the home of a Boston lawyer and its clone would be forged many years later, except for one small detail. It would not have as potent an energy substance from within, just whale oil. Buck removed it from his spare shirt and decided that it was probably best just to pawn it off or swap it while he still had it. It was rather large and bulky for a seaman. As he turned it over, he noticed the salt spray from the sea had dried into grayish-white smudges here and there.

Before attempting a cleaning, he was observant enough to notice the lid. With the strength in his arms that was twice or maybe even three times as great as some men, he tried to pry it off. It did not budge nor loosen in the least. He shook it, but nothing rattled inside. He gave up trying to open it in favor of cleaning it. He dipped a portion of the blanket from his bed into the basin of water provided for him in his room, and gently began wiping the surface. He felt that same warm tingling feeling in his hands as when he had first picked it up at Father Joey's mission.

He stopped a moment and then resumed his cleaning. When he was nearly finished, the temperature increased until the unexpected happened. He let go of the lamp and it crashed to the floor sideways, but the gaseous matter still poured forth. Since the lamp was not standing upright, the Djinni stood a few inches shorter than normal, but upright nonetheless, and still taller than Buck. Buck's first reaction was to swing his giant fist, but the closed hand penetrated nothing but air as it rode through the Djinni's formless figure. Buck stopped, stared, and listened as the creature spoke.

"What is your first wish sailor?" It was a little uncanny if not somewhat disturbing the way the Djinni sized up its new master, and then spoke in an understandable though odd, accented language that Buck did not know. Not unlike Tonara, a sailor's training centered around listening and following orders. Buck heard clearly what the chubby, somewhat formless, statue in front of him dictated.

It delivered the question in a loud, clear, commanding voice, but Buck showed no fear. He was used to others fearing him, and he could often sense it in their body language. The somewhat transparent being before him gave off no such vibe. Buck reached out his hand a second time and it once again carried on through to the rear side of the spirit-like Djinni. He pulled it back and decided to do as requested.

"Hmm," Buck grunted, "I would like a wooden chest filled with gold coins." Silence filled his small room as the lamp consumed the last of the figure. A slim minute later, a wooden chest three feet long, two feet high, and a foot wide appeared at his feet from nowhere. The chest had bright brass hinges and clasps, but no lock.

Buck bent downward and carefully lifted the hinged cover. A dusty light poured forth from the room's one tiny window, but still managed to cause quite a glitter from within the box. The bright intense beam of light refracted into Buck's eyes temporarily blinding him. He moved his head to one side to escape the light. When his vision returned, his eyes spied a fortune in gold coins. He slowly sat down and sifted through the chest forcing his beefy hands to the very bottom. The consistency in the chest from top to bottom was unchanged as he brought up two massive handfuls of coins that rested beneath those on top. They were all the same. A face that was hard, weather-beaten, scarred, and prematurely lined, broke out into a rare smile. A rare moment indeed.

Buck may not have had a formal education, but he was far from ignorant. He knew the life of the sea as well as an old, experienced captain. He had learned the use of the sextant, the compass, and the position of the stars above. He knew the positioning of the great sails, fitting out a vessel, loading a cannon, rationing food and water, and pretty much everything else that was technologically available to a man of the sea in his time.

What to do with all this gold? That was the first question to pop into his thick head. There was enough money to buy his own ship, something he never imagined in his most far-reaching dreams. He had always lived for the present, and the present only. He forgot the past as soon as it was over. The future ordinarily surfaced when his pockets emptied, and it was time to sign up on another vessel.

With this newfound fortune, he could be his own captain, be the one to give out orders, and run the ship just the way he wanted to run it. He formulated a plan to have the ship of his dreams built to his own specifications. It would take time, many months if not more depending on whether he could find available skilled craftsmen in the art of shipbuilding.

He sat thinking as never before, and then a new idea surfaced in his mind. Why not just wish for it? The magical fat man gave him a chest of gold, why not a ship? A second smile appeared in his facial features burned brown by the sun. He plotted further. He figured that he could not just wish for a ship in his room above the tavern. He would have to find a secluded spot along the ocean, but not too far from town. It would require a sailable harbor or at the very least a cove with a deep bottom.

He knew some good tough sailors too, but he would have to recruit many more. He could do it; of that, he was sure. About the only risky thing now would be to leave the chest of gold behind.

It was heavy and normally would have taken two men to lift, but Buck heaved, groaned, and managed to move it to a corner of the room. He threw his clothes and blanket on top, and the first order of business was to find a padlock to secure it. He dropped a few coins in his pocket and wallowed down the street to the blacksmith shop. A single gold coin netted him a heavy iron lock with a wrought black key. He hurried back and was relieved to see that no one had entered his room.

For the first time in his life, Buck Heidel had clear ideas and goals. He stayed away from the booze when he could have purchased hundreds if not thousands of bottles of rum. He sat down again as a million thoughts raced through his head. He locked the chest, unlocked it, locked it, and repeated the maneuver several times. Finally, he inserted the long iron key a seventh time, opened the chest, scooped out a solid handful of gold coins, and shoved them into a tattered pocket. He redid the lock, covered the chest as before, and left the room.

He walked down the muddy streets again, only this time he sought out the stables that were just beyond the smithy. He needed a horse to cover more ground, specifically to search out a choice spot for the initial location of his ship. An old man with a makeshift cane accepted four of the gold coins for use of a horse and agreed to refund two of them with the safe return of the horse. The old man selected a large older light gray Belgian draft horse that would be able to support the weight of the big man before him. The old man thought about acquiring another gold piece for rent of the saddle but thought better of it. The big man had a very dangerous look about him and two gold pieces already presented a handsome profit margin. Buck mounted the big horse and rode off.

The town he had been staying in bordered the Atlantic, so it was not far at all to the water's edge. He knew that there were many more sea towns and outposts south, so he chose north to scout the shoreline. After 2 hours of a stiff steady walk by his old rented but reliable horse, Buck saw little but huge boulders, rocky outcroppings, sand bars, shallow water, and everything possible except maybe a sharp reef to prevent a ship from navigating the region. It was no wonder as to why there were no ports or people this way. A little further, he discovered a possibility. Surrounded by what appeared to be two large rocks was a nice deep inlet, large enough with adequate room to spare for a single ship. It would never make a port or harbor with such little space, but it just might suit his needs.

He dismounted, looped the halter around a large rock, removed his clothing, and waded a little way out into the inlet. Unlike most sailors, Buck was a good strong swimmer. It was ironic that so many men that lived on and around the sea could not swim at this time. The water deepened quickly which was another good sign, and, at less than 200 feet out, the water flowed over his head. He swam out another 200 feet satisfied that there were no jutting rocks, sand bars, or any other type of visible barrier like a shallow reef to break up a sizeable ship. He returned with the contented feeling that this was his place. He rode the horse harder on the return trip and in barely over an hour, he was tying it up in front of the tavern. All he needed to do was get the lamp.

He ran up the stairs 3 at a time. When he entered his room, it did not appear disturbed by the lamp and the treasure chest resting where he had left them. He removed the lamp from his tattered spare shirt and was about to leave when a new thought entered his mind. He knew roughly what kind of ship he desired, but wondered if he would be able to wish for it correctly. He sat down a moment thinking of both the complicated and intricate details of a large sailing vessel. His mind was sharp, but his language skills were not.

What he needed was paper and perhaps he could do a rough sketch of his dream ship. Paper should not be too hard to obtain; after all, the captains he had known kept all sorts of charts and maps; nevertheless, this raised another problem. He would need a set of charts to travel the known seas. He could read sea charts, but where did one go about getting them? He considered carefully and figured that he could take care of both problems at once. He would just steal someone's charts, which hopefully would provide him with some paper in which to sketch a ship.

He rewrapped the lamp, returned the horse, and then visited a nearby merchant for two key items. With a little additional gold, he purchased an iron bar and a sparkling dagger that had caught his eye. The blade was forged in silver and had a tiny red ruby inlaid within the handle. He hid both items beneath his clothing on the way out.

What light remained of the day; Buck strode along the docks observing the various ships in port. He did find one to his liking. It had been completely unloaded and only two guards remained to watch over her; both would be taking forced naps later that night. The iron bar proved to be quite useful; not only did it knock a couple of heads into dreamland, but it was also excellent for prying the door open to the captain's berth. Buck used it again to force the locked cabinet open where the charts were stored. He grabbed them, stuffed them into a convenient sachet case that he also found in the room, and made for his own room above the tavern. He felt a wave of relief after his mission was complete and drank away the night in celebration.

By the time Buck re-entered the land of the living, the noonday sun moved beyond its zenith point. Refocusing on the task, he had a little trouble concentrating given that he sported a throbbing hangover and realized he did not own a writing instrument. He cursed, wondering if the ship he had robbed might have had a pen and inkwell, he couldn't remember with his aching head.

After getting his bill up to date and another week's rent paid in advance, he expended an additional gold coin to secure an inkwell and pen from the tavern keeper. He had formed the ship countless times in his mind over the last two days and made his first attempt to duplicate it on paper. His first try was rather messy. The second was little better but did show some slight improvement. He had little experience writing, just his occasional mark on contract papers as he had sailed out. He always made a swishy "W" like representation since he had no clue how to sign his real name. The third try was better, but still not good enough. He did have high personal standards and he wouldn't feel right with it until the sixth drawing. After spending seven hours working it over, number six was the one he wanted. It was still a little messy and uneven; however, he would have to rely on the spirit creature to fill in some of the details.

HE SET THE PAPER ASIDE. He sat rubbing his head, as there was so much to consider. Aside from the ship itself, he would have to recruit crewmembers soon. There were supplies to purchase in advance, specifically, a good deal of food and drink. He never had to concern himself with these vital details before and was soon learning that management was a whole other ballgame. Should he buy the stores now and carry them to the ship, or create the ship first and drive it into port? He thought more about that one and decided to go with the former.

It might raise many questions with the local lord if a strange flagless ship commanded by a general seaman were to dock alongside the numerous merchant and government ships. It was best to have as much prepared in advance as possible he surmised, and that included recruitment. He would wish for the ship on his own and hopefully stock it the following day, and then be off. In the meantime, an entire week would pass before he summoned the Djinni.

Buck truly had no close friends but there were always some hard men like himself that were more or less acquaintances, shipmates, or perhaps a drinking buddy even if for only a single bender. His empty growling stomach reminded him that it needed filling. He packed his charts and drawings away and headed downstairs for some much-needed food and drink. The first man he ran into that he knew somewhat was Jake O'Donnell, a tough Irishman whose past was not unlike his own, run away & sail away. Jake could drink and fight with the best of them, but more importantly, he was competent working most tasks on a ship.

"You lookin' for work?" Buck sat down next to him and got right to the point.

Jake scratched his unshaven bristly chin and said, "Aye."

"Got a boat, I need men, know anyone else?"

"Why shore laddy, I kin thank of four or five right off."

"I want good tough men, experienced ya know, I don't care what they done."

Jake rubbed the stubble at the bottom of his chin again, "Well, maybe two o' three den."

"Okay, meet me here tomorrow, 'bout the same time." Buck left and went on to visit nearly every tavern in town. He sought out those he knew and reluctantly placed his trust in a select few like Jake to network for him. He would deal with problems as they arose, harshly if necessary. He had to be careful in some of his selections; after all, there were jobs on a ship that not everyone could do. He needed a cook, maybe a butcher too, a carpenter, a sail maker, and so forth. Within a week's time, he would assemble a ragtag crew of miscreants and misfits.

The crew was only half the battle. To feed an additional 19 men aside from himself for weeks and maybe months at a time, he would require generous supplies. Buck repeatedly sunk his hands into his chest of gold and purchased cask after cask of potatoes, onions, Dutch cheeses, sugar, salt, bread, butter, vinegar, tea, salted pork, and salted beef. He even purchased some salted cabbages, but he was not that familiar with them, and they would not last long before spoiling. They didn't taste very good either.

On a typical sailing ship, food was only half the nourishment required. Beer, wine, and rum stored in forty-gallon barrels would be more important to the men than food, and even water itself. He sought out the old man at the stables and was able to rent wagons. He soon found out that if he was going to be the manager, or more specifically, the captain, it was getting time to delegate responsibility. Jake and his recruits were assigned to load up for transport as Buck had an extremely important task to perform. It was time to create the ship.

He followed a similar path as his previous scouting expedition only this time he brought the lamp and the sketch of his dream ship along. With his tattered shirt, he cleaned the lamp and the being from within did not disappoint him. It spewed forth to its full height unencumbered in the open and spoke in a deep but clear voice, "What is your second wish barbarian?"

Buck ignored the insult and spoke as he had rehearsed, "I wish for a ship like in my drawing like a galleon with two sails on the foremast, two sails on the main mast, and one on each mizzenmast. It should be 120 feet long with a very strong hull made of oak to carry much weight, and all the lines and lanyards and rooms like that of a Spanish galleon." He paused a moment to recount the number of cannons he had on his drawing as the Djinni was about to slip away. "Wait!" Buck commanded, "There should be ten cannons on each side complete with a stack of balls and powder barrels for each one. I also want one cannon up top near the stern castle." The Djinni with a look of discontent and impatience held forth and listened as Buck continued.

"There should be nine main cabins in the stern castle with the captain's quarters the biggest. There should be a table with...with...with six chairs, a lamp overhead, a telescope, compass, sextant, a place for charts, a bed, and some chests for weapons." He thought a few more seconds while holding his hand up to the Djinni in a halting motion, "I want as many as 25 muskets with balls and gunpowder in the chests and the same number of cutlasses too. I'll need 15 berths in the hold for the sailors and a small prison area with iron chains, bars, and padlock. Also, I would like...," but that was it. The Djinni's designated time at approximately three minutes out of the lamp was up, and it slithered back within. To this point, it was the lengthiest wish ever made and Buck was the first to use up all the allotted time. The Djinni would consider the ship as one wish as everything else was just details connected to it.

Buck had wanted to add a couple of cutters or dinghies to move about from ship to shore and back again in shallow water, but it was too late. He scanned his drawing to see if he had placed a rowboat or two, but he knew without looking that he had overlooked that detail. No bother, the most important items were there, and he would just have to purchase the smaller boats elsewhere.

A shadow fell over his paper and when he lifted his eyes, it was there, right in the place he had swum out to a week earlier. He had little in the way of doubts that the thing would deliver, especially after producing the chest of gold. With his mouth wide open, he stared at the ship with awe for several seconds. He couldn't wait. He tore his clothing off and was soon swimming faster than he ever had before. In a few short minutes, he was climbing the long heavy rope that held the heavy giant black anchor. Another minute he was over the side standing on the deck of the ship, no, it was his ship!

It was all there: even the two rowboats he had forgotten in the drawing. The Djinni apparently knew what a decked-out galleon was and provided. Buck strolled down the nearest ladder way to the lower deck, strutting about like a male peacock with a full muster of females. He stroked the first of the 20 cannons all gleaming in two straight rows of ten, back-to-back on each side of the ship, all black, polished iron, new, and next to them sat neat stacks of balls and powder barrels.

Another ladder way led further down into the hold of the vessel. Half of it contained spacious private rooms with wooden bunks along with the iron cage he specifically requested. The key was in the lock, and he removed it and then placed it in his pocket. The other part of the hold was empty but spacious and he estimated that it would hold at least double the initial supplies as he had ordered; then again, he might need the space for plunder as he smiled with crooked teeth.

He returned topside, and then climbed the mainmast up into the giant crow's nest to get a look around. The aerial view was awe-inspiring. The shore was empty save for rocks, sand, and the golden gleam from the bronze lamp sitting in the open on the shoreline. The sun struck it just right to provide him with a brilliant flash. He scrambled down thinking that he had better not stay on the ship too long and leave the lamp unattended. He doubted that anyone would stray along this way, but he was here, and who knew what reason somewhat else might have. He was still reeling with excitement and needed to inspect the stern castle and his own room.

The stern at the front of the ship was by far the most elaborate. The berths below had been better than anything he had sailed on, but those above were as fancy as any galleon that had ever sailed, and the Spanish did not cheap out here. The eight rooms below the captain's quarters were trimmed neatly in polished maple, including the beds. The beds sported soft sheepskin and wool bedding. Each room outfitted with a wooden desk, chair, and storage closet.

The eight rooms were virtually identical until Buck reached the top compartment, the one reserved for the captain, him! His room was a little more than three times the size of the others. A bright glossy oak table with six matching chairs was bolted directly to the floor. There was a good deal of maple in the other furnishings and paneling; nevertheless, unlike the others, his room was trimmed out in brass – door handles, knobs, a lantern fixture above the table, an oversized compass, hardware on the various chests present in the room, and even a brass telescope.

Muskets and miniature iron balls for bullets filled two such chests. Filled with ample gunpowder, little kegs, the same shape as those that sat next to the cannons only smaller, rested alongside the chests. Another smaller chest, identical to the one he had left back at his tavern room, sat in the bottom of a storage closet. The closets, the door to his room, and the chests all had locks with keys stuffed in them. He pocketed all the keys as he discovered them. Another big heavy chest contained forged iron cutlasses with skin-shearing blades and golden handles. He smiled for he knew the men would appreciate such a shiny new weapon; most sported some old rusty dull knife like his own.

Buck left his room with his heart in his throat, beating like someone amped out on uppers. He had never been quite so excited in his life. He tested many of the ropes and they were so smooth, free, and easy, that he realized they suffered no damage from use, nor fraying and discoloration from the relentless salt spray of the ocean. He had never served on a ship so new. It was strange to see new ropes, sails, shiny pulleys, and fittings with no rust. All of it sparkled like the lamp on shore as the sunlight reflected repeatedly upon it depending on his position on the ship.

Reluctantly, it was time to leave. There was so much to do yet and an unoccupied unguarded ship was a hazard in and of itself. The danger would increase with every extra minute that passed. He undid the perfect square knots and slowly lowered one of the small cutters into the water. He jumped inside and rowed once around the ship, inspecting the hull and as far as he could go along the surface line.

She was neat, clean, not so much as a chip or scratch, and no trace of a barnacle. They would all come in good time but for now, his eyes only viewed perfection. She was like a virgin girl, untouched and gorgeous as she beckoned him to be the first. He paddled to shore but could not help but glance back twice, then a third time at such a magnificent ship.

They were ready for him when he returned, and Buck was actually pleased but did his best not to show it. He only had to load his personal chest of gold and then give the order to leave. He would not let the chest out of his sight. Except for maybe three or four, Buck knew the nineteen men who would serve as his starting crew. He had trusted a very select few like Jake to gather them, and there appeared to be little cause for alarm. They were a ragtag bunch with prematurely lined and heavily weathered tanned faces, knotted hands, breeches, waistcoats, stockings, tattered shoes, some with rags tied around their heads, and all with one basic thing in common, their rough and tumble appearance.

They were sailors, the worst of the worst. Buck was already thinking of first and second mates, and perhaps the select few whom he would allow to bunk in the best rooms of the stern castle; then again, the rooms below were none too shabby. He doubted if anyone would complain, and if they did, he'd just throw them off. Perhaps he would have the carpenter install a plank for just such matters.

There was little doubt as to who would be his second in command or first mate. Jake O'Donnell was a natural leader and Buck had already placed him in charge of the final arrangements including the leading of the wagon train. The men responded to Jake almost as well as they responded to Buck. Jake was just a shade less than six feet in height, well above average for the time, and he would back down from no one, except for maybe Buck. Jake was more outgoing, gregarious, and the life of the party; in short, the guy who would drink, dance, joke, and sing along with anyone, and the more he drank, the louder he got. Jake would get one of the prize rooms topside.

Another choice room would go to a Spaniard named Vargos. No one really knew his first name; he was just Vargos. Probably like half the men assembled, Vargos was on the run. He personally had struck a Spanish naval officer, which usually meant a serious whipping was in order or perhaps even a death sentence. Some died before they could endure 40 lashes from a cat 'o nine tails, a multi-tailed barbed whip used for the severest of punishment.

Vargos managed to escape and a nice long voyage far away was about the only insurance for his livelihood and good health. He was one man that Buck trusted least but they needed him. He had a reputation as a gunner and was likely the best cannon shot available in the town at the time. He would prove to be vital in training the others, including Buck. Once a few of the others learned the art of firing cannon balls accurately, Buck could dispose of him later if he caused any trouble.

The only person with any formal education was a tall, thin Englishman named John Watson. Watson had spent some time in London studying astronomy, celestial navigation, and the use of the most modern instruments including sextants, compasses, and scopes. The only problem was his expulsion from Cambridge for repeated drunkenness. Buck needed a pilot and someone who could read. He knew Watson could handle it if he stayed away from the barrels of brew. An occasional bout was one thing; perpetual inebriation was another. Buck would keep an eye on him and already threatened to break him in half if he showed up for duty pasted. John Watson was much of a scholar and listened well, especially to this formidable and dangerous captain.

Another vital position was that of carpenter, and it went to the only recruit over 30 years of age, one who had just turned 31 the previous month. Peter Stubbs grew up under the wing of his father whose trade was that of a ship builder. Peter became bored with working on land in a harbor and longed for the adventures of the sea. He served on several vessels as a carpenter's aide or assistant.

Along with being the oldest, Peter was the shortest of the crew and lived up, or rather down to his namesake. He may have been short, but he was stout and nearly completely bald as well. He was an ugly man and had very little luck with the ladies in his life other than whores. A scar along his left cheek from a lost knife fight did not aid in his overall unattractive appearance. Buck wasn't exactly looking for pretty boys, and from what Jake told him, Stubbs could do the job, and that was all that mattered to Buck. Stubbs had his own tools too, which was good, though most of them had been pilfered from various ships; still, they were in his possession, and that too was good enough for Buck.

Like Stubbs, a second Spaniard named Lindez grew up under his father's occupation, but that is where all similarities ended. Lindez was of average height, around 5'5" or 5'6" but weighed in at 250 pounds. He was a drinking master. He had won numerous bets in taverns from northern Africa to England and had never met his match from a drinking standpoint. He would prove it several times and would turn out to be the biggest glutton on Buck's ship too. He was round, jovial, and could boom out a baritone tune quicker than Jake O'Donnell who was no lightweight from a singing or drinking standpoint. Lindez's drinking ability was not what got him recruited. He, like his father, was a sail maker. Despite his fat sausage-like fingers, give Lindez a piece of canvas, needles, and string, and he would produce a workable sail. Buck had included extra canvas within his loads of supplies.

That was it for the stern castle berths. Buck had a few left over that he could use as rewards later as needed. About the only other skilled position unaccounted for was that of cook. It was ordinarily a low-ranking position, and Buck assigned it to a man named James "Jimmy" Hall. Buck left him down below to bunk with the remaining sailors. He also had a man by the name of Jacques Marquette who was half-French and half Spanish. Marquette possessed some skill as a butcher should the need arise, and Buck housed him below adjacent to Jimmy. Marquette's father was French, and he had some rudimentary cooking skills as well. The remaining seamen received rooms below.

It took better than half the day to load the ship with the two dinghies. That was all they had available to them at the time to transport and load the cargo. Buck made a mental note to pick up a larger rowboat someday. For now, he was fortunate to have any at all. Buck had gone first with his chest, and he had taken enough gold out for supplies and transport that there was room for the lamp to rest hidden and locked within. After he moved it and locked it within the captain's quarters, Buck stayed on the ship permanently to supervise the loading and storing of the supplies.

Yet, the majority of the men had no idea what was going on. Murmurs mixed with awe as hundreds of questions surfaced in their heads, especially when Buck not only announced that he was captain of the ship, but that he owned it too! They stared at him in disbelief for he had always been one of them, a rough and tumble sailor, one of the roughest at that. They were not about to challenge him, but they were still curious.

Buck had little choice but to lie, he simply told him that he stole it from a Spanish shipyard and killed all of the guards aboard. That tidbit gained the men's respect, and some even cheered at the news. They were all riffraff in a way, the dregs of society from lowly thieves to experienced pirates, they were all there, present and accounted for. It did not take long for even the most ignorant of the bunch to figure out that they would be serving on a pirate ship. Buck gave each one of them one final chance to back out, but nearly all were on the run, dead broke, or down on their luck. They all remained, especially when they viewed the magnificent ship up close and personal.

Buck assigned jobs, and since the ship was ready for sale at the dawn of its creation, there wasn't a lot to do to get moving. Buck barked out orders and Jake added a few of his own or reinforced those of his captain. There were six main sails, two each on the mainmast and foremast, and one each on the two smaller mizzenmasts at the ends of the ship. Ten men worked on loosening the sails from undoing the knots within the gaskets to tacking to maneuver and release the great canvas. The anchor was drawn and John Watson, the English pilot, steered the massive rudder.

A slight wind caught the sails as the ship heeled to starboard. Adjustments followed loud orders as Buck noted carefully how she moved. It would take time getting used to her and feeling her out, kind of like the first time with a new woman, but so far so good. She edged along and the weather cooperated as well.

It turned out to be a fine day, more than fine, within the realms of magnificence. An hour later, Buck's next order of business was to ration out some food and drink. A gallon of beer per day per man was the most he had ever recalled receiving as a sailor, and that was measure he would use. They would have to eat certain foodstuffs first before they spoiled too badly, and the first items that came to mind were the cabbage and bread. The men needed meat and he would go easy on the salt pork and beef initially since those items tended to last the longest, as long as they were packed and sealed tightly within the salt kegs.

Buck had no particular destination in mind, just south for now along the coast of Portugal. The crew would need much training before they could accomplish what their fearless leader had in store for them. Buck believed in preparing for emergencies and already set some of his men to work. After ordering Jimmy the cook to prepare a meal and Marquette to assist him, he sought out Lindez and instructed him to begin work on a spare sail that would fit either of the two central large masts. Vargos the gunner was next, and Buck was eager to blast some cannon balls for much needed practice.

With 21 cannons aboard and a healthy supply of muskets, they needed to know how to use them if they were going to be a fighting ship. In Buck's mindset, everyone needed to learn, even the cook and the pilot. Buck took three men at a time along with Vargos to the lower deck that contained little but the heavy iron weapons. The forged coal black cast iron cannons nearly blended in with the ship, which had been finished in the darkest of oak. There were hatches and tracks to move them in and out of cover to keep them dry when stored away.

They did not fire any of the eight-pounders in the beginning; instead, Vargos showed them how to load the ball, pack the right amount of powder, and to set off the charge. They would not complete the final step for two more days. As Buck had ordered, the training was mandatory for everyone, but it was a popular order as all were eager to learn firsthand. They shot muskets before firing the cannon, or more accurately. To err on the side of caution, Buck only let on that he had a single black powder rifle, not an entire chest full of rifles let alone pistols as well. He did not know many of the men well enough to trust them with their own firearms just yet.

They hauled the sails in and weighed anchor in what appeared to be a vacant area along the coast. One by one, the crew practiced loading and shooting the musket at the trees for an entire day. Vargos proved to be invaluable as he was the only one familiar with the new flintlock technology. The new design contained a piece of flint in the cocking hammer, and when someone pulled the trigger, the flint struck a piece of steel sharply. The impact created sparks that set off the powder charge and propelled the bullet forward. When Buck was satisfied that all had learned the basic operations of the musket, he finally moved on to the cannons.

Eight-pound balls fired at a decent rate of velocity could do some serious damage to whatever got in their line of trajectory. The poor trees along the shoreline from the ship suffered significant damage; some toppled to the cheers of the amateur gunners. Buck watched closely and noted there was one whose accuracy rivaled that of Vargos himself. George Bracken was a natural; another skinny English kid, even slimmer than the pilot Watson, took intuitively to cannon firing. Aside from being the scrawniest of the lot, Bracken had one other characteristic besides his slight build that distinguished him from the others; at 17 years of age, he was the youngest.

As a kid, Bracken had been shifted from one orphanage to another, lived in the streets occasionally, and had some success as a basic pickpocket and thief. The local gang leaders and ringmasters did not appreciate little George Bracken cheating on them or working solo on their turf; furthermore, in a dispute with one of those leaders, George was quite adept and accurate at knife throwing and launched one at his boss in a fight. He only wounded his elder slightly, but consequently, he had to run away or risk facing the boss's wrath, which probably meant a sound beating, whipping, or perhaps a deep cut in retaliation. The streets of London were no longer safe for little George Bracken and at age 14, he signed up on a ship as a cabin boy, and had been sailing ever since, all of three years. He turned out to be a quick study and his aim was true.

Buck had seen Bracken in action with two knives in a tavern last year. The boy was taking bets that he could hit the center of the ace of hearts at a distance of 20 feet. Men who had never seen him do it lost their money as the regulars in the tavern laughed again and again just as they had been laughed at before. Buck readily saw the possibilities of a skilled knife-thrower.

It was a nice positive to see the young Bracken hitting trees squarely with cannon balls, especially after a single adjustment. Others could move their cannons up, down, and sideways several times over and were fortunate enough to graze a branch. Bracken's comrades nicknamed him "Bragg'in." Unlike most braggarts, blowhards, and exaggerators, Bragg'in could back it up with his knives and cannon shots. He was at least pleasant and careful not to offend his bigger shipmates, which indubitably, was everyone on the ship, especially the brawny intimidating captain.

The sailors were still at a loss as to how Buck had pulled it off. The brand-new spit- shine ship and the wealth of supplies was overwhelming to say the least from a man of Buck's background and disposition; yet, the most amazing thing of all was about to happen, Buck's final wish. Buck had been thinking long and hard about his wish. He had his well-supplied ship and a workable crew, not to mention a chest with plenty of gold remaining.

He wanted to acquire more treasure, but only in the good old-fashioned way, steal it! It was the anticipation of a fight and the thrill of the conquest that spurred him on. He did think of something that just might make his future exploits a little easier. It was an interesting idea and Buck was not sure if it would work or not; then again, he had little to lose if it didn't. He already had a well-gunned ship, extra gold, liquor barrels to spare, and plenty of ammo to blow several sailing vessels out of the water. Alone in his spacious quarters, he undid the ragged shirt that he kept about the lamp and rubbed.

"What is your third and final wish?" The semi-transparent rounded figure bellowed out at him.

"I wish for the ship to be seen only by those on it or touching it or any man that holds one of the cutlasses that you gave me before."

The formless figure vanished before Buck's very eyes never to return, at least for Buck's requests. He had not known the word *invisible* but that was what indeed he had requested for the ship. To test his wish, he had to order the release of one of the cutters. He also snatched one of the cutlasses from the locked chest within his cabin that still held 25 of the decorated blades. He had thought carefully, and the cutlasses provided him or any of his men holding one to find the ship when they were not on it.

For the third time in a row, the Djinni did not disappoint him. He left Jake in charge and took the pilot Watson and the knife-throwing Bracken down in the water in the small rowboat.

With cutlass in hand, the ship did not disappear to Buck's eyes as it did for his two companions. Watson and Bracken were downright flabbergasted and rubbed their eye simultaneously for a moment. They could hear the hustle and bustle of the ship but could not see much except for a strange pattern outline in the water. They could not use the sun as an excuse since a couple of drifting clouds currently buffeted it.

Buck almost laughed aloud but held it back to short burst until he set the cutlass down in the bottom of the boat. He saw or rather did not see what his companions were desperately looking for. He handed the cutlass first to Watson and the ship appeared suddenly barely 20 feet away. Watson passed it over the Bracken before they returned to the mother ship.

In threes and fours, Buck ordered all the sailors to experience the phenomenon. They were naturally amazed, almost unbelieving except for their eyes, confused, and a select few were superstitious. Here was magic they had never witnessed before, and some were afraid. They did not know if it was the ship itself or the cutlass that did the trick until Buck held a topside meeting for all to hear. He hauled out his chest and one by one, handed each of them a cutlass.

"As long as you hold this weapon in your possession, nothing can go wrong with you, you will always see the ship. Lose it, and you lose your way back." Buck's physical size alone along with his gruff nature automatically commanded respect, but these new developments brought fear to the eyes of many. It worked well for Buck and a mutiny would never happen on his ship if he were alive.

There was one last minor detail overlooked by Buck concerning his ship. With permission, the robust sailor Lindez suggested a name for the ship. With his nimble figures and some accurate caulking tar, they lowered Lindez down the starboard side of the ship near the front where he proceeded to do a decent job of writing considering the conditions. Lindez had his cutlass stuffed in his waistband so that the ship did not disappear from his sight while he remained suspended by ropes over the edge. When he had finished, the side of the ship stated in large block letters: "THE GHOST."

The Ghost left only a dent in the water along with a consistent wave as it plowed forward. Water splashed against and ricocheted off at weird angles it as it sped southward down the coast of Portugal at a leisurely pace. The first victim of Buck's wrath was a merchant ship. It would hardly pose a challenge considering the far superior firepower of *The Ghost*. The booty was an old two-masted Italian Carrack. It was big, slow, and looked as if it was a hundred years old. It flew the Portuguese flag and that alone was enough for Buck to consider it his enemy; then again, any other national flag gave him that same feeling.

During the afternoon, they slowly and stealthily crept up on the ship as Buck ordered his crew into silent mode. As darkness neared, Buck made his move. When they closed within sixty feet, Buck signaled Jake who in turn signaled Vargos below. Five booming cannon reports echoed in the stillness of the night as five black deadly balls found their way over to the helpless old Carrack.

The aim of Vargos and Bracken was true, as their orders were to take down the mainmast; the other three targeted the smaller foremast. The mainmast toppled easily with the two superb shots from Buck's best gunners; as it fell, it crushed three men to death and injured several others. The other hit the smaller mast once, off to the side. It wasn't enough to drop it, but it did sway off balanced.

The old ship halted almost immediately. Deemed too elderly and unseaworthy to travel on the open seas far from shore, its primary function changed to pickups and deliveries between European coastal ports. Two of the three lethal balls meant for the foremast crashed into the side of the old ship, one continued all the way through the rotting planks and created a hole of like size vertically through the entire ship. Water seeped in at an alarming rate while the captain screamed orders to halt the flow, patch it if possible, and several men began bailing. Not only was the captain of the Carrack alarmed but confused too.

The sounds of the big guns with red fire flashes were unmistakable in what little light remained. But where was the ship that fired them? On top of that, they were supposedly in friendly waters too. With his vessel taking on water and the mess on the ship caused by the busted mainmast, the captain had little time to think. If that wasn't enough, out of nowhere strange men appeared boarding his ship. It was as if they came out of the clouds themselves. He found half his men bound in ropes on his own deck before he even noticed the none-too-polite visitors. They murdered several others in cold blood, while some bled, pleading for help. About the time he realized what was happening, the huge hands of Buck seized him, and a jeweled cutlass pressed tightly against his throat. There was nothing to do but surrender.

The living prisoners were huddled together apart from four. Buck allowed two of them to continue to work on the hole in the ship and two others to hand crank the crude pumps in an attempt to bail out the ever-increasing flow of water into the hold of the Carrack, all with supervision naturally. Buck needed a little time to search and take what he could since the ship would be no use to him at the bottom of the Atlantic Ocean.

It wasn't long before Buck realized that it was a disappointing take. The main holds were empty save for a few barrels of salt pork and beer. Buck confiscated them along with a few casks of gunpowder. The Italian-built ship did sport two cannons; however, they were small ones, and the accompanying balls were about half the size of those on *The Ghost*. Buck left them and settled for the gunpowder only as far as weapons were concerned. The captain's berth on the Carrack yielded a few coins and weapons, Buck took them all.

They loaded up what they could and were gone within twenty minutes. Luckily, none of Buck's men had so much as suffered a scratch, but even more fortunate, none lost their prized cutlasses and found their way back to *The Ghost*. Those who could see from the Carrack watched as the pirates disappeared over the side of their ship as mysteriously as they had appeared. They assumed incorrectly that the intruders were just going over the side into boats below. They had no idea that *The Ghost* rested side by side. Voices came from *The Ghost* as they shoved off, but the men remained unseen by the rather bewildered surviving crew of the Carrack.

The old Italian ship struggled to stay afloat with all hands working frantically to save her. She would survive the ordeal and limp into a not-too-distant port. There was cause for celebration on the conquering ship, the first of many. Half of the confiscated food and drink acquired in the brief, but short battle was consumed that night aboard *The Ghost*. Buck did not quite collect enough coins, knives, and daggers to give every man one, but he secretly removed several gold coins from his own hoard to make up the difference; that way, every man received something for his efforts. Lindez had his first chance to prove just how much he could drink, and he did himself proud.

The Ghost continued its slow journey south preying on old and new merchant ships. They avoided the great warships of Spain and those of the ever-growing British navy for now. Buck had no set goal in mind as to where to sail, but like Tonara, he left a path of death and destruction to those in his way. The Djinni was quite satisfied with both. As Buck considered carefully, he knew in his heart that they would have to attempt the taking of a warship, maybe just for the challenge, or perhaps to restock balls and powder. He could probably do that at a seaport, but a sailing warship would be a much bigger prize.

To this point, he was pleased with his crew. The men were becoming more efficient and better trained in the art of warfare with each conquest. Moral was high as the crew profited from every conquest, even if just food and liquor. Buck was certainly providing the experience, and some did not need much in hand-to-hand combat. The exception was the powder-actuated weapons. Buck allowed more and more guns out on the raids, but he continued to lock them away in the designated chest in his cabin when finished. Their use was sparing in the first place, mostly to keep the prisoners in check while pillaging the captured ship. He trusted his men to some degree but aside from the shifty Vargos, there was one other he kept a closer eye upon, and that was Hans.

Hans was neither tall nor short, neither big nor small, and average or ordinary was about the best way to describe him. He lacked courage in Buck's eyes, and he seemed to be the only one on board who did not take well to the life of piracy. Hans was from one of the Scandinavian countries in the northlands, Denmark Buck thought, and Hans, like Bracken, had escaped an orphanage at an early age. Hans was mild, good-natured, but overly quiet. He had no friends on the ship and was the only true loner among the crew.

Buck noticed during the raids that Hans was always at the rear of the boarding party, and far as he could tell, Hans did not readily engage the enemy or more accurately, the victims with any relish like the other crewmembers. Buck was not sure if he had even fought or stabbed anyone. What kind of pirate was that? Hans did not have the stomach for what they were doing and that led to his attempted desertion. Given the secrets tied to *The Ghost*, Buck could not allow anyone to leave alive, and he often wondered if the men knew that. He doubted anyone would want to with the way things were going, except Hans.

It was during the attack of a smaller English merchant ship where Hans attempted his escape. The strategy for overtaking the vessel was like that of the other victims in that balls were launched at the masts in the dark. *The Ghost* moseyed forward until it was side-by-side, and then the crew boarded the target ship during the confusion. Hans was part of the initial assault but sought out one of the officers, a man who appeared to be the first mate on the English ship. Hans avoided the captain for that would have been too obvious; furthermore, Buck or Jake, depending on who was in charge, ordinarily hunted him down as standard procedure.

When he felt no one was looking, Hans took the first mate aside and frantically explained his situation because time was short. Hans tried to tell the English first mate in one minute how he wanted to defect and how the possession of the cutlass allowed one to see the invisible ship. The first mate nearly struck him down but when Hans handed him the cutlass hilt first, more or less shoving it into his hands, *The Ghost* came readily into view to the awestruck eyes of the Englishman. The first mate seemed to understand and since the pirates were pretty much in full control of the ship, to strike Hans would have been fruitless. The two scrambled away from where the pirates rounded up the merchant ship's crew.

Hans almost escaped in hiding with the Englishman, but the alert eyes of Peter Stubbs, the carpenter, caught them. Stubbs may not have been the sharpest tool on his workbench, but it did not take a genius to figure out what was happening. Stubbs grabbed Jake by the arm nearby and pointed in the direction of Hans and his new friend running off. They gave chase immediately and easily caught up with the two.

The ship was not that large, and the fallen mainmast and consequent tangled rigging blocked many of the walkways, which, in turn, provided little opportunity for a fast escape. With one savage blow from the hilt of Jake's cutlass, the Englishman fell into unconsciousness, but he was not dead as Jake thought he might be. Shaking and trembling, the terrified Hans received a glancing blow and Jake dragged him back to *The Ghost*. In the heat of the moment, and given the fact that it was dark, Jake and Pete did not notice Hans' cutlass under the inert form of the injured first mate.

Punishment was harsh, swift, and only delayed by the raiding of the English vessel and Hans' eventual return to consciousness. *The Ghost* did not move far from the disabled English ship as Buck and the others worried little that anyone would see them. It was close to midnight, but the moon was bright enough to see an ordinary ship at some distance, but then again, Buck's ship was far from ordinary given its unique cloaking properties; nevertheless, there was one man on the English boat on this individual night who could see it just fine.

Barely awake with his aching head, Hans found himself tied to the main mast as Buck produced the dreaded cat 'o nine tails. No one could swing it more powerfully than Buck, and with each blow, the claws embedded and ripped the back of Hans as efficiently as a velociraptor. With each flick of Buck's wrist, Hans' screams reached not only the crew of *The Ghost* nearby, but all alive and conscious on the English ship. The sharp tails cut deeply into the bare back of Hans, some to the bone.

Buck stopped after ten lashes, only to remove the flesh from the tails. A crewman threw a bucket of salt brine on Hans' back and it stung nearly as much as the whipping. Four more blows and Hans left the world of consciousness. Buck added six more to make it an even twenty. To compound his point as judge and executioner to the fate of traitors, Buck lifted the nearly dead form of Hans easily with both hands above his head, and with a mighty heave, tossed him far overboard. Walking the plank would have been too easy.

The cool salty water sent a fresh batch of raging fire up and down the back of Hans and revived him briefly. *The Ghost* moved on while Hans managed to keep his head above water for a few short minutes; however, it was enough time for the first mate of the merchant ship to attach a line of rope to himself and save the almost-dead deserter, time enough too to stay ahead of the sharks.

Another typical celebration following the raid took place on *The Ghost*. Since it was dark and since he believed there was no chance of discovery, Buck did not post any lookouts. Consequently, the rescue of Hans went unnoticed. The English transport ship happened to have a surgeon on board, and after treating his own wounded, he cleaned the horrific gouges with alcohol, and then wrapped Hans' back as best he could; fortunately for Hans, he was unconscious through the procedure. Hans would live but it would be three days before he could relate his tale. His story was nearly unbelievable except that his newfound friend verified the part about the ghost ship.

The most valuable piece of information that Hans could provide other than the ability to see the pirate ship with possession of the cutlass, not to mention the guns aboard, was the general direction and slowness in which Buck was travelling. That was a huge mistake of Buck's. A slow leisurely pace with long stops gave those aboard the broken but seaworthy English merchant ship plenty of time to inform an English admiral named Parker at a nearby post.

The first mate and new friend of Hans was also named Parker. He was the nephew of the admiral, and the tale was far more believable when recited by one the admiral knew and trusted. If that wasn't enough, there had been rumors of a ghostly ship that struck in the night up and down the coast of Portugal; Hans and the younger Parker simply provided a viable explanation for them.

Admiral Parker commanded one of the best warships in all the English Navy. It was a special ship in that it was innovative in design for the time, particularly since it was a vast improvement over the galleon. The masts were truer or straighter, a specialty-built hull was reinforced to carry the added weight of additional guns and cannons, and as many as five sails per mast were fastened where the galleon typically carried two. Despite the added weight of additional firepower, it was more maneuverable and faster with the more complicated sail network above.

Eventually it would evolve into a British ship named an East Indiaman, which would further enhance England's reign over the seas. This specific model commanded by Admiral Parker was fully 150 feet in length and carried fifteen big guns on each side. Named *The H.M.S. Destroyer* only a year earlier, it sped down the southern coast of Portugal under full sail in pursuit of Buck's elusive pirate ship.

Buck and his vessel reached the southern end of what is now modern-day Portugal, about a hundred nautical miles from the northwestern coast of Africa. He had a two-week lead on *The Destroyer*; nevertheless, there were many factors allowing the warship to reduce the distance between them. For one, Buck was never in a hurry and rarely if ever completely opened all of the sails. They had little reason to hide since they were supposedly invisible. Buck did not travel at night, nor did he stray far after a successful ambush.

Buck stopped at the port of Cadiz in northern Spain to purchase a few supplies as well as to provide his men with a little shore leave. There was nothing like drinking in a tavern or roadhouse, not to mention the whores available no matter how dirty. When a man was away at sea for weeks or even months, it was not unlike prison life when it came to female companionship or lack thereof; over time, even the scaggiest and/or fattest of prostitutes was like coming home for Christmas. The magnificent British warship made no such stops in its pursuit.

Buck was uneasy about letting his men go off on their own. They did swear repeatedly upon torture and death to keep the ship secret, but who knew what one would say after a few tankards of beer or voluminous wineskin. Then again, Buck thought, who would believe them about the invisible ship and the magic cutlasses? Still, he did not wish them out of his sight for long. Even though the ship held superior sleeping arrangements compared to what they would get on land, shore leave was still something to anticipate Aside from loose women, the ever-increasing money and booty were useless if the men could not use them in some way.

He granted them a two-day leave and a third to help restock the ship with vital supplies. Jake was one he could trust to help keep a lookout and things did seem to go smoothly other than a couple of black eyes and a broken nose for one after some fairly minor and expected tavern brawling. To Buck's relief, they were sailing south again in three days, and everyone was accounted for; still, he did not bother taking inventory of the cutlasses. If he had, he would have learned that one was missing. The only problem was that in two days after the shore excursion, a lookout holding Hans' missing cutlass in the crow's nest of *The Destroyer* would sight *The* Ghost.

The chase was on. Buck had no idea *The Destroyer* was in pursuit, even after Lindez, the current lookout, spotted the tailing ship from afar. There was no concern whatsoever since they felt positive that they were invisible to all. Only when Buck gave the order to let out a little sail and drifted further out away from the shore, and when the pursuer matched every maneuver, did he begin to worry.

He strode out on the main deck and began shouting orders to open her up, fully. The crew loosened the knots and the topsails filled; likewise, the mainsails opened completely, and after a small adjustment, which consisted of a heel to portside, *The Ghost* sped out to the open sea. Every little sail on the two main masts as well as the smaller mizzenmasts was fully opened, full speed ahead.

Little by little, *The Destroyer* gained. They adjusted too and steadily gained, not much, perhaps a foot per minute, but twenty yards every hour brought them that much closer. They closed within one-third of a mile before the light of day expired. It was then that *The Destroyer* had difficulty keeping sight of *The Ghost* and lost a good two hundred yards in the darkness. It could have been much worse had they lost sight of her altogether.

Admiral Parker may well have pulled within cannon range the next day had not a storm stunted his progress. It was not a great storm, but the wind-driven rains were just strong enough for both ships to close their sails or risk having them torn to shreds. Both could do little but ride it out. *The Destroyer* did not gain ground, nor did she lose any until nightfall once again.

The rain continued into the night and *The Ghost* disappeared from the only man on the British ship that could see it. Fortune still resided with the admiral since, by mid-morning, the storm dissipated and a new lookout holding Hans' cutlass in his pants, spotted *The Ghost* with the aid of a powerful spyglass. The chase resumed.

Buck continued in a southwesterly direction west of the coast of Africa. The charts he had stolen contained a map of the ocean including all of Africa's long coasts, both west and east. It also plotted the way to India, which was the destination of the ship from whence he had lifted the charts. His pilot, John Watson, read them accurately, but by the end of the day, they would be further west than what the maps in their possession covered. It was not long before they were on their own. Buck gambled that way hoping that the pursuing ship would turn back. It didn't. It was gaining more in the day than it was losing at night.

Buck Heidel was not a man to be frightened or run away from trouble. He had spent much of his life facing his problems head on, at least where a fight was involved. The weather was now clear and probably in a day, unless a squall popped up, they would likely have little choice but to turn and fight their foe. Although most of the men on Buck's ship were criminals, they were brave fighters who would stand and fight at Buck's command.

Jake at last figured out Hans had lost his cutlass and that it had remained on the English ship that they had plundered. An inventory check by Buck confirmed that one was missing. It didn't take a brilliant detective to realize that it had fallen into the hands of whoever was commanding the trailing ship. *The Ghost* was outgunned, but a single man on *The Destroyer* could still view it; nonetheless, that would likely be a moot point once *The Ghost's* cannon fired up clouds of black smoke to reveal their position to everyone.

After conferring with Jake, the best strategy Buck could come up with was to attempt to spot the man with the cutlass and fire away at him with both muskets and cannon. They felt for sure that the spotter would be in a high lookout post, or more accurately, in one of the crows' nests. If they could take him out, they could perhaps sneak away while shooting at anyone who approached the fallen man. If that didn't work, they would just have to fight it out the traditional way; that is, until one of the ships sunk.

The best timing for an attack would be in the darkness, Buck's usual modus operandi when pirating. He would wait until then before turning *The Ghost* around to face the intimidating English Man-of-War. If he could fire first, it might be enough to gain the advantage over the larger and more powerful ship. Little did Buck realize that *The Destroyer* had a healthy crew of seventy-six, quadruple his own since Hans had not been replaced.

It was not a good night for an attack and there would be no surprise. Half of the moon provided enough light for the lookout to keep *The Ghost* within his sights. *The Destroyer* was ready as ever, a formidable opponent with far more cannons and crew. For the first time, the two ships headed in opposite directions, *The Ghost* back to the east and *The Destroyer* west, or in short, on a direct collision course. Lindez, the best lookout using Buck's telescope, spotted his counterpart on *The Destroyer* who happened to be spying on him at the exact moment. Lindez did not see the cutlass present, nor did he see any other lookouts above. He could only assume his captain sought this one.

Just as Buck was counting down the minutes based on the range when his ship turned about broadside, as he was about to give the order, Admiral Parker beat him to the punch. Six blasts in succession sounded from *The Destroyer*, but all were short save one big iron ball that broke through the side of *The Ghost* just above one of the cannons. All ten cannons on the port side of *The Ghost* fired in random order, but all were aiming at the foremast where the crow's nest above with the lookout rested. The lookout aboard *The Destroyer* toppled as two of the ten balls struck the foremast. A lone musket ball struck the man in the leg as he was attempting to climb down. Those on *The Ghost* lost sight of him when he fell.

The fight had just begun, and more and more blasts followed, but far more frequently from *The Destroyer*. The crew's training was specifically for war at sea, and they fired in unison into the hazy black smoke from the opposing ship. It was all they could see. Despite having more men and guns, they could not employ snipers to pick off what they could not see, but they could aim their cannons at the red fire sparks from the opposing guns. Within fifteen minutes, over thirty balls had slammed into *The Ghost* while only a dozen connected with *The Destroyer*. The portside gunports on *The Ghost* were a mess as a third volley disabled six, and some balls penetrated the front lower hull area, and *The Ghost* began taking on water.

The battle raged on, and Buck should have retreated or attempted an escape, but he didn't. It was not in his nature to back down from a fight. Instead, he tried to turn the ship to utilize the other ten guns. It was slow going as *The Destroyer* punched and pounded away. Six of Buck's men were dead including Peter Stubbs the carpenter and Jimmy Hall the cook. Stubbs had his entire midsection blasted by a cannon ball while Hall died in a blast of a hundred shrapnel pieces when an opposing cannonball struck the cannon he was attempting to load.

The seagulls stayed a safe distance away from the melee, but a few unlucky fish had already gone belly-up from the shocking vibrations where some balls exploded in the water. *The Ghost* shuddered, slow to turn as it filled with water. It was only a matter of time before she would go down. In the heat of battle, Buck managed to locate Jake, the closest man he had to a friend. He pulled Jake aside and roughly shoved him into his cabin where the lamp was stored.

"Rub it!" Buck screamed above the deafening noise as he shoved the lamp into Jake's hands.

"Wha...uh...what?"

"I said rub it! Here, take the shirt, and rub it damn it all man!"

Jake did as ordered while the ship listed heavily to starboard. In the confusion, the Djinni came forth and demanded a wish from Jake.

"Quick now Jake," shouted Buck above the battle noise, "Wish for us out of here." The noise from outside had drowned out Djinni's voice and Jake had not heard it clearly.

"Wha...uh...what are you talking about?" Jake questioned.

"There's no time, just say: "I wish we were out of here.""

"I wish we were out of here," Jake obeyed.

The Ghost vanished. It not only disappeared from sight as it always did, but its physical presence and all aboard transported to the Pacific Ocean. Strangely, it was morning outside to Buck's crew and a still calm met them as a misty lazy fog rested over the water. Just as they disappeared, *The Destroyer* did likewise, at least from their viewpoint. Land was in sight to the East as Buck screamed orders loud enough as if the cannon were still firing. A reef was in sight and Buck immediately sent a leadsman to check the depth.

"Seventy fathoms!" Bracken returned the order with a yell of his own as he began estimating the depth every five seconds. In a couple of minutes, he shouted "Forty-five" and Buck did his best to try to turn the ship around, but she was heavy and nearly listless.

The main mast was hopeless after several cannon shots. It had not fallen over but it was swaying, and many ropes and sails were supporting it instead of the other way around. The ragged sails along the foremast were trimmed but not tacked effectively in time. If that wasn't enough, there was a reported four to five feet of standing water in the hold and rising inch by inch. All live able-bodied men not on topside trying to work the sails were ordered below to bail or pump.

"Thirty fathoms!" Shouted Bracken followed a few seconds later by "Twenty fathoms!." A half of a minute later, it was down to ten fathoms.

Buck had one last resort before they broke up on the jutting reef as he rushed Jake back to his cabin, "Rub it and wish for the ship to be right!"

Jake was as confused as ever and had not even seen the Djinni clearly the first time, but he at least accepted the old shirt of Buck's again. When he was about to rub it, a tremendous crash cracked the hull of the ship like a jagged earthquake line in the dirt. The stern rose high out of the water and nearly everyone below and above fell including Jake and Buck. The lamp tumbled to the floor. It was too late for any more wishes.

As massive amounts of water rushed in, those trapped below drowned in a minute or two depending on who was able to hold their breath the longest. Two of the remaining five topside fell completely overboard with the impact. Despite Buck's shouts, Jake regained his footing and rushed out of the cabin, the lamp forgotten, at least by Jake. Buck picked up the lamp along with his old, tattered shirt and made for the nearest cutter. *The Ghost* was now sinking fast, and it was time to abandon ship. Buck didn't care whether it was tradition or not that the captain be the last to leave, he was getting out, the others be damned.

Like an aftershock, a second crash into the reef sent Jake and two of the other three remaining topside overboard. None of them made it except Bracken. He, along with Buck, managed to reach one of the small boats and undo the ropes just as the top deck sunk beneath the surging waters. Buck had the lamp wrapped within his old shirt while Bracken had nothing except the clothes on his back. Just as Bracken released the last remaining rope tie on the cutter, *The Ghost* smashed into the reef one final time casting Bracken headfirst into the sea.

Buck reached out in an attempt to save him, not for the humanity of the effort, but only because he needed someone to make wishes since he exhausted his requests. It was fruitless however. Bracken hit his head on a loose plank and slipped into unconsciousness. His lungs quickly filled with water, and he died by the time Buck could maneuver the small boat in an attempted rescue.

Buck did have his cutlass tied within his waistband, but the only thing it revealed to him was the final sinking of the masts below the water's surface. Until it completely rotted away, *The Ghost*, recently pretty as a picture with a lingering touch of new ship smell to boot, would remain invisible to the creatures of the sea, at least to those with ordinary sight. The only smell that Buck could sniff was that of fire and brimstone and the smoke that went with it.

He could do nothing but row toward the strange unfamiliar shoreline in a boat that was little more than a bare sliver from the magnificent vessel it had come from. Buck had absolutely no idea where he was but ran the cutter up in a sandy area void of rocks, stepped out, and started walking inland. He needed to find water for starters, but he himself was discovered before he could complete much in the way of exploration.

Two Indians unfamiliar with white men caught up with him. One of them jutted a spear in his direction and said something, but Buck took the gesture as a direct threat and stabbed him with the cutlass. The other backed off as Buck bore down upon him, and Buck may have succeeded in disposing of him too had not a larger group appeared from over a sand dune.

The one backing off raised his own spear, shouted several words, pointed wildly at his dead companion, and then at Buck, and then the horde descended upon the lone sailor like hungry vultures on fresh roadkill. They riddled Buck's body with spears, and, as blood poured out from countless wounds, darkness overcame his eyes forever. Blood spattered Buck's spare shirt too and dripped upon the lamp. One of the Indian men wiped Buck's blood from the lamp when the smoky form within rose.

"What is your first wish redskin?"

The highly superstitious group fell into a fright. The one who had rubbed it dropped it and stepped far back with his people without speaking. A few of the older men huddled and thought that maybe it was the spirit of the white man they had killed, or maybe some other apparition. Due to its appearance, it did not look like a good spirit to them.

They stepped further back and were relieved when it returned to the inside of the lamp a few short minutes later. After a brief counsel, one of them agreed to take the lamp to a place where none could disturb it. He covered it up within the bloody shirt, and then took it to a cave inland while the rest of the group returned to their village.

PART V:
THE AMERICAN WEST

"**G**old! Gold! Gold from the American River!**" - Sam Brannan, California's first millionaire, while holding aloft a vial of gold, Sacramento, California, 1848

CHAPTER XXIV

After selling off his land in Tennessee, Jeremiah Jones purchased a team of horses and wagon and was off to California the minute he'd heard about gold. News traveled fast and in a few weeks' time after the precious 'metal's discovery, 90,000 people rushed to California. Jeremiah gathered up his wife and only child and hit the road. Many people died on their way to the far West of America by getting lost, trying to cross The Rockies in the winter, fighting with hostile Indians, and by starving. The Jones family made it by having a little extra money, a good rifle or two, and the good sense of traveling in a large wagon train with an experienced and respected guide.

Unknowingly, Jeremiah staked his first claim near the cave where the lamp lay hidden for hundreds of years. Bugs, bats, and spiders nearly as big as gold sift pans filled the tiny enclosure. It still made an excellent natural shelter for human occupation, the kind used by intelligent primates for thousands of years.

He left his wife and six-year-old son Oliver outside to gather a little firewood while he went in to clean a little house, scare the bats out, and wipe the spider webs away mostly. At about 16 feet in, the cave doglegged to the left another twelve feet or so, and Jeremiah had to duck his 6'2" frame below the low ceiling that was shorter than him by three inches or so in the rear section. His wife was tall for a woman too, but she could have fit with three inches to spare. After the bend, there was barely any light left, but he did find a small pile of rocks at the end. When he kicked a few aside, his foot made a strange tinging sound, something metal. It was the lamp. He backed up to the bend where there was more light, and then brushed the dirt and grime from the lamp with his shirtsleeve. It was enough to release the inhabitant.

"What is your first wish?" The head of the fat spectral form seemed to touch the ceiling, and this was in the section of the cave where it rose a good seven feet. The voice, however, was quite clear.

"Whoa there partner, what're you talking about?" Jeremiah inquired.

"You get three wishes, what is your first?"

"Well, I'll be, what kind of funny business is this?" Jeremiah was not frightened but could hardly believe what he was seeing. The light was still a little dim, and the figure was somewhat translucent. The Djinni remained silent and was about to return, when Jeremiah spoke again, "All right partner, I'll give it a try, I came out here for gold, so let's see some." That had been his dream and his sole reason for coming here.

The Djinni vanished and left three pea-sized gold nuggets adjacent to the lamp. Jeremiah noticed the glitter as a bit of sunlight hit them from the opening of the cave. "Well, I'll be," he shook his head. He picked up the lamp, shook it, tried to open it, and then rubbed some more dirt from it with his sleeve. The Djinni popped out again.

"What is your second wish?"

"All right partner, I'd like a little more gold this time, give me a few hundred of them there nuggets." The Djinni fulfilled the wish, but Jeremiah would not live to make his third and final wish. He did have time to buy a nice home to live in but did not share the secret of the lamp with his wife. He scooped up the nuggets, loaded them in the wagon, rounded up his wife and young Oliver, and headed for town.

"But the West of the old times, with its strong characters, its stern battles and its tremendous stretches of loneliness, can never be blotted from my mind." - Buffalo Bill Cody

CHAPTER XXV

"**D**on't shoot boy!"

"Bang!" Too late, the projectile sprang forth like a mini missile from its hiding place. Little Jimmy Johnson grappled up a steep, rocky trail to track his kill. Rifles, including the one nearly as tall as the boy, have probably been responsible for more purposeful destruction than most anything imaginable, except for millions of plump house cats running loose outdoors in the next century and beyond.

"Why boy, whaddya shoot this one fer?" A deep voice protested from a grizzled towering figure.

"Pa sure is gonna like this one!" Jimmy was beaming with pride, and who was going to tell an impatient trigger-happy kid not to shoot whatever he saw that was moving?

The big man knelt beside the dead beast to get a closer look. "She was a beauty, young, and...."

"Rrrroooowwww," came a sudden cry, and a little kitten not 6 weeks yet on the planet came shooting out. "Rrrrroowww," it whimpered again with ears down and tiny teeth exposed.

"Well, whatta we have here?" uttered the big man.

The boy cocked his big Winchester and aimed at the kitten, "I'm a ginna get two in one day, Pop'ull sure like that." With finger on the trigger, the big man grabbed the rifle, flung it miles away it seemed, grabbed the boy, and started shaking him as if he were trying to relieve him of his pocket change. The boy didn't have any.

"What ta hell's a matter wit you boy?" It's bad enough that you gone and kilt its maw, do ya have to shoot everything ya see boy?"

"Lemme go, lemme go," cried the boy, "My dad'll give me five cents for every cat I get so's they don't get the sheep and you better leave me be mister or I'll tell my dad about you and he'll come a-lookin for you. My dad used to shoot...."

"Whoa boy, take a breath, them lions have got just as much right to live around here as anybody else including you boy, and if you were busy tenden to yer sheep, ya wouldn't have any problems at all with these critters up here. You get home now boy and if yer daddy wants to see me, why you just tell'em to come up here and ask fer Grizzly Jones."

The boy headed in the direction of his lost Winchester the second Jones let go of him.

"Grrrrr," came a growl from the kitten. It sat near its mother sniffing and then trying to protect her.

"Well, yer just a killer now aren't ya and what am I a gonna do with you huh?" Grizzly Jones got down on all fours and stalked the kitten. A little paw shot out lightning quick. With amazing speed for a man his size, Grizzly shot out a paw of his own and seized the kitten with one quick stroke. The tiny but sharp teeth immediately clamped down on the nearest flesh, which happened to be Grizzly's arm.

"Ouch!" With his other hand Grizzly grabbed the thick tuft of fur at the back of its head and held it outward looking at him with as much menace as a hungry pit bull would a rabbit. The cat lurched at Grizzly's face, but the man held it outward at arm's length, which was considerable given that he was 6'5" in height.

"'bout six pounds of pure terror, that's all you be. Yer about ready to terrorize mice, but that's about it lil fella." Grizzly held the kitten immobilized and hiked back to his cabin.

Back in the Gold Rush of 1849, Jeremiah Jones was one out of hundreds or perhaps even thousands of miners, prospectors, and unrealistic dreamers who struck it rich. Of course, Jeremiah did little in the way of backbreaking labor as the Djinni had provided him enough nuggets for several lifetimes; yet he was shot and died in a robbery leaving Oliver at 7 years of age alone with his mother. Ten years later, that included a few years of schooling under his belt, Oliver would lose his mother to smallpox.

Fortunately, Jeremiah had purchased a ranch, built his home, and put a few thousand in the local bank before someone stole his remaining nuggets. At age nineteen, Oliver grew to his full 6'5" frame and was drafted by the Union. He fought in a few battles during the big war but was more of a service after it fighting Indians. The Indians were in a precarious position at the end of the Civil War, much as they were ever since the white man arrived in the New World.

Long before Europeans sailed to North America, Indians had inhabited the lands for thousands of years. The Indian way of life was a highly democratic one based on sharing, reciprocity, the band unit, and most importantly, their entire culture existed on the economics of survival. When the white man arrived, he drastically altered Indian culture, mostly in terms of materials good and outright greed. They adapted too well to European culture and became dependent on it, readily turning on their relatives and cultural ideals to obtain the toys and trinkets of the white man.

There were many crazy theories as to how the Indians got here. One is that they came here by ferry from Europe, another that they were descendants from the lost continents of Mu and Atlantis. In the 1600's, the Puritans believed that they were the lost tribe of Israel who had wandered so far that they lost all their Godly traits and became children of the devil. The Puritan view was one that settled in with Europeans for two centuries. Modern anthropologists believe they migrated from Asia some 14,000 years ago across the Bering Straits when land bridges formed during the last Ice Age. Indians believe that the Great Spirit placed them here.

Whatever the case, they clashed with the outsiders and lost their lands and cultural identity as a result.

The Europeans started in the East for that was their quickest route across the Atlantic. They came in droves, like flies to a carcass, and by the time the Indians realized what was happening it was too late. Disease and devastating wars pushed the Indians West but demands for increased land by the whites never let up.

The Gold Rush was just another piece in a large jigsaw puzzle that brought whites across the continent in search of wealth. The Civil War offered the Indians a rare opportunity to reacquire some of their lands; after all, the white men were fighting each other! How could the President or Great White Father possibly send troops to fight Indians? Since the War of 1812 when it seemed that half the Indians sided with the British and the other half with the Americans, some of the most intense Indian warfare took place during America's Civil War years.

Not all Indians wanted to fight, but some joined the Union while others joined the Confederacy. Those that did fight saw it as a battle against whites in general. Those who aided the North thought that their military service would prove their loyalty and thus lead to better treatment after the war. Those who joined the South expecting a Confederate victory believed they would continue roaming the plains instead of imprisoned on reservations.

Whites lied to them in any way possible to get them to fight on their respective side. Certain tribes were drawn into the war whether they wanted to be or not, especially those in the Oklahoma Indian Territory. There were Five Civilized Tribes there, precariously caught between western mineral sources and the eastern Union government, not to mention that the territory was on the northern border of Texas, a southern state.

In 1861, the Confederate Government decided to annex all Indian Territory within Oklahoma and sent army officer Zebulon

Pike to negotiate. Pike lied by telling the Indians that after the South won the war, all treaty obligations previously made by the U.S. Government would be honored; furthermore, Pike promised the Indians a seat in the Confederate legislature and that Indian lands would never be redistributed as private property as the U.S. Government routinely did.

Based on these lies, many Oklahoma Indians pledged their support and loyalty to the South. The North negotiated as well. Later in 1861, John Ross, a Cherokee who had learned impeccable English, went to Washington to ask President Lincoln to continue annuity payments during the war for those Indians that remained loyal to the Union cause. Lincoln warned Ross that if the Indians sided with the South, the annuity payments would stop.

When Ross returned and informed his brothers what Lincoln had said, internal division took place between the 5 tribes, and even within the tribes themselves. The Creek for instance split with half joining the North and the other half with the South. The new treaty drawn up with the U.S. Government permitted the North to take half of Creek land. At the end of the war, the federal government was quite displeased with all Indians in the Oklahoma territory. Rather than separating the loyal from the disloyal, it was easier to band all of them in the region as traitors and usurp all the land.

Oliver "Grizzly" Jones got heavily involved with the Navajo after the war; nevertheless, the Navajo were just another tribe that suffered severely during the war. In 1863 in New Mexico, Colonel Kit Carson, with an army of 650 soldiers, began a winter campaign to force over 10,000 Navajo onto a reservation. For two years, the Navajo resisted the movement by fighting and then retreating to Canyon DeChelly. The canyon was horseshoe-shaped with high cliffs running along the rear and sides; so well fortified in fact, that the whites referred to it as the "Navajo Gibraltar." When Carson reached the canyon in 1863, his horses and even some men began freezing during an unusually brutal winter, some died.

Carson worked out a bold strategy. He left part of his army in front of the canyon, then snuck the rest of it to the rear where men were lowered downward eight hundred feet by ropes. The Navajo guarded the front only and did not think a rear attack possible. Caught in between, the Indians surrendered after a short battle. The army rounded them up and marched them four hundred miles to a reservation located in the desolate lands of eastern New Mexico. Like all removals, it was tragic and downright pathetic. The reservation contained some of the absolute worst lands in the state. None of the land was irrigated, leaving it unfit for people used to farming and grazing; as a result, hundreds died.

Many officers like Captain Oliver Jones, serving under General Carlton, sincerely tried to help the Indians. They cut their own men's rations in half and even more at times to aid the starving Indians. After the Civil War, the U.S. Government decided to force all Indians on reservations. Fighting continued for two decades until all were subdued. In 1871, the government sent the Navajo back to their homeland in DeChelly canyon with new cattle and seed, but seven years had been wasted in agony and there was little else the government could do to make up for it.

Oliver "Grizzly" Jones sold off his ranch in California that he had inherited from his parents to purchase an even larger one in Colorado Territory along the Arkansas River. Two thousand acres of land cost him $1,000 along the plains of what is now southeastern Colorado roughly 200 miles west of Dodge City, Kansas. Throughout the war, the most sustained and brutal fighting took place in this region by Plains' Indians. They attacked wagon trains, stagecoaches, and settlements. In the summer of 1864, Cheyenne and Arapaho warriors controlled all lines of communication east of Denver in the Colorado territory, so much so that the Union had to communicate by ship around the southern tip of South America to reach California and other far western settlements. After the war, the army moved in and forced them on reservations too.

Befriended by Grizzly Jones, one warrior, destined to become a chief, suffered serious wounds in a losing battle against Colonel John Chivington, a former Methodist preacher. Chivington shot Graywolf twice, once in the arm and once in the leg. Both were clean wounds passing through muscles and tendons without shattering any bones, but Graywolf had lost a lot of blood when Grizzly found him. Grizzly hoisted him on his broad back and took him to his ranch, dressed his wounds, and nursed him back to health. There were still a couple of German immigrants from Denver who were there completing the finishing touches to his new home, a good-size two story structure, much larger when compared to the single-story log style homes that most were building. It took a few extra weeks to finish the home, and for when Graywolf was well enough to depart.

"Where are ya gonna go?" Grizzly inquired.

"Back to my band," Graywolf replied. He had learned English after spending many winters at Fort Lyon near Denver. A common practice before confinement on reservations was to go to the nearest fort and surrender on the verge of winter. The army would then provide food and clothing. In the spring, the Indians would escape and go back on the warpath.

"Your band's been wiped out."

"Everyone?"

"Even the women and children," Grizzly said sadly.

Graywolf put his head down in his hands. There was a young girl who could potentially become his wife.

Grizzly placed a massive hand on his shoulder and said, "Why don't ya stay with me awhile? I've got a big ranch here that I just bought and I'm a gonna need a lot of help runnin it."

With his band exterminated and remnants of neighboring tribes moving further west from the ever-penetrating U.S. Army, Graywolf accepted. Grizzly would also profit from the arrangement since the Plains' Indians were the very best cavalry that North America had ever seen; after all, they used to run down buffalo with little more than spears and bow & arrows. Graywolf could handle a horse as well as a rifle.

Grizzly had his house completed in 1872, a few short weeks after he had picked up Graywolf. He hauled all his family's possessions from California to Colorado in two separate wagonloads. The wagons were stacked with crates from floor to ceiling, some he had not even sorted. Large items like furniture he either sold off in California or left them with the former estate. One day when he was unpacking an old crate, he found the lamp. The lamp remained unused for twenty-four years, when his father last used it. His mother, even if she knew of its existence, had never discovered the secret within.

"Never seen that before," Grizzly muttered to himself. He looked it over from front to back, shrugged, and didn't think much of it. He wasn't even sure what it was but thought it would look all right on the mantel. He simply placed it there. Within a year, he had acquired two houseguests: a Cheyenne warrior, and a baby mountain lion. It wasn't his intention to pick up strays, but he was always a big man with a heart to match.

The year 1874 was when Grizzly seriously began raising cattle. With the help of barbed wire fencing—that cost twice as much as the land—and then the addition of twenty Hereford cows and four nice-sized prize bulls imported from England, Grizzly had the beginnings of a fine ranch.

His pet cat "Killer" was gradually beginning to accept Graywolf as a permanent resident. Killer was quite tame around Grizzly and slept with him every night, but Killer didn't care for most strangers. Grizzly could control the 175-pound tawny cat with a good slap or kick if necessary, but no one else dared. Killer was outside all day to hunt freely or do whatever lazy well-fed cats do, usually not straying more than a few miles from home. Grizzly, realizing that the cat might eventually attack his horses and cows as it grew, trained it at an early age to get along with the other animals. He and the cat routinely slept in the barn so that both the cat and the more docile grazing animals assimilated. Unlike wild cougars, Killer grew up hunting small game exclusively such as rabbits, squirrels, and birds.

Also, 1875 was the year that problems arose, big trouble. The nearest homestead was the Johnson Family's spread about ten miles north. Grizzly had never met them except for little Jimmy Johnson, the one who was hunting cougars at the time. With her son Jimmy in tow, Emma Johnson rode in near midnight during a cold rainy April night. When Grizzly was aroused from his sleep, he could both see and feel the terror despite the drenched ratty looking forms hovering outside of his door.

"Can ya help us mister?" Emma pleaded.

Just then, a little snarl was heard behind Grizzly, "Shut up cat." Grizzly only half turned but gave the cat a stern intimidating look and a little growl of his own. "Well, don't stand there getting wetter if that's possible, come on in and don't mind the cat, he's just a big baby." The cougar bound upstairs it what seemed like a flash of two or three steps before the Johnsons could see him. It didn't help that their heads and faces were dripping like a slow but steady running faucet. "Come on over here to the fireplace," Grizzly beckoned as he grabbed a few kindling sticks and one thicker piece of oak to get the embers going again.

"I knows him momma; he's the one who took ma gun when I was huntin them mountin lions."

"Hush child," Emma held her hand up to slap him but didn't follow through. She realized that they were in desperate need and didn't want things to get off to a bad start.

Grizzly had heard though and chuckled, "Yup, I remember you too little fellar, only you was a might smaller back then. Anyways, I want to show you somethin." He went upstairs almost as fast as the cat and found Killer hiding between the bed and the wall. "Come on ya big baby," he said coaxing and then half dragging the big cat downstairs.

Emma gasped; it was just one more thing she needed to frighten her into total lunacy that night.

"It's all right," said Grizzly, "This here is the same rascal that yer boy tried to kill that day. One of the best friends I ever had." Killer cowered behind Grizzly like a shy dog and then followed him out to the kitchen where Grizzly set a pot of coffee on the wood stove. He looked back at his visitors. The boy was fair-haired like his mother, tired, but with a little wildness to him as one would expect. Though she was getting a few lines around her eyes, Emma was a looker, no doubt about that.

By this time, Graywolf had long awoken before Grizzly, but allowed the big man to handle things while he cautiously remained out of sight. He slipped out the back to take the Johnson horse into the barn when he figured that all was safe inside. He now returned from the barn through the front door of the house.

"Ahhhh!" Emma screamed; this was just too much. The sight of the lithe wild-looking but slim Indian clad in buckskin with a dangerous looking tomahawk strapped to his waist belt was the last straw. She turned as pale as new fallen snow and sort of half fainted, partially coherent but a bit out of it too.

Grizzly took several long quick paces toward her and placed a massive hand on her tiny shoulder, "No need to worry ma'am, this is my other good friend Graywolf, he's with me."

"Howdy," said Graywolf. He had picked up much in the way of the local English dialect and rarely spoke the Cheyenne language any longer.

The big, bearded man with his pet lion and Indian pal were very odd looking now that all three were together. Emma shook her head a little to try to clear her vision.

"I don't think that we've properly introduced ourselves yet," said Grizzly. "Ya know Graywolf and my cat Killer, well I'm Oliver Jones, but ma frens jus call me Grizzly. I think it's the beard," he added as he tugged it and laughed. He thrust out a huge hand to meet her small but coarse one.

With her mind and vision cleared up some, she said, "I'm Emma Johnson as her hand disappeared completely within Grizzly's. "This here's ma boy Jimmy."

"Glad to meet ya again son," Grizzly said as he strode over and enveloped the boy's hand as well. Jimmy had been sitting wide-eyed and speechless as the cat, followed by the Indian, had all entered the living room of the big man's home. Graywolf followed and shook hands with them too, but they were a little afraid of him. In the 1870's, virtually everyone living in Indian country out West had both experiences and had heard nasty rumors, whether true, untrue, or greatly embellished, about the savageness and brutality that Indians could administer to white folks.

Grizzly finally set out to satisfy his curiosity after they had managed to shell shock their guests, "So what brings ya'll out this way?"

Emma looked over at Jimmy, and she could see that the boy was haggard and worn out, and he was young at that. She knew that her own energy level was even worse, but like nearly all mothers, the kid or kids came first. "Have you got a place where I can put Jimmy to sleep first?"

"We got an extra bed," answered Grizzly.

"The boy can have my bed," interrupted Graywolf.

Emma thought for a moment, and then accepted. She would get the extra bed upstairs and Jimmy would sleep in Graywolf's bed downstairs. Graywolf would sleep on a bearskin on the living room floor. When they laid Jimmy to rest, Emma waddled back in, sunk in the same chair, forced her eyes to stay open, and began her story.

"Me and Jimmy was in the barn when these 4 men rode up to our place. My man Jim was fixin the corral fence when he heard shots. We come runnin outside and saw one of our cows shot dead. Lucky they didn't see us. One of 'em said 'We gonna eat good tonight boys.' Jim swore at 'em and told 'em to get off our land. They jus laughed and started shootin every which way. Well Jim tried to get in the house, but they rode him down and kicked him from their horses. He picked up a pitchfork to use against when they, they, ..." Emma started sobbing.

Grizzly waited a moment and said softly, "Go on."

"They shot him, four or five times, maybe more." Emma paused as she sobbed further. "Me and Jimmy hid in the barn 'til dark and rode down here cuz we'd heard that somebody lived this way."

What could he do but help? A woman and boy had been wronged, a grave injustice to say the least. "Well Mrs. Johnson, you can stay here as long as you like. You got any other family around here?"

"Nope, my husban's family lives back East, never met 'em. My own mum died when I was ten. My dad and brothers were killed in the war. I'm alone now 'cept for Jimmy."

"Well like I said, you can stay here." He paused, a little on the shy side now. She was a beautiful woman, and her hair was beginning to dry, long and light brown, not quite blonde, but full and thick. He wasn't used to having a woman around and had lost a little of his easy-going confident manner when he stared at her too long. "Uh, uh, lemme show ya yer room," he finally said to break what was beginning to be an awkward silence.

"Thank you, Mr. Jones," she said relieved. Tired didn't begin to describe her condition.

With the Johnsons tucked in, Grizzly sat up awhile with Graywolf and said, "Whattaya think partner?"

"Big trouble," answered Graywolf.

"I'll bet ya that it's some no good bastards over from Dodge City."

"Bastards?"

"Nasty ya know, rotten to the core."

"Like a bad apple?"

"Yup, close enough." The two talked awhile longer before retiring.

In the morning, Grizzly awoke to a freshly cooked steak and egg breakfast. The eggs came from a few chickens that Grizzly kept in a fortified coop and Emma had sent Jimmy out to retrieve them, just like he would have done back home. Killer avoided the cows, but he often looked hungrily at the chickens.

"I could get used to this," said Grizzly as he tore into his food.

When they finished, Jimmy asked politely, "Is there anything I kin do Mr. Jones?"

"Graywolf might need a hand milking the cows if yer up to it." Although he generally allowed the milk of his breeding cows to dry up once the calves were of age to feed on their own, Grizzly milked a few younger cows perpetually because he liked milk. Killer also profited from this arrangement.

Jimmy sped away, which left Grizzly alone with Emma. She was certainly much easier on the eyes in the morning. At twenty-eight years of age, she was a tough lean somewhat petite pioneer woman with hair down to her shoulders and big sparkling brown eyes that lit up his table like nothing had before. Grizzly was only five years older. Although the male population plummeted during the war, women, at least those of a marriageable nature, could be scarce in the Western territories, especially with isolated settlements like the one Grizzly inhabited. Widows usually did not last long out here either.

"Is there anything else you can tell me about these fellars?" Grizzly broke the ice.

"I, I think I told you all there was last night." She thought for a moment, and to Grizzly, she was cute as a button as her forehead wrinkled as she strained to think. "Wait, I do recall one of 'em said that he always wanted a nice ranch with lots of cows."

"That it?"

"Yeah, I think so, it was dark, and we was hidin'."

"Rustlers, damn rustlers of the worst kind," said Grizzly. "Bad enough they steal cows, but to shoot a man and take his ranch is another matter."

"I been thinkin'," said Emma. "I'm gonna have to find me a sheriff or marshal somewhere to take care of them guys. I was wonderin' if I could borrow one of your horses, mine might still be done in some."

"Whoa, hold on there little lady, the nearest marshal is probably in Denver and ya probably won't find him for a few weeks even if ya make it there. Anyways, it's 150 miles north through rough mountain country, and you might run into a stray Indian or two. Me an' Graywolf will take care of this," he added firmly.

"I jus got to do somethin'," she said.

"Tell you what, you sit tight here, me an' Graywolf will go check things out." Grizzly rose from the table, found a pair of colts, strapped on his belt, put his boots on, and was off to the barn in search of Graywolf. Grizzly did nothing more than nod at his

Indian friend. Graywolf nodded back, added a rifle to go with his ever-present tomahawk, and the two saddled up horses with the intent of paying a little visit to the Johnson ranch.

It wasn't hard to find. Billowing smoke was visible for miles away as the Johnson cabin had been set afire in the morning light. It a little over an hour, they switched into stealth mode as they got within a mile. At a half a mile out, they dropped from their horses, tied them off, and approached cautiously on foot. The four rustlers were busy rounding up cattle, the only thing of real value on the Johnson ranch, aside from Emma Grizzly thought. The thought of them catching and ravishing her was enough to motivate Grizzly into passing his own death sentence on the quartet. The Johnsons had accumulated 138 head worth $25 each, a good sum of money back in the day.

It was now time to be patient and scope out the situation. They decided to wait for several hours while the round up was in progress. They could have picked a couple of them off with rifles, but Grizzly wanted to catch them all alive, together. Using boulders and high grass for cover, they edged a little closer, close enough to notice the body of Jim Johnson not far from a couple of dead cows that they had shot. Hordes of flies hovered about the bloody carcasses. One of the thieves was hacking away at a dead cow, likely slicing off a few steaks for their ill-gotten meal.

Grizzly motioned Graywolf and pointed toward the barn, the last remaining structure that the thieves had not set afire. They edged that way, crawling now through tall grass. Graywolf seemed to be naturally better at stealth and now led the way. They edged close enough along the rear of the barn to hear two of the men talking. Suddenly, the alarm sounded. The man slicing up the dead cow was yelling and pointing to the others. Grizzly and Graywolf were not those discovered, but Emma. They saw Emma Johnson in the distance kicking up dust from her horse as she rode straight for what had been her home.

"Damn," muttered Grizzly. Before Grizzly and Graywolf were in position to spring, two of the men leaped on their horses and were off to meet Emma. In her haste, she had not loaded her rifle. When she slowed to fire, nothing happened. By the time she scrambled for bullets, the two were upon her. One of them leapt from his horse to hers, struck her in the jaw, and they both went down into the dirt. A minute later, they tied Emma's hands behind her back, and led her back to her burned out ranch. She was conscious but dazed.

"Whatta we have here boys?" The man who spoke was a bit bigger than the others, though still three inches shorter than Grizzly, but he did appear to be the leader of the group. He rudely knocked Emma's hat off and brushed her hair back. He ran his fingers down a large red welt that was forming along her left jaw line.

"Will you look at that boys! I haven't seen a woman that purdy since the whores in Dodge City. I think I'll go first boys, y'all can fight for sloppy seconds! Tie her down to the ground," he commanded as he began unbuttoning his pants. Emma tried to struggle, but two pairs of rough dirty hands grabbed each of her arms and forced her to the ground.

It may not have been his initial strategy, but to Grizzly, a prime opportunity presented itself. The four men were together now in one place, and Emma certainly provided an attention-grabbing distraction.

"Well boys, I do believe that that there woman is the last you'll ever see," announced Grizzly with two big Colt.45 revolvers pointed at them. He made sure to aim one directly at the leader's heart. At this time, Graywolf remained out of sight flanking around the band of thieves to get clear open shots if necessary.

Grizzly could present a large obstacle had he approached directly in the big man's footsteps.

"Up with your hands!" ordered Grizzly.

As one man slowly started pulling up his hands from knee to waist level, quick as lightning, he drew his revolver. Two bullets pierced him before the revolver completely cleared his holster, once by Grizzly and another from Graywolf.

"Anybody else?" Grizzly calmly pointed one gun back and forth between two of the standing thieves while keeping one on the leader. The mystery of the second shot revealed itself when Graywolf came into sight with rifle raised and ready to shoot again.

"What er ya gonna do with us?" sneered the leader, caught with his pants down.

"Shut up and keep your hands up," Grizzly said as he nodded to Graywolf. Graywolf collected their guns and tied them up as Grizzly kept his guns trained on them. Once he had them subdued, Graywolf backed off some but kept his rifle leveled.

Grizzly rushed to Emma's side and untied her, "You all right darlin'?"

"No, well yeah I guess."

"Are you hurt?"

"No, not that," she said.

"Oh," Grizzly was a little concerned. Women, he was thinking to himself, but he understood some when she went and kicked the man in the head who had hit her, and then kicked the leader too for good measure. When she went to retrieve her rifle, that is when he stopped her.

"They're thieves, no good rustlers, and they killed ma husband! They deserve to die, and I'm aimin' to shoot 'em."

"Emma, let us take care of it."

"What're you gonna do?"

"Yeah," the ringleader said snidely as he had been listening, "What er ya gonna do with us?"

During the nineteenth century in Europe, men celebrated each other's cunning in stealing neighboring cattle, or perhaps ending up with a few more than they started with when they drove them to market. In the American West, men hung rustlers and murderers.

"You're gonna hang, "Grizzly promptly answered. There was a big oak tree a few hundred feet from the burned-out home. Grizzly consulted with Emma before proceeding, "Is this all right with you?"

"Hangin's too good for 'em but it's the best we kin do," said Emma. She had put her rifle down at Grizzly's urging.

Grizzly held his guns on the prisoners as Graywolf scrambled up the tree to rig up a rope. There were some nice strong lower branches, but high enough up where they would have to sit the prisoners on their horses to do the trick. Grizzly threw them up one by one on their respective horses, not really knowing whose horse belonged to whom, but it really didn't matter.

He got on his own horse to loop the rope around their necks, gave them a minute or two to pray or say any last words, and then proceeded to slap the horse out from under them. If there was one positive about hanging, it tended to be a silent execution since the rope cut off both sound and circulation, though a last gasp or two could sometimes be heard. Grizzly dropped each one after that last breath since he only had one rope. When they were finished, they lit a fire with some cut wood on hand and burned the bodies. They did take the time to give Jim Johnson Sr. a proper burial.

The Johnson farm was sold soon afterward to some English immigrants. Grizzly and Emma were married a few months later when a suitable preacher passed through. The cattle moved into one herd over to Grizzly's larger ranch. Emma did the usual womanly tasks of keeping the big house clean by sweeping the floors and whatnot; nevertheless, she was an outdoor girl and spent more time outdoors helping with the cattle and other chores. She never gave the lamp on the mantel a thorough dusting, never enough to release the Djinni.

One could wonder if the Djinni had anything to do with the rustlers. The bigger question might just center about the Djinni knowingly or unknowingly contributing to their fateful outcome. Was there a connection? If so, did the Djinni actually draw a line between deserved or righteous killings as opposed to unrighteous? Is there such a thing? Or in other words, can killing ever be righteous? Perhaps only a higher power knows, maybe the creator of good such as angels and evil like devils and perhaps Djinnis, but maybe Djinnis were just in between somewhere.

The lamp would eventually pass into the hands of their youngest daughter Catherine Jones, some twenty-two years later. The lamp always fascinated Catherine, but she never gave it enough attention in her youth while residing at the ranch in Colorado. A young clean-cut lieutenant previously stationed at Fort Lyon whisked Catherine off to Michigan when she was eighteen. Later that year in 1897, Catherine would bear her only child, a daughter that she named Rachel.

Former Lieutenant Robert Stringer resumed his place at his father's farm in Michigan when his commission ended. Stringer had also helped in placing Indians on reservations, but he was not as kind or merciful as Grizzly. He oversaw a group of men who took to killing Indians if they gave even the smallest amount of resistance. He was often involved in petty little skirmishes that at times resulted in the extermination of small bands or even entire villages on occasion.

For the most part, the Jones family had been isolated from this type of cruel behavior and the young lieutenant had seemed to be concerned, understanding, and a nice enough fellow to them;

nevertheless, outward appearances can often be deceiving. When Stringer asked for Grizzly's daughter's hand in marriage, Grizzly was all for it. His only reservation was that there was the possibility that they would never see Catherine again.

PART VI: MODERN TIMES

"The wishing gate opens into nothing." - Charles Haddon Spurgeon

CHAPTER XXVI

The first few years of the twentieth century included discoveries and notable deaths. Queen Victoria of England finally passed on after a lengthy run and Edward VII succeeded her. Leon Czolgosz, an infamous anarchist, assassinated US President McKinley in 1901. A new vibrant Theodore Roosevelt took the bull by the horns and assumed the presidency. A few short years later, Orville and Wilbur Wright flew their first airplane at Kitty Hawk while Henry Ford organized the Ford Motor Company in Dearborn, Michigan, some 90 miles south of the Stringer farm.

With young Robert Stringer in control of the farm, the elder Stringers planned on their first long trip to visit relatives in Galveston, Texas in 1900. They never made it. They took a train to Chicago where they boarded a steamship on the Mississippi River. From Chicago they travelled to New Orleans, to the Gulf of Mexico, and then on to Galveston Bay where their ship and all its occupants perished during one of the most powerful hurricanes ever to strike the eastern coast of Texas.

The year 1900 was also a bad year for Catherine Stringer. Since the death of her in-laws, her husband had been very moody and had not accepted the death of his parents well. One fall morning as Catherine was baking bread, she heard a crash of broken glass followed by a scream. Three-year-old Rachel had knocked over Robert's last bottle of whiskey, one that was nearly full. A thin trickle of blood streamed down her cut leg like a miniature rivulet.

"Damn kid, that was my last bottle," Robert said as he strode over to Rachel, picked her up roughly, and proceeded to spank her violently.

"Stop that Robert!" Catherine commanded.

"Here, you take this rotten kid," Robert answered as he forcibly shoved her to Catherine. By now, the child was wailing as loudly as humanly possible for her young vocal cords.

Catherine took Rachel into the kitchen, pumped some water onto a cloth, removed a minute chard of glass, and cleansed the wound gently as only a mother can.

"Can't you shut that damn kid up?" Robert shouted from the other room. Rachel had just settled down some when Robert staggered into the kitchen. At the sight of him, Rachel burst into tears again followed by loud wailing.

"I said SHUT UP!" Robert yelled as he approached the girl threateningly.

Catherine stepped in between them to provide some measure of protection for her daughter, "What's gotten into you anyway? Can't you see that the child is hurt? It's all your fault anyways, if you'd stay away from that bottle, we wouldn't have these kinds of problems."

"Why don't you shut up too," said Robert.

"I'll not have you talk to me that way Robert Stringer."

Rachel was still sobbing when smoke began pouring out of the oven. Catherine rushed over to the oven, shut it off, and pulled out two burnt loaves of bread. She was a fair cook, but cooking was more difficult then since ovens did not have timers, thermostats, or other modern conveniences. "Look what you made me do," Catherine said to Robert, irritated.

It was then Robert did something he'd never done before. He hit her, a solid blow with a closed fist to the right side of her face. She staggered backwards and fell. Robert left her there and headed for town to acquire more liquor. Within a few minutes, her right eye looked much like the uneatable blackened bread. When she regained full consciousness, she burst out crying. Rachel cried along with her.

It was not that difficult to understand Robert Stringer's behavior. His own father used to hit him, his mother too. The majority of wife and child abusers grew up in a family where such actions were commonplace. Robert had always been a little off, and downright mean. As a child, he took pleasure in torturing insects, burning frogs, shooting birds with his BB gun, and even mutilating cats. His detestable behavior went towards his family more often since it had little else to target. Problems with alcohol only made it worse.

As a few years passed by, Rachel grew up to be a plump red-faced homely child with thin wispy brown hair about her rounded and freckled face. Even her green eyes were unattractive; more of a murky color as compared to her mother's more brightly featured emerald eyes. Rachel constantly feared for her father, especially if she did anything that altered in the slightest way from his exacting commands. His rigid army training had taken a turn for the worse when he treated his wife and child more and more like the Indians that he once brutally persecuted.

Catherine suffered harsher treatment than did Rachel. She tried her best to protect her daughter, often stepping between the girl and her violent father. Catherine could not accept the treatment quite as easily. Rachel was raised with it, but Catherine, being the youngest, had been spoiled by her father, Grizzly Jones. It was her mother, Emma, who disciplined her most, but that was just with minor spankings and an occasional slap; on the other hand, Grizzly was a gentle giant and rarely touched her. Overall, it was nothing compared to her husband's brutal treatment, who now hit her at the least provocation. She wished that she could write a letter home, but she was too embarrassed.

It was Catherine's best friend Irene who figured out what was going on. Irene lived on a neighboring farm and put two and two together to come up with a solid four; after all, one could only fall down the stairs so many times, run into doors, trip over things, and so forth. With divorce being such a stigma in the early twentieth century, Catherine continued to hang on to Robert. Divorce was unheard of and those who went through with it faced ostracization from the community. She still wrote letters to her family in Colorado about her life embellishing the good while failing to mention Robert's increasingly ugly behavior. "Take Rachel with you an' go back to Colorado," Irene said quite often, urging her to leave him.

Catherine finally came to that conclusion on her own in the summer of 1908. The farm suffered neglect, no one made necessary repairs , nor did anyone take care of the corn and wheat, and Catherine and Rachel alone tended to the animals. For the last two years, Catherine had slept in the same room as Rachel. She learned that her husband often visited a prostitution house in a ratty part of downtown Bay City, Michigan. That was okay with her since he had been leaving her alone for some time in that regard. The love had mostly died the day he first hit her, and what remained eroded completely away within a few short months.

A new problem that arose was that Robert was becoming more and more frequently short of cash. One night, when he could not scrounge up enough money to visit the local whorehouse, he decided that he had enough of sleeping alone at night in his own home no less. Catherine was a woman, HIS woman more precisely, and he believed that she should fulfill her wifely duties as he saw fit; after all, HE was the man of the house. One night, he boldly entered her and Rachel's bedroom, forcibly picked Catherine up, and hauled her off to his room with her kicking and screaming.

"Let me down!" She screamed aloud swatting him with her open hands in the process.

He threw her upon his bed, no, their bed, none-too-gently either and said, "You'd better realize your place woman, and it's here, in MY bed." He proceeded to tear away her nightgown as she resisted.

"Leave me alone!" She screamed out as she clawed at his face. She drew blood, which only served to enrage him further.

"Shut up bitch," and he hit her several times in the face and in the side of her head. The shots drove a small bone chip above her eyebrow deeper into her cranium, so deep that it lodged itself in the outer region of her soft brain tissue as she drifted off into unconsciousness. At this time, Rachel lay with her head in her arms sobbing amidst the screams of her mother. The eleven-year-old girl was frightened, but was not quite old enough to understand completely what her mother experienced. The noise suddenly died off and Rachel could only here the grunts of her father as he did his business and then left during the night shortly thereafter.

Catherine did not wake up until the morning, and when she did, she had a splitting headache. To accompany a slight concussion, the chip was applying its own pressure; thus, causing a severe migraine. It was then she decided it was time to take Rachel and herself away from this cruel, unstable man. She sent Rachel to the barn to do the milking while she began packing that same day and, fortunately for her, Robert would not return until well into the night.

She took the dusty old lamp down from the mantel. No one had touched it since she moved to Michigan some eight years ago in the year 1900. On a farm, most did not bother cleaning the knick-knacks and baubles since there was always so much else to do. The dust was so thick on the lamp that she took a cloth and decided to clean it up some before packing it away.

Like a funeral urn, she had mostly forgotten about it. It just sat there day after day, week after week, month after month, and year after year, and now, eight years had passed. She blew on it first and a cloud of dust shimmered in the sunlight, as it too would settle mostly on the floor. As she rubbed and rubbed, a new cloud materialized in the shape much like an exotic but fat Middle Eastern man as it poured forth from the spout.

"What is it you wish wench?"

"What?" Her head was hurting so bad now that she wondered if the cold stare of this towering form was just some sort of weird illusion.

"You have 3 wishes," it bellowed out in a deep impatient voice, "What is your first request?"

Without thinking long and hard which may not have been possible given her aching head, she just blurted out more in frustration and anger, "I wish that my husband was dead." The Djinni whisked away. Had she been more alert and not stricken with a blurring pain, she may have noticed a little smile, or maybe just a slight leering grin, upon the Djinni's face right before it disappeared back into its prison.

The next day, when she was all packed up and ready to leave with Rachel, she decided to take one last look at her pathetic excuse for a husband. She peered into his room, the room that she had once shared with him. He was lying there with his clothes on, passed out she surmised. It wasn't unusual, but the next thing she became aware of was the strong smell. He wasn't moving.

She crept a little closer and noticed that his chest was not moving as it should. Then she noticed his face and screamed. He had a sickly smile with his yellowed teeth sticking out. His eyes were open wider than usual, and a putrid odor arose even stronger from his dead body. It might be that she was just closer now, but she solved that by slowly backing off.

"What's the matter momma?"

"Nothing honey," Catherine said as she closed the door, "Daddy's a little sick is all. We need to get the doctor." They went into town together and Dr. Jacobson followed them back in horse and buggy. He actually owned a new Detroit Electric, a battery-powered automobile that he used about town, but he still preferred a horse for rural travel.

"Well, it looks like his heart just stopped beating," Dr. Jacobson concluded. "Did he drink a lot?"

"Yes," Catherine answered a little hesitantly.

"Doesn't help," he said as he put his arm around her shoulder. "I'll take care of the body but might need a little help getting it into my cart." He was not elderly, but at 57 years of age, he had far fewer years ahead of him than behind. "You've got a bit of a bump on your head too Mrs. Stringer, mind if I take a look?"

"Sure."

"Put a little of this on it," he handed her a small dark amber bottle of iodine. "It'll sting some but stop infection."

"Okay."

"Does it hurt much?"

"Oh, just a little," she lied but did not know why.

"Rest is always good. Let me know if it gets any worse."

"Okay."

When the doctor rode off, Catherine had hidden the lamp deep within one of her trunks. Her head hurt terribly now, and she wished now that she had been more up front with the doctor. She sat down and decided to unpack; after all, her husband was the reason she was leaving and. She felt guilty nonetheless.

Irene Abernathy, Catherine's good friend, proved to be most helpful. She accompanied Catherine to the funeral and even sent her sixteen year-old son out to the Stringer farm since she had nine children and could certainly spare one. The boy was a little on the fat side but strong, and a good hard worker. He was not the sharpest tool in the shed, but he had a solid working knowledge of farm life.

Catherine's condition continued to worsen. She looked downright awful, but most people thought that it was due to stress from the death of her husband. Eventually, the bone chip continued to exert too much pressure as it sank deeper into her brain until it ruptured. She died of a massive brain hemorrhage two weeks and a day after her husband had passed. She never tried to use the lamp a second time.

"I was quiet, a loner. I was one of those children where, if you put me in a room and gave me some crayons and a pencil, you wouldn't hear from me for nine straight hours. And I was always drawing racing cars and rockets and spaceships and planes, things that were very fast that would take me away." - Gary Oldman

———◉———

CHAPTER XXVII

———◉———

"BRAD! BRAD! COME ON Brad, WAKE UP!"

Brad rolled over and sat upright, "All right ma, shit, just quit pounding on the door, I'm up."

"Well get your lazy ass out of bed, vacation is over with, and I'm not gonna waste my time every damn morning trying to wake you up," announced his mother in a none-too-friendly business-like manner. Mrs. Walker would anyhow, as Brad would forgetfully fail to set his alarm clock the next morning.

At sixteen years of age, Bradley Walker was of average height, a bit on the skinny side with thick dark brown hair. His hair was getting quite long, an inch or so past his ears. His mother finally relented after months of arguing and begging her to let his hair grow out. It was the latest fad and since virtually everyone else was growing it out, why shouldn't he? Long hair was the "in" thing, especially since The Beatles had invaded America a short time ago. Brad also had dark brown eyes, wore geeky looking horn-rimmed glasses, and as an average teenager, sported jeans and a T-shirt as typical warm weather attire. Since it was wintertime, it was necessary to cover the T-shirt with a flannel or sweatshirt.

Brad jumped into the shower with the depressing feeling that Christmas vacation was over. The temperature outside hovered a little above zero degrees on a cold January sixth morning in 1964. There was no concern with global warming just yet, particularly in a northern state like Michigan. Michigan winters at the time were not exactly wild, but those in the Lower Peninsula were easier to tolerate than those of the Upper. Brad wiped up half-heartedly, dressed quickly, strolled downstairs, and at 6:45 a.m., he was ready for his ice-cold bowl of cereal to match the weather outside. After inhaling the corn flakes, he returned upstairs, brushed his teeth, threw on his coat and hat, grabbed his books, said a quick good-bye to his mother, avoided her attempt at an irritating kiss good-bye, and was out the door at 6:58 a.m. waiting for the 7:02 a.m. bus.

In the four minutes of waiting, Brad smiled knowingly that by early spring, he wouldn't have to ride the bus any longer. His dad had promised to buy him an old car this month now that Brad had a job and could afford the maintenance and upkeep. It would be a delayed Christmas present but one worth waiting for; nevertheless, his dad warned him that he only had a couple of hundred dollars to spend, maybe $250, and the car would likely need a little work. Brad did have confidence in his dad however, as his dad seemed to be quite mechanically inclined. Of course, engines and the basics workings of automobiles were far simpler mechanically before the age of computers made the backyard mechanic virtually obsolete.

When the somewhat rounded 1959 Chevrolet school bus pulled up, Brad hopped aboard and scooted in with his best friend Tony. Tony Thornton sat in the middle of the bus away from the weirdoes in front, but far enough away from the burnouts in the back. Tony was a bit shorter than Brad, a little rounder, but similarly dressed. Their immediate conversation centered on Christmas.

"Whaddya get?" Brad broke in.

"My old man bought us a pool table," stated Tony who was not only referring to himself, but his little brothers too. He was dark complexioned and came from a big Italian Catholic family. "My mom got us the usual shit, you know, socks, underwear, shirts, and pants."

"Yeah, that's a drag man, I got that stuff too; you know they have to buy that shit any way."

"Yeah man, what did your dad get you?"

"Nothing," answered Brad saving his little surprise for affect.

"Aw come on Brad, you guys ain't poor, so what'd he get you?"

Brad couldn't hold out any longer, "He said that after Christmas when it warms up some that he's gonna get me a car!"

"Wow! My dad told me that I couldn't have a car 'til I'm eighteen and have a job too. Any ways, I can't even get my license 'til March, won't be sixteen until then. What kind of car are you going to get?"

"I don't know yet, but since my dad works for Chevrolet and likes GM cars, it'll probably be a Chevy or Pontiac or something like that."

They arrived at school at 7:22 a.m. They shared the same locker and after dropping some books off, they parted at 7:30 a.m. as the first warning bell rang. Nothing like the old school bells to prepare one for factory life. Bay City Southern High School was essentially a lower to middle class, perhaps working-class school located near Saginaw Bay on Lake Huron in central eastern Michigan.

Bay City was primarily a factory town with strong union ties with both the United Auto Workers and the Teamsters. Out of the 450 high school students of driving age, only about forty of them were regular drivers to school while thirty-two of these owned the cars that they drove. Out of that thirty-two, only a handful were juniors and Brad contemplated joining that select few as he drifted off during a boring first hour of English Lit. Thinking of cars was certainly more interesting than the age-old drama of Romeo and Juliet. Seven-thirty-five in the morning was way too early to get into the swing of high school especially the first day after a nice, long winter break.

"Pay attention Brad," commanded Mrs. Jenson. Brad was off somewhere with the radio playing loud and his arm out the window when she broke his reverie. He looked up at the old, wrinkled face of Mrs. Jenson and tried to look attentive, but the minute she looked elsewhere, his mind wandered back to where he would park his car in the student parking lot: maybe next to fat Sandra Poleski's Volkswagen, or Jimmy Dickerson's '49 Mercury, or maybe Eugene Sanilac's brand-new Chevrolet Corvair. He jumped back into reality when Mrs. Jenson began assigning parts in the play that each one of the students would have to read aloud in class starting tomorrow, bummer.

Second hour was much brighter than first. Physical Education was usually fun and if you were bored, you could at least look at the girls in their shorts, the shorter the better. Mr. Givens at least kept you active, and for the next two weeks, they'd be playing floor hockey indoors. Indoors would be the norm for a good three months. The first day or two of a new sport was usually dull since that was when the coaches explained all the rules, boundaries, and whatever.

Third hour Geometry wasn't that bad either. Tony was in this class with him, but since the class sat in alphabetic order, the arrangement kept them apart. Mr. Peterson wasn't too bad. After his basic lecture of the day on similar polygons, he would let the students move freely about the class if they settled down, weren't too loud, and didn't cause any trouble. They could work together in pairs, groups, or there were always a few weird loner-types like the fat girls or the total nerds, a rare few of whom would grow up to be anarchists or reds.

Fourth hour consisted of World History and lots of 8mm or 16mm monotone black & white movies. Mr. Slater had the distinction of being the most boring teacher in the entire school. At least 3 times out of the 5 days of class per week, he showed old black-and-white history movies on an old rickety projector which undoubtedly like clockwork, broke down thrice during each movie. Some of the films had more spliced scotch tape than actual film cells.

Mr. Slater liked war movies and some of the WWII footage wasn't bad at times; nevertheless, the movie today was exceptionally terrible since it consisted mostly of still images and a narrator who was talking about some war in Spain in the 16th century. When the projector broke down the first time, everyone clapped. Mr. Slater became quite irritated, especially since he thought he was doing them great favors by showing him these movies, many which he personally owned. Back in the day, he didn't see movies as a student and felt that he was far ahead in a technological sense as a teacher. To avoid smacked smack in the head with a yardstick, Brad managed to keep his eyes open at least, and pointed at the old freestanding tripod screen.

Lunch break was a welcome relief after that movie. Brad met Tony in the cafeteria and exchanged banter about the day so far. The food was miserable, consisting of bloated noodles with chicken or chicken-like gravy, Jell-O for dessert, and a small carton of milk to drink. There wasn't much chicken in the gravy and small of the bones remained; as a result, every third or fourth person received one. The line went fast as the cooks had grown quite efficient with slapping globs of food on hard plastic trays that they rudely shoved in front of them. For the extreme derelicts, it would be good practice for when they ate later in prison. After receiving their food, Brad and Tony sat down to eat. A few seconds later, a sharp crunching sound emanated from Tony's mouth.

"Shit, it's a damn bone."

Brad laughed and then cautiously ran his fork in his own gravy. He didn't find anything suspicious. "Have you tried the Jell-O yet?"

"No," answered Tony.

"It's rotten, er, I mean bad, tastes bad." Brad finished his milk and opened the carton completely at the top from both ends. He proceeded to spoon his Jell-O into the carton.

"That bad huh," said Tony. Tony ate half of his, looked about cautiously for any authority figure, and then did the same thing as Brad with the rest. He quickly folded the milk carton back into its original shape. This was trick to fool school employees who were strict about wasting food. The monitors forced into cafeteria duty usually insisted that students clean their plates. To protest, the students in the know simply stuffed their unwanted food into their empty milk cartons and folded them back up.

Fifth and last hour consisted of Biology. It was not an easy class, especially when Mrs. Cramer tested them on all those bizarre Latin phylum and species names. It was not a class for the squeamish either. So far, they dissected sheep hearts, worms, and crayfish, but the coming attractions for the New Year meant bigger and better things like frogs, cats, and possibly pig embryos if Mrs. Cramer could secure them.

The room always stunk of formaldehyde especially with all the glass jars of preserved animals lying around like snakes, rats, hearts and other organs of various creatures, baby deer, turtles, and so on. Mrs. Cramer was just a bit creepy and collected these things as ambitiously as Mr. Slater did with his old films. It looked like the last thing they would be cutting up were frogs before the first semester ended in a few short weeks.

School ended at 1:10 p.m., which was a little unusual. Due to overcrowding from those annoying baby boomers, the school ran on split shifts, morning for the high school, and afternoons to early evenings for the middle school. Brad usually worked two or three hours after school each day and more on weekends at the Bay City Children's Zoo. His job was to feed the animals and shovel the paths to and from the barns. The business was more of a petting zoo that closed in the winter, and many of the animals lived in cages within barns during the cold season. His mom usually picked him up from school and dropped him off at the zoo, which was just a few short miles from their home.

Brad had keys to the padlocks on the barns and ordinarily saw his boss on Saturdays. The first barn contained electricity and the only running water. Brad started his routine here. First, he fed the nine rabbits in their sizeable 6x8-foot pen with a half a pail of pellets, and then filled their bucket full of water. Second, a smaller pen two feet less in linear dimensions housed a few guinea pigs. They ate the same food as the rabbits, only less. Further down in the barn another pen or stall held geese and they were watered and fed cracked corn. Adjacent to the geese were some exotic chickens who received cracked corn and water too.

The petting zoo was more like a farm since it contained little more than farm animals. The outdoor animals consisted of a few cows and a bull, some goats, a couple of horses, and some sheep. They too had barn shelters but could roam in and out since the doors were either open or nonexistent. All had to be watered from buckets carried from the barn with electricity to their containers. Two buckets each for the goats and sheep, while it took ten or twelve to fill the troughs for the cows and horses.

The second barn in line after the one with electricity contained hay and straw bedding. Brad occasionally placed a little straw in the respective shelters of the outside animals. Hay distribution happened daily and an adult horse or cow could easily munch more than a bale in a single day. There was one additional storage barn for tools like shovels, hoes, and wheelbarrows. Brad was fully familiar with the wheelbarrows since he used one of them to clean out the pens of excrement on weekends.

Brad finished at about ten minutes to four and would have to wait an extra ten minutes for his mother. He was thinking within those minutes that he'd be pulling his own keys out of his pocket, unlocking HIS car door, starting the ignition, and then blowing some dirt as he spun his rear tires. With a car, he wouldn't have to wait, maybe even finish by 3:30 if he rushed through his chores, log out at 4:00 just the same, and get paid for that half an hour he didn't work.

Who would know? If the boss wasn't there and better yet, the animals fed and watered, he could cruise that extra half hour. His thoughts drifted to spring and summer where he envisioned driving along, arm out that window, and waving to his friends while he bobbed his head to the car radio. The girls would be lining up too since a cool car certainly meant more dates. His mother broke his reverie when she pulled up in her spacious 1960 Chevy station wagon.

That night as the family sat around watching television, Brad was both pumped and anxious about the car; it was about the only thing on his mind. "Hey dad, when are we going to start looking at cars?"

I forgot to tell you son, my buddy Joe at the shop has an old Buick for sale, and we ought to mosey on over there this weekend, whaddya say?"

"What kind of shape is it in? Brad said excitedly.

"Well, he said that he hasn't driven it in a couple of years since he ran it onto a tree, but he says it still runs all right."

"Oh," Brad said somewhat disappointedly as he conjured up a car with severely smashed front end.

"Well, you know son that you're certainly not going to get anything new."

"I know, so when can we take a look at it?"

"I'll talk to Joe tomorrow about next weekend maybe."

The week went by slowly. Classes seemed to drag on and on while Brad found himself counting the minutes down more and more while repeatedly staring at the various generic classroom clocks. He had some timed down to the second for when the bell would ring. Somehow, the days crept toward the weekend. Saturday was extremely busy since he had to accompany his boss to the Farmer's Mart to pick up bags of feed. They did this monthly and since it had snowed several inches, extra shoveling was necessary as well.

Things were a little slower on Sunday and this was the big day. There was no additional snow and Brad was done with his rounds at the zoo by noon. His father picked him up so they could go check out the old Buick. The man who owned the car lived about fifteen miles away, right near the factory where Brad's dad worked. When they arrived, Joe was expecting them and pretended he had been shoveling his driveway.

"Well, the car's back here alongside the house, just follow me," Joe motioned with his arm. They walked along until they came to the car encapsulated in a mound of snow, or rather a snowbank with a car. It further proved Joe's inactivity with the shovel.

"I didn't have time to get her shoveled out yet and I haven't started her up in a few weeks either," he said somewhat apologetically. He wasn't sounding too optimistic, especially since he should've been if he had any hope of ridding himself of the car. He produced another shovel which looked new along with an ice scraper. The three of them set to work on uncovering the car.

When they finished, neither Brad nor his dad were in the best of moods. Brad's face crinkled into a frustrated frown as they could see much of the car now. The front fender on the driver's side had been smashed in along with the corner where the bumper and grilled met the fender. It was an older car, early '50's thought Brad, much more rounded than those of the later '50's and early '60's. He didn't know the exact year offhand, but it did sport four trademark Buick ventiports in the front fenders. That likely meant that it had a big eight-cylinder engine, that much he knew; had there only been three on each, then it would maybe only have had six cylinders. There were exceptions to those rules but that was the first positive he could see.

His father did all the talking as if Brad wasn't there, "Well, how about if we can hear it run?"

"Okay," answered Joe, "But we might have to jump it. Like I said, I haven't started it in a few weeks." Joe had to enter on the passenger side since the driver's side fender had pushed back into the door; thus, jamming it from opening. It was cold outside and had been very cold the last couple of weeks with a few nights where the temperature fell below zero degrees Fahrenheit. Joe turned the engine over a couple of times, a painful "Rrrr Rrrrr" sound and then it promptly died.

"Let me get my car and the jumper cables," replied Joe as he scrambled out of the passenger side. He pulled up near the old Buick with his Pontiac Tempest, popped the hood, hooked up the cables, and signaled Brad's father to get into the Buick. As he revved up the Tempest, Brad's dad turned the key in the Buick's ignition. After several groans, the starter seemed to kick up a notch with the added power, and it started with a puff of bluish black smoke from the tailpipe.

Joe got out of the Tempest, unhooked the cables, and said, "She runs great and lookie there," he pointed to the odometer, "Only 42,000 miles, I kind of wish I wasn't getting rid of her. Tell you what, why don't you take her around the block a couple of times?"

"All right, hop in Brad." They took it for a little spin, checking to see if everything was working like the AM radio, the inside lights, the wipers, speedometer, and so on, listening for any abnormal engine noises. Everything seemed all right. When they returned, they checked the outside blinkers and lights. They all worked. The brakes seemed okay, the car steered okay too except for maybe a little deviation to the right, the tires had some tread, and there was no visible rust on the body.

Brad didn't like it at all. It seemed a bit out of style and the front driver's side corner had been smashed. It just looked terrible at the front driver's side corner. Maybe fixed up some, it might have some appeal from a retro standpoint, perhaps even likeable; now, it just looked like a piece of junk. The inside, however, was somewhat all right; there was a small tear in the driver's bucket seat and a crack in the left side of the dash where Joe's knee had hit when he crashed into that tree.

Bob Walker, Brad's father, was still doing all the talking, and he did like the way the car ran. It was tough to find a good runner that old for not much money. "Well Joe, so how much are you asking for this junker anyway?"

"Two hundred fifty dollars."

"I don't know, it's beat up a bit, might take some green to fix 'er up some, how about $150?"

"Nope, got to have at least $225."

"Maybe $175?" Brad's father questioned hopefully. Bob Walker could see that they would have to hound the junkyards for body parts.

"Nope, $225," Joe seemed to be holding firm.

"Well, I don't know; she'll need a bit of work; the most I think I can handle is maybe $190."

"I guess that I'll take $200, but not a penny less," Joe countered.

They both knew from the start that it would probably sell for $200, but this ancient style of bartering and haggling always took place, especially during the sale of a used automobile. Lu Lin's parents would have related well.

"Well, Brad, looks like you've got yourself a car."

"Thanks dad," answered Brad with a hint of sarcasm. The heap wasn't exactly the car of his dreams in its present condition.

"Hey Joe, if anybody asks, tell 'em you sold it for 50 bucks, that'll save me a few bucks on taxes."

"You bet Bob," Joe said as they shook hands to seal the deal.

"Can you handle that thing on the way home?"

"Sure dad. Remember I passed my driving test and got my license a couple of months ago."

"Just checking, she pulls a little to the right. I'll follow you home since we don't have plates yet."

"It takes about 30,000 parts to assemble an automobile, but only one nut to scatter them all over the road." - Mark Pickvet

CHAPTER XXVIII

"Look at that thing Bob, just look at it! It's a piece of, a piece of... JUNK!" Nancy Walker, Bob's wife, exclaimed.

"Now listen dear, I bought it for the motor, and we have plenty of time to fix it up, be good for the boy to learn a few things," Bob replied.

"He's not going to want to drive it like that," stated Nancy, "Hell, he can't even get in the driver's side."

"I know, I know, but trust me, we'll work it out."

Nancy just shook her head and went back into the house.

Brad had mixed feelings initially about the car. It was a 1953 Buick Series 70 with a 322 V8 engine. It could probably go fast given that it was a V8, and Brad thought that maybe he could race some of those seniors who were always boasting about their cars. It needed a lot of work though. Brad had helped his dad some with cars but not all that much. He was more of a gopher as his dad did the actual work. All the expenses for parts would have to come from Brad's job to make it somewhat respectable.

The next week of school seemed to drag slower than the last, like a snail going uphill against the wind. Tony at least showed some excitement and enthusiasm about his car and dropped by Wednesday night to look at it. He acted as if it was all right, but Brad sensed that he thought it was a piece of junk. Brad did have faith in his father and if his dad thought it was all right and fixable, then Brad would go along with that.

Finally, the weekend had arrived at last, a time for father and son to bond over the one thing perhaps outside of fishing and hunting, that held more weight, and that was working on a car project. A good deal of routine maintenance took place. They gave the old Buick a complete tune-up with new spark plugs, a distributor cap, ignition wires, points, and condenser. The timing was set, the carburetor cleaned and adjusted, the oil changed, the car well lubricated, the front wheel bearings packed with grease, the tires pumped up including the spare, and Brad spent some time just washing the exterior and cleaning up the dusty interior. All in all, he was out a little over $20 so far.

"You know, she's kind of a luxury old boat," his dad laughed. "Did you know Brad that for GM, Buick was always #2 behind Cadillac in the high-end market? Chevy was always at the bottom with Pontiac not far behind. Oldsmobile is in the middle."

"What about GMC Truck?"

"Not really sure, but they've always been similar to Chevy trucks. I think we'll go see what we can find at the junkyards next weekend."

"Okay."

The next week of school was awful, more so than the previous one. With the coming end of the semester, final exams were now looming above the horizon. Brad usually made the honor roll with mostly B's and an occasional A, but this semester things weren't going quite as well. Playing the part of Capulet, Juliet's father, was not exactly awe-inspiring and Brad fell into daydreaming during the passages in which he had no part. In gym class, his highlight of the day, he would definitely get an A, but some of those history quizzes based on Mr. Slater's obscure movies did not go over well. Volumes of three-dimensional figures were not sinking in, especially when Brad was getting more and more lax with his homework. The muscles of frogs with those long Latin names that were hard to memorize and even more difficult to spell were not sinking in either.

The problem was instead of visions of fairies and sugar plums and everything magical, 188 horsepower, 322 cubic inches of V8 power, a top speed he had looked up as exceeding 100 mph assailed Brad's mind. He envisioned himself racing down Euclid or Huron Street, pedal to the metal, with the wind pumping through that big electric shave style grille.

Another weekend rolled around, and Brad was looking forward to visiting his first junkyard ever. Since the car seemed to be running smoothly, the junkyard goal was to obtain body parts. Brad had easily viewed the wrecks from highways at a time when fences around them were not mandatory, but never as close up and personnel as he perceived them now. Piles of twisted rusting metal such as decimated Dodges, mangled Mercury's, pulverized Pontiacs, bashed-in Buicks, crappy Caddy's, and on and on; nevertheless, above all else, it was a parts' heaven. Water pumps, alternators, blown tires, leaking radiators, emblems, blown engines, stripped gear transmissions, shattered glass, and an almost infinite list of every car part imaginable was there.

As they were searching specifically for Buicks, Brad's heart almost stopped when he came upon a smashed Studebaker. The engine had passed completely through the firewall into the interior shoving the steering wheel into the front seat. Brad peered for a closer look inside and saw a piece of clothing attached to the steering column with an old rusty-looking stain. It was immediately apparent to Brad as to what had happened to the driver. He backed away realizing that both car and driver had ended up in their own respective graveyards. It shook him up some, but he snapped out of it when he heard his father's voice.

"Hey Brad, over here!"

Brad followed the voice and came across his father several rows back, being careful to side step the junk and broken glass that seemed to be everywhere. Walking in a junkyard could be a dangerous proposition, especially if one veered from the semi-cleared paths between the vehicles. His father had found the front end of a '53 Buick, pay dirt.

"Well Brad, that bumper and grille look pretty good to me. What do you think?"

"I guess so," answered Brad who really couldn't tell the difference between a Buick and a Ford, at least where only pieces of bodies were found without hood ornaments or lettering. He marveled at his father's ability to pick out a grille and a bumper from a front end that had one fender missing, with the other fender and hood smashed beyond recognition. The rest of the body was long gone too like Ernie Harwell announcing a home run. Brad realized that he'd walked right past it. "How do we get it off?"

"It'll cost you a couple of bucks to get it removed since it's still attached to a piece of the frame down there."

They walked back and asked one of the mechanics, a grimy grease-laden man in faded denim coveralls, for assistance. The guy probably had more toes than teeth. He wheeled out a set of tanks, one containing acetylene, and the other oxygen. He played with the valves, made some sparks with a little flint device, and in no time at all had a seething bright blue flame protruding from the nozzle of his cutting torch after bumping up the oxygen valve. In a matter of minutes, he freed the rusted and now threadless bolts from the frame. After haggling over the price for a short time, which Brad felt his father excelled at, Brad had his bumper and grille for $38, an entire week's pay.

Do you have any other '53 Buicks around here?" Bob Walker inquired.

"That's gettin older now. If we did, they'd probably be right 'round back here, nearer da end. We try to keep things somewhat togetter, but you know how dat goes!" He gave them a big toothy grin with about four visible teeth and enough gaps to floss with the wrong end of a toothbrush. "Call me if ya need me," he added as he left.

"All we have to do is get you a fender and a hood and you'll be all set Brad." They spent another 20 minutes searching to no avail before giving up. "I know of some junkyards down off Dort Highway in Flint, one is supposed to be one of the biggest in the state. We'll head down there next weekend and give it a try."

"Okay."

Unfortunately, report cards arrived before the Flint trip. Brad missed the honor roll for the first time in his high school career. Close, but that C- in Geometry and the D in Biology hadn't helped. His mother was worried while his father was angry.

"Don't you know that if you want to get anywhere in this world, you're going to need an education? What's the matter with you getting a "D" in biology? You'd better shape up or that car might stay up on blocks in the garage longer than you expect." That last threat really sunk in and forced him to do better. Brad promised he'd never miss another honor roll again, and that was enough for his dad not to cancel the trip to Flint.

Flint—the town where Chevrolet and Buick were born, and made virtually every Buick for almost one hundred years, until 1999—earned its nickname Buick City. If one couldn't find parts there, where else would one look? Flint was about forty-five miles south of Bay City. In a little under forty minutes, they drove up to Well's Auto Salvage on Dort Highway. The Bay City junkyard was nothing compared to this one. Twenty acres of cars going back to the 1920's and '30's seemed to spread out for miles. They asked for assistance first before wandering on their own.

"1953 Buicks? Oh yeah, no problem, should have a bunch of 'em. Go down the right side, maybe sixteen or seventeen rows over, and keep walkin' back, ya can't miss 'em."

Brad and his father were off. Things seemed better organized here. Where they had tried in Bay City, they succeeded here in keeping the Chevrolets with the Chevrolets, the Chryslers with the Chryslers, and even some of the odd stuff too like Hudsons, Packards, Nash models, Kaisers, and Willy's Jeeps; many produced from companies that had long gone out of business.

His dad spotted the Buick section right away and no less than five 1953 Buicks sat right in a row; nevertheless, the problem with junkyard cars is that they have been mortally wounded, invariably smashed well beyond repair and four of the five were no exception. These four were smashed beyond recognition in the front end, the fifth however was only destroyed on the passenger side as it had been severely T-boned, the driver's side was intact, just the one fender they needed. The fender nonetheless wasn't perfect. It had a small rust hole in the front at the bottom. The hood had four small dents, more like round one-inch holes that hadn't gone through all the way. Brad's father assured him that both could be body-worked with a little Bondo. For another $35 Brad had what he needed to complete his budding hot rod.

As February passed away, the weather remained cold. March could come in as a lion or lamb and go out the opposite way as they said, this year, in 1964, it came in like a lion. To combat the icy cold garage despite the shelter of having walls, Brad's dad had a portable kerosene heater to warm it up while they worked on the car. The fenders, grilles, bumpers, and hoods bolted on back popped right off after a little lubricating, drilling and cutting, the old ones popped right off.

After a trip to the hardware store for some bolts, the junkyard parts bolted on nicely. About the only problem was that the car was originally dark blue in color; but now the front driver's side fender was green, and the hood was black. Brad didn't realize that the car would have to be painted, but his father had. Although his father had an air compressor, Bob Walker had never painted a complete car before, but he was willing to try. The only necessary item that he lacked was a pneumatic paint gun, but Generous Motors, as some called it, provided him with one for free if you knew and trusted the people you worked with, especially those in the paint department. These fringe benefits were not exactly legal, but it seemed like most everyone did it at one time another, a small tool, chain, paint gun, or what have you.

Brad's life was quite busy. Weekdays were spent working after school and doing homework for a change. There was some precious time on weekends to prepare the car for its pending paint job. Aside from sanding away the rust, filling in the holes, and then sanding them smoothly, all by hand no less, there was lot of prep work before the big paint day.

Brad was given all the grunt work, namely the sanding and just prior to painting, his dad gave him some fine grit paper, wetted down which confused Brad some, and had him give the entire body a light wet sanding. With tack cloth, the light bulb went on in Brad's head as the cloth picked up the fine particles on the Buick's body. He still had to tape off the parts with masking tape and newspaper that were not to be painted, and this included the long chrome trim that went from the front fender nearly to the rear tire. He would have to tape the little trademark Buick ventiports carefully as well.

Brad had wanted the car painted black like the hood, but his father warned him that every little scratch and sloppy or uneven bodywork which there had been a little of, would tend to be very noticeable in such a color. His father suggested fire-engine red so that people would take notice, but Brad didn't really want a gaudy color and red didn't seem to fit the style of the Buick. They compromised and decided upon the original somewhat dull dark blue. This had the added advantage that if any new paint ever scraped away, then the identical color would show underneath apart from the hood and front driver's side fender. They had ordered the paint from a local parts store to match as closely as possible.

They poured the paint, was with some thinner, into the spray gun. The canister on the gun held about a quart. Brad's dad closed the garage door about three-fourths of the way leaving about two-and-a-half feet open at the bottom. For ventilation, they used a couple of electric tabletop fans to blow air outward, and opened the one small, screened window. March was not such a bad time to paint since there would be little in the way of dust or leaves kicked up outside. They donned their crude respirators, which were nothing more than ineffective dust masks and were ready to go.

Brad held the hose and trouble light as he followed his dad around the car. His dad sprayed very lightly, overcompensating some to avoid drips, as auto paint was quite thin and prone to running like rainwater or tears down one's face. They stopped three times to reload the gun's reservoir and continued slowly around the car several more times. The little electric air compressor had trouble keeping up and they had to pause now and then to let it build up adequate pressure.

After circling the car some 18 times with the dark blue paint, they stopped to clean the gun, and then went around three more times with a protective clear coat. After finishing, they had a feeling of euphoria and light-headedness, and that was due to the inhalation of paint fumes. Since it was getting on well into early Saturday evening, they left the car with the garage heater on to aid it in drying. They closed the overhead door but left the small window partially open, screen only.

First thing in the morning, they inspected and evaluated their work. Aside from a couple of minor drips, a blemish or two, and a little evidence of bodywork if one looked closely, it was a halfway decent job, maybe not professional, but a good amateur attempt. From a distance, it looked great, up close; it was okay.

After feeding the animals in a near record time, Brad spent the rest of his Sunday removing tape and newspaper from the tires, windows, door handles, locks, lights, grille, bumpers, chrome strips, mirrors, and vents. The total investment for the paint job and bodywork had cost another couple of weeks' worth of pay; license and insurance would pretty much eat up the rest of March's paychecks. To Brad, it did seem to be worth it. The car was whole again, and he could get into the driver's side as one would expect. There was an awesome feeling of satisfaction in doing much of the work himself.

"When can I take it to school?"

"I'll stop by tomorrow and get your plates and insurance. You'll need money for gas too," his father chuckled. As usual, when one purchased an old used car, the gas gauge was naturally either on the empty mark or barely a half of a millimeter above it. Brad was down to his last couple of dollars; nevertheless, at twenty-seven cents a gallon, he could probably get the tank half-full.

With the plates on front and back the next day, it seemed like Tuesday morning would never make it, but it did. Brad even remembered to set his alarm clock, so no wake-up call from his mother would be necessary. She checked anyway and was shocked to see him up and about. His grades had improved in the third marking period, but something else held him back. It had been two weeks since they started the car and the battery, an old, weakened model, refused to turn the starter motor. Poor Brad ended up sitting with a surprised Tony on the bus.

Tuesday, March 24, 1964, could very well have been one of the worst days of Brad's life, at least for the year so far. The car hadn't started. He had boasted repeatedly about it and was supposed to show it to all his friends and others he hardly knew at all. Lunch hour was a major disappointment since he planned to eat in the car with Tony while they listened to the radio.

Later that same day at the zoo, the guinea pigs had somehow chewed a hole in their pen and the little bastards escaped into every conceivable crack and crevice in the barn. Rounding up the speedy little furry critters was difficult at best since they had a taste of freedom and did not want to lose it, who would? He wasted an extra hour and a half mending the pen and chasing down the little devils. With any luck, his dad was going to pick him up a new battery and probably have the car running by the time he got home.

"Mom?" Brad asked when he called his mother to pick him up at 6 p.m.

"No Brad, it's me," his dad answered.

"Whoa, where's mom?"

"Her mother er your grandmother died, she's out."

"Oh," Brad really didn't know what to say.

"I'll come get you."

"Okay." Just a bad day Brad thought, and he would soon learn that his dad hadn't had time to pick up a new battery for his car. Bummer.

Brad had not been close to his grandmother on his mother's side for the simple reason that the 68-year-old woman had passed from mere eccentricity to virtual insanity over the past few years. After her husband had died 4 ½ years ago, she put on even more weight to a body that was already rotund to say the least. She had become so obese that she was smelly, gross, and suffered from poor health. She had diabetes but refused to follow her prescribed diets which led to poor circulation, neuropathy, and failing eyesight, not to mention heart trouble. Her heart had enlarged too in the time since the death of Brad's grandfather, and she died of heart failure before they could amputate her dead feet.

The timing of it all was just bad for Brad. Since the family was preoccupied with funeral arrangements, the Buick would sit in the garage for the next several days. He would have to buy a new battery anyhow and wouldn't have the money until Friday; still, had it not been for the untimely death, his dad would have picked one up and Brad would have reimbursed him.

The actual funeral took place on Saturday. After work on Sunday, Brad's mother insisted that he accompany her to his grandmother's shack as they referred to her old tiny, dilapidated farmhouse. The little farmhouse, once quite cozy in its day, was now a disaster. A saggy leaky roof with torn shingles, a couple of broken windows covered by taped plastic, paint virtually gone from the rotted, grayish-colored wood siding, the porch half gone, and other areas of neglect all made it worse than a handy-man's special. Old Rachel Abernathy had refused to give up her retirement home. It was probably for the best since foreclosure would likely have happened before the end of 1964.

Brad got attic duty with specific instructions to throw anything out of no little or no value. With a ladder and a lantern, he approached the attic. He carefully lifted the three-foot square board, shoved it aside, and thrust the lantern upward as he bobbed his head just above the attic floor through the opening. The first thing he noticed was two things running along the back wall that reminded him of guinea pigs.

"Damn rats!" He said aloud. He brushed some cobwebs aside and hoisted himself up on the rafters. The rats scurried further away from the blinding light. The attic was a mess full of dust, dirt, mold, and must from leaking water, and the cobwebs were so big, it looked as though they could trap a grown man or maybe even a small cow in places.

Several old, blackened cardboard boxes stood in a pile atop an old wooden ship trunk with most of its wood rotten and fragile but still intact. He gingerly opened the trunk and the cover held. There was little except moth eaten clothes. The boxes held some clothes too that were filled with mold and mildew and some other useless junk. There was an old Polaroid camera, odd car parts, plumbing pieces, pipe joints, a rusty single-barrel carburetor, and other metal long since oxidized into worthless rust.

As he dug around, flashing the lantern every so often in case the rats came for him, but they did seem to have mysteriously disappeared, he came across a bundle of old letters that were no longer readable, the pencil and pen markings were far too smudged. He found some broken lanterns, some rotted windowpanes, torn screens, chipped porcelain dishes, rotted strawberry baskets, the thin wood kind, and more junk. One particular box that interested him was filled with some odd metal items including a couple of sets of stirrups, a pair of spurs, a riding crop, some hand tools, a copper pot, brass doorknobs, brass handles, and an old antique looking brass or bronze lamp.

Brad proceeded to hall the junk out saving the camera and the box with the metal items that he placed in the trunk of his mother's car. His grandparents had a fire pit in the backyard and there were still the remnants of a woodpile that his grandfather had probably last cut five or six years ago. The rotted wood had lost most of its mass; nevertheless, it was dry and would burn fine, just not all that long. They would build a fire and burn the old boxes, trunk, clothing, and about anything that would burn.

His mother in the meantime had gathered the usual family keepsakes such as pictures, jewelry, and other memorabilia. There was an English sterling-silver, slightly tarnished tea set, and his mother took that as well. In 1964, silver was around $1.29 an ounce and gold was going for a whopping $35, and, on top of that, sterling silver wasn't even pure silver, just 92.5%, the rest copper. U.S. coins, namely the dime, quarter, and the new Kennedy half dollar were still made of ninety percent silver, 1964 being the final year. Overall, there just wasn't all that much valuable or even salvageable. Most everything else that wasn't burnable she would donate to the Salvation Army or Goodwill.

They didn't replace the battery in Brad's car until Monday evening. The last day of March, right before Fool's Day, would finally be Brad's big day to exhibit his car to Bay City Southern High School. It started without a hitch and Brad shoved the column gearshift up and in for reverse. He revved it up a bit too much and then let the clutch out too fast. It lurched and stalled. It started right up again and this time he let the clutch out painstakingly slow, riding it a little too much.

In 1964, driver's training was all about the manual transmission and he had learned how to work a clutch; nevertheless, every vehicle was different and took some getting used to. He backed out of the garage all right, dropped the gearshift down and in for first, up and out for second, and then down and out for third came naturally. In ten minutes, Brad proudly parked his ride in the very back corner of the student parking lot.

Contrary to last Tuesday, this new Tuesday turned out to be one of the best days of Brad's short life. It seemed like the whole school wanted to see his car. It wasn't really a hotrod, but more of a big luxury model, maybe not as cool as some of the later '50's or early '60's models, but classy. Tony was more enthusiastic, knowing once how terrible the car had looked, but now it had gone from junker to jewel, if one didn't look too closely. Even girls that hadn't given him a second glance now seemed to take notice. The crummy food at the cafeteria would no longer have to be eaten if he so chose; he could drive anywhere else in town or just pack a bag lunch in the car.

"It's not a throttle – it's a detonator." - Jeremy Clarkson

CHAPTER XXIX

With the coming of spring, Brad explored virtually every possibility or opportunity that his wheels presented: going to movies, drive-ins, bowling alleys, diners, and various places with Tony when girls weren't available. His extracurricular activities with the car ate up his paychecks faster than his car repairs had. One day in particular, after school, on his way to work, Brad experienced one of the first real thrills of his life. On a small two-lane highway, Jimmy Dickerson, with a gang of friends packed in, went flying by in his '49 Merc. The car was the oldest in the high school parking lot, four years before Brad's, which wasn't exactly new. Jimmy hovered a little as he passed by and someone in the backseat urged Brad to catch up if he could.

Any inexperienced, somewhat immature, sixteen-year-old would not ignore a challenge, no matter how firmly Bob Walker hammered warnings about excessive speed into his brain. In the heat of the moment, he thought nothing about his dad. Brad pushed the pedal to the floor and in no time at all, just a matter of seconds, he was roaring past an unprepared Jimmy Dickerson. Jimmy floored his Mercury in return, but Brad had the momentum, and no matter how hard he tried, Jimmy couldn't catch him. With a rush of adrenaline, Brad hadn't realized just how fast his car could go, a little over a hundred miles per hour he found out that day.

In an attempt to save his honor and reputation, Jimmy Dickerson challenged Brad to a real racing making the excuse that he had had too much weight in the car with 4 of his friends, nearly half of a ton extra. Against his better judgment, Brad accepted; anything less would have been complete cowardice. Chris Johnson was the most popular guy in school because he had dropped a souped-up small block 327 V8 in his '57 Chevy and claimed the title as "Man with the Fastest Car in School." It couldn't hurt Brad to enhance his reputation some a bit with a road victory or two. The quarter mile race would take place immediately after school on Patterson Street, not far from the bay, which students occasionally used as a drag strip.

Brad had never raced from a dead stop before but had spent a little time practicing to speed shift just to be cool, Elvis-like cool though Elvis had pretty much been replaced by the likes of The Beatles and The Rolling Stones; still, Elvis was always cool. Beginning at a little bridge over a creek and ending at a large telephone pole marked the boundaries of the popular racing strip. There were no houses near, and the street was isolated, good solid pavement as well, no potholes or uneven areas. It was closer to three-tenths of a mile, but no one knew any better and if they did, they wouldn't have cared.

One of Dickerson's friends stood a foot in front between the two cars and held his hand high up in the air. When he counted to three and dropped it, they were off. The engines roared as they had revved them up, and then squealed their tires as they popped the clutches, hard. The more experienced Dickerson got off slightly faster, about a car length less a few inches. When Brad shifted into second, popped the clutch as fast as he could, he gained ground as his front tires gained a little past Dickerson's rear wheels.

Exactly like the day before, when Brad floored it in high gear, he flew past Dickerson and ended up three car lengths ahead at the telephone pole. An old Mercury flathead V8 from the '40's, even with the Ford-Holley split float and dual downdraft carburetor, was no match for a Buick V8 from the '50's. Aside from winning the $5 bet, Brad's reputation now had a root, significant enough to qualify as a taproot.

"Straight roads are for fast cars; turns are for fast drivers." - Colin McRae

CHAPTER XXX

B rad saved the box that he'd gotten from his grandmother a second time since his mother decided it was virtually worthless. She had gotten the tea set and had polished it with some chrome cleaner that the boys had recently used on Brad's car. Brad took the chrome cleaner and the box of metal objects up to his room. He first cleaned the copper pot, which could hold something, maybe pennies, since people tended to hoard them for no good reason. Some of the car and plumbing parts were probably worthless given their high degree of corrosion.

What looked like an old oil style lamp to Brad was of some interest; it indeed was quite old, older now than anyone would ever imagine. If it was an antique, maybe he could sell it for a few dollars, enough to fill up his tank. He was always thinking of his car. First, it required polishing. He poured a little chrome cleaner on a rag and began polishing the lamp. He rubbed hard and it didn't get far at all when the sound of something like a small valve opening as a grayish-white blob of smoke poured from the lamp's spout.

"What is your first wish boy?"

"Holy shit! What ta Hell?" Brad about fell off his bed, frightened at first, then thought that maybe it was just a gag, a joke like one of those new whoopee cushions Tony had used on him last year. The cushion had been a deluxe model, and when sat upon, produced a thick puff of smoke and rank odor along with the ripping noise. Brad studied the harsh looking rounded face with thin moustache and goatee that confronted him. He then decided to ask it something to see if it could truly communicate.

"What's your name?"

"I am a Djinni, I have no other name." With Brad's request interpreted as a wish, the Djinni slithered back into its home.

"Hmmm," Brad considered aloud, "Must be some sort of antique toy like that old Zoltar fortune-telling carnival machine." The very one that showed up at the Bay City Fair & Carnival every year, it even looked a little like the satanic face of Zoltar, only it spoke whereby in contrast, Zoltar spewed out paper messages like fortunes.

"Brad! Brad! Come and get it!"

It was time to eat, and he rushed back down the stairs. He mowed through a dinner of spaghetti and meatballs and was strangely silent. His thoughts were on the old toy. After dinner, he ran back upstairs to investigate further what he believed to be an antique talking toy of some sort. He wondered if it was worth quite a bit more than he originally thought. He turned it over, looking for some sort of button or switch, but he didn't find one. He tried prying off the lid, but it didn't budge. He shook it lightly, but nothing rattled inside. Finally, he picked up the rag and chrome cleaner and started polishing it again and WHOOSH, it popped out again.

"Do you have a second wish boy?"

To Brad, this was the second time that it was asking for wishes. "Funny," Brad thought, he was just playing around and said, "Sure, I'll take a million dollars." How many people, somewhere along the line, especially the unrealistic lottery dreamers, wished they had a million dollars? One is more likely to be struck by lightning; nevertheless, the lucky few that win often can't handle it and ruin their lives. Before Brad's very eyes, ten bright crisp black and white $100,000 bills appeared in front of him with the portrait of Art Linkletter. Unfortunately, Brad had not been too specific. The bills were nothing but play money from the game of Life. Still, it was some weird magic as the Djinni thing had at least produced something tangible. He put it aside, confused, and maybe it was best to sleep on it some before he went any further.

As April was slipping away, Brad won two more races on Patterson Street against easy opponents. Eugene's Corvair was embarrassing while the race against Larry's 1959 Dodge Coronet had been a closer one, just a one-car length lead at the end. The Coronet had the straight six only; if it had been equipped with a bigger V8 such as the 354 Hemi, he could have dusted Brad.

The ultimate challenge finally came from Chris Johnson. Chris Johnson was married to his car much like the growing attachment Brad was beginning to feel for his old Buick. The biggest problem was that Chris's car was not stock like Brad's. Chris had the cylinders professionally bored out to accommodate larger pistons, a new racing camshaft, exhaust headers, high performance valves, dual exhaust, an intake manifold with a big 4-barrel Holley carburetor, and a long list of high-performance parts. Chris's '57 Chevy had a fancy jacked-up rear-end with fat slick tires too. Chris could reportedly do fiften second quarter miles and Brad was at least three or four seconds off from that. It was like running the one-hundred-yard dash where differences were measured in tenths and even hundredths of seconds, not full seconds. Brad didn't have a snowball's chance in hell, or did he?

He accepted the challenge. After school and work at the zoo, he rushed home, driving sixty-mph on the city subdivision streets. He had to get to the lamp, hoping beyond hope that it would not trick him again. He really had no other option knowing inside that he'd be about as well off as riding a bicycle against Chris Johnson's Chevy. He had to eat dinner first—pork chops and canned beans—but flew up to his room on the pretense that he had to study for a geometry test. He grabbed the lamp, the little metal can of chrome polish, and the rag, and then stopped. He wasn't racing until tomorrow, after school, and thought maybe it was not wise to wish too soon. He decided to pack the stuff up instead and throw it in the back of his car on the floor.

On the day of the big race, Brad took off at lunchtime in order to inspect Patterson Street. He had already raced here three times and thought for the first time about how dangerous it was to be racing down a two-lane road. It was flat and straight and there would be plenty of time to slide back into the right lane if a car happened to be coming in the opposite direction; that is, if the car he was racing was not immediately adjacent to his own. It wasn't a busy street either, a little isolated with no houses along the racing zone. He had left Tony behind and brought out the lamp along with the rag and cleaner. For a third time, he poured a little of the liquid on the rag and started rubbing it on the lamp.

The Djinni came forth for its final appearance with Brad: "What is your last wish boy?"

"Listen closely," said Brad, "Today after school I'm going to race Chris Johnson. We're going to start at this bridge and end up at that telephone down there. By the time I get to that pole, I wish that my car is doing 150 mph." He figured that would be plenty of speed to win.

The Djinni left and Brad wondered if he really had any chance of winning. "I hope that he got that down," Brad muttered to himself. Just in case, he rubbed the lamp again, but nothing happened, "No matter," he thought and drove back to school. The worst that could happen he thought was that he'd just lose the $5 bet. He was wrong on that score.

A little over two hours later, Brad returned to the bridge on Patterson Street. His Buick would be lucky to reach eighty mph in the quarter with a seasoned and professional driver, of which Brad was neither. Chris could reportedly exceed ninety mph in the same distance. When the arm fell, it was Chris who jumped out ahead with his nifty aftermarket positraction rear-end. By the time Brad shifted into high gear, Chris was already several car lengths ahead, but then something amazing happened. A little past the halfway point, Brad's car, with the lamp on the floor, like a missile, accelerated from fifty mph to 150 mph in two seconds. It was difficult to judge who was more shocked; Brad, pressed tightly against the back of his seat hanging on to the steering wheel for dear life, or Chris Johnson, who saw nothing but Buick taillights as Brad whizzed on by and consequently won by his widest margin yet.

At the finish line, Brad took his foot off the accelerator pedal, pushed in the clutch, and then tried to apply the brakes. Nothing happened. The car was severely rattling and shaking but continued to travel at 150 mph. Cars, even into the muscle era of the later '60's and early '70's, were often not aerodynamically capable of sustaining such speeds for long, and the old '53 Buick was no exception. Brad held it straight as best he could, but the car was shuddering to such a degree that it felt like it was about to rip apart at the seams.

The road was straight for a couple of miles, but it did have a bend or two further up. Doing two-and-a-half miles per minute didn't give Brad much time to think or react. He tried the clutch and brake again—nothing; he turned the key off—nothing; he pulled the emergency brake—nothing, not so much as a grinding sound or a slowdown in the least. The damn car just kept going and going shaking like an out of control washing machine.

The first curve was approaching fast, no, super fast, maybe in maybe thirteen or fourteen seconds. He tried slamming the brakes again as most people automatically react to in an emergency, but once again, they did not compress into the drums—ten seconds. Only one last thing to do, he tried to jump out, the door wouldn't open, five seconds. There was no way the car would ever be able to negotiate that curve, no way in hell. The new fender had not jammed like the old one, so the door should have opened, it didn't. 150 mph created a lot of wind resistance and consequent air pressure, and Brad, nearly paralyzed with fear, pressed his entire body against the door. He did not have seatbelts since they were not standard or even mandatory equipment back then, but the door opened! Just an inch but relatched itself from the pressure, three seconds.

Brad then experienced the first panic attack of his life, drifted into shock, and THREE, TWO, ONE, CRASH! Seven is ordinarily considered a lucky number but not for Brad that day, for that is how many times the Buick rolled over, scattering parts for 200 yards, bumpers, mirrors, wheels, chrome trim, fenders, and on and on. With no seat belts or air bags, Brad bounced around like a steel ball in a pinball machine; the third roll propelled him through the front windshield like a chunky stone through a thin glass-walled house.

On the fourth roll, the old Buick rolled over Brad's body, but it had already gone limp. The fifth roll only managed to scatter Brad's broken body into a few extra pieces. On the sixth roll, the engine and transmission broke loose, and an entire new set of parts flew about like shrapnel from multiple grenades. At the conclusion of the seventh roll, the entire driver's side ended up in the trunk, with the steering wheel protruding far away from where it should have been.

On the passenger side, the dash crashed through the front seat and wedged the lamp between it and the surviving half of the rear seat. Strangely, the lamp remained intact, not as much as a dent when most of the car would soon be unrecognizable. The gas tank had dislodged and bounced around in the grass, but there was no explosion. There was no spark near enough though the 4 gallons left in the tank spewed out; about all it would do would leave a dead brown spot in the grass for several months. As a result, there were no explosions, just a dirt and dust cloud and faint sounds of the car rolling and rolling and rolling.

The student spectators had only seen the car from a distance, past the curve. It disappeared from their view as it began rolling in a shallow ditch before being scattered across a grassy field. There would be no body for the viewing. Emergency services collected Brad's remains in a bag and tagged them like a war victim, then placed them a closed casket. His casket went to one graveyard while what was left of the car and the hidden lamp went to another, barely more than a partial chassis with some connected interior components.

"How are we to conduct ourselves, lord, with regard to womankind?

As not seeing them Ananda.

But if we should see them, what are we to do?

No talking, Ananda.

But if they should talk to us, lord, what are we to do?

Keep wide awake, Ananda." - Digha Nikaya, ii, 141, 3rd Century B.C.

CHAPTER XXXI

A few years later, Armstrong, Aldrin, and Collins were walking on the moon, a first, and quite a giant step for mankind. A few weeks later, the music festival of the century took place at a dairy farm in Woodstock. Four years after those two monumental events, twelve years of unnecessary fighting in Southeast Asia ended with the loss of nearly 60,000 American troops; those that survived were largely ignored or forgotten back home. Watergate ended the next year with President Nixon resigning, the first American president ever to be so humiliated. Finally, in 1977, Little Joe Monroe's conscience rested much easier when President Carter pardoned all Vietnam draft dodgers. After six years working for a lumber company in northern Canada, Little Joe could finally return to Michigan, his true home.

In the city of Flint, sometimes known as "Little Detroit," Joe got a job as a factory worker at $9.75 an hour, a decent wage given that he had no education beyond high school and little in the way of skills except for running a chainsaw and other power equipment. His job consisted of installing the same three chassis bolts on identical Buick Skylark frames minute after minute, hour after hour, day after day, and time moved about as fast as a fat sloth on a hot day.

The assembly line was relentless, boring, drudge-like, and mind numbing. It had taken him a few missed bolts to get the hang of using the fancy pneumatic powered wrench, but that was no big deal, virtually every vehicle had something missing. When it was up and running, the assembly line moved quickly, and another chassis appeared a minute or so after the previous one floated away.

Despite the boredom, the money was good, a big factor in why he and others like him were stuck with monotonous jobs that they despised.

Little Joe was named that way as a kid since his dad's name was also Joseph, Big Joe and Little Joe. He never lost the name and that's because he never grew beyond 5' 2 ¼". His dad was a big guy, around six feet tall, but he must've inherited his height gene from his 4'11" mother. Little Joe rented an upstairs apartment for $250 a month with all utilities paid in Flint's crime-ridden East side. It had only four rooms: a kitchen with built-in appliances, a bedroom, a living room, and a bathroom.

The room was close to 400 square feet, but not altogether bad for a single guy; a wife and only one kid would likely have made it unbearable. With cheap rent and no heating or electricity bills, Joe was able to save a good deal of his earnings. In 1978, there was no such thing as the Internet, at least for the masses just yet, no pay TV or cell phones either, and a single landline was about $9 a month.

The summer of '78 turned out to be a good one for Little Joe. He made a few new friends, shop rats like himself, as well as meeting up with a few old acquaintances. A new ice cream stand opened across the street called "The Dairy Nut" in a red building that resembled an old gambrel roof barn without the loft.

Joe got into the habit of visiting The Dairy Nut about once a week at first, and then nearly every day when he met Sally. Joe had always done poorly with girls, figuring his height and smallness turned them off. How many girls really fell in love with 120-pound guys that barely stood five-two? In a way, they could be just as shallow as men when it came to physical characteristics. Sally was shorter than him, but did weigh a little more. She was homely with a large, hooked nose, freckles, premature lining around the eyes, and thin stringy hair; nevertheless, she was sweet, polite, and always greeted Joe with a warm friendly smile, and that is why he asked her out.

He got up the courage one day and just blurted out, "How about dinner Friday night?"

"Okay," she answered shyly. It had been two-and-a-half years since her last date.

"What time do you get off?"

"Around seven."

"Pick you up then?"

"Okay," was another meek reply; her knobby knees nearly buckled.

Their first date was a huge success. Although they both leaned toward the side of shyness, they talked a good deal and went to a movie afterward. They even kissed goodnight on her doorstep, or rather her mother's doorstep, an awkward peck, but it was a start. Sally lived alone with her mother. They followed up with a Detroit Tiger baseball game, more movies and dinners, and a round of putt-putt golf where Sally beat him soundly. She even teased him about it, but Little Joe just laughed it off, commenting on how useless a skill it was to hit orange golf balls through tunnels, under windmills, and into the nose of a gaudy clown face. It was all good fun.

Two months and three weeks later, they made love for the first time on Joe's single bed in his apartment. Like the first kiss, it was a little awkward, but they did all right. Sally had to guide him to the right spot, but with only two pieces to the puzzle, it wasn't that difficult to fit them together. In fact, they did so good that Sally became pregnant that very same night.

They married three months later and spent their honeymoon at Niagara Falls on the Canadian side. Niagara Falls was only a little over a four-hour drive due east from Flint. They visited tacky wax museums, went up the Skylon Tower, and were soaked on 'The

Maid of the Mist' boat ride near the base of the falls. It was a nice honeymoon and since Sally wasn't showing much yet, they made love every night during the four nights they were gone.

Joe abandoned his apartment when the six-month lease expired. He invested in a bit of a fixer-upper, but at least it was a fair sized three-bedroom home, much bigger than the apartment. With a new wife and a boy on the way, they would need more room. It was a typical single-story frame three-bedroom home built in the 1940's with wood siding and a shingle roof. The basement leaked some, it needed painting inside and out, the front porch was in three separate pieces, and the attached two-car garage needed a new roof. It was only $38,000 and Joe had saved enough to make a ten-percent down payment. If there was one drawback aside from the repairs, it was located on Flint's East side, a notorious white trash area.

By 1982, the house was in much better shape though the neighborhood was not. As the nation's Hispanic population rose, Michigan was no exception. The barrio came to the east side of Flint, mixing and merging with the poor whites; in the meantime, the blacks stayed more on the north end. In time, all would clash to make Flint the murder capital of America, at least from a per capita sense. At least Little Joe and Sally fixed up their house. They had completed all the painting on their own; Joe did the outside and helped with the inside. The professionally sealed basement came with a twenty-year guarantee against leaking. They paid a roofing friend of Joe's $1,200 to have the garage roof reshingled.

The neighborhood was about the only part of their lives that leaned toward the negative. Along with three-year-old Bobby, they now had one-year-old Suzy. Little Joe got a promotion from line worker to one of the new inspector positions. To compete with thre ever-growing superior-made Japanese and German imports, quality control became the WORD for American car manufacturers as they bled market share to their overseas competitors. Joe's new job was to carefully inspect cars and tag them for anything missing on the chassis, which had become quite familiar to him. He also started taking night and Saturday classes at Mott Community College to become a licensed mechanic. It was fortunate he did so because the factory laid him off the next year. Two short months after the layoff he received his certification and mechanics were in great demand, especially the new ones who could do electrical work on most of the new computerized cars.

Joe hired in at a local Buick dealership. Within two years of evening courses, he obtained his master mechanic certification and made more money than he had in the shop. With the house in good repair and a little money to spare, Joe took on a new project – restoring an old Buick from the fifties, 1953 to be exact. His would be a professional restoration from the ground up.

This literally meant taking off most every part down to the frame, and then putting it all back together with new or used parts if necessary and removing every speck of corrosion or rust. He had been sifting through the classic car section in the want ads of *The Flint Journal* when he saw an ad that read "'53 Buick Roadmaster for parts or restoration, runs, $400 or best offer, 555-1031." He called the number, set up a meeting, and after looking it over, offered the guy $350. The guy took it. Little Joe towed it home in the summer of 1985.

The following summer while working on the interior, he found the lamp. He was simply looking for a couple of dashboard knobs at the junkyard on Dort Highway, just a mile and a half up the road. When he removed a radio knob, he noticed a faint glimmer on the floor, brass or bronze or something somewhat gold in color as he was rummaging around. It was jammed between the dash and rear floor, strange he thought, must have been one heck of an accident for the dash to be so far back. It was none other than the remains of Brad Walker's decimated Buick.

After pushing a good portion of the dashboard forward, a little more than half of the lamp exposed itself. At first, he thought it was some odd part of the car, but on closer examination, it was something else. With a couple of hard pulls, the whole thing came out. Curious, he brought it up front and asked what they wanted for it and the three knobs he was able to salvage, they settled on $5, $1 each of the knobs and $2 for the lamp.

"What you got there?" Sally wanted to know.

"Looks like one of those old antique oil lamps, I found it at the junkyard, but the top is stuck on."

"Maybe if you rub it a genie will come out," she joked and giggled.

"Funny," Little Joe laughed too.

"What are you going to do with it?"

"Don't know for sure, not even sure why I bought it, it just looked interesting I suppose. You know, it's in pretty good shape considering the condition that Buick it was in, not much left of the car."

She laughed again, "What'd I tell you Joe about picking up junk? I just filled up 2 big boxes for mom's rummage sale next week, and you bring more of it."

Bobby came running in, nearly 8 years old toting another kid's book on space, "Whatcha got daddy?"

"Just an old lamp I guess."

"Kin I have it?" Bobby asked pleadingly.

Joe looked it over, tugged the stuck cover one last time to no avail, shrugged, and said, "Sure, why not," and handed Bobby the lamp.

Bobby ran off with it in one hand while clutching his space book in the other. Sally had asked him just yesterday what he wanted to be when he grew up, his answer had been, "An Asssstronaut!" His teachers and half the boys in his class had given the same answer. Ms. Robin, his third-grade teacher, had done a module on space and had all the boys pumped up at least.

"Now what's he going to do with that thing?" Sally questioned.

"I don't know, I guess he'll play with it a couple of days and forget about it soon enough," Joe answered. "Maybe when he gets bored with it, you can steal it away for your mom's yard sale."

"That's not a bad idea," stated Sally making a mental note to box it up in a few days.

The lamp had a long history of sitting around for years collecting little more than dust and dirt and the last 22 or so years was no exception. Bobby took it outside to the water faucet and hosed it off. He ran back in for a towel to wipe it with and lo and behold, magic!

"What do you wish for little one?" The Djinni almost asked in a kindly manner, but the leer was still there.

"Whoa! Wow!" Bobby was excited now but not the least bit scared, why should he be? In his world, he had experienced video games and special effects in all the latest movies. Virtually every toy he had ran on batteries and did something, lit up, crawled, or moved in some manner. He was a bright kid and seemed to understand what the cloudy mass of a fat man was asking him.

"I want to be an Asssstronaut! I want a spaceship. I want to be an Asssstronaut!" He repeated excitedly. It hadn't bothered Bobby one bit that the last six U.S. astronauts died in the Space Shuttle Challenger explosion back in January, including a teacher. The Djinni registered two requests as it retreated; Bobby wouldn't get a chance at a third.

Bobby immediately fitted into a tiny flying saucer with a bubble top, just the kind of spaceship he was thinking The Jetsons would use to cruise. The glass was extremely thick and overall, the ship could withstand the rigors, pressures, and extremely hot temperatures of leaving the Earth's atmosphere at escape velocity. The craft promptly whisked him into space with an hour's worth of oxygen. He sat in awe with his mouth open. He was able to see the moon up close and personal, lots of stars, and the Earth itself looked like a big blue swirly marble with streaks of white and tan. He experienced the most thrilling hour of his life even though it was his last. To this day, the itty-bitty ship continues to drift further out into the universe like one of the old Voyager Spacecraft.

Twenty minutes after Bobby left, Sally found the lamp partially wrapped in one of her good towels, which now had large black smears ground into its green dye. "He's going to get it for this," she said aloud, "Oh Bobby! Bobby!" But he never did answer. She threw the lamp into another box clearly marked "RUMMAGE" while Bobby became nothing but a picture posted on a milk carton.

"I mention this fact as tending to support what I have often heard stated, namely, that a shark's sense of smell is so keen that, if men ever bathe in seas where they are found, a shark is almost sure to appear directly afterwards." - George Grey

CHAPTER XXXII

FOR SOME REASON, MARGARET Fellner continued to let her ex-husband Roger sleep with her. She felt ruined for all other men. In nine years of marriage, they had eight children; something about the lack of birth control combined with the stars lining up in terms of fertility. She'd have a baby, recover in a week or two, have sex, and then bam, pregnant. One problem is that she did not have time to lose some of that extra weight between pregnancies, and she was not a small woman in the first place.

Roger was a bit of a bad boy with an old Yamaha motorcycle and a rusty Pontiac GTO, but in both the short and long run, he turned out to be a bum and a criminal. Police caught him stealing cars at the ripe old age of seventeen and spent a year of time in the Genesee County Jail. When he got Margaret pregnant, he did offer to marry her, no big wedding, just an appointment at the old Justice of the Peace. He had to wait until he was released, which happened to be after the birth of their first child. Roger would brag that his wedding cost $30, $20 to see the judge and $10 for the license.

With his criminal record combined with his lack of skills, unless hot wiring cars counted, it wasn't easy for Roger to find any work. As a result, they lived on welfare and the government handouts increased with each newborn child; the more kids they had, the bigger the checks. It was a sweet deal in America, the land of opportunity; some places like China, withdrew benefits or even imposed huge fines if a couple decided to have more than one child; not so in the god ol' USA.

As part of his welfare situation, it was necessary for Roger to report to Michigan's Unemployment Bureau every so often. They would try to match him with a prospective employer, but Roger either came up with an excuse or got fired, usually for stealing something as small as paper clips, a stapler, other office supplies, or even toilet paper. Roger took up fishing, partied constantly, and spent a good portion of those checks on cigarettes and the cheapest beer he could find. In the 1970's, cigarettes were only about 40 cents for a pack of twenty, maybe $3 or $3.50 for a carton of ten packs. Unbranded beer in plain white cans with black lettering stamped "BEER" sold for as little as $4 a case. He didn't mind since he felt that most cheap beer tasted the same anyhow, especially after one had downed a few.

Roger was a scammer. He figured out the welfare system, sold a little weed on the side, and worked under the table for cash only at a local auto repair shop; all the while avoiding the hassles of a real job. He and Margaret bought damaged merchandise at the grocery store for about one-third or even one-fourth the normal retail prices, mostly dented cans, and partially opened boxes.

The '67 GTO rusted so badly that one of the front fenders and rear quarter panels flapped in the wind when they traveled over 40 mph. Flint, along with most cities in Michigan's Lower Peninsula, salted the roads heavily during winter ice and snowstorms. Salt, one of the worst corrosives, particularly with metals, ate away car bodies like flesh eating bacteria. The Pontiac, though a classic in its day, burned a lot of oil, backfired, and perhaps ran on six and sometimes seven cylinders out of its original eight.

To get a license plate for the car, Roger would visit a different insurance agent each time, use a separate insurance company, get a policy written up, perhaps make a small deposit, like $10, and then asked them to bill him for the rest by mail. With a temporary proof of insurance in hand, he would then take it to the Secretary of State's office to get his plates. When the insurance bill came in the mail, he'd simply ignore it or cancel with the company; thus, obtaining his plates for a year's time without carrying insurance as mandated by law. He kept a list of insurance companies to be sure that he didn't use the same one twice.

Roger and 'Margie' as he called her, had their first child in 1973 and divorced in 1980 when Roger was busted for peddling marijuana to high school kids. As Margie got bigger over time, Roger was not awesome in the attraction department either. He developed a beer gut, smoker's cough, and he just never cleaned up well. He looked ratty, had bad breath, often didn't shave for days on end, and wore the same clothes repeatedly without washing them; nevertheless, he still seemed to project that masculine bad boy image complete with bulky arms filled with garish blue biker tattoos. He liked his faded, partially torn jeans and an old leather jacket with more creases than a-hundred-year-old man. He carried his wallet and keys on separate chains that he hooked to his belt loops, too cool.

Except for the sex life, which the pot enhanced, the marriage had never been a good one. Margie was constantly saddled with kids while Roger, at times, could be gone for days, whether it was fishing with his buddies or just on a drunkfest, or as in most cases, the two usually went together. He was ordinarily drunk or high at home or both and squandered what little money they had.

She needed clothes for herself, diapers for the kids, always more food, and the bills tended to pile up to the point that their phone and power were periodically shut off. She found out that Roger was sleeping with one of her friends, but there were others too that she didn't know about. Her prospects in the same department were dim as she gradually crept over two hundred pounds, smoked a good deal herself, wore glasses that she got from Goodwill, and had a pudgy, large, pasty, rounded face with moist chin rolls. Her complexion always seemed to be red with her face dripping sweat.

After the marijuana bust, Roger was back in jail, for two years this round. Margie used the opportunity to catch up on bills, buy enough food for the brood, and acquire clothes at garage, yard, and moving sales. As the auto factories started to close in Flint, more people were moving out than in. She was able to push the divorce through since having a repeated felon for a husband was reason enough. When Roger got out of prison, she continued to sleep with him.

By 1986, problems arose with their thirteen-year-old daughter. Anne Fellner, living in a bad neighborhood in an apartment where she shared a room with her four sisters, became a carbon copy of her mother. It hadn't helped in her basic upbringing that her father was a lazy absent drunken bum, while her pudgy haggard welfare mother of twenty-nine looked more like forty-nine with deep premature lines from the stress of her life. When her father went to jail four years prior, her mother provided them with a bounty of surplus food. Margie still bought the dented cans but also received the government surplus goods for low-income families. Margie never had a job. Consequently, skinny Annie put on pounds faster than a steroid-injected hog in a fast-finishing operation.

Annie had been a tiny six-pound nine-ounce baby and a skinny grade school kid, but her eating habits never were the best. This was because of her upbringing, as items like fresh fruits & vegetables, lean cuts of meat, whole grain breads, and so forth, are all quite expensive and often beyond the reach of low-income families. She grew up eating white bread, cheap sugary cereals, fatty meats like hot dogs and bologna, and any fruits or vegetables she got came out of a dented can laden with sugar and salt respectively. Food surplus from the U.S. Government consisted largely of five-pound bricks of cheese, which Annie loved, plastic bottles with honey, and pound packages of pure fattening butter. Whenever she acquired a quarter or any other loose change, it was undoubtedly spent on a candy bar or junk food. Her mother had a penchant for potato chips and ice cream, and Annie delved into those too when she could sneak them past her mother.

Aside from sharing a weight problem, Annie, like her mother, became pregnant as a high school teenager. Statistically, Annie was right on course since unwed teenage mothers are invariably children of young unwed teenage mothers. At least her mother had gotten married after her birth even though it was a big mistake. Annie had no idea who the father of her child was since she slept with virtually anyone who offered. She naturally did it for attention.

Annie's own father was always gone while her mother had divided hers between the eight children with the youngest always getting the most. None of the boys wanted her for a girlfriend, but they would sleep with her given their hormone-induced thoughtless ideas when it came to sex. Annie became known as the "pin cushion" since she put out. Junior high and young high school boys gained experience with her and then cast her aside.

It was about two months later when Annie Fellner realized that she was carrying a child. She had been waking up sick the last few weeks with headaches, stomach cramps, and morning sickness. The biggest clue was when she missed two periods in a row even though she had only started barely eight months earlier. Judy Crampton, her best friend, was only 14 years old and had already had an abortion.

"I missed two in a row," Annie said gloomily.

"You're pregnant," said Judy.

"Yeah, I think so."

"Whatcha gonna do?" Judy asked between bubble gum pops.

"Don't know."

"When I got pregnant, I told my mom."

"What she do?"

"She went crazy Annie; she hit me an' knocked me down. She was yellin' an' screamin' and wanted to know who I'd been messin' with an' I told her I wasn't sure an' she hit me again an' gave me big bruise on my shoulder." Judy went on rapid-fire like.

"Whaddya do after that?"

"She sent me to my room upstairs an' waited 'til dad got home an' then she told him an' they talked for like a real long time like ya know? Dad was real mad an' told me that I was like getting an abortion an' they set up an appointment like you know? Just three days after."

"How much was it?"

"Hundred fifty bucks."

"Wow!" Exclaimed Annie, "I ain't got that kind of money, didn't you want to keep your baby at all, like you know?"

"I don't know, dad was gonna kill me an' I wasn't gonna argue an' like you know, I just got it done."

"What else did they do?"

"Dad like grounded me like for two years, said I couldn't go anywhere, do anything with guys for like two years, an' said that if I did that, he was gonna beat me an' like kick me out of the house."

"Did it like hurt any when you got it done?"

"It wasn't too bad, it hurt some, but like I got it over with you know? Listen Annie, maybe you should like tell your mom, you can't like get an abortion without your mom or dad signing up for you."

"I can't," said Annie. "I ain't seen my dad in a month and mom 'ull kill me sure. I can't have a kid, I just can't." Annie began to cry, big wet splotchy tears that smeared an overabundance of cheap eye makeup in the corners of her pudgy reddened face.

"Well you like gotta do somethin'" said Judy as she put her own flabby arm around her equally flabby friend.

The next day was Saturday and Annie Fellner thought long and hard about her condition. She couldn't get an abortion at the clinic, it was too expensive for one, and since she was still a minor, she needed parental permission. She could tell her mom, but her mom just might kick her out. She didn't really want the child since there would be no place or no room to keep it, let alone the expense associated with a baby. She was ignorant of the fact that the State of Michigan funded abortions for low-income families like hers, but it would still involve telling her mom.

She put off the decision and walked down to a rummage sale a few blocks away. She had fifty cents in her pocket when she approached Sally Monroe's mother's sale. She found a large T-shirt that had the word "Gucci" written on it and she bought it for a quarter. She noticed four or five other people walking around the card tables and picnic tables filled with assorted junk when she noticed the lamp. She picked it up, turning it over and over; on the bottom, it had a price tag marked $1.00.

There was something about it that fascinated her, even called to her, much like collectors who find a new object for their collection whether it's a paperweight, dinner plate, shot glass, thimble, ornament, or whatever. She didn't have enough money for it but while the old lady was busy selling an iron for a buck-fifty to another customer who was trying to get it for a buck, she blocked the lamp with her none-too-small body, wrapped the Gucci T-shirt around it, picked it up, slowly turned around, and walked off with it. No one took notice.

Back at the house, most of her little brothers and sisters were watching cartoons on an old fuzzy black and white television with broken rabbit ears that only pulled in three or four channels. Her dad had put some black electrical tape around the antennae to keep it upright. She walked into the empty bedroom and sat down on one of the mattresses lying on the floor. She made a half-hearted attempt to remove the T-shirt from the lamp, but she pulled it down instead of up. One sleeve caught on the spout, the other on the handle. She then yanked it up, brushing more than half the lamp as she finally released it; that wasn't the only thing released.

"What do you wish girl?" A rounded cloud of smoke had poured out into a fat Mideastern looking man with a long pencil thin moustache and short goatee. What was totally weird was that he was speaking to her.

Like so many others, it frightened her at first, but she recovered, "Dude, are you like for real?"

"I am ready to obey you as your slave, so what is your first wish?"

The seven-foot mass seemed to take up a good portion of her room as it was not exactly thin in the middle either. The ceilings were originally seven feet in height too, but they sagged and were crooked or uneven in places, particularly where the Djinni was standing; as a result, his turban touched the ceiling and three inches of it disappeared.

"I want to get rid of my baby," said Annie.

A loud whisper-like noise filled the air...Psssshhh," as the Djinni retreated once again back into the lamp.

Although she missed her next time of the month due to her pregnancy, she had what she thought was an unusually large one that night. She woke up around 1:00 a.m. with terrible cramps and an abnormal amount of bleeding.

"Damn, it hurts!" She said as she staggered into the bathroom at the end of the hall clutching her lower abdomen, dripping like a leaky hose as she walked. She managed to find a raggedy stained towel, wet it some with a little cold water from the sink, clean herself up some, but she could not stop the bleeding. In the bathroom closet, she found a box of unbranded maxi-pads; there was only one left. She put it on, but both the pains and bleeding intensified.

After half an hour of misery, the pain let up a little and she was able to walk hunched over clutching her lower abdomen back to the girl's bedroom. As she went to lie down, a sharp pain struck in her most private area. She moaned quietly trying her hardest not to wake anyone up. The pain continued to jab her like a skilled boxer until it settled more into a persistent throbbing. She couldn't sleep. It hurt so much, god did it hurt.

She remembered the lamp and wondered if that nasty looking thing in there had anything to do with her present condition. She crawled over to the closet, careful not to upset any of her younger sisters spread out across the three mattress tops that covered most of the floor. She took out the Gucci T-shirt where the lamp was hidden and managed to half crawl and walk back to the bathroom, leaving a thin trail of blood wherever she went.

She felt her way with one hand while clutching the lamp inside the T-shirt in the other. In the bathroom, she groped for the light switch, found it, and pushed it upward, smearing little splotches of blood on the wall and switch plate. She yanked the T-shirt off the lamp, but nothing happened. She pulled, cursed, clawed, and beat the lamp; still, nothing happened.

"Come out you bastard!" She screamed and cried as a mixture of tears fell from her eyes mixed with blood from her hands. The pad had been overflowing and when she removed it, there was more blood on her hands. She used the T-shirt to wipe the blood and tears from the lamp and this time it came out.

"What is you second wish?"

"God it hurts! It hurts so bad!" She tried to muffle her screams, but her mother woke up this time. "Make it go away, oh please make the pain go away." She was delirious now. "Let me go away too, anywhere in the world but here." She was still hanging on to the lamp as the Djinni retreated inside of it.

She did have two wishes left and why not take care of both at the same time? That was far from her thoughts, but the Djinni interpreted them that way. The pain immediately stopped, then Annie disappeared with the lamp before her mother could discover the source of all the commotion. The Djinni figured that the middle of the Atlantic Ocean was an appropriate place, one of the largest and most likely geographical features on the planet if one were going to go somewhere by random chance; after all, she had said anywhere in the world, right? About seventy-one percent of the Earth's surface was ocean and all the oceans flowed into one another.

There were no boats or no shipping lanes where she was at, nothing but an endless infinite view of flat water in every direction. She had gone under but came right back up on the surface, spewing saltwater as she caught her breath. Given her relatively large body mass and high percentage of fat, she was quite buoyant and treaded water easily. She was a natural floater not a sinker. She still held on to the lamp, but the pain was gone. Unfortunately, her clothes and hands were a bloody mess, and it wasn't long before the smell attracted several sharks. A typical shark can detect a single drop of blood in a million drops of water and they descended upon her like starving ants on a candy bar.

As they battled for the prize, a smaller white shark and a hammerhead squared off; the white bit the hammerhead on one of its lower front fins; it started bleeding too. Soon, the other sharks ate it, another wounded shark, and the girl. Coming late on the scene, a fifteen-foot, 2,000-pound female Great White Shark swallowed Annie's lifeless right arm fiercely clutching the lamp with its right hand. Female sharks were on average a little larger than male sharks and could consume more. They often didn't chew much, just enough to swallow pieces as big as their respective throats and stomachs would allow.

"Poker exemplifies the worst aspects of capitalism that have made our country so great." - Walter Matthau

———◉———

CHAPTER XXXIII

———◉———

THE FOUR OF THEM HAD met up as junior high students when they all joined the "Explorer's Club," sort of a sophisticated coed Boy & Girl Scout outfit in Littleton, Connecticut. Anthony (Tony) Andrews, James (Jimmy) Baldwin, Robert (Bob) Polaski, and Mark (Mark) Miller would all go on to the same private high school in New Haven. They were all spoiled rich kids from wealthy families and would likely be Ivy-League bound next year in 1987, possibly Yale, but maybe not since it was local, perhaps Harvard or Brown or Princeton or some other super expensive ultra-prestigious Eastern school. It was summertime now and school was the last thing on their minds.

Tony sat down in his father's den, which his father referred to as "The Trophy Room." It was in a large finished open room in the basement, but with climate controls and dehumidifiers so as not to upset the dead animal trophies. He looked up and admired the stately lion's head whose blank lifeless professionally stuffed face stared back. Sometimes it was a little creepy since it sported Mona Lisa eyes, the kind that followed you about the room whether it was the den or The Louvre.

There was a beautiful carved mahogany three-in-one game table that you could play cards, bumper pool, or just leave it with a flat surface which they had built puzzles upon when he was younger. Several stuffed decorations hovered above, some acquired legally, but others not quite so. There were heads of eland, rhinoceros, hippopotamus, bear, moose, deer, elk, goat, ibex, and so forth, both from the Old World and New, mixed as his father acquired them. Given the rise of numerous national parks in Africa, the governments banned a good deal of hunting, but one could easily bribe officials, rangers, and poachers. Local guides would take you anywhere for a price and a few hundred dollars American was equal to thousands in rural parts of Africa. The world is a large place to police and all bets are off when the police and game wardens are corrupt.

Tony was reading an old Max Brand western in a big comfy leather lounge chair before his 3 friends were due to show up for a poker game in a half an hour or so. His mind wandered up at the products of wasteful killing, next to a girl named Jackie who had turned him down for a date, and then back down to the light easy reading of a classical western. It was a book that did not require careful reading, as he read a page or two without really following along.

He had gone with his dad hunting elk in Wyoming, white-tailed deer in Michigan, moose in Canada, mule deer in Colorado, but never beyond North America. He'd done more fishing in one of his dad's boats with his friends than hunting. He had been raised on guns. On hisnineth birthday, his dad bought him the Daisy Buffalo Bill model BB gun, a step up from the classic Red Ryder, and then offered to pay him a dollar for every bird that he killed and $5 if he could get something a little bigger like a small rabbit or squirrel. He made a quite a few bucks killing off songbirds not realizing much in the way of ethics since his daddy readily encouraged it.

He grew up with the same god-like attitude, especially when it came to hunting. To alleviate the boredom of the woods, he and his father would at times shoot at anything that moved whether it was legal or illegal, doing as much damage to the local wildlife as a swarm of house cats turned loose outdoors. They shot birds, chipmunks, squirrels, possums, raccoons, snakes, frogs, and even large insects to improve their marksmanship. Tony thought about this and smiled as his mind wandered to the book, then to hunting, and girls, and what not. He was lazily finishing another chapter when the doorbell rang. He raced up the stairs to answer it.

"What's up Tony?" Jimmy said as he walked in.

"How's it going?" chipped in Bob who was one step behind Jimmy.

"Not much" and "Okay" were Tony's answers. He led them downstairs and two steps from the bottom, the doorbell rang again. It was Mark this time, and after similar greetings, Tony led him downstairs too.

"Mom and pops are gone, right Tony?" Mark asked as he cracked open a can of beer.

"Don't worry about it; they're up at the cabin for the whole weekend. Anyways, my dad doesn't mind if you have a beer or two." Tony's parents owned a summer cottage up in Maine.

"Mine does though," answered Mark.

"You're a wimp," said Jimmy, "Maybe we ought to call your old man and tell him that you're drunk and can't drive home!"

"Uh huh, and if you do, I'll kick your ass," said Mark good-naturedly. "By the way Jimmy, I'm surprised that Marcia allowed you to come here tonight."

"I took her to the drive-in last night and as she usually goes shopping most of the day Saturday with her old lady."

"What did you see?" Bob Asked.

"I'm not sure, we really didn't go there to see the movie if you know what I mean," said Jimmy with a boastful devilish grin on his face.

"Good man!" Said Tony, "Well boys, let's get the cards out, that's what you're all here for, right?"

"We certainly didn't come here to see you," said Bob.

"Aw shut up Bob, why don't you guys get the top off the table while I round up some chips." Tony came back with a fancy revolving chip dispenser stuffed with heavy clay chips while the other guys pulled off the flat tabletop to reveal the poker level underneath. That poker section had pockets for money or chips, built-in coaster indentations for beer cans, and ashtrays too, which were needless since none of them smoked.

"Let's have your 50's and remember that the white chips are a dollar, the red are two dollars, and the blues are $5," stated Tony.

Yeah yeah, we know what they are, so just get them out here," answered Mark impatiently as he dug out two twenties and a ten.

"Just want to make sure you know what you're losing," Tony said as he gave each of them four blue chips, ten red, and ten white. It was quite a bit of money when compared to the lower and middle classes who often gambled with nickels, dimes, and quarters. Tony and his pals played $1 ante and $5 maximum raises. They were after all, the sons of lawyers, bankers, and corporate executives.

They cut for the first deal and Jimmy's Queen of Spades was the highest. "All right, ante up," said Jimmy, "The name of the game is five-card Draw with deuces wild." Jimmy dealt them out one at a time after each of them deposited a white chip into the pot.

Bob sat next to Jimmy on the left and had the first bet. He glanced at his cards surreptitiously and observed a pair of tens. "It'll cost you a dollar to stay," he opened by spinning another white chip into the center of the table.

On Bob's left sat Mark whose hand was full of five non-matching cards, all under 10 at that, but he threw a dollar in because one of his cards happened to be a deuce.

"What ta hell, I'll stay in," said Tony. His hand contained nothing much, but he had an ace and would take advantage of their special ace rule allowing him to draw four cards when the usual draw limit was three.

Jimmy's hand was the worst of the lot, no aces, no deuces, but with the chance of three new cards, plus no one had raised the bet, he could hardly refuse. "What's a buck?" He questioned as he rolled his chip into a growing sea of white.

"I'll take three," Bob said as he saved his pair of 10's and threw out his other cards. Jimmy promptly dealt him another ten and two useless cards.

"I'll have three too," Mark said as he saved his wild card and his other highest card, which happened to be a nine. Jimmy dealt him an eight, a seven, and a five. Mark quickly arranged his cards in order from lowest to highest placing the deuce in place as a six; it was a straight.

"Give me four," Tony said.

"Well, show us that ace," Jimmy said as he eyed him suspiciously.

"Give me the damn cards," demanded Tony as he flipped over his lone ace of spades.

"Ooo, the death card," Jimmy whistled as he dealt him another ace, a king, an eight, and a four. Jimmy then threw out his three lowest cards while saving his queen and nine. He drew a deuce, a three, and a jack; the best he could come up with was a pair of queens despite the wild card, the worst hand again.

"It'll cost you two this time," said Bob confident that his natural three-of-a-kind would win.

"Here's your two plus three more," chipped in Mark with a single blue $5 chip. Tony and Jimmy promptly folded knowing that there was little hope of winning with their measly pairs. It was a game with wild cards and there were already two avid bettors.

"Three more and call you," said Bob.

"I've got a straight," Mark laid it out nicely on the table as he spoke.

"Shit, beats my three tens."

As Mark scooped in the chips from the pot, the cards went Bob's way and since it was dealer's choice, Bob decided to play five-card stud.

The game started at 8:00 p.m. and they decided to break up around midnight. Like all card games, poker is a game of chance and does not require serious or deep thinking like chess. There is a little psychology involved in knowing your opponents; nevertheless, for those who know the basic strategies and probabilities, it really comes down to luck as the most significant factor in winning. It was simple, if you received good cards, then you were more likely to win; if you received bad cards, then you were more likely to lose.

In Texas Hold 'em for instance, are the world's greatest tournament poker players truly the best? All things being equal, bluffing, betting, and a little mixed-up strategy could be important factors, especially if the cards were consistent for each person, but they are invariably not. A high pair in the hole instantly puts a player in a favorable position, especially if another is consistently getting two mismatched small cards like a two and a seven in different suits. Even the little guys can win with a lucky draw.

Jimmy was having a bad night. After a little past 10:00 p.m., he cashed in a couple of twenty-dollar bills for a fresh batch of chips. Tony and Mark were about even while Bob was having a very good night. Jimmy continued his losing streak and was becoming increasingly irritable; nevertheless, it wasn't the total fault of the card gods.

By 11:00 p.m., Jimmy had been drinking excessively, much more than the others, and the way he was playing showed. It was a trick often employed by the big-name casinos – give free drinks to those gambling and they'll bet foolishly. Jimmy didn't fold anymore and just went along with every hand, matching bet after bet. He caught the others trying to bluff once or twice, but they were bright lads and were on to him. In response, they cut down or eliminated their bluffing altogether.

The big blow came to Jimmy on the final hand before they called it quits. Tony was dealing a hand of seven-card stud with nothing wild. He dealt two cards face down to each player and then one up. All three of Jimmy's cards were diamonds, including the ace dealt up.

"Five dollars," was all that Jimmy said as he tossed a blue chip into the center of the table.

Bob was next. He had an ace up and another proverbial ace in the hole, so it didn't take him much to stay in despite Jimmy having an ace exposed as well. On second thought, since it was the last hand and he was having a good night, he decided to raise. "Here's your fiver Jimmy plus two more." He added a red chip with the blue.

Mark, who had three totally unmatched cards decided to bail out early though he had less than half the total of expected cards. Tony, using the same logic, decided to stay for just one more hoping to better his hand before bailing out. $7 was still a stiff opening round bet.

With $25 in the pot already, Tony dealt the three remaining their fourth card. Jimmy received another diamond, four toward the flush with three more cards on the way. He was feeling good despite the bleary way the cards were beginning to look. Bob got a five to go with his two aces and a jack, not much help. Tony bettered his hand with a matching six.

"Five dollars," replied Jimmy who added another blue chip to the pile as wildly as the first. It rolled on its side, but Tony stopped its progress and dropped it back toward the central area of the table. Bob and Tony both called the bet without raising this time while Mark was content to stay out of it; after all, he would end up a few dollars ahead for the night.

The fifth card was dealt up as Tony laid them out for the three of them who were still in. Jimmy didn't get his fifth diamond to complete his flush, but he still had two chances yet. Bob got the last ace remaining in the deck to go with his other two, revealing a pair for all to see. He still held that ace in the hole. Tony added a four to his up cards, which now gave him two-pair though no one could tell. He had a four, six up, a four, and a six down.

The bet shifted to Bob whose two aces up was the best hand showing now. "We'll keep it consistent," Bob replied as he made sure that the others observed the blue chip that he craftily rolled into the pot. It made a clatter as it fell on top of the growing pile. He was feeling pretty good with his three aces.

"I'll stay," said Tony as he placed his own blue chip more carefully in the center with hardly a sound.

Jimmy was again low on money and out of blue chips. He reached into the front pocket of his designer jeans and pulled out a couple of crumpled twenty-dollar bills. He shoved them at Mark and said, "Give me a few more chips will ya an' make'm all blue." His voice was deteriorating at a rate directly proportional to his alcohol consumption. When Mark returned with eight shiny blue chips, Jimmy snatched them rudely and threw two of them in the pot, "I'm raisin' ya five."

Throughout most of the night, they had hardly used their blue chips except for Jimmy. All of a sudden, there were ten blue chips in the pot, three reds when Bob had raised $2, and four whites from the original ante: a grand total of $60. Bob and Tony called as they each added another blue chip, now the pot stood at $70 even. Bob was down to his last blue chip, Tony was out of his, and Jimmy had six left that he had just acquired.

Tony was the dealer. As was his style, he dealt the last two cards out together, one down, and one up, for one final round of betting. Jimmy got his fifth diamond, the king. That made it a strong virtually unbeatable flush with both ace and king, at least from a flush standpoint. Bob did not improve his three aces, but he still felt confident; there were no other three-of-a-kinds that could match him. It was Tony, however, who struck pay dirt. He dealt himself another six in the hole, which gave him a pair of sixes and a four in his down cards, nicely matching the six and four in his up cards. Though a bit on the small side, it was a full house, better than a flush and far superior to three-of-a-kind.

"Five dollars," said Bob whose two aces showing allowed him to bet first and throw in his last blue chip.

Tony picked up five red chips in a neat stack and slowly dropped them into the pot one by one saying, "I'll see your five and raise five."

Jimmy quickly picked up three blue chips and said, "Here's your ten plus five more." He somewhat aggressively and even violently thrust them into the pot.

With a hundred dollars in chips resting in the middle of the table, Bob was the one who was getting worried the most. He already had a significant amount of money in the pot, and it would take at least a straight to beat his three aces; furthermore, Tony was only showing a six of spades, a four of clubs, a king of hearts, and an eight of clubs. "Not too promising," Bob was thinking to himself. Jimmy's face-up cars didn't look much better with an ace of diamonds, the eight of diamonds, the queen of hearts, and the nine of clubs. "I do wish that I had that ace of diamonds," Bob almost muttered out loud. His lips moved but the words were unheard.

"Let's go, shit or get off the pot," Jimmy nearly screamed with impatience.

"All right, all right, hang on to your drawers, here's my ten bucks, I'll just call," said Bob as he scattered in ten white chips.

It was Tony's turn, "Here's my five plus another five." Tony promptly deposited four reds and two whites.

Before Tony's chips settled, Jimmy quickly threw in a blue to match, then another for a final five-dollar raise. The pot now was at least double any they had had earlier in the evening. They had passed the point of no return, so Bob reluctantly caught up with ten more dollars and called. Tony added his five white chips and called as well. Tony thought about raising but he was getting low on money too. The pot now held an assortment of good ol' American red, white, and blue chips; a total of $145.

"Well, what've you got Jimmy?" Mark questioned as an innocent bystander who was very glad that he had folded early on. Jimmy slammed his down cards to reveal his flush and made a move toward the pot as if to reel it all in.

"Aw shit, I knew it," said Bob who immediately threw his cards in angrily.

With that, Jimmy had his sweaty fingers on the outer limits of the chip pile.

"Hold on a second!" commanded Tony.

Jimmy froze with the tips of his fingers on top of the pile, "What?"

Tony slowly turned his hole cards over one by one revealing his full house.

"Son of a bitch, goddammit to hell, look at that shit!" Jimmy shouted about every expletive he could think of. "Son of a bitch," he repeated one last time as he gradually eased his hands back from the pot. The others became a bit more uneasy with Jimmy's temper tantrum as Tony scooped in the big pile of chips.

"Well, it's getting late," said Mark who gladly accepted his money and left. Bob's remaining chips netted him $34 while Jimmy only had $9 left to cash out. Tony was glad that they all left quickly, especially Jimmy who was still grumbling but at least didn't throw anything. Jimmy, however, would remember little in the morning.

The four met together again at 10:00 a.m. sharp on Wednesday morning for their weekly summer golf outing at an exclusive private course called The Brookshire Country Club. It was a beautifully maintained course with rolling freshly cut bright green fairways, aerated clear ponds, immaculate white and finely raked sand traps, and old stately hardwoods mixed in here and there: massive oak, maple, and birch; then again, nothing less was expected of it by the members.

The houses that dotted the fringes of the course, including one by Bob's parents, started at about $500,000 for a small one and a half story cape cod, and ran up to several million for some of the five thousand and six thousand square foot three-story mansions. There was some variation in style as one could find a turreted Victorian model here, a columned Greek revival there, a massive Colonial further up, and so forth.

The country club itself was once a large thirty-two-room mansion built by some lumber baron. Now, it housed a restaurant, a large indoor swimming pool, lockers, a pro shop, and a few rooms people could rent under the auspices of a bed & breakfast inn; those rooms rented for $400 a night, but did include all green fees. In a separate building connected by a two-story habitrail-like walkway, there were tennis courts and a racquetball court as well. It was at the pro shop where the four boys met.

"Give me a pack of those prostaffs," demanded Jimmy as he reached for a 10-dollar bill.

The cashier gave him his pack of three golf balls plus a $1.92 in change, "Need anything else? Tees maybe?" The man questioned in a friendly manner.

"Sure, why not," answered Jimmy. He surrendered another $1.75 plus fourteen cents in tax for a pack of twenty wooden tees. The same materials would have cost half that amount in a department store. They had all purchased their clubs from the little pro shop for hundreds of dollars more than they could have elsewhere; nonetheless, it was just the way of the wealthy.

They hauled all their bags down a steep incline to get to the electric-powered golf carts owned by their fathers. They placed their clubs in the bag holders in the back of the carts and Bob & Mark rode off together to the first tee. They ordinarily played on teams of two for a relatively small wager based on their combined team score. Bob was by far the best golfer, primarily because he lived on the course and practiced more. To even things up, he paired with Mark who was the worst of the lot. The usual wager was five dollars per stroke. To date, the highest margin of victory had been twelve strokes in a match last year. This cost Jimmy and Tony sixty dollars each.

The course itself was relatively short. The par threes were less than 175 yards, there was only one par four over four hundred yards, and there was only one par five on the front nine and it was barely over five yards. Par for the course was only seventy since there were three par threes on the back nine to go with two par fives there, par thirty-five per nine.

Jimmy and Tony held the honors since they had won by three strokes last week. The first hole was a 370-yard par four that doglegged to the left. Jimmy teed up first but teed his ball up a little too high. He got under it a bit on the downward swing and skyed it too much. It landed about 170 yards in the middle of the fairway, short, but at least it was straight. Jimmy would be satisfied if they went that way all day.

The others followed in a leisurely fashion, taking a few practice swings, acting like pros, which they were not. Tony promptly shot one into the rough thirty yards further than Jimmy had. Bob smashed one right on the sweet spot and it landed 230 yards down the fairway. None of them was physically overpowering. They didn't lift weights and they had rarely done any hard labor in their lives to develop their muscles. Bob would continue to hit his shots further but that was due to the smoothness and correctness of his swing, not because of any physical advantage. Mark was the last to tee his first shot and he swung somewhat awkwardly on top of the ball.

"Wormburner!" Tony laughed as Mark's shot skimmed along the tips of the grass. It came to rest barely over a hundred yards.

"Lucky they cut the grass every day," laughed Bob who had been trying for years to get Mark to alter his swing.

They were all tied up at the halfway point. As usual, Bob shot in the upper thirties and posted a thirty-seven, just two above par with a respectable seven pars and two bogies. Mark ordinarily hacked out somewhere in the high forties and ended up with forty-nine; together, he and Bob totaled eighty-six. Tony and Jimmy shot forty-two and forty-six respectively. So far, no big surprises, but the back nine would prove troublesome for Jimmy. Holes ten to fourteen remained quite like one through five in terms of scoring. Bob continued his fine round with a single bogie stuffed between two pars on each end. Mark even hit a couple of pars thanks to a single putt on a par four, and a nice tee shot on a par three that landed him nine feet from the pin; he lipped it out barely missing a birdie. Tony and Jimmy fell behind a couple of strokes with a combination of pars and bogies, but nothing quite disastrous just yet. The final four holes would set Jimmy off.

The fifteenth hole was a 550-yard par five with a small pond about 250 yards strategically placed in the middle of the fairway. The idea was to hit the first shot short of the pond, the second over it, and thethird on the green, two putts, easy-peasy-lemon-squeezy.

That's how Bob did it at least. Mark accidentally hooked his first shot so far to the right that the pond was no factor for him at all. He took two more hacks in the right-side rough just to finally make it back to the fairway. It took him two additional shots to make the green followed by two putts for a double bogie seven.

Tony successfully nailed his second shot over the pond, albeit short, and then took out a four-wood for his third shot to reach the green, still over two hundred yards for him. He hit the wood perfectly; but it landed twenty yards over the green. He was able to chip it up to the green between a couple of trees and two-putted for a bogie six. Jimmy's drive was one of the best of the day, just a yard or two short of Bob's and perhaps only fifteen yards from the central pond. To outdo his drive, he selected a number two wood, and then proceeded to overswing terribly. His club connected with the turf nearly two inches behind the ball, and then two plunks were heard after he did manage to come forward and nick the ball; one for the splash of the shiny white ball, the other for the massive divot-like clump of dirt that followed the ball into the water.

"Oh shit! Motherfucker!" Jimmy cursed as he flung his club back into his bag. He walked up the edge of the pond, backed up two steps, and dropped a new ball over his shoulder. With the penalty stroke, he was now technically shooting his fourth shot. He decided to give the two-wood another try, tried to concentrate, but rushed it, and swung too hard again. The same old thing, déjà vu, two concurrent splashes as he cut up the sod while barely striking the ball.

"SON OF A BITCH! Goddamn, motherfucker!" He roared out as he hurled the golf club a full thirty yards out into the middle of the pond. The club cartwheeled nicely as it made a tremendous splash. Mark, who was still way off to the right, was the only one who missed the club throw; nevertheless, he did hear the expletives quite clearly after the plop.

Tony, who happened to be near Bob, walked up to him and said quietly, "Dang, Jimmy's really losing it lately, don't you think?"

"I almost said something Saturday when he lost his temper at the card game. I thought he was a bit drunk, but he was the biggest loser of the night. I think you're right, he's never thrown a club like that before, and those are expensive clubs."

"I'd hate to see what happens if he hits his next shot in the pond," said Tony, "He might throw the whole bag in then."

"I don't think he's that stupid," said Bob. Just then, Jimmy hit a decent 3-iron shot far over the pond. "Well Tony, looks like he'll keep his clubs at least until the next hole."

"I hope so."

Jimmy placed his seventh shot barely on the edge of the green and a putt exceeding 50 yards by a foot or two. His first putt took him within three-and-a-half feet from the hole, but the second one came up an inch short.

"Son of a bitch! Cocksucker!" Jimmy screamed and ranted again as he pounded his putt onto the sensitive green, making several deep dents before throwing it off several yards in the general direction of his golf bag. "A Goddamn ten, a Mother Fucking ten!" He shouted so loud that other players on adjoining fairways and tee areas were taking notice.

As they were exiting the putting surface, a greens keeper pulled up to check on the numerous complaints from other golfers. There was a certain etiquette standard in all golf, but even more so on a private course. Jimmy was not exactly following the expected customs. The driver of the John Deere Gator was a well-seasoned weathered man in his mid-50's, heavily wrinkled but muscular from engaging in a good deal of outdoor work. He mowed, cut trees, raked, moved the holes about the greens, and did the heavy grunt work ordered by his boss, the head groundskeeper. He never did get used to these stuffy rich folks, but he tried; nevertheless, the punk kids were always the worst.

"Listen here kid, if I hear that language again, or so much as one more complaint, I'm gonna pick you up and personally escort you off the place, capeesh amigo?" He directed his attention to Jimmy, now identified as the cursing culprit.

"Yeah, yeah," said Jimmy sarcastically.

The groundskeeper looked as though he was debating whether to get out of his cart and throttle Jimmy, when Bob stepped between them, "All right, all right, we'll take it easy," Bob said in a somewhat irritated voice, though his irritation was toward Jimmy.

"Good, and just remember that this is a peaceful, quiet, respectable place, try and keep it that way," the groundskeeper said and then abruptly drove off before any of them could reply.

With his quintuple bogie, Jimmy and Tony lost four strokes or twenty dollars on that par five. The sixteenth hole was a 395-yard par four straight away, but with four deep sand traps artfully placed around the green. Bob was getting to be a little irritating to the others, even so to Mark, his very own partner. Bob played it right: a nice drive, a short iron shot to the green, two putts, and an automatic par.

Mark hit another grass skimmer that either burned or scared the worms back underground; it only landed 105 yards up the fairway. He selected a three-iron and hit it further than the initial drive, and then used the same three-iron for his third shot that amazingly landed him on the green. He two-putted for a bogie five, which was fine by his standards.

Tony hit a decent drive that traveled over two hundred yards but dubbed his second shot. His third shot with a six-iron was a thing of beauty and one of his best shots of the day; it hit the somewhat sloped green twenty feet in behind of the pin, then spun backward toward the hole a good fourteen feet. He sank the six-foot putt for par. Jimmy's drive was a lot like Tony's, but his second shot landed in the bunker in front of the green.

"Shit," Jimmy muttered in a normal tone of voice; loud enough for his friends to hear, but it did not carry over to the adjacent holes like his very recent outbursts. He had a sand wedge in his bag, but one of the special rules of being in a sand trap was that one could not "ground" the club; in other words, one had to suspend the club in the air rather than resting it on the ground behind the ball as one usually did. Course rules prohibited golfers taking practices swings in the sand as well.

Jimmy did everything correctly except for getting the ball out of the trap. It had rolled in and hence, was not buried; thus, it should not have been that difficult to punch it out. Jimmy reared back and topped the ball terribly with the sharpest and steepest sloped club of all. The ball obtained little in the way of height, not enough to escape or clear the trap, and then rolled back down, actually a few feet further back in the hazard from the green than before.

"Motherfucker!" Jimmy partially yelled; it wasn't a full rebel scream, but it was about fifteen more decibels over normal conversation. Without gathering his thoughts, cooling down, or taking any time at all, he impatiently rushed back in, stepped back, and took a vicious swing at the ball. This time he sent it roaring across the green and into another sand trap behind it. Without saying a word though his face was a near-bursting deep crimson color, he hurled his club without looking or caring where it had gone.

"Watch what ta hell you're doing!" Mark yelled out as he had barely dodged the club in time to avoid being cross-whipped.

"What's gotten into you lately anyway?" Tony questioned as Jimmy was storming out of the initial trap.

"Sorry," was all that Jimmy mumbled, not really meaning it. He picked up his thrown club, now slightly bent, and was able to place his next shot on the green. Two putts netted him a triple bogie seven, another ten-dollar loss for the team.

The seventeenth hole was a 158-yard par three with a sizeable pond in front of the raised tee area. It did require one to hit a shot about seventy yards in the air to clear the water hazard. As usual, Bob had the honors again, and selected a six-iron. The pin was pretty much in the center of the green, an ideal position for the players. Bob hit a masterful lofty shot that landed on the front part of the green, took two hops forward of all things, struck the pin on the second bounce, and rebounded barely a foot short of the hole, nine and a half inches to be exact, a sure gimme for a birdie.

"Nice shot!" Tony praised him.

"Beautiful Bob! Just beautiful! Damn near a hole-in-one," Mark added.

Jimmy said nothing.

Tony was up next, selected a five-iron, and hit a low liner that barely cleared the pond; luckily for him, the tee off area was up on a hill. Had it been level, the ball probably would have skimmed and then died in the water. He did get a favorable roll, but his ball still ended up resting several yards short of the green.

Afraid of the pond and his ability to clear it, Mark selected a three iron, which he hit rather well. It landed in some scattered trees behind the green, but at least he had a clear path coming back through, and more importantly, he got it over the pond.

Jimmy kept fighting with his temper, but he was losing that as badly as he was the match. Like his partner Tony, he ordinarily used a five-iron on this hole, but today, he thought he'd try thesix. If Bob could do it, then he figured that he could do it too. As frequently happens when one selects a higher numbered club, particularly at the amateur level, one tends to push or swing just a little bit harder to compensate for the expected loss of distance.

Jimmy pulled back further on his backswing than normal, and then on his follow through, he pulled his shoulder and head up higher than usual. The result was that he did not quite get under the ball. By topping it, he hit a soft liner about fifty yards straight ahead, Ker plunk! A poor little water bug minding its own business lost its life instantly as it failed to move out of the way of the giant heaven-sent spherical white destroyer. Smooth ripples upset the still water as other bugs desperately scooted away from the scene. With a nice wide crease in it, this ball would end up in the driving range buckets when the grounds crew dragged the pond, too damaged to try to resell.

"Aw Shit! Son of a bitch!" Jimmy sounded off nearly at the top of his voice while he swung his club wildly like a baseball batter trying to swat flies. The others were looking around uneasily for the dude in the Gator.

"Take it easy now, Jimmy," said Tony, "Everybody has a bad day now and then: we'll get them next week."

Jimmy said nothing in return, teed up another ball with the same six-iron, and hit it some 16 yards short of the green, but at least he had cleared the water hazard. They all hit their next shots on the green except for Bob who was already there. Bob simply backhanded his putter with one hand to tap in his birdie, his first of the day. The rest of them two-putted. Mark and Tony ended up with bogie fours while Jimmy scored a six, his second triple bogie in a row. Comparing Jimmy's six to Bob's two, the team of Tony and Jimmy lost another twenty dollars.

The eighteenth and final hole was a 377-yard par four with a slight dogleg to the left. Bob and Tony played it right with two shots to the green, two putts each, and two pars went solidly in the books, or at least on their respective score cards. It took Jimmy and Mark three shots each to make the green, but where Mark two-putted, Jimmy three-putted; thus, going down a final five dollars. The others collectively held their breaths as it looked like Jimmy was going to hurl the putter at the clubhouse for an instant, but he held back. Since they were so near to the clubhouse and a few people were out on the second-floor veranda eyeing them, Jimmy finally exercised a little discretion and cursed quietly to himself rather than one of his screaming temperamental outbursts. The others were finally relieved when Jimmy put his putter back into the bag and walked off without further incident.

Bob had shot par for the back nine; an impressive thirty-five with seven pars, a bogie, and a birdie; his final total was a more than respectable seventy-two for an amateur, about three shots better than his usual five-handicap. Tony added a forty-one on the back to boost his eighteen-hole total to eighty-three, not too shabby for a typical weekend amateur golfer. Mark did a little better with a forty-seven, which gave him ninety-six altogether, a score more typical of the weekend duffer. Computing Jimmy's score took an extra minute or so. Jimmy's back nine netted him a fifty-two, the first time he had shot in the fifties for nine holes in the last two or maybe three years. His grand total tied him with Mark. All in all, Jimmy and Tony lost by eleven strokes for a fifty-five-dollar loss, a record since they had teamed up the way they did.

They parked their miniature electric cars in the appropriate spaces and went inside for a soda. Bob left early muttering something about picking his mother up at some gallery because her Mercedes was in the shop. Mark made a detour for the restroom, which left Tony alone with Jimmy.

"What's the matter with you lately anyway Jimmy? You blew up at the poker game the other night, and we could understand that since you were kind of drunk, and you did lose a big hand. You acted the same way today only worse, is something bothering you man?"

"I may as well tell you Tony, me and Marcia finally broke up last night. We've been or were fighting a lot lately and well...," Jimmy broke off at this point.

"That's too bad," was all Tony could think of saying.

"What's too bad?" Mark questioned as he sat back down.

"I broke up with Marcia."

"Oh," said Mark, "How come?"

"I don't know, she said something about needing to meet new guys, needing time, and going out with her girlfriends looking for guys, whatever. Of course, the bitch said that we could still be friends, what ta fuck is up with that bull shit?"

"Hey listen Jimmy," said Tony, "My dad said that we could take the boat out Saturday. Since it looks like you're free this weekend, why don't you come along?"

"Maybe, I don't know, I've been kind of a dick."

"It's all right," said Mark, "Can you promise to keep it cool?"

"Yeah, I suppose, I promise to keep my temper in check, okay?"

"Great, we understand," said Tony. "Then it's settled, anyway, quoting an old saying, there's plenty of fish in the old seas and we're going to get some real ones on Saturday out in the boat, who needs a regular chick anyhow? Just cramps your style man, now you can play the field."

"Right I guess," Jimmy answered none-too enthusiastically.

Thursday and Friday passed by quickly and the four were together once again at the New Haven Yacht Club. The yacht owned by Tony's father was thirty-two feet in length, powered by a 120-horsepower Mercury outboard motor. It had a neat little cabin area much like the inside of a recreational vehicle. It had a three-fourths-sized bed, a tiny stove, a tiny bathroom, a tiny sink, a few wooden cabinets, and a few ship gadgets including sonar and radar.

Aside from being loaded with the finest quality stainless-steel-plated bamboo fishing poles bolted in, all four of the boys were hunters, and they had their guns packed. They brought a couple of coolers crammed with beer and a picnic basket stuffed with sandwiches and snacks. The basket was a gift from Mark's mother who purchased the finest deli meats & cheese on bakery quality buns no less.

Tony started the engine with a quick twist of the key and then slowly eased out of the harbor into the ocean. They rarely traveled more than a mile or two from the sight of land. None of the four were expert sailors but at least Tony could navigate, read a chart, and operate the devices on the ship including radar and sonar; GPS tracking systems would not be standard equipment for at least another decade. Around 11:30 a.m., after an hour and a half of cruising out, then in circles, Tony cut the engine and dropped the anchor. He grabbed a beer and said, "Anybody else?"

"Sure, why not?" Jimmy answered. They all ended up having one to go with the eight sandwiches doled out, two each.

"These are great!" Exclaimed Bob as he bit into lettuce, tomato, and Swiss cheese all nicely sandwiched between thinly sliced meats of turkey, corned beef, and roast beef.

As they finished eating, they decided to bait their poles and do a little leisurely fishing, but in the act of doing so, Tony noticed something out of the corner of his eye off the port side, "Hey! Look guys! Over here or I mean over there," he motioned out into the water.

"Looks like dolphins," said Bob.

"They're headed our way," added Mark.

"I'll get the guns," said Tony as he leapt down into the cabin. He emerged but struggled handling four shotguns that he doled out. "Hall the anchor in," Tony said as he hit the ignition.

The chase was on or more accurately, a meeting was about to take place. The unsuspecting dolphins had experienced man and his boats previously, and they were not afraid. The strange upright figures had given them food too and as they approached the boat, they expected nothing less; nevertheless, they were in for a rude awakening.

When the dolphins were in close range, several shot gun blasts and stinging buck shot pellets peppered the unsuspecting school of nine. Four managed to get away but not without some injury; one lost an eye while another had part of its dorsal fin cut off. The one with the broken and busted up fin struggled to retreat with the other three. The four that sped off were still better off than the other five suffering repeated shots as the excited boys pumped more and more shells their way. Their blowholes filled with blood and a couple drowned while the other three bled to death.

The world is a cruel place. The four boys were from a class of wasters and takers, not givers. This behavior was natural to them, especially Tony, whose father had built a gaudy trophy room. Tony's dad had taught him that the world was in his hands, and that man had the right to kill virtually anything except his fellow man; nevertheless, there were even exceptions for that.

Tony had influenced his friends with some of this senseless killing attitude and they came to love it almost as much as he did. There they were, the four of them, cheering, laughing, and high fiving as they watched five harmless dolphins in the prime of their lives, bleeding, dying, while they enjoyed and even reveled in the destruction. Dolphins were some of the most intelligent animals of the sea but destroyed by those arguably more ignorant than them.

The slaughter was neither subsistent nor commercial, just for the sport, if you could call it that.

"Look at that," said Tony surveying the crimson pool, "We let four of them get away."

"That one doesn't look so good, let's go after it," Bob said as he pointed at the one listing somewhat with the wounded fin.

"Forget it," said Tony, "Let's watch what happens to the dead ones." They lacked the slightest amount of decency to put the one out if its misery that was obviously suffering. A true hunter does not leave the wounded to suffer.

Approximately twelve minutes later, a small hammerhead shark moved in to feed. Tony and Jimmy shot the unique shape of its head, with its creepy eyes, off in a simultaneous blast from their guns.

Mark was the one getting nervous, "We had better cool it a little with the guns, you never know, the Coast Guard might have heard."

"Maybe you're right," said Bob as he leaned his gun against the cabin.

"Let's watch the show!" Jimmy said as he leaned his down too.

Tony wasn't happy, but he put his gun down too with the others, at least for the time being, but not before racking another shell just in case. Soon, several more sharks appeared, mostly hammerheads and a feeding frenzy took place. Five dead dolphins and a medium-sized shark made up a lot of food. The swarming action became so violent that one shark mistook his cousin for a carcass and took a large bite out of its underside.

Fresh blood drew more bites and soon some of them were eating each other, which often happens in a feeding frenzy. A beautiful blue shark showed up, bigger than the hammerheads, and a few backed away from it giving the big gun a little more room to feed. Out of the distance, an even larger dorsal fin, bigger than any present, even the blue, closed in on the scene. It was a great white, about the second most feared predator in the sea next to the killer whale.

Jimmy noticed it first, "Hey! Look at that!" Jimmy ran to pick up his gun.

"Wait a second! Tony yelled out, "Let's see if we can catch it!" His mind raced back to his father's trophy room and centered on the giant swordfish mounted on the wall. "My dad always wanted to get a shark to add to the wall downstairs."

"You can't be serious," said Mark, "Look at the size of that thing!"

"I don't know," said Bob, "That ain't no little fish out there, how do we get it on board?"

"Well," answered Tony, "Sharks usually only come this far north in the summertime when it's warm, so it's not always easy to find them here. My old man's been wanting to capture one like I told you, and he's got a small hoist set up in the back." The others had not paid attention to it in the back of the boat off near the motor. It was a block and tackle affair with a crane arm and chains like that of a 'cherry picker" used to remove and install car engines, only a little bigger.

"I still don't know," said Bob, "Even if we get it on board, how are we going to kill it without messing it up too badly?"

"We shoot it once or twice in the head," answered Tony. "Too bad I don't have dad's old 50-caliber buffalo rifle with me, that'd probably do the trick, damn thing is like an elephant gun!"

"Aw what to hell, let's give it a try," said Jimmy as he grabbed a shotgun.

"How are we going to get it away from that crowd?" Bob asked, noticing how the great white and moved in and was feeding as viciously as the rest of them.

"We need to be patient," said Tony, "Wait 'til he moves away from them some." It was in all reality a "She."

"Who's going to shoot him?" Jimmy inquired.

"Tony should," answered Bob, "He's the best shot. Any ways, if he blows his damn head off or messes him up, then he can't blame it on us."

"Okay, all right with me," said Jimmy somewhat reluctantly, he had wanted a crack at it himself.

"Fine by me," said Mark who was backing off and didn't even go for his gunThey pulled the anchor in again and Jimmy fired up the motor as he took hold of the wheel in the driver's seat. Bob figured out the workings of the hoist and passed a second rope to Mark in preparation for the capture. Tony had both barrels of his Benelli filled with shells, turned the safety off, and sighted a line on the shark. "Edge over here a little" Tony pointed.

Jimmy would move the boat, "A little this way now," Tony directed as his gun moved with the shark. Finally, when the great white had taken several massive gulps of food, it broke out of the pile temporarily. That's all the motivation Tony required. In an instant later, Tony shot twice vertically right into the top of its head. In about 13 seconds, a nice round lucky number, it bellied up and appeared to have died.

"Quick now Jimmy!" Tony sat the gun down as Jimmy maneuvered the craft over to the side of the great white. Bob bent far down into the water and managed to wrap the chain around the top of the shark, which was now the underside. Mark wrapped his length of rope inside and about the tail fin and tied it to the boat. With a little group effort, they were able to roll the shark over to secure the chain and rope. Bob started turning the crank to raise the arm of the hoist, which in turn was lifting the shark, inch by inch, but it was rough going.

"Hey! Somebody give me a hand," shouted Bob. It was getting more difficult to crank as the shark was edging out of the water.

"Coming!" Tony raced over help.

With all four of them on the same side of the boat along with the shark, the boat suddenly tossed violently on the starboard side. Bob lost hold of the crank. The tension built up in it caused it to reverse course several times, striking Bob hard in the shoulder while the shark dropped two feet back into the water.

"Shit!" Bob cursed as he rubbed his severely bruised shoulder. The rope slid some back too and Mark suffered some light rope burns.

Tony was there immediately. "Are you all right?"

"Hurts like hell, but let's get this damn fish aboard," Bob said.

This time, both Tony and Bob gripped the crank while Jimmy and Mark tugged on the rope. The boat lurched again and was leaning at a steep somewhat dangerous angle, but the hoist manned by the two boys now kept the shark moving steadily upward. The little yacht did possess excellent buoyancy, much improved from the old wooden whalers from centuries past that could support forty tons of whales on their sides. The shark was probably a ton and a quarter, maybe a ton and a half. Bob and Tony were doing most of the heavy work. When the shark was high enough, they concentrated their efforts on swinging the hoist to drop the big fish into the boat, and they did it successfully.

"Ouch!" Mark exclaimed. While removing the rope he had been pulling, he rubbed the shark the wrong way. A shark's skin is very smooth, provided one strokes it from its head to its tail; going against the grain from tailfin up felt like coarse sandpaper. The bloody abrasion leading from Mark's wrist to his elbow was direct evidence of that fact. The boat righted itself some but still leaned to the starboard side because of the immense weight of the shark that leaned that way.

"What's the matter?" Tony asked.

"Damn, I just cut my arm a little," answered Mark, "Have you got a first aid kit?"

"Yeah, I'll go get it," said Tony as he ran down to the cabin area to retrieve it.

Mark fixed up his arm wiping the blood with a gauze pad and applying some ointment.

Bob was holding his shoulder and Tony said, "How bad is it?"

"I'll have a nasty bruise, but I think the bones are still in place," muttered Bob.

"Holy shit! We did it!" Jimmy was ecstatic, "We Fuckin-A actually did it! Look at the size of that bastard! You got a tape measure Tony?" The shark filled a good portion of the flat bottom space in the boat.

"No, I don't think so."

"I can just see it now hanging in your basement Tony," said Mark appreciatively. "You'll have to invite us over for a game once you get it hung up."

"Well, it's going to take some time for that, the guy that does my dad's stuff takes at least a few weeks, maybe a couple of months for something big."

"How long do you think it is?" questioned Jimmy.

Mark took a guess. "Let's see, the boat's thirty-two feet, right Tony?"

"Uh huh," said Tony.

Mark continued, "Well, it looks a little longer than half the boat, so I'd say what, maybe 17 or 18 feet?"

"I think that's pretty close," stated Bob.

"I hope my old man doesn't get mad, look at the mess that thing is making," Tony said pointing to the blood and other fluids pouring out of the shark's head wounds.

"Don't worry about it, we can hose it down when we get back to the docks," Jimmy said. "By the way," Jimmy continued, "Can I cut out one of its teeth?"

"Sure, why not?" Tony answered. "His face and head are all messed up anyway. That taxidermist dude is going to have a lot of work fixing up that head. I think sharks are supposed to have hundreds of teeth, rows of them."

Jimmy approached the massive sea denizen with a jack knife, somewhat matter of fact like and unsuspectingly. They all made the same mistake. Since they shot the shark point blank twice in the head with a 12-gauge shotgun, and had shown no further movement when they had hauled it out, they assumed it was dead. Its wounds were fatal, but it was not yet dead. They also forgot or did not know that fish can survive out of water for some time before drying out too much.

Jimmy knelt down by the shark's head. The great white was lying on its back with its huge jaws facing the sun. He pried its mouth open a little to get a better view of row upon row of sharp-edged nasty looking razor-like teeth. Jimmy eyed one large front tooth in particular and attempted to saw it off. This activity seemed to revive the shark somewhat, but it still did not show any outwards signs of life. Jimmy tried to cut and then made another sawing motion with the small jack knife, but it was proving difficult to remove, so he changed his angle of attack. In doing so, he placed his entire right arm across the now partially open mouth of the beast.

With a sudden spasmodic movement, the shark instinctively opened its mouth wider, jerked forward, and closed tightly on Jimmy's arm. The razor-like teeth snapped the arm as easily as Jimmy had once done to the frail frozen branches of a birch tree. A similar crackling sound followed as the humerus, radius, and ulna all shattered simultaneously.

"Ahhhhhhhhhhhhhh!" Jimmy wailed loudly as he instantly went into shock, and then passed out.

The others stared horrified with mouths dropping nearly to their chests. Tony was the first to react. He raced over to Jimmy shouting back to Mark: "Get that first aid kit over here, now!" He grabbed Jimmy's legs and pulled him away from the jaws of the beast.. Jimmy's blood was now pouring out from where the severed arm has been, and mixing with the sharks on the deck. Mark rushed over with the kit.

"We've got to stop the bleeding," said Tony. "Damn, we're going to have to make a tourniquet."

In the meantime, Bob was standing there gawking, "Come on Bob, find me something to tie off this arm!" Tony commanded.

The attack sliced Jimmy's arm neatly, halfway between the shoulder and elbow, right through the bicep, tricep, and other muscles in between. A chainsaw couldn't have done a better or cleaner job. Bob came rushing back with some fishing line on a spool and handed it to Tony, "Is this okay?"

"Maybe, worth a try," Tony said as he quickly unspooled some 20-pound test line and tied it tightly around what was left of Jimmy's upper but small bicep. "It'll bite into his skin but at least it'll cut the flow of blood. Help me take him downstairs."

Jimmy was fading in and out of consciousness, just enough to mumble and screech incoherently as the three managed to get him to the cabin bed. "Keep pressure on it," Tony added to Bob and Mark, "We're going to have to get him back fast."

Tony raced up topside, started the engine, got moving, and then pushed it to full throttle. With one hand on the throttle, he hit a few buttons on the radio with the other and issued a mayday to the coast guard. There were no government ships in the area, but the coast guard at least alerted the harbormaster and sent for an ambulance. A couple minutes short of a half an hour, they landed at the harbor as paramedics rushed into the cabin.

"Damn, he's lost a lot of blood," one of them said, "Pressure is weak."

"He's in shock too, set up an IV immediately," said the other one, "Get that in and we'll haul him out." Once they hooked Jimmy up with a combination intravenous fluid and blood bag, they pulled him out carefully and laid him on a stretcher. Tony, Bob, and Mark were staring awkwardly trying to stay out of the way when one of the paramedics started shouting at them.

"Are any of you hurt?" He said looking them over carefully. They all had some of Jimmy's blood in various places on their clothing.

"No," said Tony stating the obvious, "It's just Jimmy's blood."

"Okay, we've got to hurry now, where's his arm?"

"What?" Bob raised disbelief as the others seemed to freeze.

"Shit, it might be too late already, where's the damn arm?" The paramedic shouted.

Tony finally spoke up as he seemed to be the one who acted best under pressure, "I think, I think it's inside the shark," he pointed. "The shark ate it," he added.

"Jesus Christ! What ta hell are you doing with that?" The paramedic yelled. So intent were they at getting to Jimmy, they had not noticed the massive form lying motionless on the bottom of the boat.

"Well, let's just get him to the hospital, his vital signs are weak. We'll leave the rest of it up to the coast guard," said the other paramedic. A small coast guard cutter had followed them in, and the captain had entered the scene. The paramedic had a quick word with the captain about the arm and then bolted with the ambulance.

The captain was forty-eight years of age, short, burly, and obviously the superior officer in charge. He selected a tall and skinny subordinate named Patterson who was around thirty to board the boat with him. "All right Patterson, tie that thing's mouth shut, we don't want any more surprises," he commanded as he pointed to the shark. "You boys stick around here, don't go anywhere." The captain produced a huge Crocodile Dundee type knife with a blade nearly a foot in length. He immediately noticed the shotgun pellets plastered all over the shark's head.

"All right Patterson, get ready just the same." Patterson also produced a rather large blade as the captain neatly sliced the shark open from its lower jaw all the way down to the tailfin. He stayed as far back from the mouth as he possibly could. The shark didn't move an inch; it had passed on for good during the return boat trip.

"Nice cut sir, she seems to be dead."

"Aye, but you never know Patterson, you never know." The captain deftly made a few additional shorter cuts and laid open the entire digestive system including the bloated stomach. Throughout history, hunters have found bizarre items in sharks, such as shells, rocks, anchors, shoes, tools, and human bones on occasion. This one had a few bones, a pair of pliers, and of all odd things, an old bronze lamp. The captain discovered the arm long before it reached the stomach. The rest of the junk lay in a gooey pile in the bottom of the boat.

"Get the car Patterson!"

"Yes sir."

"You boy, grab me a sheet or towels or something," the captain said to Tony who was the closest. Tony raced back down into the hold.

"There any ice left in that cooler?" The captain spoke sharply to Bob who was next in line.

"Maybe..., I don't know."

"Just get it, bring it here."

Bob did as told. Tony produced a sheet, and the captain yanked it out of his hand, poured the half-melted ice from the cooler into it, wrapped the arm, and disappeared in a flash. He moved fast for his relative thickness and age. He dropped the package on the floor of the backseat, slammed the door, and waved Patterson off. Patterson would be just a few minutes behind the ambulance. The captain did not go with Patterson but came back to the boat.

"That was a pretty stupid thing to do," he lectured. "If your pal makes it, he'll probably lose that arm. I also saw what you did to her; don't you know that it's illegal to just shoot anything out in the ocean as you please? I'm going to cite you all, including your injured friend, for unlawful use of firearms. You'll likely have to make a court appearance, but I'm sure your daddies have good lawyers, you'll probably get a little probation and a nice fine." He wanted to cuss them out royally and threaten them further, but he had to be careful since they were indeed rich kids. After writing up four citations, he pocketed one with Jimmy's name on it and left. The boys would end up with 6-month probation sentences and $500 fines after their parents' lawyers negotiated them down to misdemeanors and fines.

Tony drove the boat back to his father's slip, then breathed a sigh of relief. "Damn," was all he said.

"Well Tony, do you need any help cleaning up this mess?" Mark asked.

"Nah, we've got a small pump and I'll hook up the hose to wash her down. Why don't you guys get cleaned up and then go over to the hospital to see how Jimmy's doing. I'll clean up some here and meet you there in a couple of hours."

Tony had grown up hunting with his father and the general entrails of what they killed and gutted did not bother him. He dumped larger chunks overboard and hosed down the deck. He found a scrub brush and bucket, added some soap, and then scrubbed the deck. He discarded the shark's indigestible artifacts into a large garbage bag with one exception, the lamp.

"Strange," he thought aloud, once rinsed, the lamp was somewhat clean and unmarred compared to everything else. He soaped it some, rinsed, and then began wiping it off with a towel when it started hissing. He dropped it and stepped back as if there wasn't enough drama for one day.

The smoky grayish-white cloud morphed into a fat Middle easterner with slightly monolid eyes, and it recited: "What is your wish boy?"

"Holy shit!" Tony gaped at it. He looked down at the carcass of the shark, and then back up at the figure waiting impatiently before him. Tony laughed a little too hysterically, "A wish you say?" The more he stared at it, the more he laughed. It certainly was a sad excuse for a genie if that's what it was. The ones he had seen on television were always fat, fatter than this one even, far more colorful with exotic costumes, and maybe more oriental looking. This one was kind of a murky gray color with bold blackened eyes and a cruel snarling mouth, kind of like seeing a more colorful one on a black and white TV.

"Must be some kind of joke," Tony said aloud, "Of course I'd love to be away from here now, maybe out hunting big game somewhere, can't wait 'til my dad finds out about this, he's going to be pissed. Why am I taking to you anyway?" He stared back down again at the shark just as the Djinni was about to leave. "Actually, I wish that we'd never have found you." Tony was referring to the big fish carcass, but the Djinni understood differently as if the boy were referring to the lamp. The Djinni had registered three separate requests and proceeded to grant them as its form returned to the inner chamber within the lamp.

The wounds of the four boys ranged from virtually nothing to minor, then to serious, and then to fatal, but not for Jimmy. Mark skinned his arm and suffered nothing more than an abrasion. Bob bruised his shoulder, but no bones were broken. The arm arrived too late for Jimmy, but he survived the ordeal less one appendage. It was Tony who lost his life somewhere in Tanzania on a big game hunt in Africa before the summer was over. He and his father were tracking a lion that Tony had wounded, but the lion got to Tony before his father could finish it off. In the meantime, the shark carcass had mysteriously disappeared, as did the lamp.

"Little League baseball is a very good thing because it keeps the parents off the streets." - Yogi Berra

CHAPTER XXXIV

Charles Jensen III, better known as "Little Chuckie" at a young age or just plain "Chuckie" as time went on, smacked the ball over fifty feet in the air. He was four years old, big for his age, and it showed in the way he smashed the baseball with uncommon vigor with a twenty-eight-inch aluminum bat. They were hitting the ball off a tee, but Chuckie had some experience with piñatas. At the last birthday party, he was the only one who could break through it in his age group. Many of the same preschoolers were here having a lot of fun whiffing or barely contacting the ball; not so for Chuckie, he hit the ball twice as far as anyone else.

It was a hot ninety-two-degree Sunday in Cedar Rapids, Iowa. Smack! A sixty-two-foot shot by Little Chuckie got the spectators "Oooing" and "Ahhing."

"Good boy Chuckie, Yessssssssss!" His father praised him repeatedly, almost embarrassingly so.

They owned an eighty-acre farm a little south of the city and three-fourths of it was ordinarily planted in corn, what else? Charles Jensen Jr. did allocate a few acres to vegetables which he hauled to the farmer's market in an old rusty '63 Chevy longbed stepside pickup. The truck had 120,000 miles on it with a slipping transmission, a rusted floor, holes in the lower doors, and fenders that were getting close to being wind-flappers except for some life-saving spot welding; yet, it had been faithful going on for more than three decades. The original wood bed had long since rotted and been replaced with a couple of sheets of three-quarter plywood. They only lived a few miles outside of town, so the old truck didn't have to work too hard. The Jensens had their own rented spot at the market, which was open Tuesdays, Thursdays, and Saturdays. His wife Susan generally acted as the cashier during these days; Saturday was the busiest.

The farm had once been much larger under Charles Jensen Sr., but near defaults on loans had forced the elder Jensen to sell off 560 acres that once served as collateral backing. Consequently, Charles Jensen Jr. did not make his primary living off the farm. He worked as a telephone repairman full time and ran the farm part-time a few hours each weekday after work and on weekends. He tried to take it easier on Sundays unless it was planting or harvesting time.

A good chunk of Sunday was devoted to family time now with Little Chuckie; he had more time with the boy now that his three daughters were grown up and moved out. He was forty-five now, not a bad age, but one where pains and recovery time from hard labor increased little by little especially with that extra bit of stiffness in the morning after a hard days' work, particularly in the lower back. At 5'10", he was about average in height but large in the shoulders and chest and built for low work like picking vegetables. He had married young at the age of twenty and his wife was even younger at the time, only eighteen. Little Chuckie was not exactly planned, but Susan had no delivery problems at age thirty-nine, and Chuckie seemed just fine. Susan came from a taller family, and she was only two inches shorter than her husband.

A year later, at five years of age, Chuckie was able to play ball in the Pee-Wee League. He was as big as an average seven-year-old. Tallness ran true on his mother's side as his mother's father, or his grandfather, had reached 6'6". Chuckie would fall short of that mark by a couple of inches, but where they were thin, he inherited some girth from the Jensen clan. Chuckie hit the first home run of his life that summer. It didn't clear any fences by any means, and if official scoring was taking place, then it likely would have been ruled a single. To the Jensen family, it was a homerun, sure enough.

Chuckie hit a little pop fly that dropped in behind the shortstop, barely reaching the outfield. The left fielder awkwardly rushed in, nearly fell before he even got to the ball, then picked it up when it rolled to a stop. He threw it to second base, only it sailed way over the head of the little pygmy covering the bag. Chuckie ran on to second at the urging of the first base coach and was halfway to third when the first baseman picked up the ball. The first baseman lobbed the ball perfectly to the third baseman; unfortunately, the third baseman was not quite well versed or skilled in catching the ball just yet. He held his glove out too far and the ball flew neatly between his face and the mitt. Chuckie rounded third and headed for home while the third baseman retrieved the ball. The throw the third baseman made to home plate was so terrible that it actually came closer to first base rather than home plate. Chuckie ended up sliding needlessly to make it look good.

Chuckie's team won twenty-three to twelve that day and there were more errors than runs, but no one was keeping track or cared much for that matter; after all, they were all six and seven-year-olds except for Chuckie. At age five, Chuckie looked like an average peewee out there. At six, he was better than average. At seven, in his final year of peewee, he was by far the best in the league; then again, there were only six teams in the league with ten to thirteen players per team. One had to be bad not to play. To be the best out of sixty-seven players was still an accomplishment, but much of it was due to his size. Besides being tall, the hard labor of farm work over time contributed as he grew older, adding muscle and tone to go with his father's wide shoulders.

Sundays were a great time with dad. Chuckie's dad practiced with him for hours it seemed, playing catch, pitching to him, and hitting balls for him to field. After three daughters, it was somewhat of a relief to have a son. With sixty acres in corn, four in vegetables, and another ten with woods, there remained a few acres in some odd, uncleared brush. His dad had cut out a couple of acres of that brush with a cutter attached to a big 230 Massey Ferguson tractor; the same tractor that now had a sizeable sweeping grass cutter attachment to keep it trim, perfect for a makeshift ball field.

Soon, Chuckie's cousins and neighborhood friends, and some of their friends too, began meeting virtually every Sunday afternoon at Chuckie's house for a pickup game of hardball. They utilized old license plates for bases, and brought a few bats to Chuckie's house. At times, they could only round up seven or eight kids, but they still played with only three or four on a team. In these situations, the pitcher's hands substituted for first base; that is, if the pitcher got the ball before the batter reached first, then he was out, the old, "Pitcher's Hands are Out" routine.

One Sunday, only three kids showed up, so Chuckie's dad held a little competition playing five hundred. His father hit fly balls, which were worth a hundred points, grounders fifty, and first hops off line drives counted seventy-five. The first one to get to five hundred points would win; however, if a player committed an error, the entire accumulated total to that point was lost and the player had to start back at ground zero. Chuckie won better than half the games, but he did have a distinct advantage. It not only was his home field, but when his father finished work early some days, Chuckie invariably talked him into hitting him a few balls to improve his fielding. As he got older, Chuckie took on more of the fieldwork, especially in the summers. This too allowed for a little extra ball-playing time.

At eight years of age, it was on to Little League. Boys could play Little League if they were under thirteen. If they turned thirteen before September first, then they couldn't play that summer. Chuckie was lucky in that his birthday was in October; that way, he could play a full five years when most were restricted to four.

Chuckie was far above average from a size standpoint; nevertheless, he was not quite as advanced as the eleven and twelve-year-olds.

Even into the early 1990's, Little League was still quite competitive in Cedar Rapids, Iowa. There were twelve teams with fifteen players each. Each team played the others twice for a total of twenty-two games for every team not counting playoffs. Chuckie spent most of his first year on the bench. He was a back-up left fielder and only played a few innings here and there, usually late in the game if they had a big game or their opponents blew them out. The only positive was that the current starting left fielder was twelve years old and wouldn't be around the following year.

The league divided into two separate divisions of six. In Chuckie's first year, his team finished second. Since all the teams were from the same city, they only had single names like Dodgers, Yankees, Cubs, and so forth, borrowed directly from the Big Leagues. Chuckie played for the Tigers and his season had been disappointing to say the least. Like a high school freshman playing with seniors, he was not used to sitting out, but he did make up for some of it by practicing more at home.

The baseball season ended in late August of 1992, just before the start of school. The corn harvest wasn't far behind, and by the middle of October, Charles Jensen Jr. was doing his final tilling of the soil for the year. He was in fact using an old disker hooked up to the Massey Ferguson to work and turn the soil. He began with a straight path down the middle. When he reached the end, he would swing around to the far western side and make another straight run down the edge. At the corner, he would swing back east to the middle plowing along adjacent to his initial run.

Back and forth, 'round and 'round like a merry-go-round, he moved up and down looking back at the disker now and then to make sure that nothing caught or got stuck in it. Sometimes a stone might cause him to stop and remove it. Most farmers had a nice little rock garden or stone-laden driveway edge with the rocks they pulled out of their fields. Damn glaciers left all kinds of crap.

The rolling metal disks turned and sliced smoothly and deeply into the well-worked soil as the old thick cast iron engine chugged onward. The ultra-thick blocks, low gearing, and low rpm's made old tractors virtually indestructible. On one of his glances back when he was nearly finished, he caught a glimmer of something stuck between two disks that had ceased to rotate. He pressed the clutch in and shoved the transmission lever to neutral. He leapt down to remove the obstruction. It was the lamp. He picked it up curiously, stared at it briefly, shook his head, and then set it down on the floor of the tractor near the clutch pedal. He had a job to finish and no time to play now.

After a few more passes, he swung into the pole barn off the west side of the house and parked the tractor indoors. He was a bit tired from the noise and vibrations from the old somewhat rough-riding tractor. The tractor did not have an enclosed cab like newer models, and consequently, no stereo or climate control. His ears continued to ring some several minutes after shutting the old motor down.

He swung himself down and reached across to grab the lamp. He picked it up, turned it over once, then twice, and examined it more closely. It was dusty and dirty but surprisingly not dented, or even scratched much despite its position between the disks of the plow. He did not try to wipe it but did tug at the lid; it did not budge at all. He figured it was probably just dirt encrusted or maybe even rusted on, but he was too exhausted to spend more time with it in the barn, so he just carried it up to the house.

"Whatcha got there?" Susan asked as she stood in the flowerbed up in front of the house. There was a hoe in her hand since she was cleaning the weeds from her petunias.

"Some old piece of junk I found in the field," he answered as he handed it to her.

"Looks like an antique or something." She mused, "Maybe an old tea pot?"

"Could be," he said, "I don't know."

Chuckie rounded the corner of the house with glove, bat, and ball in hand, "Hey pop, will you hit a few to me?"

"I don't know, how long before dinner Suey?"

"About a half an hour maybe," she announced.

"All right Chuckie, just a few." He decided that he had enough energy left to hit Chuckie some fly balls. If he didn't, then he'd waste just as much energy trying to refuse him. Chuckie could be irritating but relentless.

Before they headed to the ball field, Chuckie noticed the strange object in his mother's hands, "Hey ma, what's that?"

"I think it's an old tea pot. Why don't you clean it up for me later Chuckie?" She placed it on the porch decking.

"Okay, sure ma, but hey dad, let's go!"

When he was alone with his father, they played a different version of five hundred. Grounders, first hops, and fly ball were all worth fifty, seventy-five, and one hundred respectively as always, but the number five hundred wasn't important. Chuckie would accumulate points until he made an error, and then start back at zero. That evening he set his own personal record at 1,875 points before he charged in after a line drive and he blooped it. It hit a small rut, took a bad hop, and skipped past him. Unless it was hit far over his head, anything that got past him was an error no matter how unforgiving the ground.

"Time for dinner!" His mother shouted.

The half hour went by quickly, at least for Chuckie, and they strode together up to the house. The three of them ate alone, a nice pot roast lined with baked potatoes and carrots. Chuckie was more like an only child since his three older sisters were all in their 20's and had left the nest. After dinner, Chuckie dried the dishes as his mother washed them. When he was finished, she reminded him about the lamp that was still sitting on the porch. She even filled a 3-gallon bucket with two gallons of water mixed with a spray of dish soap, along with a thin hand-sized sponge and a rag. To keep the last few remaining bugs out of the house, she latched the screen door and went back into the house to watch the evening news with her husband.

Chuckie slopped the sponge over the lamp. The second round he wrung it out and wiped off the soapy watery mess from the first round. When he started to dry it with the rag, the Djinni slithered out. "Do you have a wish boy?"

It was not difficult for Chuckie. He was still young and had seen enough cartoons that included things like animated genies on TV not to be afraid. Unlike many who hesitated, disbelieved, or hemmed and hawed, Chuckie's wish came very easily to him. He lived for baseball, playing it in the daytime, thinking about it when he could not play, and dreaming it during the night.

"I want to be a baseball player!" he demanded.

The Djinni squeezed back inside. It was the easiest wish the Djinni ever had to grant. The Djinni did absolutely nothing to do because Chuckie was already a baseball player.

There was still some soapy water left dripping on the lamp, Chuckie wiped it off and the Djinni popped out again: "What is your second wish boy?"

Chuckie strained his neck to look up at it, "I told you already, I want to be a ball player."

The Djinni disappeared a second time. With the soapy water removed, Chuckie still held the rag and wiped it clean. The smoky cloud poured forth once again: "What is your third wish boy?"

Chuckie, with about all the reasoning an eight-year-old could muster, sat for about twenty-two seconds with a thoughtful but confused look upon his face. He seemed to be getting nowhere and then a light bulb came on and his face lit up, "I want to play baseball in the big league like the guys on TV!"

The Djinni retreated finally with something to do. Chuckie finished drying the last few remaining wet spots, but the Djinni did not come out anymore. Chuckie shook it a little, knocked on it, but nothing. He sighed, brought it into the living room, and handed it to his mother.

"Well, it looks nice and clean Chuckie," she complimented. She took it in her hands examining it. It was a dark somewhat worn bronze color. She tried the lid like her husband had but it stuck. She looked at it again and decided that she really didn't like it that much. She tugged one more time at the lid; it didn't budge.

"I couldn't get it off either," remarked Charles.

"Well, I guess it ain't good for much then, maybe Maria would like it. She's always collecting old junk like this." Susan was referring to her oldest daughter. "Here Chuckie, why don't you throw it that box in the closet, there's some other stuff in there I need to give to your sister."

Maria Smith, who was once Maria Jensen until she married, had two small children of her own. She came over for a visit on a warm late October Saturday. It was windy and the leaves were nervous, scattering about as if a fire was coming for them. She arrived with her two kids but no husband. She had been having problems with John, but gladly accepted the box that contained the lamp or the "bronze teapot" as her mother called it.

"Found it in the field," Susan had said.

"Thanks mom, but it's not me, John just doesn't like kids. He never really did like children, but I thought when he had some of his own, he'd change his mind."

"I don't know," declared Susan, "Maybe when they get bigger, he'll do more things with them, like your dad does with Chuckie; after all, Billy's only two-and-a-half years old and Betty's just a baby."

"I hope so," said Maria, "He hardly ever gives them any attention."

"Give it time, that's all you can do. You know, if you ever need a home, you know you've got one here, for the babies too."

"Thanks mom, but hey, it's about time for us to take off, thanks for the teapot."

"Okay now, we'll see you soon." They hugged, Susan kissed the grandkids, and they left, kids, box, lamp, and all.

In his ninth year, Chuckie was the starting left fielder for the Tigers. He batted eighth in the lineup since his hitting was still a little below average for Little League, but not by much; then again, the entire team was not very good that year, 1993. They were a young team since they had lost nearly all of their eleven and twelve-year-old starters from the previous year. They would finish 1993 dead last in their six-team division.

A good deal of their problems centered on their starting pitching. The best teams had power pitchers. Things like forkballs, screwballs, curve balls, sliders, split fingered pitches, knuckle balls, and the like were virtually unheard of at this level. The Dodgers won because they had two twelve-year-old pitchers who blew the ball past batters, and even registered complete game shutouts here and there. Blanking a team in Little League was a little easier since games lasted only six innings.

With his level of dedication, size, and constant practicing, Chuckie became an above- average little-leaguer at the ripe age of ten. His dad helped a lot as Charles Jensen Jr. improved Chuckie's hitting by pitching faster and harder than Chuckie's peers could do. Consequently, Chuckie moved up to the fifth spot in the batting order. Little League ball fields were much smaller than the major leagues; straight away center field was still a good 325 feet, but the lines were only about 260. The power alleys were a few feet less than three hundred.

In 1994, Chuckie hit his first triple that year missing a home run by a matter of inches. He was a left-handed batter though he threw the ball with his right hand. He was able to slam a fastball off the fence down the right line after pulling it strongly. He also hit several doubles that year up the alleys. Home runs were rare, and the Tigers only had one boy with enough power to hit a ball that far. Mike Hunter hit two of them that year, but 1994 was also his final season at that level. Chuckie would take Mike's spot in the clean-up position in 1995.

At age eleven, Chuckie's father continued to work with him from both sides of the ball. He could still pitch faster than Chuckie's peers, and Chuckie was routinely scoring over 3,000 in their version of five hundred without making any errors. The Sunday game at the Jensen house had grown through the years and many too old for Little League, the thirteen- and fourteen-year-olds were routinely showing up to play if the weather was feasible. At age eleven, Chuckie hit and fielded as well if not better than most. He was also as big as they were. In his eleventh year, Chuckie went through a growth spurt, growing nearly half a foot and adding power to go along with it. In 1995, he led the Tigers to a division title.

Chuckie hit a home run in every other game and even two in the same game once. It was in the playoffs with the Cubs that he was injured. In late summer 1995, the playoffs were a best two out of three. The Cubs' best pitcher, twelve-year-old Dennis Williams, was just a little nervous and started out pitching wild, overthrowing, and missing the strike zone by a wide margin. The first two Tiger batters received walks on four straight pitches each, ducking and dodging the errant throws. His coach came out to talk to him and Dennis seemed to settle down briefly by striking out the third batter; nevertheless, the batter for the Tigers had been overeager too and swung at a couple of bad pitches, one in the dirt.

With two runners aboard and only one out, Chuckie stepped up to the plate and the Tiger fans present gave him a roaring cheer led by Charles & Susan Jensen. Often, the parents sitting on the cramped bleachers became more excited and involved than the players themselves, screaming and shouting at the players, coaches, and particularly the umpires when a certain judgment did not favor their child or the team.

"Ball one!" The umpire bellowed out as the Cubs' catcher snagged the pitch a good foot and a half outside the plate. The second pitch went way over the head of the catcher as well as the umpire. The catcher flagged it down as the base runners advanced to second and third respectively. The third pitch going nearly 80 miles per hour headed straight for Chuckie. His immediate reaction was to duck and the hard ball smashed directly into his right elbow.

Crack! The sound was terrible, and the bone broke an inch or two outside of the skin where it had not been before. Chuckie dropped the bat and went down, clutching his arm. Within two seconds, his mother, father, coaches, and then the entire Tiger team rushed out to him as the crowd thickened.

The coach took control, "I think it's broken," he stated the obvious. "I think you had better take him to the hospital Susan."

A pinch runner took Chuckie's place as the Jensens headed for the hospital. The Tigers ended up winning the first game eight to two because of Dennis Williams' continued wildness; nonetheless, with Chuckie out, they lost the next two mostly due to the absence of their star clean-up hitter. In the meantime, Chuckie's elbow was in worse shape than it looked. Dr. Peterson, the family doc, had to call in an arm specialist, a man by the name of Dr. Hall, to survey the x-rays taken of the elbow.

"Will you look at that," said Dr. Hall as he pointed to the chart. "Besides fracturing out below the elbow, it chipped up here, and you see these little specks here, here, and here," he said as he pointed, "We'll have to remove these, and there might be some nerve damage too. First things first, we'll need to get those chips out and then set the arm."

"I agree," said Dr. Peterson, but he was only a general practitioner. "I'll go tell his parents."

"It'll like heal or go back to normal, won't it?" Charles questioned.

"Well, it's hard to say until Dr. Hall is finished with the surgery. It doesn't look too badly but...."

Susan cut in, "But what?"

"There could be a little permanent nerve damage."

"Are you sure that you just can't put a cast on or something like that? It's just a broken bone, right?" Susan added.

"Well yes, there's no ifs, ands, or buts, the chips must be removed, and he'll probably have to wear a cast for a good 6 months. From there, we'll see if he regains full rotational movement; like I was trying to say, there is a possibility of restricted movement."

"Well, how about his baseball? Will he be able to play as good as before?" It was Charles, the dad, who naturally brought up the sports angle.

"I can't make any promises until after the surgery, and then it will still be an educated guess. We likely will not know for sure until the cast is removed and after a little physical therapy just to get it mobile again."

Chuckie's ball playing for the rest of the year was over with, not just the two playoff games, but all the backyard activity as well. When the cast came off in early February of 1996, the doctor thoroughly examined him, x-rayed again him, and finally assigned him four weeks of therapy at a separate facility owned by the hospital network. The Jensens were able to speak with the specialist after Chuckie's stint in rehab.

"The arm is nearly back to normal, but the bone is slightly shorter than it once was," stated Dr. Hall. He was pointing to an x-ray that the Jensens did not understand; it just looked like most any elbow to them.

Chuckie beat his father to the punch, "Can I play baseball?"

"Sure you can. The arm is about ninety percent of what it used to be, but with a lot of practice, you'll probably never know the difference. The only problem is that it's a little sensitive now. Dr. Hall turned to Chuckie's parents and spoke more business-like, "The bone is somewhat restricted in movement, but the chance of breaking the same bone is rather slim; still, if he does continue to play ball, and does break it again, the use of his arm will be even more limited."

"What are you saying?" Charles asked.

"Another break there and his baseball days will be over with."

"But he can play?"

"Yes, of course, I am not sure if I would advise for or against it; obviously he is young and enjoys the game, but think of this injury as two strikes; a third and he'll be out." Dr. Hall laughed inwardly to himself with the baseball metaphor.

Chuckie continued his therapy at home with small dumbbells. His slightly smaller right elbow caused him to alter his throwing slightly. On the downward motion of his arm, he had to go slightly lower which helped him some. It taught him to follow through more. He also had to lift the elbow up slightly higher when batting to compensate for the bone's reduced size. In a way, it improved his swing too. He swung more on a level plane rather than upper cutting the ball. At age twelve, he stood over five feet in height and would reach the height of his father by the time he was fifteen with a good six inches more to go.

His last year of Little League would prove to be his best. He had tied the all-time record last year in 1996 by hitting twelve home runs; he would nearly double that total in '97. The velocity of his throwing improved so much that the coach decided to try him out as pitcher as well as catcher, where they could use a good strong arm. During his final Little League season, he would spend the first three innings pitching and the last three catching; nevertheless, he preferred the outfield.

The Tigers went all the way in '97 and Chuckie earned three separate trophies: one for which every member of the team acquired for winning the championship, one for MVP in the league, and one for MVP in the all-star game. The all-star game took place after the playoffs, and each coach chose two players from their teams to participate. Chuckie was the first choice, scheduled to play in the outfield since the other coaches selected enough pitchers and catchers. In the final game, Chuckie almost hit for the cycle missing the triple as most do in that endeavor. His defensive play was equally impressive as he threw out a runner at home from deep left field on a sac fly attempt.

Chuckie's promising career took off like a freight train on a tight deadline once he got to high school. His rapid physical growth accelerated him to the junior varsity team as a freshman. In the tenth grade, he made the varsity team; like his first year in Little League, he mostly sat the bench as a sophomore. Eleventh and twelfth grade were a different story as he continued his road to stardom. He had been good enough to play as a sophomore; however, the coach favored the older players more. Eleventh grade proved that he was much better than the average high school baseball player. He improved as a power hitter smacking line drives with good contact with an occasional home run.

Scouts were often present during high profile high school matches, mostly college recruiters; nevertheless, that changed during Chuckie's senior year in 2001. Though his grades were moderate, B's and C's with an occasional A or D, he at least became more of an intelligent hitter. High school pitchers were still power pitchers, but they also learned how to throw curves and changeups among other tricky pitches encouraged by their coaches with no thought to the damage of their still developing arms.

As a junior Chuckie adjusted; as a senior, he now had experience. He hit so many homeruns in his final year of high school that he had full scholarship offerings from over a hundred universities. Major league scouts got wind of his abilities and baseball is one of the few sports where high schoolers could make the leap directly to the bigs. It wasn't long before he received minor league contract offers.Since he was only seventeen, Chuckie talked it over with his parents as they had to be present with any scouts, either college or pro. They preferred he go to college since numerous universities offered him scholarships, and it was something he could fall back on if baseball didn't work out. The talent was there despite the deal Chuckie had made with the devil; then again, the elbow could turn out to be an Achilles Heel.

Chuckie just wanted to play ball, maybe set some records, and make some money too, pretty much in that order. College to him would be a potential waste of four years or at least two or maybe three depending on how long it would take him to make it through the minor leagues. The decision was easy. Since he didn't care for school, he signed a three-year contract with the Chicago White Sox for $375,000; $100,000 for the first year, $125,000 for the second, and $150,000 for the third, all guaranteed for playing in the minors with incentives for renegotiating at a much higher rate if or when he made the majors. It did take him a year to move from single A to triple A.

In the year 2003, his second in the minors, he got the call up to the majors in April only two-and-a-half weeks into the season. He started at a torrid pace, hitting.400, smacking six homers, and driving in eighteen runs in his first five weeks of playing. He cooled off some, but hit.308 at the All-Star break, with seventeen homers and forty-seven RBI's: not bad for a rookie.

He made the All-Star team but struck out his only at bat later in the game. The problem, however, was a mistake he made a long time ago, one over which he had little control. For how much he had devoted his life to baseball, how he practiced, played, and lived it; he may well have made it on his own; however, he had made a fatal wish as an 8-year-old that he had long forgotten about. Three weeks after the All-Star game, a wild split-fingered fastball came in hard on him before he had time to react. He tilted backward and the ball smashed his surgically repaired right elbow dead on. After two rounds with the best sports surgeons in the country, he could only bend the elbow about a third of the way like the average person. He could still swing a bat some but couldn't hit a ball beyond two hundred feet. Dr. Hall was right.

"I have spent a goodly part of my life in study and research. During the last thirty years I have read every single piece of literature on the subject of Spiritualism that I could. I have accumulated one of the largest libraries in the world on psychic phenomena, Spiritualism, magic, witchcraft, demonology, evil spirits, etc. some of the material going back as far as 1489, and I doubt if anyone in the world has so complete a library on modern Spiritualism, but nothing I have ever read concerning the so-called Spiritualistic phenomena has impressed me as being genuine. It is true that some of the things I read seemed mystifying but I question if they would be were they to be reproduced under different circumstances, under test conditions, and before expert mystifiers and open-minded committees. Mine has not been an investigation of a few days or weeks or months but one that has extended over thirty years and in that thirty years I have not found one incident that savoured of the genuine. If there had been any real unalloyed demonstration to work on, one that did not reek of fraud, one that could not be reproduced by earthly powers, then there would be something for a foundation, but up to the present time everything that I have investigated has been the result of deluded brains or those which were too actively and intensely willing to believe." - Erik Weisz aka Harry Houdini

CHAPTER XXXV

What about the lamp? It rested in a box among tons of other boxes in Maria Smith's crowded basement. Chuckie's older sister collected knickknacks, porcelain pieces, vases, glass objects, old irons, brass, cups, saucers, ceramic animals, souvenirs, paperweights, toys, shoes, stuffed animals, jars, bottles, books, and about anything a compulsive hoarder might keep without throwing out, even old newspapers and magazines, or anything she felt that might have the slightest chance of possessing a potential monetary value. She dreamed of opening a store one day but would have difficulty parting with her things.

Maria's husband, John Smith, built shelf after shelf throughout the entire house for Maria's things. He put up with her OCD and even made an effort to accommodate her whims, but he did not give their children the same latitude. He was a good husband but somewhat of a mean father. He never physically abused his kids beyond normal corporate punishment with a paddle, applied with a light touch; he dished out mental abuse.

He never praised, encouraged, or spent much quality time or any time at all with them. To Billy and Betty, he was indeed intimidating, not easily approachable, and even hostile and threatening. They learned early on that it was just best to stay out of his way. John Smith did his best to return the favor. With Maria's junk combined with the fact that he really didn't like kids, including his own, he spent more and more time away from home as the years crept by. He spent his free time bowling, golfing, playing softball tournaments, at the bar with his buds, and fishing as far away as Lake Michigan.

It had been thirteen years since the lamp had been used by Chuckie back in 1992, and now, the genie was about to come out of the bottle once again. On a rare weekend spent at home, John finished installing two additional rows of shelving above the fireplace in the living room. It was probably one of the last few open spaces on any wall left in the home. Before he had even put his tools away, Maria had half of it filled with ceramic or porcelain animal figurines. She sent nine-and-a-half-year-old Billy and seven-and-a-half-year-old Betty down to the basement to find more so that she could fill or even overfill the new shelves. She gave them each a roll of paper towels to clean and dust off whatever they might find.

It was a neat job for the two curious youngsters to explore their mother's junk, with her permission for a change. It would keep them busy for hours rummaging through stacks of dusty dark boxes in a somewhat sour or smelly lightly damp basement. If John didn't keep the gutters clean of leaves, they could plug up the downspouts, and cause water to collect along the house; and thus, trickle into the basement causing a minor amount of mold and mildew. The kids didn't seem to mind as they uncovered dogs, cats, a tiger, and even a ceramic octopus of all strange things. By chance, they happened to uncover the lamp.

"Ew!" Betty nearly screamed and stepped back as a big black hairy wolf spider slid along the fused cover of the lamp.

"Squish! Got'em!" Bobby said as he proudly squeezed spider guts with a piece of paper towel. He kept going with the paper towel. There A neat spider web was on the side of an open box where the lamp leaned. Inside the box, between the lamp and an interior wall, was an entire network of artistic webs. Bobby wiped them off vigorously and a final flourish on the lamp's surface was enough to release the Djinni. The sound of air escaping from the pressurized inner chamber filled the damp but solid block basement. A smoky monster was asking them for wishes but neither was sure to whom it was speaking.

Television, the all-encompassing day care, nanny, mother's little helper, babysitter, teacher, and mind-rotter all rolled up into one had always been Maria's crutch when it came to raising the kids. At this moment, perhaps all that time in front of the TV paid off for the kids. They already had a good deal of experience with wild animals, creepy monsters, and hundreds of other scary things, especially when Bobby did a little channel surfing when his mother wasn't watching them too closely. Ironically, despite dispatching a spider nearly as big as a cup holder, Billy was the one who was now frightened. Betty wasn't at all and was the first to speak up.

"I wish that my daddy would go away." He paddled her barely an hour earlier and she was still holding a grudge.

The Djinni vanished and so did her father. There was one significant difference: someone would see the Djinni again, but none would ever again see John Smith. The kids looked at the lamp, looked at each other, and Betty just shrugged. Billy shook it and nothing happened, so he just shoved it back into the box; after all, it was their mission to find ceramic animals for their mother's shelf.

In 2006, the following year, Maria lost the house. John had been the primary wage earner and with him gone, Maria's barely-over-minimum-wage job could not support their middle-class standard of living. First, the bank repossessed the car once three payments lapsed. The living room furniture, acquired on credit, was next to go. She had several credit cards charged to the limit and her phone was ringing off the hook by the sponsors.

Overdue bills piled up and those who came to claim the furniture politely took them off an end table and carefully laid them onto the floor. The insurance company stalled on any payout of the life insurance policy since John was not definitively dead. With her savings exhausted and creditors constantly demanding payment, she declared bankruptcy. She auctioned off her precious collectibles, with each creditor getting a portion or percentage of the goods.

The ensuing auction lasted seven hours and the lamp appeared on the podium during the fifth hour.

"What do we have here?" Ollie's son of Ollie's Auction House bellowed out to no one in particular. He recognized the object for what it was, "It appears to be an antique lamp!" He said as his father raised it up to him. The two took turns as auctioneers. "Who'll give me ten dollars? Humba Humbila Humba Humbila Who'll give me ten? Can I get ten? Do I hear ten? Humba Humbila How about five, just five dollars? Humba Humbila…"

There was no response yet.

"Who'll give me five?"

Still no response.

"What about two dollars? Just two dollahs….Humba Humbila…..Well come on folks, this is an antique! Q_U_A_L_I_T_Y Bronze!" he droned slowly and then picked it up from his father's outstretched hands and brushed it off as he tried to open it. The Djinni came out in front of the little crowd of 103 potential buyers.

"What is it you wish?"

A quiet hush fell over the crowd. The Djinni had spoken directly into the microphone and all heard the deep, raspy, evil-toned distinctly. Oliver Jr. had been holding the lamp a good five feet off the two-foot platform and the seven-foot Djinni was now standing an astounding fourteen feet from the floor to the tip of its turban-covered head. Oliver Jr. recovered quickly from the surprise.

"Look at that folks! Will you look at that! It's like a hologram or say, it's a magic lamp!" After the initial surprise, it was the year 2006 where special effects and gimmicks ruled. Oliver Jr. really didn't believe it was magic nor did the spectators, yet the Djinni certainly looked like nothing much that they had seen before. Genies always had kind faces and the most recent experience with one for most had been the blue one in Disney's "Aladdin" released over a decade ago; nonetheless, this one had a mean look about it.

Oliver Jr. went back into salesman mode; after all, he and his father got a direct commission on everything sold, so the more money he could get for the objects on hand, they more they got paid. "Lookie here folks! It even asked me to make a doggone wish. Can you believe that? Well, I'll tell you what, I wish that we'd sell this thing for twenty bucks." The Djinni heard and vanished in a wisp of smoke. "Lookie there! He must've heard me! Now let's start back where we left off. Who'll give me two dollars? Humba Humbila Humba Humbila...." A dozen hands popped up.

"Three dollars here, four, got four now, five, do I hear five, five here, five there, 7.50 once over here, humba humbila, do I hear ten? Got ten, twelve here, twelve there, got twelve, do I hear fifteen? And a fifteen, fifteen, fifteen, fifteen yup! Twenty now, twenty, twenty, humba, humbila, got fifteen, gimme twenty, who'll gimme twenty, twenty, and a humba, homba, homba, humbila, twenty? Yes sir! Got twenty, got twenty now, humba humbila, gimme twenty-five, who'll gimme twenty-five, got twenty, got twenty, humba, humbila, lookin' for twenty-five, twenty-five once?" No answer, "Twenty twice? Do I hear twenty-five? Sold to number eighty-seven for twenty dollars." He banged the gavel with his final words as his father held up a faded barn painting. Number eighty-seven happened to belong to twenty-eight-year-old Matt Hunter and his mother, Theresa Hunter.

The two lived alone together in a medium sized three-bedroom home in Cedar Rapids. Matt shared expenses with his mother ever since he handed her his first one hundred dollars check earned at a high school talent show some ten years earlier. Matt was a skinny

150-pounder nearly six feet in height. His slenderness enhanced his flexibility, which in turn aided him in his chosen career. He was a performer. His act was a combination magician, juggler, escape artist, and clown. When performances or bookings were hard to come by, he spent time painting houses in the summer and plowing driveways in the winter with an old '93 Jeep Wrangler.

Matt the Magnificent had a face that was lean with hollow cheeks and a black pencil thin moustache that he curled at the ends. As he had told his mother, the moustache was somewhat a part of the act of making him look slick or exotic. He walked slightly stoop-shouldered probably because he was always cramped inside so many props, many of which he routinely escaped from, like crates, bags, cartons, coffins, trunks, and a metal vault. The majority opened from the inside with hidden hinges and/or latches. A few opened from the bottom so that no matter how many chains, nails, locks, or ropes they fastened up top, "Matt the Magnificent" could creep out the bottom. These escapes always happened behind a curtain, and many wrongfully believed t there were trap doors in the floor or on the stage, or people came out like a fast-acting split-second pit crew to let him out.

Matt had been showing off since childhood. In grade school, he had purchased magic cards at a toy store. In fifth grade, just a few months before his dad had left them, his dad had taught him how to triple cut a standard deck of cards with a single hand. Matt practiced with both hands. In junior high, he read every book on card tricks that he could get his hands on, and then expanded to other small props like balls, rings, and handcuffs. It was easy palming the key to the handcuffs to escape from them. Maybe secure it handily within his back pocket from which he could easily reach it.

Escape artists and magicians often became good lock pickers as well and Matt was no exception. He read all that he could and purchased books on magic as funds allowed. Like all magicians, he created some of his own tricks, a few with cards that he did not even share with his mother. Many a trick died with its performer since they failed to tell anyone how they did it.

Matt's mastered juggling three tennis balls at age thirteen, and a year and a half later, he added a fourth. It took him another four years of steady practice to handle five. He would never exceed that amount but juggling five tennis balls nonetheless was still impressive. He would start with three, which was no big feat, and his audience watched unmoved until he announced, "Now I'll do four balls!" This began to get their attention since only few out there could juggle three; four was beyond the realm of most part-time amateurs.

"Now I'll do five balls! That's five balls ladies and gentlemen!" This was far more difficult, but with hours if not days of practice, combined with quick hands and supreme concentration, he succeeded if only for a minute or two at most. When he had everyone's undivided attention, he'd end by catching all five balls in his top hat.

When he received favorable applause, he would make one last juggling announcement, "Now ladies and gentlemen, you haven't seen nuthin' yet! As an unprecedented fete, a miracle in a way, I will not attempt to juggle eight balls!" Now the crowd was superlatively intrigued, as a typical hush followed them. Matt would then reach into a box with three pool balls and begin juggling them easily; after all, they were just black 8-balls, but only three of them. This ordinarily made the crowd laugh and ease up some of the critical attention, if any, that they were giving him. His was a variety magic, performance, and comic show, all under the auspices of "Matt the Magnificent."

The talent show during his final year of high school opened the door to his career. He had a half an hour act where he escaped from a wooden coffin-like box and from handcuffs too. He performed several card tricks as well, and his three, four, five, and then eight-ball juggling act, all mixed in with a few jokes. He was awarded first prize which included a trophy, a hundred dollars, and local media coverage that led to his being asked to perform at birthday parties, hotels, amusement parks, and other events. He added a clown suit and learned to tie animals with skinny balloons too.

For the next ten years, he continued his theatrics eking out a living, adding more props and acts in his spare time, but supplementing it with painting and snow plowing. He learned how to fake eating fire by breathing out gently to keep the intense heat of the flames from the soft tissues within the roof of his mouth. When he first attempted this, the fire partially destroyed his moustache, which required a solid month to return.

At a convention in Chicago, Matt learned the art of retroperistalsis, which is the technique of letting an object pass down his esophagus halfway or so, and then fetching it back up again by way of controlled muscle contraction. He practiced with cherry tomatoes tied to a string. If he allowed one to travel too far down, then he could pull it back with the string. If the tomato dropped into his stomach, that was no big deal. Once he felt confident that he could do it, he partially swallowed coins, marbles, and even with a live goldfish without gagging or vomiting. He never advanced beyond goldfish although he saw masterful performers in Chicago do it with frogs and mice.

He and his mother both liked auctions, she with an interest in antiques, and he was always on the lookout for a new prop, crate, or whatever might be used in his show. At the auction where the lamp was presented, he and his mother were there seeking an old oak table to replace the rickety card table in their kitchen that they currently used for meals.

The presence of the lamp had been a pure stroke of luck for the young man who thought that it might have some potential in his act. If the genie thing inside could ask for wishes, he figured that he could pull something out of his hat or sleeve to match it. The oak table sold for $240, and Theresa Hunter stopped bidding at $200, which had been her upper limit. With Matt getting the lamp for $20, they at least did not go home empty-handed.

His mother dropped him off at the house as she continued to the supermarket to do a little grocery shopping. Matt took the lamp to the spare bedroom, converted to a storage room for his business materials. He placed the lamp on a roll top desk where he did his studying, paperwork, and general planning for upcoming events or shows. Like all magicians, he studied it thoroughly, every square inch of its outer surface.

The mystery of a magician's act was only for the audience, not for the magician himself. He turned it overand upside down. The top didn't budge, not even when he tried to pry it open with a screwdriver. He could not discover its inner secrets or basic workings. There was no button to push and no string to pull; nothing seemed to turn the thing on. Perhaps it was voice activated? he thought about what the auctioneer had said, but nothing useful came to mind.

"There must be a way to get inside," he muttered aloud. He found no screws, no bolts, no rivets, nor any other fasteners holding the thing together. It couldn't be magic as magicians were by far the biggest doubters of anything magical. Harry Houdini himself, one of the greatest magicians ever, had spent a good deal of his efforts, decades in fact, debunking the work of others.

The lamp appeared to be one solid piece except for the lid. He tried to gaze down the spout using a pen light, but the long flowing curve of it only allowed him a view of about three inches downward. The only logical conclusion was if the lid was permanently fastened, then it must open from the inside like many of his own escape contraptions. On second thought, maybe it was just rusted or corroded.

He began prodding, poking, twisting, and finally rubbed it with a cloth rag. That was enough. A noisy swishing sound filled his quiet room as the entity from within filtered out. The Djinni's smoky form morphed from the top of the desk, up the wall, and across a couple feet of the ceiling where it gazed wickedly down at him. A good part of its chunky body blanked out the wall too.

"What is your wish?"

"Whoa!" Matt about fell out of his chair and pushed back some as it frightened him at first. He still wheeled back a little more, looked up at it staring menacingly down at him, and then tried to ration out that it was some kind of neat trick. His first thought was that it might not be good for little kids since it was kind of scary or aggressive looking or both.

"That's the same tone of voice that it used at the auction, so there must be some little recording device in there somewhere," he said aloud. He edged tentatively forward in his chair looking down at the lamp but could not identify anything. The hologram picture, or whatever it was, tailed down into the spout as nothing else had opened, not the lid for sure. He tilted his head back and looked up at the dark penetrating eye surveying him. "Same facial expression," he muttered in sort of a neutral scientific way. He tentatively reached out his hand to touch its body and his hand passed right through it.

"Ah ha!" Matt said more forcefully, "Just as I thought, this is just an illusion or an image from a little camera device inside I'll bet."

"Tell me," he spoke up at it, "Can you say anything else?" To his amazement, it did!

"I am ready to obey you as your slave, so what is your first wish?"

He thought it over again and said, "Of course several messages could be recorded on one tape. I had a girl friend who had a talking Barbie doll, seems like her little sister had one of those talking stuffed bears too with something like a 500-word vocabulary." His time was up and a sucking noise like that of a quiet vacuum cleaner interrupted his thoughts as the monstrous thing streamed back into the lamp.

Matt contemplated its disappearance, "If it was an image, then how did it get sucked in instead of simply disappearing? Strange," he thought. He continued to think aloud, "Maybe there is some kind of power source like batteries that pulls the image back in. Maybe it's not an image." It looked like smoke, but it didn't smell or drift away; it did go up, and then form into a distinct figure; yet, still attached or bound to the lamp.

"Let's try to activate it again." He tried to remember what he had done to release it, so he poked it, prodded it, shook it, and finally rubbed it with the cloth again, that did the trick. He made a mental note that it was the rubbing that triggered it. Maybe it was much like a touch lamp, just needed a little extra pressure. The thing popped out as before.

"What is your second wish?"

Matt sat back confused again. A touch lamp just turned a light on and off, or maybe it did have varying degrees of brightness, but his was definitely different. He caught the "second" part, as this was indeed his second time that he had released it. "Hmm," he said aloud, "This is more confusing that the Chinese Water Torture Cell and I wouldn't mind having one of those instead of this stupid lamp." The Djinni finally registered a wish and faded back into its home.

As he sat confused and a little frustrated, out of the corner of his eye, he noticed a voluminous upright aquarium-like structure materializing across the room. He spun his chair around to view the device. "Holy shit!" He couldn't believe his eyes and nearly ran to it. It rose higher than his own height as it was perched on a metal stand. It was fully five feet lengthwise across the front, but perhaps only a single foot in width on its side. It had ankle-locking devices at the top and water filling it partially.

The Djinni had prepared it perfectly leaving out just enough water for a person of about Matt's slim weight to get in upside down without it overflowing. It was set up in a very tempting position. It was indeed a Chinese Water Torture Cell, an exact replica of the one Harry Houdini first used in one of his numerous escape acts. The water cell was one of the few mysteries of Houdini's act never solved by another performer. Houdini's device now belonged to a personal collection, reported to be in rough condition. The cell could no longer hold water due to the cracks in the glass. The board at the top was missing, the locks were rusted shut, and most notably of all, the key or rather the keys to solving the puzzle had long gone missing like a lone pilot in an Alaskan storm.

Matt's brand-new device had the board at the top. The function of the board was to hide one's toes, which faced forward, all with the occupant suspended upside down. The reason to hide them lay in the design of the keys. The keys were long, simple skeletons purposefully bent into right angles to hang over the toes of the submerged person, who could then push up on them in order to release the ankle locks. The locks were also very basic in design and needed only a firm push and slight twist of the key to swing them open, something that required only a minimal amount of dexterity with one's feet; in fact, they were so uncomplicated that one could open them with a flathead screwdriver.

The torture cell was certainly dangerous since one had to escape while holding one's breath while perched upside down no less. Once the ankle locks at the top released, there yet remained the difficult task of getting out of the chamber feet first. There was not enough room widthwise to turn around and exit headfirst. One had to grope out with one's feet while controlling the odd buoyancy of the human body. With all thoughts forgotten about the lamp or Djinni, Matt had the urge to try it out.

With his mother out grocery shopping, Matt strode over to the bathroom to grab a towel or two, then on to his bedroom to strip. He removed his clothes except for his underwear. If he ever did this on stage, he'd wear a bathing suit, but at home, it really didn't matter. He now knew how the cell operated but he was going to play it somewhat safe. For one, there was no way he could lock himself in without an assistant. He removed the keys and swung the ankle locks back out of the way. He tested the lukewarm water with his hand and then walked over to his desk to obtain the chair. He would have to stand on it to enter the tank. As he laid his hands on the chair, he stopped a moment and stared at the lamp. He had been too excited about the water cell and had forgotten about it.

"My God, did you do this? Nah, it couldn't be, things just don't happen like that." But the torture cell was physically there, and he knew in his heart that it had not been there before. It was real, not an illusion, but there had to be a trick, right? Magicians make this stuff up to fool others. But how did it fool him? There was a remote possibility that his mother had bought it for him as a surprise and placed it there, or had it delivered by UPS, FedEx, or somebody else. Maybe he had just missed it when he entered the room. He didn't believe that; after all, it was awfully big. "Hmm, I'll deal with you later," he said to the lamp as his curiosity wandered back to the water torture cell.

He rolled the chair over and made another bathroom trip for some additional towels to spread about the floor around the iron stand. He balanced on the chair, placed his hands on the rim of the cell, and heaved his body upward gracefully. For a split second, he was worried that the strain on the top edge might break the glass, but it was very thick, like an upright aquarium. He slid in headfirst and strove for the bottom. His feet hit the ceiling of his room as he entered the tank, but that didn't hurt anything; nevertheless, he made one additional miscalculation, and this one was far more significant.

Matt stood 5'11" but the tank's was for a man of Houdini's stature. Harry Houdini happened to be only 5'5". To get his entire body into the tank, it required a little extra bending and contorting on Matt's part, which literally put him in a jam. He was in great physical condition and could hold his breath for two minutes and some change, but could he get back out?

Matt was in a seal position within the tank, only reversed from the front. His face was pressed into the bottom rear of the backside; his chest rested partially on the bottom of the tank; his stomach was contorted sideways against the front side, about a foot from the bottom; and his hips and legs bent at an odd angle up so that his feet were jammed in the top rim of the tank straight up vertically from his head.

In short, his lithe frame was both contorted and stuck. There was absolutely no room to maneuver. The buoyancy factor continued to bend his body as much as it could, swaying his midsection a few inches back and forth, but his head and feet did not budge. After a minute and 40 seconds, bubbles started escaping from his mouth; he needed air in, not out. If he just had a few more inches, then he could have broken free, but there was no room.

Then he did not hear but felt a vibration. His mother came home just in time to save him, but alas, it was not meant to be.

Precious moments were wasted hauling in bags and stocking the perishables into the refrigerator and freezer section. He wanted to and even tried to cry out in desperation, but the only sound was additional bubbles floating upward in less decibels than a whisper. When she finally took the time to inquire about his well-being, it was too late.

"Matt? Matt? Are you home?" She checked his bedroom first, not there. When she entered his workroom, she couldn't help but notice the new object.

"Never seen that before," she said as she approached it. Then she saw movement, some gentle swaying; it was Matt's stomach and knees bobbing up and down, but only an inch or so. Since he was in the tank in reverse, she couldn't quite make it out until she realized a full body was in there. She rushed around to the back of the tank and saw his nose plastered against the glass with bubbles streaming upward. "Oh my God! My God!" She jumped on the chair, and it rolled partly away. She almost fell, but caught herself and came back. She dipped her hands in, pulled on his feet, but could not free him. He was stuck.

She jumped or rather tentatively got off the chair without rolling it, then raced back to the kitchen. She fumbled under the sink where she kept an old hammer, rushed back, and shattered the glass on her third strike. The water swept shards of glass on its way out as two hundred gallons spilled forth, soaking through the carpet to the floor beneath. In less than a minute, it was raining in the basement.

Avoiding the sharp-edged glass pieces as best she could, she dragged his body into the hallway and began pumping his stomach frantically. She altered the pumps with mouth-to-mouth blasts of air trying to perform the old cardiac pulmonary resuscitation, just like she learned at a class at the Red Cross.

For a moment, she thought that she heard a faint heartbeat when she rested her ear upon his chest. It was just a little gas gurgling about, but she did not know that. She began to tire and realized that she could not keep this up on her own forever. She dashed to the phone, dialed 911; and when the paramedics arrived a scant 11 minutes later, they found Theresa Hunter still trying to revive a dead man.

"We think sometimes that poverty is only being hungry, naked and homeless. The poverty of being unwanted, unloved and uncared for is the greatest poverty. We must start in our own homes to remedy this kind of poverty." - Mother Teresa

CHAPTER XXXVI

A month later, well after the funeral, Theresa placed an ad in the classified section of the *Cedar Rapids Express News* for Matt's possessions, namely the ones he had used in his various acts. A magician from Chicago who knew of Matt answered the ad. He had heard of Matt the Magnificent's death and had even seen one of Matt's performances. Was there a better way of adding to one's own act than borrowing, or in this case, buying the props of another, especially when that significant other would not be using them any longer? Alex Blake couldn't think of one and he purchased the entire lot for $500. Theresa took Matt's clothes and a few other miscellaneous items to the Salvation Army. It cost Alex $125 plus the favor of a friend to rent a truck and move the goods.

Alex lived on the twelfth floor in an apartment complex on Madison and Fifty-second. The lamp had been part of the deal, now packed in a large box with cards, balls, top hats, capes, and a variety of other tools of the trade. Alex had the pleasure of sorting the keepers from the throw-outs. As he inspected the lamp, he did little more than turn it over, tug at the fused lid, and then toss it into the throw-out pile. He saw or found no practical use for it.

Since he lived in the big city where such events as yard and garage sales did not exist, he tossed what he could not use into a big garbage bag, then hauled it down to the apartment community dumpster in the alley behind the complex. The waste management company, or more simply the garbage truck, ordinarily came by early Wednesday morning between 2:00 a.m. and 3:00 a.m. Alex dropped it in on a Sunday afternoon.

This dumpster happened to be in Emma's territory. Emma was a bag lady evicted from her welfare apartment two years earlier. Like most of the homeless, she was more of a mental case, unable to manage a small apartment despite the government assistance. Life for her was not much worse than her former place of residence.

The late 19th century apartment had been dirty with peeling paint, rarely had operational plumbing, but when it did the water came out a brown sewage color and nearly smelled as bad; and then, it was filled with monstrous cockroaches. One of Emma's five children, a four-year-old girl, had died from lead poisoning from munching on the old paint chips. Emma won a lawsuit but ended up with $2,000 when the unscrupulous lawyers landed six figures.

Emma's children had four different fathers and the kids had gone by the time they were 15. One boy died from a stab wound while brawling in a gang war; another still alive in a different gang. Of the two surviving girls, one lived in a group home and the other was a drugged-out prostitute. One of the men didn't even know he had a child while another falsely believed that he was the father of two, not the one who was the true biological father of the other two. Emma had never married.

Unbeknownst to her, she had just turned forty-nine years of age; nevertheless, her wrinkles and hard life made her look like she was in her early sixties. A stocking cap she wore in cold weather covered her thin, dirty, prematurely gray hair. She ordinarily found her clothes, including shoes, which were currently one size too big, in dumpsters, just like the torn duffel bag in which she carried them. She had used one of those donation drop boxes in the past to clothe herself, but large homeless black chased her away. Her most prized possession was a shopping cart she stole from a grocery store parking lot.

Most people avoided her as she cackled and panhandled for change. She was scary looking. Over half of her teeth were gone and those that were left were discolored and rotted, which in turn, left her face distorted, especially since the six teeth that were still in a row and somewhat serviceable were all on the lower right side of her mouth. Her pockmarked cheek jutted out on the left side, which served to squeeze or scrunch her left eye further up. The result was that her left eye looked much thinner than the right. Combined with the dental problem, her face was just plain freakish. People either ignored her and hastened their steps around her or dropped her a quarter but still sped on more swiftly. They were usually gone by before she could utter an incomprehensible "Than you."

Emma had two primary sources of moneymaking. One was begging which snagged her some loose change, maybe a few dollars total on a good day. The other was what she picked up in her shopping cart and could possibly sell to a lady at a flea market several blocks further west of town. The lady was kind and paid her anywhere from a dime all the way up to a dollar for whatever she deemed worthwhile that Emma brought her. The lady worked in a massive, converted warehouse, but met Emma behind it once a week. The lady sold the stuff for as much as a thousand percent mark-up; still, a thousand percent on a dime was still only a dollar.

One of Emma's faults was that she rarely purchased food with her money. She purchased booze instead. Alcoholism forced her and her kids out of her shabby apartment. She bought liquor instead of paying the bills or food for her children. There were corner liquor stores that sold cheap wine for as low as $3 a bottle or two for $5, Mogen David or Boone's Farm often. Still, she had to eat something to survive and the various dumpsters and garbage cans, specifically those by the restaurants in her little territory, served just fine. America wasted food in abundance.

One of her favorites was a busy fast food chicken joint where the garbage dumpster was in the back corner of the parking lot.

It had its own roof, three walls built around it and a tiny patch of rare city trees for shade. She could hide within this clump of fourteen trees and spy on a lackey minimum wage employee who emptied the trash about every half hour to an hour or so depending on how busy the place was. When the employee left, she made her move. Combing through the bags, she found biscuits, mashed potatoes, and chicken; some of it was even whole, uneaten and untouched, but she really didn't care. Mixed in were little salads and coleslaw packets, some unopened. She could actually consume a rather balanced diet. She felt safe with this dumpster, as she no one forced her to defend it in some time.

She once strayed nearly a mile away and was beaten and run off by a homeless man crazier than her for interfering with his dumpster; it was a McDonald's, one of the best. Aside from other homeless, it was often older children who abused her the most, taunting, teasing, and sometimes throwing things at her. One boy had even tipped over her cart and kicked her duffel bag. It was not an enjoyable life and what little thinking she did, she sometimes wondered why she just didn't sneak into a tall building, take the elevator up, find an open outdoor spot, and then make like a bird and jump.

On a cool October morning in 2006, she found the lamp while dumpster diving behind a Chicago apartment building. She was semi-sober or semi-drunk depending on whether one was an optimist or pessimist when she picked it out of a smelly bag. It was even cooler to the touch than the weather, but her face perked up and she even managed a crooked scary looking grin of excitement upon its discovery. The woman at the flea market might give her a whole $1 for it; that, combined with the $2.15 she currently possessed in change just might snag her another bottle of Boone's Farm. She still had a half a bottle of MD in a brown paper bag that she was working on.

Emma rushed it over to the old warehouse that held the flea market, but it was too early. It happened to be 9:30 a.m. but the place didn't open until ten. She had no idea of the time, thought about waiting around, and then began wandering aimlessly south with no specific goal or destination; perhaps she had life figured out after all. She found a back alley near the University of Chicago, parked her cart, retrieved her brown paper bag with the wine bottle, and grabbed the lamp too before she sat down.

She stared at the lamp admiringly, noting that it could likely snag her another fresh bottle, enough to drown her misery for another day. She took a swig and a full deep gulp, "Ahh," she muttered. "Iffen I coul' onla die" she slurred out incomprehensibly. The worst time of the year for the homeless was approaching, and Emma was no exception.

It was getting progressively colder, nights were beginning to dip below freezing, and as winter neared, the dumpsters would become part of her sleeping arrangements. They were certainly warmer than a cardboard box. She had become little more than a half-wit, but somehow, she gathered up a little human spirit and survival instinct, and went on. There were many like her in big cities throughout the world, the forgotten or ignored or both. With her wine bottle down to a fourth, she drifted off into slumber but there were no sugarplums dancing in her head.

She woke with the bottle in her hand and the lamp in her lap. She took another swig, looked down, and noticed some dried-up liquid that stained her newly found bronze relic, a little orange juice from the dumpster. She used her filthy dress to wipe it, but only smeared it around some making it dirtier than before. Instead of cleaning it, she managed to release the Djinni.

"What is it you wish for wench?" The Djinni towered far above her sprawled body on the pavement, with her back slumped against a wall.

She was now a little beyond the half-drunk stage, but her eyes widened, one about twice as big as the other, since her left eye was permanently squinted. She would have fit in well with the upcoming Halloween parade. She blubbered as she did before, "Iffen I coul' onla die."

This seemed extraordinarily easy for the Djinni. As he slithered back into the lamp, Emma's bodily functions ceased as she drifted off into a permanent, peaceful slumber.

Two other people in the neighborhood noticed the Djinni's odd appearance. One was a little poor girl peeping around the corner; the other was a university student who shortcutting through the alley scarcely in time to view a blob of smoke flowing or something like that. The male graduate student approached it tentatively both noting and ignoring the dead woman; he mistakenly believed that she had passed out in a drunken stupor even though she smelled like roadkill. Another tiny pair of eyes continued to observe from a low spot at the corner.

William "Willie" Lewis bent down to pick up the lamp out of curiosity. He had spent roughly the last nine years at one college or another. He received his first bachelor's degree from the University of Michigan, followed up by a master's degree, the former in General Studies, the latter in History. From there, he moved to Indiana, picked up a 2nd BA in Philosophy; nevertheless, as financial aid and funds were dwindling away, he returned home to Chicago to live with his parents. They had helped with tuition, and to this point, he had gotten through with some aid and their support without racking up any debt, but that was about to change. He secured a student loan and earned a second MA at the University of Chicago, Philosophy again, a most useful subject for little more than debating or arguing; then again, he felt that this subject was his official calling. There was little choice in his mind except to pursue a PhD.

Holding the lamp somehow brought back a strange memory of his very first semester at Michigan. It was in his English 101 class with Dr. Sheila Hosenburgh. It was his first published work even if it was in a rarely read obscure campus newspaper that employed one of his friends. The Djinni, if it really did possess any emotion, would have been proud of it.

One of their first assignments by Dr. Hosenburgh was to make a list of 50 or more items but keep it under one hundred. That was it. They had to keep a journal for the class and the professor simply wanted them to write and write and write no matter how obscure. Others wrote grocery lists, movie lists, their favorite CD's or musicians, book lists which buttered up the professor, sports lists, and even one wrote a brand-name athletic shoe list and had to work hard to reach fifty. Willie went over to the dark side and wrote about death with many involving or influenced by man:

Death Progressions by William F. Lewis
Prologue: In the beginning, there was no life.

1. One man murders another.
2. Two dogs mortally wound each other in a staged fight.
3. Three newly hatched robins were raided by an untethered house cat.
4. Four frogs + one tadpole eaten by a snake.
5. A crow snatches and eats five white cabbage butterflies.
6. Six gray whales harpooned in a single whaling expedition.
7. Seven flies landed in a spider's nest, and all died the same day.
8. Eight endangered snow leopards killed in March for their precious fur.
9. Nine red foxes all caught in the same foot trap within one year.
10. Ten deer killed illegally by one hunter in a single season.

11. Eleven trout hooked in a stream on a good day of fishing.

12. A dozen peacocks strangled for their feathers.

13. Eight frogs, four birds, one butterfly, one bee, and one praying mantis all shot by a 9-year-old in a single day with his new BB gun.

14. An entire pride of nineteen lions shot for sport.

15. Twenty-two roosters gouged and pecked to death in one staged cockfight event.

16. Twenty-eight mice were poisoned under a house.

17. A mass suicide for 31 beached whales.

18. Thirty-six dead on May 6, 1937, when the Hindenburg exploded in fire.

19. An entire herd of 39 African elephants were shot for their tusks which only seven possessed.

20. A bus in Quebec in 1978 plunged into a lake drowning 40 handicapped theater- goers.

21. Forty-four various bugs captured and suffocated in glass jars by one kid.

22. Four dozen worms mutilated as bait during a fishing expedition.

23. One small hornets' nest sprayed, 54 casualties.

24. Five dozen minnows were destroyed on an ice-fishing excursion.

25. Indians run 61 buffalo over a cliff.

26. Seventy-two garden-raiding rabbits shot in one day on a farm.

27. Seventy-eight alligators unlawfully captured for their skins.

28. In 1955, a racecar at the Grand Prix in LeMans, France, hurtled out of control into the grandstand, 82 spectators dead.

29. The Ocean Ranger, an oil drill rig near Newfoundland,

capsized in a storm 200 miles at sea, 84 dead.

30. One lone anteater took 7 minutes to lap up 93 ants from a hill.
31. Three freshly hatched sea turtles made it to the ocean, the other 228 did not.
32. The Great Chicago Fire in 1871 killed 250 people.
33. Six hundred baby seals clubbed for their fur in a good days' work.
34. Eight hundred lobsters were captured in their traps in another good days' work.
35. In 1912, the Titanic sank, 1,513 declared dead to the sea.
36. Two thousand sea snakes taken for their skins.
37. Five thousand butterflies collected on one jungle expedition.
38. The hurricane in Honduras in 1974 claimed 8,000 lives.
39. Nine thousand shellfish destroyed for a few odd pearls.
40. Anthills set afire in Texas; 10,000 ants perished.
41. Thirty thousand fish trapped in one massive drift net.
42. One huge bees' nest wiped out: 50,000 bees gone.
43. In 1864, a killer cyclone in India accounts for 70,000 human lives.
44. A flood in Holland in 1228 drowns 100,000 people.
45. 200,000 mosquitoes poisoned to death in one spraying.
46. 400,000 American deaths in World War II.
47. 600,000 Armenians massacred by The Turks in April of 1915.
48. 800,000 killed in an earthquake on January 24, 1556.
49. 1,000,000 potato beetles ruined by a crop duster.
50. 3,000,000 chickens killed in America daily.
51. 6,000,000 Jews annihilated during The Holocaust.
52. 8,000,000 turkeys killed for Thanksgiving.
53. 9,000,000 deaths in World War I.

54. 10,000,000 non-Jews (Gypsies, Slavs, Poles, Ukrainians, Belarusians, etc.) also exterminated during The Holocaust.
55. 15,000,000 deaths in World War II.
56. 1,000,000,000 organisms killed by acid rain in the 1990's.
57. 5,000,000,000 life forms killed in a typical oil spill.
58. 10,000,000,000 life forms killed in a typical forest fire.

Epilogue: Nuclear War decimates the planet; in the end, as in the beginning, there is no life.

Although Dr. Hosenburgh found it a little on the disturbing side, she could at least appreciate some of the thought and research that went into it. One could search this stuff on the budding Internet, but in 2006, Google was still not yet a household name and search engines at the time were quite weak in comparison. Willie received an "A" for doing more than most, and it was at least original.

The next journal assignment was to select ten items from each individual list, and then write a paragraph or two about them. This was particularly difficult for the one who had listed shoes. The following journal entry for this topic was to actually select one of those paragraphs and expand it into a three-to-five-page essay. Willie ended up writing in defense of turkeys and the result of his research turned him into a vegetarian. Turkeys were often crowded 10,000 strong in a 100x500-foot barn, fed for a few months until they reached a certain size, usually about fifteen pounds for hens and twenty for toms, and then rounded up and taken to the slaughterhouse. Most never saw the light of day during their short lives.

Why he thought about this for a few minutes of holding the lamp was a bit of a mystery to him; oddly enough however, the lamp seemed to have warmed up significantly, more so than just the heat generated by his hands. His hands and fingers were lightly perspiring, and it was barely forty degrees outside, enough to see the fog from one's breath. His fingers were sliding a little, adding to the smudges made by the orange juice and Emma's greasy fingers. He focused on the lamp while keeping a wary eye on the old bag lady. She didn't move and he was satisfied that she was sleeping or passed out, how deeply he never fully realized. Two little eyes were still peeking at him from around the corner when he produced a wad of tissue to wipe some of the grime from the lamp's surface.

Willie was on the short side at 5'6" and had long hair at the sides that could not quite hide his prematurely balding head. He could comb it over he surmised but did not worry about it just yet. He sported a thick brown moustache that matched the color of his hair. The wad of tissue that he placed every morning in the front left pocket of his jeans served two purposes. One, it was useful for cleaning the thick lenses of his glasses, and two, it served as some relief to his sinuses which flared up on occasion. Today, October 26, 2006, the tissue served a third unexpected purpose: it released a smoky monster.

"So, what is your first wish?"

"Ah!" Willie was barely alarmed and laughed aloud. "So, this is what I saw back here, I suppose you can grant me anything," he added somewhat sarcastically.

Willie decided to test it jokingly of course; he was far too rational to believe that this was anything more than a toy, though the thing sure had a nasty look about it. Halloween was coming soon, and it was probably just a gag or prop. He whipped out a crumpled dollar bill from his front right pocket and said, "Here, you see this? Give me a thousand like it." Immediately, ten neat bundles of a hundred 1-dollar bills each clasped in paper holders appeared at his feet while the Djinni did its own vanishing act. The

First Bank of Chicago came up a grand short in one-dollar bills at the end of its mandatory accounting audit that very same day.

Willie sat down and flung his backpack on the ground. "Holy Shit!" He said aloud. He glanced around suspiciously and thought that he caught a glimpse of something around the corner but dismissed it as he did with the unknowing corpse a few feet away.

This really flew Willie for a loop. He did not believe in gods, demons, ghosts, monsters, the afterlife, or anything remotely supernatural. Sure, there were things unexplained and unanswerable philosophical questions about the universe, but here was a thing offering wishes. He was not super interested in money or material gain though an extra thousand could pay a little on the old tuition bill.

He further thought about taking the lamp with him; however, it was not his, and above all else, Willie lived with strict morals and ideals. Perhaps he could not take it, but maybe, just maybe, he could wring another wish or two out of it like water from a soaked rag. With his wad of tissues, he vigorously rubbed the lamp again with the same result. The tall overweight form materialized above him and demanded a second wish.

Willie was somewhat prepared. Thinking of a biblical reference regarding King Solomon combined with the meaning of life, he said, "I wish for knowledge." The Djinni dissolved from view; Willie developed a vast encyclopedic knowledge as well as a basic working knowledge in all subject fields taught in a standard American four-year university.

Willie immediately clutched his head as it was far too much at once. Innumerable facts severely overloaded his brain. He could see himself as never losing another debate at the debate club nor any pickup chess matches at the Union Building, but the way his head was hurting, he wasn't sure if he could even make it there, just a few short blocks away. While his first migraine was about two-thirds of the way through its development stage, he rubbed the tissue on the lamp a third time.

"What is your third and final wish?"

Willie clutched his head and said, "I wish to know what's in store for me in the future, say ten years from now." Willie expected at some point to have a brilliant career as a noted professor, perhaps a Nobel Prize winner, maybe a wife and nearly as brilliant kids, and a nice house of his own. Instead, the Djinni showed him darkness, emptiness, and nothing.

As the Djinni dissipated, so did the sunlight from Willie's life. Total absolute darkness descended upon him as his wish came true. Just darkness or blankness, no heaven, no hell, nothing in between, no reincarnation, nothing, nothing but darkness, deep space darkness with no stars for light centuries away, a place where light could never hope to penetrate, like a black hole for instance, utter desolation. It filled Willie's present and his future world, and then it was gone. It didn't take any precise genius, even his own, to understand where his existence or lack thereof had gone. No more Willie.

"No, it isn't fair," he clutched and pressed hard as the migraine was nearing its climax. "I can help the world. I can make it better. No!" He shrieked as his head pounded like a jackhammer.

He frantically began rubbing the lamp repeatedly until his fragile tissues fell apart; nothing happened. The more he thought he believed he should have used that third wish to cure his growing headache, one progressing at an exponential rate as more knowledge swelled.

His head ached and throbbed so badly that his vision began fading in and out, more out than in. He violently threw the lamp against the hollow concrete block wall, clutched his backpack, and staggered off in his original direction. By the time he entered the courtyard at one of the university halls, he had to sit from the dizziness and sensory overload, partially blinded as his vision alternated from one collapsing eye to the other. The headache had reached its peak, but unfortunately, it did not come down from there.

Suddenly, he had trouble seeing out of both eyes. It had been blurry in one, then the other, but not both, until now. His left side felt weak and tingling as he lost feeling in his arm, shoulder, and then leg on that side of his body. The left side of his face involuntarily drooped; he could not raise it, and he started to drool. So great was the demand on his system from his brain, that not enough blood could flow upward to meet it; thus, his brain cells began to die. Within minutes of sitting down, he passed out, and then passed away from a massive cerebral hemorrhage; in short, he stroked out.

"Be kind whenever possible. It is always possible." - Tenzin Gyatso, the 14th Dalai Lama

CHAPTER XXXVII

A few minutes after the strange man left, Jenny cautiously approached the sleeping woman and the lamp, which, surprisingly, bore no dents despite its collision with the wall. Jenny was in little more than rags but knelt beside the old woman. "Are you okay, Misses?" She asked the lady who of course did not and could not respond. Jenny tapped her shoulder lightly, but there was still no response. A tear exited one of Jenny's eyes and flowed down her smooth baby-like cheek. "You poor old woman," she said. Jenny had the idea that the old woman would not be getting up again.

Jenny possessed a rare combination of bright blue eyes and dark brown hair. Her future beauty would be her ticket out of the lower classes, but for now, she was just a poor street urchin of eight years. What had originally caught her attention, even before the man had arrived, was the action of the lamp. Her mind was quick, and she had a fair idea of what was happening. She picked up the lamp and took it home.

She lived alone with her grandmother whose social security check supported them both. The house was a tiny five-room affair complete with kitchen, bathroom, living room, and two bedrooms located in a run-down neighborhood on a tiny, fenced lot. Luckily, they paid it off some years ago.

After the housing crisis in the first decade of the twenty-first century, it was likely under five figures in value. They at least had a postage stamp lawn, an island of green in a sea of concrete. The one advantage of it all was that the fencing and yard allowed them one small luxury, and that was Coco, Jenny's mixed mutt. Coco was just a fifteen-pound male dog, a little brownish Jack Russell terrier mixed with some other terrier or two, perhaps a little poodle and beagle too.

Jenny let herself in the gate where Coco greeted her with a friendly bark even though he had one paw raised and was limping around on three legs. He had sprained his left front paw yesterday and Jenny was not sure how bad it was; after all, they did not have the money to take him to the vet. Jenny thought that it might be broken. Jenny dropped the lamp off on the back porch and snuck into the house just as she had snuck out.

She wasn't supposed to leave the yard, but grandma was not in a position much to know. Her grandmother was in bed suffering from lupus, an autoimmune disease that rarely allowed her mother to go outdoors. Grandma had most things delivered directly to her home such as groceries and most other essentials could be mail-ordered. It may have cost more, but it was convenient. Jenny peaked in and noticed that her grandma was still asleep, and then went back outside to tend to Coco.

"You poor little boy Coco," she soothed as she aided him in getting to her lap, "I'm going to make you better. Just a minute Coco, I gotta go get somethin.'" She ran to the bathroom, unrolled some toilet paper, and came back in less than a minute. She hefted the lamp to her lap and rubbed it with the tissue. Coco let out a low sounding hostile warning growl, the one he reserved for unwanted strangers when the Djinni poured out of the lamp.

"What is your first wish girl?"

Jenny had already seen the spirit four times and spoke confidently, "Please fix my doggie's leg." The Djinni withered away about the same time that Coco stopped growling. Miraculously, he started running around the yard on all fours, as good as ever, barking and yipping happily as he leapt and bound about, chasing butterflies and rainbows or so it seemed.

Jenny felt a little angry and even ashamed for forgetting to say "Thank You" to the Djinni. Her grandma had taught her to say that whenever someone was being nice to you. She vowed not to forget the second time as she wiped the surface of the lamp again, just like the man had done in the alleyway.

The gray matter poured forth again and said, "What is your second wish?"

"I wish that my grandma wasn't sick anymore, thank you!" She managed to invoke her best manners before the cloudy figure disappeared as quickly as it had appeared. Without even checking, like Coco, she was sure that grandma would be feeling better, but now she faced a grave dilemma. She had wished for two things that she had really wanted, to help Coco and grandma, but she was having trouble coming up with a third. She thought long and hard and finally came up with a solution, another wish, not for herself, but for someone else again. Her tissue was fraying, but when she rubbed lightly, it did the trick. The Djinni appeared for her final request.

"What is your last wish girl?"

"It must be lonely for you in there, you poor old thing. I wish that you didn't have to live in there anymore," she said as she pointed at the Djinni's long time what seemed like its forever home. "Thank you!"

The Djinni was compelled to leave for two reasons: one, because the little girl had wished it; the other, because all through the centuries, Jenny was the first to make three unselfish requests. The Djinni swished out, but instead of leveling off at seven feet with an attached tail, it continued to rise, onward and upward. The connection with the lamp was broken and the lamp immediately collapsed into metal dust. The cloudy-like figurine rose higher and higher out of the sky, into space, from infinity and beyond Jenny thought.

"What are you doing out there, Jennifer?" Grandma was up and about, and seemed to have a little extra kick in her step.

"Just playin' with Coco is all!" She answered with a devilish grin.

"We shall not cease from exploration, and the end of all our exploring will be to arrive where we started and know the place for the first time." - T. S. Eliot

CHAPTER XXXVIII

About nineteen years later, on October 7, 2025, a meteorite slammed through the roof of Dr. Billings' house, which no longer contained an antique lamp. Did it come from the same meteor as before, or was it different? Did it contain some or perhaps the same matter as the previous one?

One can only wonder.

"When I was a beggarly boy,
And lived in a cellar damp,
I had not a friend nor a toy,
But I had Aladdin's lamp."

- James Russell Lowell, *Aladdin*, 1868, st.1

MARK PICKVET WAS BORN in Pinconning, Michigan and graduated from the University of Michigan where he received his Bachelors' and Masters' Degrees. He went on to obtain a PhD in History and has written many books, especially on the history of glassware and the State of Michigan, and several works of fiction.

ALSO AVAILABLE FROM NIGHTMARE PRESS
BREAKING THE DEVIL'S BREAD:
DARK WORDS AND SHADOW TALES

Satyros Phil Brucato

Our lives are made of stories.

Some of those tales get pretty damn dark.

In the following "13 stories and an Oops," award-winning dark fantasist Satyros Phil Brucato (*Red Shoes, Mage, Valhalla with a Twist of Lethe*) explores shadows, cries, and silence.

Careless haunters, elite collectors, secretive enforcers, lip-synching goths, hapless custodians, strange children, subterranean exiles, tortured fiends, harried jesters, haggard coulrophobes, ragged batterers, joyous hikers, carnal mystics, and exploding cosmos tell their tales as sardonic darkness swallows all.

If mortal dread is the Devil's bread, then we're all welcome at the feast.

THE HURDY GURDY MAN
David Turnbull

Set in London in the summer of 1969, *The Hurdy Gurdy Man* follows Kath Dunn, who has left her home near the seaside town Berwick on Tweed, and finds herself homeless on the streets of Piccadilly. Here she encounters the eccentric Gordon Urquhart-Scott, who persuades Kath to accompany him to his large crumbling home on the edge of Hampstead Heath, where he claims to run a hostel for homeless women.

Kath finds herself inducted as one of twelve formerly homeless women who reside free of charge in the house in exchange for obeying the Hurdy Gurdy Man's strange rules, including nightly musical performances on the hand-cranked hurdy-gurdy from which his nickname derives.

Kath befriends Ruth. Together they secretly unravel terrible truths linked to the British Class system, the establishment, and the gruesome Scottish borders legends of the Redcaps. After witnessing how deep the horror within the decaying home truly runs, the two women decide to confront the evil at its source. Enlisting the help of other women, they engineer a terrifying conflict they hope will send the evil back to whatever foul region of darkness from whence it came.

BELINDA'S KEYBOARDS
PART ONE: DED'S LINE
Dedham Pond

Dedham Pond is a journalist in his fifties rediscovering how to do his job responsibly in an era that appreciates bias over truth and influencers over experts. While investigating the death of an old friend's son, Ded discovers Belinda Blessing, who is part of a conspiracy of people who enjoy injecting discord and chaos into the culture wherever they can. Now Ded must find a way to stop the destruction caused by Belinda's keyboards and bring her to justice.

SARAH CORBIN'S BLOODY REVENGE
Coyote Wallace

When Sarah Corbin and her family are killed in a midnight robbery gone wrong, she makes a deal for her mortal soul - in exchange for the chance to hunt down the men who burned her world to ash.

Violent, unflinching, and tinged with supernatural overtones, *Sarah Corbin's Bloody Revenge* takes readers into the dark heart of Texas, where the air is heavy with gun smoke and the streets run red.

On the other end of Sarah's revenge is Lono Talbot, a murderous cutthroat who has parlayed stolen gold into a position of power in the small town of Gehenna. His network of gunslingers and outlaws, reinforced with his ill-gotten gains, has made him one of the most powerful men in the Texas underground. Too well protected for lawmen, Lono continues to grow his influence and power....

....until the mistakes of his past come calling.

MURKY SHADOWS
Belinda Brady

———————●———————

WELCOME TO *Murky Shadows*, a deliciously dark world where ghosts, ghouls, monsters and all-too-horrifying realities collide, and vampires, ghosts and things that go bump in the night rule. From a vengeful fairy, to a bloodthirsty roommate, to the ghosts of a serial killer plotting their revenge, no supernatural stone is left unturned in this captivating collection of spooky tales.

Murky Shadows, by Belinda Brady, is a treasure of short stories that will take you to places you never dreamed possible, and introduce you to characters you would only meet in your worst nightmares. So sit back, relax, perhaps put a light on, and delve into this chilling mixed bag of dark stories, one that not only brings the supernatural to life, but also taps into the darkest corners of the human psyche.

Which story will be your favorite?

NO ONE CAN SAVE US
Kendall Phillips

Adam always keeps his powers in check. As the world's only superhero, he must know his limits. Defeat the master criminal, repel an army, stop a natural disaster, but never let himself go too far.

Until Syangnom.

The world has grown accustomed to the feats of its only superhuman. Adam's wife, Sara, a celebrated journalist and periodic hostage, regularly reports his exploits, and the agents of Extra-Judicial Affairs handle all the legal issues.

But when Adam becomes enraged in the reclusive regime of Syangnom, he leaves 14 million people dead and the world recoiling from the destruction he has wrought.

Now Adam's wife Sara and EJA Agent Kia Mercado must track down the conspiracy behind Adam's breakdown and discover the otherworldly source of his powers. Their search will bring them face to face with supervillains, eldritch gods, and the mysterious figure who defends Chicago from the shadows, the armored hero known only as No One.

A SOUL A DAY
Todd Sullivan

What lengths would you go to save a soul?

In the shadows of South Korea, Min Jae rebels against the Gwanlyo, an organization of vampires that tempts mortals with power, money, sex, and the promise of immortality. The catch? An eternity in Hell.

Min Jae will stop at nothing to prevent another human from becoming a vampire. He embarks on a holy quest to save those marked for damnation. Next on his list— Desmond, an expat in Seoul who lives an ordinary life of work and friends.

To stave off the Gwanlyo hellbent on acquiring Desmond, Min Jae enlists the services of Hyeri, a serial killer turned vampire who hates the organization for her own insane reasons. Will the unlikely pair be able to rescue Desmond before he becomes a vampire? Will the undead organization keep the duo from disrupting their plans?

Find out in A SOUL A DAY, a tale of violence, madness, and redemption.

SCROLLS OF RAMOSE, SCRIBE OF EGYPT
James Arthur Anderson

———————◉———————

ACCORDING TO THE BOOK of Exodus, God cast ten deadly plagues against Egypt and the Pharaoh for his enslavement of the Israelites. One wonders what it must have been like to be an ordinary Egyptian, innocent of Ramesses II's transgressions, yet still suffering the wrath of the Almighty.

Scrolls of Ramose, Scribe of Egypt retells the story from the point of view of the chief scribe of Ramesses the Great, and relives the suffering the people of the Two Lands endured during the plagues of the bloody Nile: the infestations of frogs, insects, and boils; the terror of fiery hail and darkness; and finally, the death of the eldest sons.

You have heard the stories, now see them through the eyes of the innocent merely trying to survive the deadly hand of an angry God.

STITCHES AND OTHER STORIES
J.M. Heluk

———◉———

NOTHING IN *Stitches and Other Stories* is what it seems, leaving the reader to speculate on the origin of its horror—to root out those subtle connections and, ultimately, stitch each tale together on their own.

Stitches and Other Stories was designed to make the reader an active participant. In the end, you decide the genesis of the horror.

From a family stranded by an unnatural force on their Montana farm in "Two Miles as the Crow Flies," to "Stitches," the story of a young boy terrorized by his dead grandmother. Meet a temperamental little girl from a New York City slum who possesses a deadly talent in "The Wishman and the Worm." In "The Ovid," something has come home to roost in a less-than-quaint seaside town.

Sit back and let *Stitches and Other Stories* guide you through a frightful landscape while you read deep into the night.

JENNY'S SPOOKY LITTLE TALES: VOL. 2

THE FRIGHTENING FLOYDS have been researching and writing about the paranormal and all things strange and unusual for ten years. To celebrate, Jenny recently compiled ten of her favorite stories from the many books she has written with her husband Jacob, which became *Jenny's Spooky Little Tales: Vol. 1*. Now, she has compiled ten more for *Jenny's Spooky Little Tales: Vol. 2*.

In this collection, you'll find ghosts, a meat shower, a haunted Disney World attraction, spirits of Hollywood stars and starlets, the Bermuda Triangle, and even spooky tales from Louisville's famed Churchill Downs. We hope you enjoy *Jenny's Spooky Little Tales: Vol. 2*.

READ MORE NIGHTMARE PRESS!!!

Visit our website at nightmarepress5.wordpress.com

Also, follow us on:

Facebook: https://www.facebook.com/nightmarepress1
Instagram: https://www.instagram.com/nightmarepress1